Stand By Your Man

Stand By Your Man

GIL McNEIL

BLOOMSBURY

First published 2004

Copyright © 2004 by Gil McNeil

The moral right of the author has been asserted

Bloomsbury Publishing Plc, 38 Soho Square, London W1D 3HB

A CIP catalogue record for this book is available from the British Library

ISBN 0 7475 6139 7

10 9 8 7 6 5 4 3 2 1

Typeset by Hewer Text Ltd, Edinburgh

All papers used by Bloomsbury Publishing are natural, recyclable products made from wood grown in well-managed forests. The manufacturing processes conform to the environmental regulations of the country of origin.

Printed by Clays Ltd, St Ives plc

ACKNOWLEDGEMENTS

With thanks to Dad, Jane, Jo, Katie, Mary, Minna, Mum, Rose, Ruth, Sarah, Sheila, Vicky, and everyone at Bloomsbury, Brunswick Arts and PiggyBankKids.

For Joe

Sometimes it's hard to be a woman
– Tammy Wynette

CONTENTS

CONTENTS

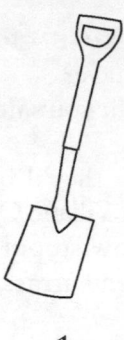

1

JANUARY

The Wrong Trousers

Garden Diary

The gardening book Mum gave me for Christmas says that vital garden tasks for January include cleaning all garden tools, ordering seeds, digging over all beds and borders, planting rhubarb and pruning everything in sight, especially wisteria and fruit trees.

I try to wash the mud off the filthy old spade in the shed, but the nozzle comes off the hosepipe and fills my wellies with freezing-cold water. Alfie thinks this is fabulous. Decide to have a go at a bit of digging instead, but the ground is frozen solid, so I end up balancing with both feet on the spade in an attempt to get it into the ground. Fall off and land in a bush with prickles, some sort of bramble possibly, or a very large thistle. I give up and move on to a nice spot of pruning, and since I'm not completely sure what wisteria looks like I hack away at the rambling climber thing covering the fence. Mum tells me later that it's a spring-flowering clematis, and all the bits I chopped off were the flowering bits. Marvellous.

'WHAT UNUSUAL SEXUAL CHARACTERISTICS does the Patagonian hare have?'

'Christ, Molly, I thought you said the questions were going to be easy.'

'Well, how did I know they'd be so competitive?'

That's the trouble with Village Quiz Nights. The rest of the village gets to see just how stupid you really are.

'It's going to be really embarrassing if we don't get a single question right.'

'Where did Frank and Pat go for their honeymoon in *EastEnders*?'

'Bugger, we haven't answered the last one yet.'

'Who invented obstetric forceps?'

'That's easy. A total bastard.'

'Shall I write that down?'

'Definitely.'

I've got a feeling total bastard isn't actually going to be the answer, but I write it down anyway.

'How many degrees are there in each internal angle of an octagon?'

'Come on, Alice, you should know this one. Didn't you do angles at architect school?'

'Sort of.'

'What did Wonder Woman's lasso always make people do?'

'Beg for mercy?'

'Molly, we've got to get at least one question right. Look, you write the answers while I work out the angles thing.'

'In golf what is the term for one under par for a hole?'

'Bloody hell.'

'Which country invented the duffel coat?'

'Oh good, I know this one. It's Belgium.'

Molly looks very pleased with herself.

'I organised a school trip to Belgium a few years ago and I had to do the worksheets.'

'I bet that was a lovely trip.'

'Oh it was. We lost two year-nines on the ferry coming

home and the deputy head nearly had a heart attack. We had to get an ambulance and everything. But he was fine – I think he was just putting it on so no one could blame him if the kids had gone overboard.'

'And had they?'

'No, shame really. One of them was Wayne Tompkins, and he's a nutter. He Super-glued a supply teacher to his seat last week in DT.'

'Well, at least we'll get one question right.'

Actually, we manage six in all. Out of thirty. Which isn't great, but we're both so drunk by the time they've worked out all the scores that we don't really care. Molly is bracing herself for sarcastic comments about teachers not knowing as much as you'd think, but luckily nobody seems to have the time to come over and be patronising because they're too busy bickering about their own scores. And at least we now know Patagonian hares are completely monogamous. Bless. And Pat and Frank went to Hawaii. Although the woman on the table near ours is still trying to convince one of the judges that it was Spain. Some of the teams are taking it all very seriously and all the judges have gone bright red. But the really good news is we've failed to get through to the next round, so technically we can go home, having done our bit for village funds, and rescue Dan from looking after two three-year-olds who didn't look very tired when we left.

'Shall we go then?'

'No way. I'll get some more drinks and we can see who wins.'

'Great. I was hoping you'd say that.'

Molly gets the drinks in, which takes ages because the pub's completely packed.

'I got triples – I thought it'd save time.'

'Good thinking. Blimey, that's strong.'

I can feel the vodka sort of softening the edges a bit. Perhaps I should put some more tonic in. Although on second thoughts it's quite nice, actually.

'How's work?'

'Crap. And we've got a trip to the Natural History Museum next week. Thirty-two stroppy fourteen-year-olds on a coach – I might as well alert the emergency services now. What about you?'

'Double crap. I've got a barn conversion for a client who hates barns, and more kitchen jobs than bloody IKEA.'

'Nice.'

'I mean what the hell's the point of buying a barn to convert if you hate them?'

'Can't you just knock it down and start again?'

'That's not really the point, Moll, and anyway it's listed – the planning boys would have a fit. And the chairman of the local Parish Council lives right opposite, and every time I go round there he's lurking behind a bush.'

'Maybe he's a flasher.'

'Probably. That'd be just my luck. If we so much as touch a single brick he'll have a heart attack. And it could be so beautiful – if the client wasn't such a total pillock. Anyway, what's so crap about school at the moment? Apart from the coach trip, I mean.'

'Oh just the usual. Too many kids, not enough drugs. That sort of thing. Nothing special, it's all right really. And some days it almost feels like I'm making a difference, you know. It's home I can't cope with. Give me a load of dysfunctional teenagers any day. But persuading Lily that she can't wear her party dress to playgroup again, forget it. It took me nearly three-quarters of an hour to get her dressed this morning.'

When I met Molly when we first moved down here I thought Lily was going to be one of those children who make you feel very bitter about life. You know the type, she's sort of the opposite of Alfie really. She always looks immaculate, and she's very polite and likes things nice and tidy. But then I realised that the thing she really likes best is annoying her mother, so that cheered me up a bit. Molly's a dungarees and

4

Birkenstocks kind of mum, organic, vegetarian and a bit of an old hippy, but in a nice way, without any chanting or joss sticks. Lily on the other hand will only wear pink, or other pastel shades at a push, preferably with sequins, and wouldn't be seen dead in a pair of trousers. She's a bit like a mini Dame Edna Everage.

'How was Janice today?'

'New lacy tights.'

Janice is Molly's childminder. She takes Lily to the same playgroup as Alfie, and collects her at lunchtime. She's always wanted a little girl, but got three sons instead, so she makes do by dressing Lily up in My Little Princess outfits, and knitting things in peach, or sometimes an unpleasant shade of aquamarine.

'Oh and I haven't told you the latest. She's started cleaning.'

'Who?'

'Lily. She trots round with a duster, and she's really into standing on a chair by the sink and doing the washing up. Janice has got her a little mop.'

'Oh dear.'

'I know. But she loves it. It's so humiliating. It makes me feel like she's judging me. I just don't get it – how come I've ended up with a post-feminist three-year-old who likes having a good go-round with a duster? Dan thinks it's hysterical.'

'Is it post-feminist then, to like cleaning?'

'Yes, it bloody is. And I'm fed up with it. I've just about got Dan to realise it's not my job to rush round after him with a dustpan and brush, and now Lily's letting the side down.'

Molly is very anti post-feminists. She thinks they're a Disgrace.

'Maybe you should hire a cleaner? Or is that not allowed?'

'Oh no. Exploiting women poorer than you is timeless really, and if you pay them properly I suppose it's all right – redistribution of wealth and all that bollocks. But we haven't got the money, and even if we did no cleaner in their right mind would work for us. Dan's started on the fireplace downstairs now, so there's a load of old bricks and bits of plaster piled up in the corner, and a great big hole in the wall where the old one used to be. I wish he'd finish one room before he starts demolishing somewhere else. It's driving me crazy.'

Dan's a builder who does mostly renovations: which means he can spend hours choosing the perfect plaster moulding for a cornice, but he's not terribly good at actually finishing boring jobs at home.

'Handy Lily likes dusting then, isn't it? You can drop her round with me any time, you know, for a session with the Pledge.'

'I might take you up on that. Oh, and that reminds me, Janice says she saw the new people moving into the big house today. The woman was getting into a Range Rover outside the shop, with two kids. All tinted windows and black leather, apparently. So you'll have to go up and say hello, and then report back.'

'I can't just march up there and nose about.'

'Yes you can, you're their nearest neighbour. Take a cup of sugar or something.'

'Alfie would eat it before we got out of the door.'

'Well, a bottle of something then, as a housewarming present. Look, I need to know. I told Janice you're bound to have met them. I have to have info soon or she'll think I'm crap. Well, more crap than usual.'

'I've got a bottle of wine somewhere, I think, but it's not very posh. What if they're über-snooters and laugh at my plonk?'

'Oh go on, please, I'll owe you one.'

'OK, but only if you promise to come round next weekend when Patric's here, and help me annoy him.'

'Pleasure.'

'He's bringing Cindy.'

'Wanker.'

Patric is Alfie's dad. Sort of. I mean technically he is, but

6

since he left us when Alfie was five months old he doesn't exactly win a Father of the Year award. Patric with a C, but no K, unlike in prick, as my brother Jim points out whenever he gets the chance. Sometimes when Patric's actually in the room.

We met at college, and he said he liked independent women, and marriage was bourgeois. Children were better off being brought up in a family based on trust and equality, which sounded quite good at the time, until he left me for his secretary, Cindy, who wears very tiny fluffy jumpers and has a collection of soft toys on her desk. And they all have names.

We'd just moved into the cottage: Patric thinks all children should grow up in the country. So there I was, stuck in a cottage that needed doing up, not knowing anybody in the village, in the twilight zone. Alfie wasn't sleeping much, and neither was I. Meeting Molly in the village shop was a lifesaver.

'I was thinking about him last night, actually.'

'Oh god, don't tell me you and Mork are getting back together again. I'll have to stab you or something.'

Molly, for some reason best known to herself, calls Patric and Cindy Mork and Mindy. Even my brother Jim's started doing it now.

'Christ no, I'm not completely mad, no. I was just thinking about how stupid I must be, to have spent so long with someone who's such a total wanker. And I never knew, while I was with him, I mean. So I must have been mad, and maybe I still am, mad, I mean, and I just don't know it. It sort of makes you worry, you know. There should be a course you can go on, maybe a night class – Manky Men and How to Avoid Them. My name is Alice and I'm a mankoholic.'

'Don't be so hard on yourself – we've all been there.'

'Yes, but not as bad as Patric.'

'Oh I don't know about that. The man I was with before Dan was pretty special. He said monogamy was a patriarchal plot, and then shagged half my friends. And I just let him get away with it because I thought he was a free spirit.'

'Nice.'

'Yes, and then I got drunk one night and snogged one of his friends, and he went tonto. And I was really shocked, you know. It was like I'd been wearing the wrong glasses, and suddenly I'd got the right ones and could see clearly what a total prick he was.'

'Just like Wallace and Gromit.'

'I beg your pardon?'

'You know, *The Wrong Trousers.*'

'Oh, right. Well, yes, if you put it like that, yes, we've all had our fair share of boys in wrong trousers. And any woman who hasn't is a total Stepford Wife.'

Molly divides women into Proper Women and Stepford Wives, and I think she's right. Proper Women have crumpled clothes, are late for playgroup, and don't know how to make meringues. Stepford Wives always look immaculate, are never late for anything, and make their own mayonnaise.

'Patric used to have a pair of leather trousers, but his legs are too thin. They sort of flapped round the ankles. He looked completely ridiculous.'

'I bet he did. But it's character-forming, you know. Shagging retards. It makes you a proper woman.'

'Good. Well, that makes me mega proper then. I'll drink to that. To men in the wrong trousers.'

'Or no trousers at all.'

By the time the winner of the quiz is announced, and presented with a rather squashed-looking box of chocolates donated by the village shop, we're all completely pissed. One of the judges looks like he's passed out, and Elsie Thomas is singing a medley of very rude songs from the Second World War. Molly's having a long chat with Mrs Pomeroy, who runs the local Garden Society and is very bossy, and I've been on the verge of nodding off while Ray Jenkins tells me all about his career with the Water Board.

Molly's at the bar when I make my way back from the loo, which is proving more difficult than you'd think because my boots have gone all wobbly. I don't normally have any problem walking in them, but for some reason tonight they're proving a bit tricky.

'Um, Moll. Wasn't one of us supposed to stay sober, so they could drive home?'

'Bugger.'

'I know.'

'Shall we ask someone to give us a lift?'

'All right, but not Ray Jenkins. There's only so much drainage a girl can take.'

'He's very keen.'

'He's also very bipolar.'

'We could walk.'

'It's nearly two miles.'

'Yes. But it's not that cold. It'll do us good.'

'Molly. It's absolutely bloody freezing.'

'Well, pick someone else then . . . Ooh. He's all right. Where did he come from? I haven't seen him before.'

A tall blond man is standing at the bar, quite near to Molly, wearing nice jeans and an old leather jacket.

'He's got a lovely arse. He's definitely not wearing the wrong trousers.'

'Molly. He'll hear you, stop it.'

The man turns round, and goes bright red.

'Great. He did hear you.'

'I don't care. He has. Men needs compliments too, you know, Alice.'

'If a man said you'd got a lovely arse, you'd smack him in the mouth.'

'Well, yes. Stictly spleeking, I would. Possibly.'

'Spleeking? I think we must be quite drunk, you know, Moll.'

'I know. It's lovely, isn't it? He has, though. And look, he doesn't look too frontal-lobe or anything, not like poor old Ray. Go on, go up and ask him if he'll give us a lift home. Go on.'

'I can't just walk up to a perfect stranger and ask him to drive us home.'

'Why not?'

Oh God. He's coming over. He walks towards us, and hesitates, and goes bright red again and sort of smiles, in a rather sweet, apologetic kind of way. He doesn't look like the sort of man who's used to being told he's got a gorgeous arse by women in pubs. Maybe he's going to come over and say something: or maybe he's going to make some kind of formal complaint to the committee. Oh god, how embarrassing. We'll be hauled up before the Parish Council for making dodgy comments in a public place. But in fact he walks straight past us, and out of the door.

'Oh. Well done, Batgirl. You really reeled him in. Nice to know we're going to be driven home by a handsome stranger.'

'I didn't notice you saying anything.'

'I was leaving the field open for you. I don't think Dan would like me bringing home strangers with nice bottoms.'

'Probably not. So, it looks like we're walking then?'

'Oh bugger it, I'll ask Mrs Pomeroy. She won't mind. She's been telling me all about the Garden Society, and she's really keen on new recruits. So I told her we'd join – there's a meeting next week. That should be worth a lift home.'

'Oh no you don't. I never said I wanted to join. You're the one who wants to grow things.'

'But you said you wanted to sort out your garden.'

'I know. But I meant saving up a bit and then paying someone else to do it.'

'But we could do it together, go to a few meetings and pick up some tips. It might be fun.'

'No it bloody wouldn't.'

'Go on, Alice, please. I can't go by myself – they might all be nutters. She's very bossy, that Mrs Pomeroy. If I buy you another drink, will you?'

'Oh all right then, but only for one meeting.'

The journey home with Mrs Pomeroy takes ages, partly because it takes her about forty-eight manoeuvres to get her Renault Clio out of the pub car park, because she's not exactly what you'd call a natural driver, but mainly because she's filling us in on the history of the Garden Society, and how vital it is to attract new members. Apparently there's bitter rivalry between our village group, Lower Bridge, and the Upper Bridge one, and they've hated each other ever since Upper Bridge won the Best Village in Bloom competition years ago.

Mrs Pomeroy says there were accusations of corruption and rumours about judges being bribed, but last year she won the Best Hanging Basket competition in the regional finals, by cramming forty-eight salmon-pink begonias into one basket with a cunning contrast planting of ivy and lobelia. I think lobelia is that blue stuff, and if it is then that basket must have been quite something. Although I'm not really sure what a begonia looks like, so it might not have been as bad as it sounds.

Dan is fast asleep on the sofa when we get back, with Lily and Alfie draped over him, and a *Peter Pan* video still playing. He looks exhausted, and wakes up with a bit of a start when Molly trips over a discarded Barbie.

'Oh thank god, I thought one of them was up again. Did you have a good time?'

'Lovely, thanks. What about you?'

'Just don't ask, all right?'

'That bad?'

Molly's smiling.

'Yes, I'm bloody knackered. Next time you two want a girls' night out I want back-up, all right, proper professional back-up. Alfie was fine – he fell asleep quite early, in our bed. But then Lily woke him up. And he got his second wind.'

'Oh dear.'

'And then Lily wanted to do painting.'

'You didn't let her, did you?'

'I'm not completely stupid, you know.'

* * *

We sit and drink tea in the kitchen, and Molly tells us about her plans for the garden, and gets quite excited and says she wants to grow vegetables, and possibly fruit, especially rhubarb, and she wants chickens, and then she starts going on about how organic vegetables taste so much better and Dan says if she doesn't stop going on he's going to bed and anyway he hates rhubarb. Dan's not really into gardening – he's too busy doing up the cottage, which overlooks the village green: they've only got a tiny front garden but the back's huge and as far as he's concerned it's a really useful place to put skips and piles of bricks. Not that mine's much better – I practically had to use a machete to get to the washing line last year. I think I might need a flamethrower or something if I'm really going to make a difference, but I don't think the Garden Society would approve, and anyway those dinky little things you use to make crème brûlée go brûlée would take hours, and anything bigger would probably be lethal and I'd end up with no eyebrows.

Dan drives us home, and Alfie surfaces long enough to have a bit of a shout and refuse to have his shoes back on, so I have to carry him to the car, which isn't easy because he weighs a ton, especially when he's half asleep. Getting him indoors and upstairs without any major incidents on the kicking and shouting front isn't easy either, and I'm so out of breath by the time I've got up the stairs anyone would think I'd just been out jogging. And every time I lie down everything whirls about a bit, so I end up sitting up in bed with a cup of tea, and a woolly hat on because the house is freezing. The central heating went off ages ago and I can't face going back downstairs and trying to coax the boiler into having another go. When we bought the cottage we had all sorts of plans for taking down walls and adding on a new kitchen and bathroom, and at some point a new boiler was going to put in an appearance, but somehow I've never got round to it, mainly because I haven't really got the money. Patric did some plans for the kitchen, which I hated, and that was that. He was still sulking about it when he left.

Patric's very keen on minimalist spaces with lots of light, which is fine, but his designs tend to include curved walls of glass and daft sinks that are so small you can only fit a plate in at an angle. When you walk into one of his buildings, instead of getting that slightly dizzy breathless feeling you get when you're standing somewhere really special, you just end up feeling irritated, because there's always something rather smug and self-conscious going on. Although there seem to be loads of people who want self-conscious houses, with sinks that you can't wash up in, which is probably just as well because according to him he's only just managing to hover above the breadline, which is why he can't afford anything regular in the way of child support for Alfie. So how he affords the new BMW he was driving the last time he came down is a bit of mystery. Perhaps it was a present from a grateful client. Or maybe like Molly says he's just a tight bastard. But to be honest I haven't really pushed him on it because I'd rather walk barefoot than ask him for money: although not in the winter obviously, and definitely not on gravel.

And anyway it was my flat we lived in, in London, so it's my money that bought the cottage, and I've still got a bit left over, for emergencies. The money Patric was planning to spend on doing the cottage up, actually. Which I'm now saving for a rainy day. And maybe a new boiler.

The humiliation was the worst thing about it all really, once I worked out that I wasn't actually heartbroken. And when I thought about it Cindy was welcome to him. I just felt so stupid, because it turned out that everyone thought he was completely hopeless, almost right from the start. And it's a bit embarrassing when you realise that all your friends have been going oh god, isn't he awful, behind your back, and not telling you, and it's only after he's gone that they say oh well, we always thought he was crap, and you're better off without him. But I suppose it's notoriously tricky telling someone that you think their new bloke is a disaster, because the minute you do they nearly always turn round and marry them, and then don't speak to you for years, not until after their divorce.

The only thing I still mind about is Alfie. I really feel like I've let him down. Jim says he's bound to be better off growing up without Patric in his life every day, and that's got to be true, I suppose, but it's still hard. Especially when Patric turns up playing Mr Bountiful, buying him all sorts of presents, and I'm the Wicked Witch who makes him eat broccoli and wear socks. Whichever way you look at it you end up feeling a failure; and if Alfie grows up to be a crack cocaine addict or something I'll know it's all my fault, and the really annoying thing is so will Patric. And it does feel a bit like someone has stamped Reject in the middle of your forehead and put you back on the conveyor belt, like some lost bit of tat in *The Generation Game*, but you still have to try to be civilised when he turns up for a visit, for Alfie's sake, just in case one day he might actually turn into a half-decent father and give Alfie a vital bit of male bonding. How to do a wee standing up, or something crucial like that. So you're sort of stuck being accommodating to someone you really want to poke in the eye and never see again, which is a complete bugger really.

Making fairy cakes with three-year-olds when you've got a hangover is definitely one of those things that are much better in theory than when you're standing there clutching a wooden spoon trying to persuade them not to put cake mixture in the pocket of your pinny. Alfie's pretty keen on cooking, but only if he can do it his way, which usually means a great deal of bashing about with a wooden spoon and eating half the mixture before you can get it into the oven.

We've done the creaming-the-ingredients-together thing, which took slightly longer than usual because I forgot to take the butter out of the fridge. I tried putting it in the microwave but it disappeared except for a small brown stain on the plate, so we had to start all over again, and now we're at the bit where you put a spoonful in each paper case, as quickly as you can before Alfie eats it.

I've still got to light the fire in the living room so we don't get hypothermia before bedtime, and try to finish the plans for the Dawsons' kitchen extension, which has to include space for their gigantic new American fridge. They're coming in for a meeting tomorrow, and I really need to have something to show them. And if they tell me one more time that they can't decide if they want to go Shaker or Provençal I'm going to shut them in that bloody fridge.

And then the phone rings. It's Patric. Hooray.

'I'm not going to be able to make this Sunday.'

'Right.'

'I'm terribly busy at work, but I'm sure next weekend will be fine.'

'Alfie will be thrilled.'

'Do you have to be so difficult? Honestly, Alice, you do seem to take pleasure in making things as adversarial as possible.'

Adversarial is one of Patric's new words. He got it from his solicitor, who handled our non-divorce divorce – since we weren't married, although it bloody felt like it from where I was sitting. Not being adversarial is terribly important, apparently, especially if there are children involved. And especially if you're the one who's doing the leaving, and don't want to be made to feel guilty about it.

'I'm rather busy at the moment, actually. We're making cakes.'

'Well, I'd better let you get on with it then. I wouldn't want to interrupt anything vital.'

I put the phone down, muttering to myself. He's such a bastard. That's the second time he's cancelled this month. Not that Alfie really minds, but he might. I mean Patric doesn't know he doesn't sit there with his face pressed up against the window waiting for Daddy to arrive. Well, actually, to be fair, he probably does, but I don't see why I should be fair where he's concerned. The truth is Alfie's pretty sanguine about Patric's non-appearances, although he likes getting presents, and Patric usually brings at least one guilt-assuaging bit of plastic crap that makes a loud noise or shoots things into the back of your legs.

'Look, Mummy, I'm being Peter Pan.'

'That's lovely, darling. Let's just wash your hands and face.'

'Peter Pan doesn't have his face washed.'

'Of course he does. If he's been making cakes, he does.'

Peter Pan's wooden spoon misses my nose by a few millimetres.

'I'm Peter Pan and I can fly.'

He runs off down the hall. Oh god. I charge after him and manage to catch him just as he launches himself into mid-air from halfway up the stairs and begin, for the umpteenth time, to explain to him why he can't actually fly, even if he is wearing a green felt hat.

'Alfie. We've talked about this. You can't fly off the stairs – you hurt your leg last time, remember.'

'Yes, but I'm a much better flier now. I can fly off the slide at playgroup now, I can, I did it yesterday. Mrs Taylor said I was very clever.'

'Yes, but the slide has a proper bouncy mat at the bottom, doesn't it?'

'You be Captain Hooker and I'll run away.'

'It's Hook, Alfie, not Hooker.'

It's important he gets this right because he keeps asking me to be the Hooker when we're at the swings, which makes people give me very funny looks, although I suppose I could just slap on a bit of extra make-up and sit twirling my handbag: it would definitely be easier than charging around swashbuckling.

'Would you like to watch a video?'

16

'*Peter Pan*, *Peter Pan*, please can we watch *Peter Pan*?'

'OK, but only if you don't keep jumping off the sofa.'

I hate Peter Pan. I think Wendy should have locked that window and told him to bugger off. It's enough to make you nostalgic for *Thomas the Incredibly Boring Tank Engine*.

I try to give the living room a quick tidy while the cakes are in, but Alfie's not really helping, and then he starts hopping up and down making whining noises because he's hungry. He's a really good little eater, as my mum would say, which is a nice way of saying he's a complete little porker, which is what Jim calls him. I'm trying to do that thing where you ignore them, until they get bored and stop doing whatever it is that's driving you round the bend, only he doesn't seem to have noticed, which is quite annoying actually.

He eats his tea in about thirty seconds flat, and is still clamouring for more cakes as I get him ready for a walk up the lane, so we can check out the new people in the big house, which takes rather longer than I'd planned because one of his wellies has gone missing, although I finally find it in the vegetable rack.

I'm not really looking forward to trailing up the lane and introducing myself to perfect strangers, just so Molly can keep her end up in the gossip stakes with Janice. But there are pretty much no limits when it comes to keeping whoever looks after your kids happy, I suppose: it's the Achilles heel of all working mothers. I'm so lucky Mum looks after Alfie: at least when it's your mum you can have the occasional whine about how you'd prefer it if they didn't let your child eat chocolate, and there's a slim chance she might pretend to listen before she slips him another KitKat.

It's freezing cold outside, but at least it's not raining, and a little walk might just get him tired before bedtime. He might miraculously fall asleep early and I can get some work done, instead of traipsing up and down the stairs getting him back into bed and bringing him drinks of water.

But whenever I've got work to finish he's bound to be

bouncing on his bed for hours. I'm seriously thinking of getting him a futon. At least he wouldn't bounce quite so high, and it would probably be terribly good for his posture. But there's probably some rule about not putting three-year-olds on futons. And anyway Mum would never forgive me – she's only just got over Jim getting a water bed.

It's only six o'clock but it's already pitch-black outside so we have to take the torch, which I bought for the power cuts that happen every couple of months round here for some reason, usually when I'm in the middle of cooking tea. Alfie is thrilled to be out in the dark, and has brought his sword in case we meet Captain Hooker.

The house is just up the lane from ours, and every single light appears to be on and the front door is wide open. Alfie bolts for freedom and attempts to climb into the back of one of the two huge removal vans parked in the drive. Big lorries are another of his passions. I grab his hand and pull him towards the door just as a woman appears.

'Hello, stop that, Alfie, I'm Alice, I live just down the lane so I thought I'd come up and say hello and welcome, and, Alfie, Stop That.'

'Oh how lovely. Do come in – we're all over the place at the moment, and the removal men have screwed up completely. Half our stuff's still in London.'

My god, how much stuff can they have? Our entire house would fit in the back of one of these lorries.

'My name's Lola, Lola Barker. Lovely to meet you. Oh there you are.'

A man emerges from the darkness as if he's been trying to hide.

'Stop skulking behind that lorry and tell me what's going on. Have they tracked him down yet, or what?'

'Well, as I've said, madam, we are very sorry. He shouldn't be much longer – he's just outside Maidstone. The battery on his mobile's gone but he phoned from a call box. And head office want us back at the depot, so if it's all right by you we'll be off.'

'No, it is not all right by me. Jesus. You can wait right here and help unload the bloody thing when it does turn up.'

'But, madam, I'll have to call head office again and they won't like it.'

'Funnily enough, I don't give a damn. I'm not feeling too happy myself. Not since you've managed to lose half my furniture.'

'Nothing has been lost, madam. I have explained. The puncture put him back a bit, and then he took a wrong turning. He'll be along shortly – he's just outside Maidstone.'

'Yes, but heading in what direction, I wonder? He's an idiot. You know it. And I know it. The only difference is I'm paying him to be an idiot. It doesn't seem possible that you could screw up such a simple process. Put stuff in boxes, deliver them, unpack them. Even a gibbon could do it.'

The removal man is walking backwards now.

'I tell you what. You ring up your head office. Maybe they can send out sniffer dogs to see if they can find him. But trust me. You are not going to be leaving here until the entire job is done. Is that clear?'

'Yes, madam.'

'Good.'

'Any chance of a cup of tea while we're waiting?'

'I don't think so. Do you?'

'No, madam.'

The removal man now seems frozen to the spot.

'I'm so sorry about that – do come in. Charles, where are you?'

She yells up the stairs, and I half expect a Labrador to come bounding down, but I'm pretty sure she's calling her husband.

Alfie's been silenced by the sheer force of her tirade, and he's been trying to sneak back towards the lorry, but then he spots a *Star Wars* light-sabre lying on the floor and picks it up seconds before a dark-haired boy belts down the stairs and grabs it from him.

'That's mine.'

What a charming child.

'Oh Ezra, don't be horrible, darling. Let him have a go.'

'No.'

'Aren't small boys foul? He's had a long day – he's not normally this revolting. Actually, that's not entirely true. Oh there you are, Charles. What on earth have you been doing?'

A man appears at the top of the stairs carrying a little girl who's squirming to be let down. He carries her down the stairs and puts her down, whereupon she toddles towards her brother and starts poking him.

'Trying to stop Ezra locking Mabel in our wardrobe, if you must know.'

Oh my god. It's the man from the pub. The one Molly said had a gorgeous arse. At least I think it is. Oh Christ. I wonder if he'll recognise me. I mean it was only a few minutes, and it was mainly Molly who was making all the noise.

'Charles, this is Alice.'

'Hello, Alice.'

I'm pretty sure he recognises me. He's sort of smirking. Bugger. How annoying.

Ezra decides that this is the perfect moment to shove his little sister with his light-sabre, but she's obviously tougher than she looks because she retaliates by whacking him so hard he almost falls over. And then they both start yelling. Really loudly. Alfie looks very impressed.

'Oh for Christ's sake. Look, I've got some chocolate buttons in one of my bags in the kitchen, but only for people who aren't yelling.'

Not only can this woman terrify removal men, but both children shut up immediately and even Alfie stands up a bit straighter in an effort to put in his bid for some chocolate buttons. The children all charge after her as she heads off towards what must be the kitchen. The house is enormous.

'Magic, isn't it? God, we'd be fucked without chocolate, wouldn't we?'

How brilliant. A new neighbour who's not a Stepford Wife, and says fuck. Molly will be thrilled.

'The kitchen's this way.'

Charles is holding the door from the hall open for me.

'Thanks.'

'Did I see you in the pub the other night? I was down sorting out the builders and we popped in for a quick drink. There was some quiz on, I think.'

'Um, possibly, yes. I'm afraid me and my friend drank slightly too much and it's all a bit vague.'

God. I sound like I'm thirteen. Me and my friend.

'Well, it looked as if everyone was having great fun.'

Oh good. He's not going to repeat the arse thing. Good.

'And it was very nice to hear such appreciative comments from your friend, I must say. Quite made my night.'

I think the best thing is probably to ignore it, and hope he thinks I don't really know what he's talking about. But he's still doing the slightly smiling, smirking thing. Double bugger.

The chocolate buttons are distributed, and a young woman called Sam appears and Lola tells her to take the children off to watch television. She doesn't look that keen.

'God, I hate sulky nannies, don't you?'

I don't really know what to say to this, since I've never had a nanny, sulking or not. But I sort of nod and try to be non-committal because apart from anything else I'm not sure she can't still hear us.

But Lola doesn't seem to care.

'I'll be glad to see the back of her, although finding another one will be a total nightmare as usual. Charles, is there any gin?'

'I don't think so. I think it's in the other van.'

'How come everything is in the other van? Jesus, do I have to think of everything?'

There's an awkward silence. But Charles doesn't appear to be too bothered at being told off in front of perfect strangers. I get the feeling it probably happens quite often, because he just ignores it.

He's rather handsome in a mildly public-schoolboy sort of way, with lovely blue eyes, and a friendly sort of face. Lola is dark and exotic-looking, fashionably skinny and wearing velvet trousers, which must have cost a fortune, and the kind of cardigan that you can't buy in Marks & Spencer.

'I've brought a bottle of wine – just cheap stuff, but it might be all right – as a little housewarming sort of thing.'

'Fabulous. What an angel.'

It turns out the corkscrew is also on the other van, but the glasses have been unpacked, and with a bit of shoving and poking Charles manages to get the cork out with a fork.

'It's like being a student again, isn't it? I spent half my life at college opening bottles of wine with forks.'

'Did you, darling? How sweet. Why didn't you just buy a corkscrew?'

Charles goes rather pink, but Lola doesn't seem to notice.

'So, Alice, have you lived in the village long?'

'Oh only a few years, but I grew up round here – a couple of villages away, actually.'

'Charles had a country childhood too. He's always banging on about the pleasures of a rural childhood, aren't you, darling? That's why we moved really. Well, that and the fact that you can't buy a decent house in London for under a million any more. It's getting beyond a joke.'

We talk about London house prices, and how much more you get for your money in the country, and I pick up all sorts of info for Molly. Lola works in an advertising agency in London, and clearly earns a fortune, and she's going to set up an office at home so she'll only have to go up to London a couple of days a week. Her father's some sort of famous composer, who I've never heard of but she's clearly very proud of him because she mentions him twice during our conversation in slightly reverential tones, although she's less keen on her mother, who she says has devoted her life to The Great Man, and can't be relied on for much in the way of motherly behaviour.

Charles's parents are obviously very rich because they

seem to own a large chunk of Hampshire, which is why Lola decided to move down here, so his mother can't pop round too often. She breeds Labradors, and is very bossy, and Lola says she's a complete cow.

And Charles is an art dealer, who buys paintings in local auctions and then gets them restored and sells them, apart from the ones he falls in love with, which judging by the number of paintings propped up in little piles all over the place must be quite a few. He's completely different when he talks about paintings, and gets quite carried away when he starts showing me a landscape, covered in layers of grime, he's just found in a job lot at an auction. And then he finds a picture of a bowl of cream roses that's really lovely and he starts telling me all about the artist, until Lola tells him to shut up, because he's being very boring. Which actually he isn't, but I can't quite work out how to say this without being rude.

Lola seems very impressed that I'm an architect, even though I explain that I spend most of my time coming up with plans for extensions rather than knocking off plans for a new Tate Maidstone. She then launches into the inevitable What Can I Do With My Kitchen conversation. That's the trouble with being an architect: people tend to ask you for ideas even if you've only been in their house for five minutes. I suppose it's the same if you're a doctor, and people roll up their trouser legs and show you their rash in Sainsbury's.

My favourites are the ones who launch into a speech about the evils of modern architecture, and expect you to defend the Millennium Dome for hours. I wish I'd known about all of this before I went to college. Sometimes I just avoid the issue altogether and say that my main job is being Alfie's mum, because that tends to make people look at you like you're an idiot, give you a condescending smile, and then wander off.

'Now tell me all about the village, Alice – I want to get to know people. Is there lots going on?'

Somehow I can't quite see Lola enjoying the WI or joining the happy clappers at the church.

'There's a Garden Society – my friend Molly's joining and there's a meeting next week, I think. I'm going along too. I'll ring you with the time and everything if you're interested.'

'Great. And if you know of any good nannies knocking about, do pass them my way. I'm supposed to be interviewing soon, so if you can think of anyone, tell them to give me a call, but not anyone too needy or neurotic. I've had enough of those.'

'I can't think of anyone at the moment.'

'Is yours any good?'

'Sorry?'

'Your nanny?'

There's something about the way she's smiling at me, in a slightly menacing, too-much-teeth-on-show kind of way, that makes me think Lola might just be the kind of woman who'd nick your nanny off you if you weren't concentrating, without a second's hesitation.

'Oh I don't have one – my mum looks after Alfie for me on the days I'm working.'

'Good god, does she? How fabulous. Do you think she'd like any more? Only Ezra's at school most of the time, so it's only Mabel really.'

Christ. I can just imagine Mum's face if I tried to foist another toddler on her. I mean she has Lily sometimes, but only as a favour to Molly. She's not in the business of setting up a crèche or anything.

'Oh no, she's got her hands full with Alfie.'

'Really? He seemed so sweet, I'm sure she wouldn't notice another one. Maybe she could pop round for tea and see what she thinks. Shall I ask her?'

'I'm pretty sure –'

'Yes, but she could just come round and see, couldn't she?'

'Lola, do stop trying to get Alice to sort out our childcare arrangements. I've told you, I'm more than happy to cope while we sort something out.'

'Yes. Thank you, Charles. But your idea of coping and mine are slightly different, aren't they? I mean if I don't want the house to look like a smart bomb has hit it we need a professional on the job, don't we? Anyway, Alice, do ask her, I'd really appreciate it, because I'd prefer someone local if possible – they won't want the ridiculous amounts of money the London ones charge.'

Right. So that's told me then.

'I'd better let you get on – you must have loads to do – but if you need anything I'm just down the lane.'

Anything apart from sorting out her childcare, although to be fair maybe she didn't mean to be quite so domineering about it all. I know how desperate people get when it comes to finding childcare. Molly says she seriously thought she'd have to give up work before she found Janice, or hide Lily under her desk or something.

We find the children watching telly, and Alfie seems to have gone into a sort of trance on the sofa while Sam sits stroking his back. He's a total sucker for having his back stroked. Sam says he's a lovely little boy, and looks rather pointedly at Ezra, who is busy unravelling the sleeve of his jumper, but then Alfie begins to whine and we make a swift exit before Sam changes her mind. Lola says Alfie can come back tomorrow and watch the rest of the film, which appears to be something extremely violent involving kung fu.

I manage to get him out of the door and halfway up the lane before he realises we are heading home to bed, where-upon he kung fu kicks his way into an epic tantrum, hurls his sword into a bush and then demands I retrieve it, and by the time we get home he's exhausted.

I put him straight into pyjamas, and read to him from the most boring books I can find until he falls asleep. And then I end up falling asleep in front of the fire and wake up at midnight, with a crick in my neck. I'll have to get up early tomorrow morning to finish the bloody plans. Excellent.

*　　*　　*

Molly and I are due at the garden thing at eight, and it's pouring, so I pick her up in my car and we arrive just as Lola is getting out of an extremely posh-looking brand-new Volvo. She immediately puts us both to shame by appearing to be on a first-name basis with far more villagers than we are, after only living here for a few days. She seems very confident about marching up to people and introducing herself, which is very impressive although I can see Mrs Pomeroy is rather surprised to find herself being upstaged quite so early in the evening.

Lola's wearing a fabulous purple tweed suit with very trendy boots, which makes me feel rather drab in my boring old jeans and jumper, but I hope she's got thermal underwear on because the hall's going to be freezing. I try surreptitiously to put on some lip gloss, but it's quite tricky in the dark and I end up putting too much on and then I have to rub it off so my fingers end up all greasy. I hope we don't have to shake hands with fellow gardeners, or they're going to think I'm a very messy eater or something.

Quite a few people have turned up already, and are sitting down on the chairs in front of the stage. Most of them are wearing scarves and what looks like at least two jumpers under their coats, and a couple of them are wearing woolly hats. A committee of ancient villagers is starting to assemble round a table up on the platform, with one man needing the help of two others to get him up the steps. Molly says she thinks we might have got the wrong night, and this is Help the Aged.

'If they start playing bingo, let's make a run for it.'

Lola laughs.

'God, it's freezing in here. Tell me if anything happens. I'm just nipping out to get my coat.'

She returns wearing a rather startling orange duffel coat, with what looks like real fur round the collar.

'Before you ask, Charles's mother gave it to me. I think she hoped someone would throw paint at me in Sloane Square. It happened to one of her old-bag friends once when she was wearing her mink. Christ, I wish I'd been there. Anyway I thought it would be perfect for the country – I mean it practically glows in the dark. And anyway the fur's fake, thank god.'

'Oh, I'm so glad you said that. Are you anti-fur too?'

Molly used to be a hunt saboteur at university, and once got chased for nearly a mile by some chinless hooray riding an extremely large horse and blowing a bugle.

'No, darling, I couldn't give a fuck – I'd wear hamster if it was fashionable – but it's totally verboten, isn't it, wearing fur.'

'You'd need an awful lot of hamsters to make a decent coat.'

Lola laughs, and so does Molly, but I notice Lola giving her a rather hard look.

Then some bossy-looking woman in a startling green hat claps her hands and Mrs Pomeroy begins reading out the agenda and asks everyone to remember to pay their subscriptions, because the new membership cards are ready.

The final announcement is that someone called Mr Channing had brought his photographs, and if anyone's going in for brassicas this year they should see him after the meeting. An elderly man waves a packet of photos in the air and looks encouragingly at the audience. One or two members of the committee shift uncomfortably in their seats.

Lola whispers, 'What are brassicas?' rather loudly and Molly says she thinks they might be cabbages.

'You can't be serious. Good God, it's like the twilight zone.'

I wonder what the correct response is when you're presented with a photograph of a cabbage. You're probably just supposed to go oh how lovely, like you do when people show their baby photos, even if the baby looks like a piglet. In fact especially if it looks like a piglet.

The meeting moves on to a discussion about the plant stall at the Summer Fair, and things get a bit lively. A woman in a navy-blue padded jacket says she thinks we should try something different this year, and make up some pots of herbs, and another woman, sitting a few rows away, says personally she doesn't think you can beat a nice geranium and she doesn't care who knows it, and she's won prizes for her geraniums, and people look forward to them. It's a lot of work getting them all potted up, but if the committee don't want her to bother that's fine by her.

Mr Cabbages then enters the fray and says he thinks herbs are a lovely idea, and would be a welcome addition to the stall, but they couldn't possibly do without the geraniums as well. Things calm down a bit after that, and there's a discussion about a new plant-share scheme, but I don't think I've actually got anything to share except for weeds, which I don't imagine is quite what the committee had in mind.

Just when I'm hoping they're about to wheel the tea trolley in a nice-looking woman stands up and begins talking about rose gardens, which is very interesting, if slightly incomprehensible, due to her use of phrases like hybrid-teas and floribundas. She has some pictures of her favourites which she circulates round the audience and they all have lovely names like Iced Ginger, and Old Blush China, and then she announces that you have to be careful if you're going in for a lot of Golden Showers, which gives the three of us a bit of a start, but it turns out to be the name of a perfectly nice-looking yellow rose. Lola is snorting with laughter by this point, and Molly has got the giggles too.

Two women finally wheel in the tea trolley, and the rose woman is thanked, and Mrs Pomeroy announces a National Design a Garden competition, run by the BBC and some magazine, and says it would be wonderful if the village could come up with an entry because she happens to know that Upper Bridge are already working on their entry, and everybody tuts and says how typical.

While Molly and I queue for tea Lola goes off in search of Mrs Pomeroy. She comes back and says she thinks she might enter Charles for the competition.

'I mean we've got stacks of land, far more than we know what do with, and it's all boring grass.'

'Is he a keen gardener then?'

'Not really, but he could learn. It'll give him something to focus on. He spends far too much time wandering about with those bloody paintings, if you ask me.'

'Mightn't it be better to start off with something simple?'

'Possibly. And I suppose his bloody mother would be bound to stick her oar in. But we've got to do something with it – it's so boring, just lawns and a few old flowerbeds. Totally suburban. I know, maybe you could design us something fabulous, Alice?'

Bloody hell.

'I bet you could, Alice.'

I could kill Molly sometimes.

'No, not really. I mean I'd love to help, of course, but I don't know the first thing about gardens.'

'Oh what a shame. But the Garden Society could help you, couldn't they? You could do the design, and they could do the plants. We'll donate the land, and then the village can enter the competition. Perfect.'

'We could make it a community project, and get everyone involved.'

'Oh I don't know.'

Actually, I do. It's a ridiculous idea, I don't know the first thing about designing gardens, and I don't know what Molly thinks she's up to agreeing with Lola, but I feel quite tempted to give her a kick.

Lola looks very pleased.

'Brilliant. Everybody's always going on about all this community bollocks and some of this lot are well past their sell-by dates. That'd get us extra points with the judges, I bet.'

'You know what, we could do a kitchen garden, and then we'd learn all about veg and stuff while we did it.'

'I don't want to learn all about veg, Molly. It's you that wants to grow veg, not me.'

But Lola thinks it's a great idea and gets even more enthusiastic.

'I'd adore a proper kitchen garden, with herbs. I love herbs. Excellent. So we'll donate the land, and you'll do the design. Brilliant.'

Lola gives me a dazzling smile, which is a bit scary, to be honest.

'Let's get that woman over.'

Before I can stop her she's marched off to retrieve Mrs Pomeroy.

Bugger. Apparently we now have a new village project. I will be designing a new kitchen garden for Lola and Charles's garden, and the Garden Society will come up with all the planting ideas. They're forming a special sub-committee, and Charles has been volunteered to help, and Molly says she'll bring her books round. Mrs Pomeroy's thrilled, and I've already been commended for my community spirit. Bloody hell. I think I'll just do a plan with lots of steel pipes and unusual-coloured cement. That should sort it. Or acres of gravel and a steel hammock.

I have a bit of a meltdown moment back at my house with Molly, after Lola has gone home triumphant and we've drunk the best part of a bottle of wine. Actually Molly didn't really fancy any, and Lola was driving, so basically I've drunk the best part of a bottle of wine, and I'm feeling slightly wobbly.

'I can't do it, I really can't.'

'Yes you can, and anyway it's too late now, you've got to do it. It'll just be a couple of walls and a few beds. Nothing too tricky. We'll look through the books – there's bound to be something.'

'Molly, just looking through a few books isn't how it works.'

'I know you can do it, and I'll help you, I really will. Ooh, I've just thought, we've got to have a water feature.'

'A what?'

'A pond, or a fountain or something.'

'Oh great. Maybe we could have a well, a really deep one. So I can chuck myself down it when it all goes pear-shaped and the whole village hates me.'

'Pears. Brilliant. We could have fruit trees.'

'Who said anything about trees? Bloody hell.'

'All the traditional kitchen gardens have fruit trees, I think. Quinces, that sort of thing.'

'I'm not even sure I know what a quince looks like.'

'Neither am I, but it'll be fine, I'm sure it will, and it'll do us no end of good in the village. Blimey, is that the time? I'd better go. I've still got notes to do for tomorrow.'

Great. So now I've got to obsess about trying to design a garden on top of everything else. On my way up to bed I notice the collection of empty wine bottles by the bin: I must move them before Mum arrives tomorrow. Last week she gave me a long speech about how Nobody Likes Drunk Women, and when I said most of the men I know seem rather partial to them she went all huffy. I keep forgetting to go to the bottle bank, and last time I went I ended up feeling like a team leader for Alcoholics Anonymous.

But having her looking after Alfie for three days a week is so great, even if she does drive me round the bend and is addicted to bleach. She even cleans behind the fridge. I don't know anyone else who actually cleans behind their fridge, and if there's ever a bleach shortage she'll have to be taken into care. But she loves Alfie, and she's much more indulgent with him than she was with us, and never makes him eat liver and onions: Jim used to hide his down his socks, which was easy for him because his socks were grey, which was pretty much the colour of the liver, but mine were white so of course when I tried it I ended up with a lecture about ungrateful children.

And she's been so great about everything really, once she got over the shock of Patric leaving. She got a bit upset at first, but that was mostly Nan's fault. She was round for tea and gave us all a bit of a shock by announcing that she thought it was probably a good thing Patric had left because she'd never liked him, he had shifty eyes, and anyway times had changed and I'd got a proper job and could take care of myself, probably better than with some man hanging about, causing more work and wanting his tea cooked for him.

And then she made the whole thing worse by saying if she had her time again she wasn't sure she'd have bothered with men, because they made such a mess and that sex business wore off after a while, and when you got to her age you realised that what really mattered was taking your chances when they came along, and having a bit of fun. And she'd seen some lovely blue wool, and did Alfie want a cardigan or a jacket, or a nice little hat and some socks, although to be honest she wouldn't mind if I wasn't keen on socks because they were quite fiddly.

Mum had to have a couple of tablets after that but by the time I was leaving she and Nan were bickering about whether balaclavas were more practical than bobble hats, and whether boys could wear lemon.

While I'm brushing my teeth Alfie wakes up and shuffles into my bed and I'm so knackered I give in. He grabs the entire duvet, rolls himself up inside it like a mini-sausage roll, and I have to wrestle him back out again and then grip on tight so I won't wake up in the middle of the night with hypothermia.

He sleeps in a sort of starfish position, taking up most of the bed, and flinging his arms about in an entirely random manner so I keep getting slapped on the back of the head just as I'm drifting off, which is fabulous and really helps me get to sleep. Perfect.

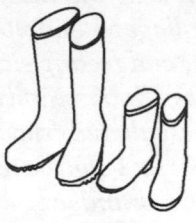

2

FEBRUARY
Tea with Mussolini

Garden Diary

A month of very chancy weather. Prepare herb and vegetable gardens ready for planting when weather permits. Order asparagus plants, sow parsley, and early peas. Finish winter pruning of fruit trees. Aerate and scarify lawns.

I try to have another go at digging, but the constant rain over the past few weeks has turned the flowerbeds into mini quagmires and my wellies get stuck in the mud. According to my book scarify means jabbing the lawn with a fork to improve drainage, so I give it a go but the fork gets stuck in the mud and I end up slipping and sliding about like someone in a Benny Hill sketch. Alfie sits in a huge puddle in the front garden, which is actually more like a small lake. I plodge through it to retrieve him, and end up soaked, and then he takes his wellies off and has another stamp round. Give up and go indoors and sit by the fire thinking about asparagus, but end up having a major panic attack about the garden-design project. If I can't even dig

*my own flowerbeds how can I possibly have the cheek
to attempt to design a whole new garden on behalf of
the entire flaming village? I end up eating half a packet
of digestive biscuits, and feeling sick, and then I look at
some of the gardening books Molly has brought round,
but the sections on espaliered fruit trees and pollination
only make things worse. I eat the rest of the biscuits and
end up feeling very sick indeed.*

LOLA'S ASKED ME ROUND for coffee to talk about the
garden, so I walk up the lane after I've dropped Alfie off
at playgroup, but manage to pick the perfect time to arrive,
slap in the middle of a domestic moment with the new nanny
Susannah, who's only just started and is already causing
ructions. Charles says that she seems to have some problem
with ironing, and sure enough as we walk into the kitchen
she's in the middle of explaining to Lola that she doesn't
think doing Lola's ironing is part of her job.

'Actually, I shouldn't really be doing the children's ironing
either. You did say at the interview that you employed a
cleaner. I'm a fully qualified childcare professional, you
know.'

Charles and I both sit down at the kitchen table with our
mouths slightly open at Susannah's sheer nerve. I wouldn't
disagree with Lola unless I was on very firm ground, and
even then I'd think twice about it.

'Yes, but Mrs Bishop is away for a few days, and you do
seem willing to bend the rules sometimes, don't you? Because
spending ages on the phone talking to your friends isn't
actually part of your job either, but you seem bloody keen on
it. You're part of the family now, Suzy, and we all have to
muck in, all part of the same team, if you know what I mean.
Actually, do you know what I mean? Because sometimes I
wonder.'

Lola has narrowed her eyes and has a rather formidable
look on her face. It's a bit like watching a car crash: you
know what's going to happen but there isn't time to do

anything about it. I just hope there's an airbag somewhere in this kitchen because it looks like Susannah might be needing one.

'Of course I do. I have worked as a nanny for nearly six years, actually, but my last family employed a cleaner, and someone to do the ironing. And actually I'd prefer it if you called me Susannah.'

'Oh. I see. And is there anything else you'd like to share?'

'Well, yes, now you mention it, there is.'

Charles mouths 'Oh god' at me, and pretends to duck under the table, which sort of makes me snigger, only I end up making the kind of noise you'd make if you were trying to do an impression of a pig, which is very embarrassing, and makes Charles laugh, so Lola glares at both of us, which is even more embarrassing.

'You did say I would have the use of a car, but every time I ask you say it's not convenient. And it's not really fair – I need a car. I do have a social life, you know.'

'Oh I know. And I'm sure my phone bill will show us just what a busy girl you are.'

'I've already told you, I use my mobile most of the time.'

'Yes, but the thing is, Susannah, while you're chatting away on your mobile I'm actually paying you to look after my children. You're meant to be helping them, giving them learning opportunities, that kind of thing. But unless they're going to grow up to be telephonists you're not offering them very much in the way of skills, are you? Apart from advanced sulking, which they're pretty good at already, thank you very much. And then when I ask you to do the simplest thing you refuse. It's ridiculous, I can't imagine how your previous employers put up with it. Maybe they weren't very good at closure. But luckily I am. So here's what we'll do. You go and pack your bags, and Charles will drop you at the station. I think we can officially say your probationary period is over.'

'What?'

'Communication skills aren't really your strong point, are they? I've noticed that before. OK, let me make it crystal clear. You are fired. And if you could get a move on I'd appreciate it because I'm rather busy today. Now, do you need me to ring you on your mobile to explain it to you again, or do you think you've grasped the basic idea?'

Susannah bursts into tears and runs from the room.

'Oh for fuck's sake. I've got a good mind to ring that bloody agency and give them a piece of my mind. That girl's a total nightmare. Oh and by the way, Charles, you'd better go to the shop once you've dropped her at the station. We've run out of apple juice. Don't just sit there looking at me like that. If someone doesn't get Mabel out of her high chair soon she'll start throwing things. Take her up with you and see what that bloody girl's up to. She's been paid for this week already, so don't let her con you into giving her any more money.'

Charles looks slightly dazed, but picks up Mabel and goes off upstairs.

I'm half in awe of how tough Lola's been, and half appalled. I mean apart from anything else it can't be exactly relaxing for the children if new nannies keep turning up all the time. I can't believe Lola's being so calm – I'd be in a complete state. It took me nearly six months to pluck up the courage to tell the woman in the village shop that my name wasn't Alison. But Lola seems quite cheerful, as if she's almost enjoyed herself.

'Look, I can come back, Lola. This obviously isn't a good time.'

'Oh yes it is. I'd much rather be talking about the garden than thinking about bloody nannies. Where have you got to so far?'

We talk about circular walls while Lola makes the coffee, and I tell her that I'm thinking about a kind of secret garden in one corner of the main garden, with trees and an arched doorway. Although obviously it won't be madly secret, since half the village will be busy drawing up plans for the flower-beds.

Lola gets very excited and starts talking about some garden she's seen at a posh country-house hotel, which had lots of stainless-steel walls and unusual types of lettuce.

Charles and Susannah depart in the middle of our chat, in total silence, although Charles does give Lola a pretty filthy look, which she totally ignores.

'I knew that girl was going to be trouble, as soon as she said she was a vegetarian. I mean, not that I've got anything against vegetarians as friends, but I need someone who can grill bacon for breakfast without going all sulky. It's a complete nightmare though, because now I'll have to get back on to the agencies, and they're all useless. The only thing they're really good at is cashing your cheque. Bastards. Still, at least Charles can cope for a bit – he seems to quite like looking after the kids. God knows why. Oh fuck, I've just remembered, she was supposed to be organising Ezra's birthday party. You will come, won't you? We're having an entertainer, and loads of people are coming down from work. I thought I might as well use the opportunity for a little open-house sort of thing. Sushi might be fun, and we can have our first gathering of the garden people too.'

'Oh yes, lovely.'

I can't imagine what the old men from the Garden Society will make of sushi, but I can't wait to find out, although it does seems a bit hard on Ezra, having his birthday party turned into a sushi event. I'm sure he'd prefer *Batman* or *Bob The Annoying Builder*.

'I'll get my PA to send out proper invitations, and Molly must come too, and all the gardening lot. You don't happen to have their names and addresses, do you? If you have them on disc that would be great.'

I'm not really sure why she thinks I might be the sort of person who has address lists on disc. I wish I was.

'I only know half their names really, but I bet Mrs Pomeroy's got a proper list.'

'Good, I'll get Sophie to call her, and she can liaise with the magician. Bloody hell, I feel tired just thinking about it. And I've got nothing to wear.'

We start talking about clothes, and end up upstairs in Lola's bedroom in her walk-in wardrobe, which is bigger than Alfie's bedroom, and much more interesting, while Lola rifles through countless fabulous outfits. I've never seen quite so many designer labels, or quite so many pairs of gorgeous shoes.

The bedroom is stunning, with acres of pale-wood flooring, and tiny Persian rugs, and the bed is vast, with a white duvet and an enormous pale-cream blanket draped over the end. It looks suspiciously like cashmere. God knows how much a cashmere blanket that size would cost but I just know it would be the kind of money that would make Mum fall into a dead faint. There's a big chocolate-brown velvet sofa at the end of the bed, with grey woollen cushions. It's like being in Heals, but without the annoyance of other customers going, 'Oh Jocasta, that's just perfect for the villa.'

The bathroom's pretty stunning too, with a pale-cream marble shower that you could fit the whole family in, and Italian spotlights in the ceiling, which I happen to know are a complete bastard to fit because I used them on a job once, and they nearly drove the electrician demented. They short out every two nano-seconds if you don't get them fitted exactly right.

I end up getting a quick tour round, and the children's bedrooms are just as gorgeous as the rest of the house. Mabel's is a homage to the White Company, with pastel waffle blankets and pink gingham bedlinen, which I rather fancy for myself to be honest, and Ezra's is similar, but in yellow, with one of those beds in the shape of a racing car. The playroom is full of every toy imaginable, including a giant panda, and an enormous giraffe. Alfie will go into a complete swoon when he sees it.

'This house is fabulous, Lola. I only came in once before, but I remember lots of floral paper downstairs.'

No wonder the builders took six months to get the work done before Charles and Lola moved in. It must have cost a fortune.

'Oh yes, it was awful. We practically had to gut the place. It's a bit smaller than we wanted, though.'

There are three spare bedrooms, and there must be more room up in the attic, so I'm not sure how much bigger she could possibly have wanted.

Lola's mobile is ringing and vibrating itself round the kitchen table when we get back downstairs. Just before it vibrates on to the floor she grabs it, says, 'Oh fuck, it's the office,' and takes the call. It turns out there's some crisis that needs her to make a call to someone called Adrian or he's going to leave in a mega-sulk, and take all his business with him.

'They're complete morons. I told them not to tell him about the box idea – I knew he'd hate it. And now I have to sort it out. Typical. Anyway, let's do this again – I can't wait to see the garden plans. I wish I could work out how to turn this fucking thing off vibrate. It's new, I dropped the other one in the bath, and that stupid girl hasn't set it up properly. Do you know how to work these things?'

'Sorry, mine's ancient, but let me know if you need help with the party, won't you? If there's anything I can do.'

Please don't let her ask me where to get sushi round here.

'Oh you are sweet, thank you. I might take you up on that – I'm not really sure which kids to invite. Could you have a think? Nice children, Ezra's age especially, from the village. Just a few though – I don't want hordes of screaming kids charging about. I've got the names of a couple of his friends at school, but I want local children too.'

Ezra goes to the local posh prep school, where he has to wear one of those ridiculous uniforms based on Victorian chimney sweeps or something, with trousers in mustard-yellow corduroy.

I promise to think of names of 'nice' local children, and walk back down the lane wondering how mixing advertising types with villagers and the Garden Society is going to work out.

And I've got no idea what to wear either, which means I'll have to go shopping. I'd better ask Mum to look after Alfie, because going clothes shopping with him is like being in *Mission Impossible*, but without Tom Cruise. Maybe it won't really matter what I wear, as long as we get a really nice present for Ezra, and Alfie doesn't decide to try to smuggle out that giraffe. And Lola doesn't sack half the catering staff in the middle of the party.

Molly's come round for tea and seems more distracted than usual. Once we've settled the kids in front of cartoons with a packet of Hoola Hoops each we take refuge in the kitchen.

'Are you all right?'

'Yes.'

'You seem a bit quiet.'

'Well, the thing is –'

And then she bursts into tears, sort of quietly and not in a hysterical way or anything, which is a good job because I've got no idea what you're meant to do with someone who's hysterical, but I bet that slapping thing is a really bad idea. Molly's really not the tearful sort, so something awful must have happened.

'The thing is, I think I'm pregnant, and I just don't know if I can cope with two. I mean I know Dan will be pleased – he's always said he wanted another one, but it's not him that's got to have it.'

'You mean you haven't told him?'

'Not yet. I'm only a few weeks late.'

'How many's a few?'

'Nearly two months actually – well, two months on Saturday. I just wanted time to think about it before I tell him. I mean it makes it so official once he knows, like it's definite. And I'm not ready for that.'

'Have you done a test?'

'No, I couldn't face it. I've got one, it's in my bag. I've been sort of putting it off.'

'Well, come on then, let's do it. I'll make some more tea or something, boil some water. Oh, sorry.'

'It's all right, but come up with me.'

We go upstairs and Molly does the weeing-on-stick thing while I wait outside the bathroom door, feeling rather nervous all of a sudden, and then she re-emerges, waving the stick in the air. We both peer at it. A very bright blue line appears in the window, almost immediately.

I hug her, and she half smiles as we go back downstairs, but she looks rather pale and tired.

'I think it's lovely, Molly, I really do.'

'I'm sure I will too, once I get used to the idea. And Dan's a great dad, he really is.'

I wish she didn't sound quite so downbeat, like she's trying to convince herself it's going to be all right.

'You're all hormonal, and it's bound to take a bit of time to get used to it.'

'I suppose so. What should I do with this?'

She waves the pregnancy-test stick in the air.

'Put it in my bin if you like, although we'll have to wrap it up, because if Mum sees it she'll have a fit. Unless you want to keep it. I carried mine around for weeks.'

'No, I don't want to risk Dan finding it, not yet. I might tell him tonight, but I'm not sure. I feel like I need a few more days.'

Oh dear. That doesn't sound good.

'Do you want some tea?'

'No thanks, I should go really – I'm totally knackered. I'd forgotten how tired you get.'

I give her a hug as she's leaving and she hugs me back, quite hard, like she doesn't really want to leave, but then she seems to cheer up and starts talking about the garden again, and promises to bring another book round on her way home from school one night this week.

She says she'll call me later, but she doesn't, which I hope means she's talking to Dan or getting used to the idea or something. I'll call her tomorrow, just to see how she's feeling. God, I don't envy her. I mean having a new baby to cuddle will be lovely, obviously – there's something so wonderful about newborns. But it will also be lovely knowing that someone else is doing the night shifts.

I'm having a horrible time at work, and Janet's being extra annoying because Malcolm is away at some conference. She runs the business with Malcolm, and is also married to him, and she's completely obsessed: the way she carries on you'd think he was some major creative genius.

I don't think she was terribly keen when he announced he wanted to hire a bright young thing, especially when the bright young thing turned out to be me, and she's been pretty revolting ever since I started. At first I thought it was me, and I was feeling pretty sorry for myself at the end of my first week until Brenda, who works on reception and has been around for years, took pity on me and told me that everyone hates Janet and she's always horrible to new people, especially women, because she thinks they're after Malcolm, which made me feel a bit better. Although it's very annoying how women like Janet always seem to assume you're after their husbands. I mean you'd have to be so desperate to go after Malcolm you'd probably be on some sort of special medication.

And just to make work even more perfect than usual my barn-hating man and his wife have turned out to have such bad taste it's completely staggering. Every time I try to steer them towards something that won't make people actually faint when they walk through the door, they manage to screw it all up again. The latest is some tiles they've found for the kitchen, with random splashes of colour that look just like vomit. And a giant blue-plastic whirlpool bath with gold dolphin taps, which they think is lovely. Sometimes I really don't know why I bother.

Molly comes round with more gardening books, and we're trying to cheer each other up while the children play and watch videos for half an hour. She's told Dan and he's delighted, and she seems to be getting more into the idea too, which is great.

'Has your mum got over it yet?'

'Only just.'

The other night when I got in from work Mum was standing at the door with her arms crossed, and a face like thunder. She asked me if I had anything I wanted to tell her, like she used to do when Jim and I were little and we used to steal biscuits and hide the ones we didn't like under the carpet. I thought she'd seen the parking ticket I got a few weeks ago, so I said I didn't know what she was making such a fuss about and she nearly went into orbit.

It turned out she'd found Molly's pregnancy test. She says it fell out when she was putting something in the recycling bin, but I bet she was having a quick rootle about to see if there was anything interesting, because she's always telling me off for making Alfie oven chips instead of peeling potatoes and making proper ones. Anyway, she'd rung her friend Phyllis who used to work in Boots and found out that a blue line definitely means you're pregnant, and she wanted some answers. I ended up having to offer to ring Molly before she would believe me.

'How's Dan – still mad keen?'

'I think the initial excitement's worn off a bit.'

Oh dear. I thought she was looking a bit fed up when she arrived.

'I mean he's pleased, really, but he started going on about money yesterday, and how much another baby will cost, and how we'll have to get the bedroom finished, which bloody annoyed me, actually, so we ended up arguing. We made it up, and he said he didn't mean he'd changed his mind, and he does really want another one, but he just wants the house finished. And I feel sick all the time.'

She's chomping her way through a packet of ginger biscuits.

'And my clothes are getting tight already – it's ridiculous.

Look.' And she hoists up her jumper, to reveal her jeans are unzipped.

'Did you get big with Alfie?'

'Elephantine. Taxi drivers used to make me promise not to go into labour before they'd let me into their cabs.'

'Me too. They thought Lily would be huge.'

'That's what Caesareans are for, trust me. No sitting on rubber rings with stitches in your undercarriage, as my gran would say. And lots of morphine for the first couple of days. Perfect.'

'I had a water birth with Lily – it was lovely. Well, most of it. I did a lot of yoga too, and I think that really helped. I must find out about classes.'

'I wanted to do something like that, but the hospital didn't have a pool. I think it had a puncture or something, and anyway Patric wouldn't come to the classes.'

Actually, even if there had been a pool I'm not sure it would have really done the trick. I know everyone says you're supposed to want to be all elemental and go for as natural a birth as possible, but I quite liked my Caesarean. And I'm not convinced that telling everyone the ideal way to give birth is squatting on a bean bag with a cup of nettle tea isn't just another way to make us all feel like failures if we end up with epidurals.

'I'd like to go for a home birth this time – I think I'd feel more in control. But Dan's not keen. He thinks if something goes wrong you're better off in hospital, and I suppose he's got a point.'

'It's tricky, isn't it, knowing what to do, but at least you'll have more idea second time round. And just think, all those lovely cuddles. And those first smiles. And the way they cling on when you pick them up, and curl their little legs up.'

'Did you find it easy to breastfeed – at first, I mean? I was so sure it would be easy but I couldn't get the hang of it for ages, and Lily was really fussy, and wouldn't latch on. You feel such a tit, don't you?'

We both laugh.

'Yes, I suppose you do. Although Alfie was such a guzzler I think that sort of helped.'

'Do you want another one, at some point?'

'In theory, yes, I suppose, but Mum would never forgive me, not if I hadn't nailed down a husband by then. Two would look like I was doing it on purpose. And I love it just being me and Alfie, and I don't know if I'd want to risk screwing it up. Anyway, it's not like I'm overwhelmed with offers at the moment, apart from the occasional builder, of course, and I don't think fatherhood's exactly what they've got in mind. And I'm not really sure I want one – a man, I mean – not at the moment. Not full-time anyway.'

'I was thinking about it the other day, you know, and sometimes I think I would have gone for it, if I hadn't met Dan – gone solo, I mean. There's this woman at school, Fiona, and she's with this really boring man. I mean he's not terrible or anything, just boring and sort of grubby, and he's always criticising her and bringing her down, but she wants kids, so she's marrying him. It's so sad.'

'I know. Mind you, maybe I'd do the same if anyone was asking me.'

'You wouldn't, you know. You're too sensible. And anyway you're too much of a good mother – you wouldn't do that to Alfie.'

'True. I might have put up with a load of retarded boyfriends, but when it comes to dads I've discovered I'm rather choosy. It's bad enough saddling him with Patric without picking another nutter. I'd really hate that.'

'Dan's a good dad.'

'I know. He's lovely.'

'It's just, well, I just wish it was a bit more exciting sometimes.'

'It's bound to be like that though, isn't it? I mean it can't be exciting all the time, can it?'

'No, but some of the time would be nice. I mean I know he loves me – don't get me wrong – and I love him too. But sometimes I can't help thinking it would be easier on my own. I wouldn't have to worry about what he thinks, or if he's OK. Sometimes all I can cope with is myself and Lily. God knows what it's going to be like with another one.

'And I just can't be bothered worrying about him too, and then he sulks. I know it's hard for him, and with the baby it's only going to get worse, but it just feels like I'm being stretched thinner and thinner. The head's asked me to apply for one of the deputy headships – did I tell you?'

'Molly, that's great.'

'I know. And I really want it. But what with school and Lily and Dan and now this one, I just don't think I can cope. I feel like I'm disappearing. It's such a cliché, but it's true: I feel like the invisible woman sometimes. Like I'm on some sort of treadmill – get up, go to work, come home, play with Lily, fall asleep, get up, go to work. And school is such a big deal, it really is. The kids deserve someone who's totally there for them, not someone who's too knackered most of the time. I don't want to turn into one of those teachers who treats it like some part-time job, just because it fits in with their kids' school holidays. We've got enough of those already.'

'You're a great teacher, Moll – you know you are. They're really lucky to have you.'

'Not all the time I'm not. Sometimes I just coast through – I can feel myself doing it. And it's not good enough. And I think Dan half wants me to give up work, or at least want to give up, if you know what I mean. I think he'd be happier if I was longing to be at home more, baking bread and having his supper on the table and all that bollocks. Sometimes I think he's jealous of the kids at school, because they get so much of my attention. And I feel guilty about that too. And anyway, if I was a really good mother I'd want to be at home all the time, wouldn't I? But I don't. I really don't. I mean I wouldn't mind doing part-time, like you. But I wouldn't want to give up altogether, even if we could afford it.'

'Oh neither would I. I'd go mad. There's only so much finger-painting a girl can take.'

'School's the only place where I feel I'm getting it right, at least some of the time. Where I really feel I make a difference. Half the time with Lily I just feel I'm not good enough.'

'Oh but that's the deal, isn't it? It's the same with Alfie. Anything he gets right is because of him, and it's his triumph, but anything he gets wrong is my fault. You just can't win.'

'I know, but it just feels so bloody hard sometimes.'

There's a crash from the living room. Alfie has jumped off the sofa during an especially lively bit of *Winnie the Pooh*. He was being Tigger but didn't quite get the bouncing right. We make a huge fuss and confirm that no, his head is not broken off, but he might have a bump tomorrow to show Nana. This cheers him up because he loves showing off bumps and scratches, which always makes me feel like a negligent mother: even though Mum swears Jim spent most of his childhood covered in sticking plasters and she had to bulk-buy Germoline until he was at least twelve.

'We should go. Come on, Lily. Let's get you home – it's nearly bath time. Shall we have a lovely bath, with bubbles?'

'No. I want to stay here. No.'

Lily begins to scream and hurl cushions off the sofa. Alfie is most impressed and joins in. We finally manage to subdue them, with the help of two tubes of Smarties and some nifty footwork, and while I help Molly get Lily into the car Alfie has a nice little stamp about in puddles, in his slippers. Perfect.

Lily is practically inhaling her Smarties now.

'You'd better get going – you're getting dangerously close to a non-Smartie zone.'

We go back indoors and I rinse out his slippers while he has a last burst of *Peter Pan* before bed. I know what Molly means about how hard it is, and how you never feel you're getting it right. And I know what she means about work too. Sometimes I actually look forward to my days in the office, just so I can feel I'm halfway competent at something. And in some ways it's much easier for me, with just myself and Alfie to worry about. I mean obviously it would be nice to have a man around, but it would also make everything so much more complicated. Whatever you do you seem to end up feeling guilty, and poor Moll seems to be finding it especially hard-going at the moment. Which isn't like her because she's usually pretty upbeat: it's probably just that hormone soup you slosh around in for the first few months.

Alfie's got really tired after all his leaping about, and I've got my timing wrong, again. He refuses to lie down while I read him a story in bed, and keeps doing head-over-heels which he's just learnt at playgroup, so I lose my temper and shout at him and he bursts into tears. I end up giving him a cuddle lying on his bed, and wake up an hour or so later to find my left arm has gone numb, and the fire has gone out. So much for a relaxing evening watching telly. I'm in work again tomorrow, and the kitchen is filthy. I must remember to have a quick squirt of Dettox before Mum arrives.

Of course I forget the Dettox, and Mum asks me what on earth I've been doing to Alfie's slippers. Like I went out on purpose and dipped them in the nearest muddy puddle. I leave her trying to persuade Alfie to eat his Weetabix, and fussing over the bruise on his head, which you can actually hardly see but still makes me feel guilty, and then I arrive late at the office, due to being stuck behind some pillock in a tractor.

Janet is standing waiting for me when I arrive, looking rather pointedly at her watch.

'Mr and Mrs Prentice are in the meeting room. Where on earth have you been?'

'Stuck in traffic – sorry. I'll go through, shall I?'

I walk straight into the meeting without giving her a chance to answer, and I've just started discussing the plans when she comes in.

'I just thought I'd check everyone was happy. Alice is a relatively new member of our team, but rest assured we have every confidence in her. And if there's anything you need, I'm just outside.'

Mr and Mrs Prentice look confused and I'm furious: Janet's notorious for barging into other people's meetings and undermining them. I've been practising what to say in case she does it to me, and it looks like this is my moment.

'Thanks, Janet, I think we're fine, but I'd love another cup of coffee.'

Mr and Mrs Prentice say yes, they would like another cup too, and then turn their attention back to the utility room. Janet looks thunderous, but has to go and sort out more coffee, so I give her what I hope is an encouraging smile, but suspect is more of a smirk, and feel very pleased with myself. Brenda brings the coffee in and gives me a wink as she pours it out.

As soon as the meeting is over Janet corners me.

'Did they like the plans?'

'Loved them.'

She doesn't look happy.

'Good. Actually, I've been meaning to have a word with you about your desk. It just doesn't give the right impression. We like to run a tidy ship here, you know, Alice – it saves so much time in the end. And if you could pick up some milk at lunchtime when you're out, that would be helpful. Brenda will be busy, and we didn't realise you would be using quite so much milk for your visitors.'

I poke my tongue out at Janet's back as she walks away, which makes Brenda laugh, and then tidy up my desk.

It would be so nice if Janet could just be a tiny bit more supportive, since she's a working mother too, but it's more like the opposite really. When Bill left at lunchtime last week to visit a nursery for his two-year-old she couldn't have been nicer, like he was in the finals for some sort of fatherhood award. But when I had to leave ten minutes early one day last week, so Mum wouldn't be late for the dentist, she made a huge fuss and said she wanted a little word but she supposed it could wait until tomorrow. I spent the entire night rehearsing things to say to her but it turned out she just wanted to tell me I'd used her favourite coffee mug, the one with flowers on, and could I please not do it again.

She seems to think that the only way to be taken seriously if you're a woman with children is by pretending they don't exist, so not surprisingly her children are dreadful: Brenda says they behaved so badly last time they came into the office everyone was praying for them to fall down the fire escape.

The job's all right apart from Janet, and at least it pays the mortgage. But that doesn't stop me wishing I could just tell her where to stick it sometimes.

Jim arrives on Friday night, having decided on a whim to come and stay for the weekend. I wish I could still do that, without having to pack enough bags of clothes and snacks that by the time we're ready to leave I don't want to go any more. But it doesn't seem possible to be spontaneous with kids: not unless you've got the kind of child who'll sit quietly in the back of the car and amuse himself for hours with a glove puppet and a packet of fruit Polos. And Alfie's almost the exact opposite of this kind of child, if they actually exist. He'd eat the sweets in five seconds flat, and he's not keen on puppets, unless they have weapons, although he quite liked the Punch and Judy we saw last year at the seaside, but that was only because Punch spent most of the time hitting things with a stick. He ended up bashing the back of my seat with his new plastic lobster and chanting 'That's the way to do it' at the top of his voice all the way home. I had to stop the car and put the lobster in the boot in the end.

Jim's on the run, again, from one of his countless ex-girlfriends who he says has turned into a stalker.

'Maybe I should move down here, and get a nice little cottage. I quite fancy the country life.'

'Don't you dare. Not round here anyway. I don't want to be besieged by hordes of women trying to track you down.'

'Hardly hordes. Stella's away for two weeks, at some big

conference, and I haven't seen Amy for ages. And work is driving me crazy – Steve keeps signing up new clients all over the place. I was in bloody Birmingham all last week.'

'My heart bleeds.'

'What about you? Any fit farmers hanging about, longing for a bit of action after dark that doesn't involve sheep?'

'No, and I haven't been looking. The only night-time action I can cope with at the moment involves finger puppets and a *Bob the Builder* night light.'

Alfie, who's been milling about trying to get Uncle Jim to play cars with him, now starts singing the theme tune to *Bob the Bloody Builder*. Excellent.

'Kinky. What do you do with the finger puppets then? That's a new one on me.'

'You're a sick man, you know, James. Sick.'

'Yes, but Alfie loves me. Come here, Alf and poke your tongue out at your mother. Look, like this – horrible Mummy.'

Alfie sticks out his tongue so far he almost dislocates his jaw.

'Oh thanks, Jim, that's just great. You could teach him to swear next, if you like. And then Mum can come to your office and slap your legs.'

'Don't you dare. Steve would love that. All right, no more poking out our tongues, Alf, or Uncle Jim's going to get in big trouble. Is there any food? I'm starving.'

We make supper and Jim says he'll give Alfie a bath.

'I'd watch out for nipping, if I were you. He's quite keen on it at the moment when he's getting tired.'

'Oh lovely – nice bit of nipping, just what I need. Does he need a drink?'

'Yes, I'll bring one up, and check you've got him in the right pyjamas.'

Last time Jim managed to put him in an old pair that were at least three sizes too small.

'You're never going to let me forget that, are you?'

'No.'

*   *   *

I sit by the fire, which is lovely, although the romance of real fires has certainly started to wear off now I know how much they involve – scuttling about with piles of logs and buckets of coal like a demented scullery maid.

Jim comes back downstairs, looking shattered.

'Well, that went well. Little bugger took hours to go to sleep. Every time I thought he'd gone off he'd sit up again and start chatting.'

'I know. It's really annoying, isn't it?'

'Slightly, yes. He was telling me all about Peter bloody Pan for ages. He still thinks he can fly, you know.'

'I know. I've hidden his hat and green trousers – it was driving me crazy. He kept leaping off the stairs. There's more wine left if you want some, or coffee?'

We talk about work, and I tell him about the plans for the new garden.

'How did you manage to end up doing that?'

'I don't know really. Lola sort of volunteered me – she's very bossy – and Molly didn't help, she's really into the idea. I've got to meet a load of nutters from the Garden Society, and they're doing all the plants. They've formed a sub-sub-committee for herbs, and one for vegetables, and Mr Channing's making sure everything goes together, so I'll have to come up with the bloody plan soon. It makes me feel sick every time I think about it. Oh and talking about being sick, Molly's pregnant.'

'Blimey, you have all been busy, haven't you? Good for Molly.'

Things are so simple in Boy World. Molly's with Dan, already has one child, so she must be pleased to be having another one. Simple.

'Do they know you don't know anything about gardening?'

'Yes, I've just told you – the Garden Society are in charge of the plants. I just do the walls and stuff. I'll show you what I've got so far, if you like.'

'Oh I can't wait. God, you're really getting into this

country-life bollocks, aren't you? You'll be learning to shoot next.'

'Don't tempt me.'

'Who's this Lola?'

'My new neighbour, I told you. You'll meet them on Sunday, at Ezra's birthday, so I need something to wear. Will you come shopping with me tomorrow?'

'No. Never again. I told you last time, I hate going shopping with women – they shop differently to men.'

'What, you mean we actually spend more than five minutes choosing?'

'Me and Alf will stay in, watch a bit of football, and you can go out and drive yourself crazy trying on forty-six different outfits and then buy another pair of black trousers. Deal?'

He can be really sweet sometimes, my big brother.

'Patric's supposed to be taking Alfie out for the afternoon, with Cindy. If he turns up.'

'Oh good. I haven't seen him for ages. Excellent. Well, that's something to look forward to. You can go off shopping and I'll stand by for Mork and Mindy.'

'Or we could go in the afternoon and you could help me choose. Alfie needs some new vests as well.'

'You're hopeless – you know that, don't you? Hopeless. You've got the chance for a nice girly Saturday trying on make-up and obsessing about shoes and you end up buying new vests for Alfie. I've a good mind to bring Stella down with me next time – she could shop for Britain. Do you know, I counted how many different shades of pink nail varnish she's got once, and you'll never guess.'

'Six.'

'See, you are officially hopeless. Fourteen. I'm not kidding, fourteen different-shaped bottles and different brands, but all bloody pink. It's a mystery to me how anyone could need that much pink nail varnish.'

'How many pairs of trainers have you got now, by the way?'

'That's different. You need different pairs for different things – I've told you. And anyway, it doesn't take me four hours to decide which ones to wear.'

'Shut up.'

'Oh charming. When you can't win, you just say shut up. That's so like a girl.'

'Shut up, or I'll find one of my bottles of pink nail varnish and paint your nails while you're asleep.'

I did this to him once, and I wouldn't lend him my nail-varnish remover until he promised to take me to the school disco, and get his friend Gary Davies to dance with my friend Karen.

'Fine by me. I'll wear pink nail varnish to your friend's posh party, and you can introduce me to the entire village as your gay brother, Jimmy. Bet that'll go down well with the gardening mafia.'

Patric turns up just as we're finishing lunch, and is wearing a new black suit, which seems to be a few sizes too big for him. He says he's been meeting a client this morning, and Cindy's been left at home because they're having a dinner party tonight. She's probably making water lilies out of napkins or something.

'I'm so busy at the moment, it's ridiculous. Oh, and I'll need to drop him off slightly early, around four if that's OK, because Cindy will need a hand getting everything ready. We've got some really important people coming.'

He always does this. Whatever arrangement you make he either arrives an hour late, or has to leave early. But somehow if I try to make a fuss about it, it comes out sounding all needy and desperate, which is the exact opposite of how I feel. But luckily Jim doesn't have this problem.

'That might be tricky, Pat, to be honest. We're planning a mega-shopping expedition. Alice has got a rather hot date coming up and we're on the hunt for a killer outfit. So you leaving early won't really be an option, because we won't be back here until sixish. That all right, mate? I'm sure Cindy will understand.'

Patric hates being called Pat, and he's not too keen on mate either, which is why Jim does it. He went through a phase of putting a *Postman Pat* video on every time Patric was around, or whistling the theme tune. In fact he's doing it again now, whistling 'Postman Pat' as he goes off to make coffee. Patric looks thunderous.

'Coffee, Pat? Or are you keen to be off?'

Jim's really pushing it now, which I have to admit I'm enjoying.

'No, I think we'd better get going. Come on, Alfie, find your coat.'

This is my cue to run round getting him ready; but somehow I just don't feel like it today. I don't see why Patric can't put Alfie's coat and shoes on, just this once.

'His coat's on the peg by the door and his shoes should be there too. Oh and his swimming things are in his bag, if you're planning on swimming today.'

'Yes, I thought we might.'

Actually, it's what they always do. Patric's pretty hopeless at planning Alfie-type activities, so I found out about the weekend programme at the local leisure centre, which has obviously been designed with weekend dads in mind. Swimming sessions with inflatables, a bouncy castle and soft play stuff in one of the gyms, and all sorts of classes where you can stick them for half an hour and still get to read the papers. Tumble Tots, trampoline, gymnastics, that kind of thing. I take him myself sometimes, although the trampoline's a bit nerve-racking. And there's a café where you can have tea afterwards.

Jim comes back in with his coffee and starts tormenting Patric about his new car.

'Nice little motor, mate. Must have set you back a bob or two. I thought Alice said money was a bit tight at the moment?'

Patric purses his lips and tries to get Alfie's shoes on.

'I'm not sure about the colour though. Isn't black a bit passé now?'

'Classic colours never change.'

'Oh, is that right? Well, good for you. Nice to meet a man who knows how to spoil himself. Most of the blokes in my office with kids get all sensible and start buying estate cars, or saving up for school fees. It's tragic.'

Jim winks at me and goes back into the kitchen. Patric's gone white with fury.

'I'll see you later, Alice.'

He stamps off down the path with Alfie, who's so excited about going swimming he's barely given me a second glance, which is nice but vaguely upsetting too. Half of me wants him to refuse to go anywhere with Patric, and say he'd rather not go swimming with someone who's treated his mother in such a shocking fashion, which would be pretty unusual for a three-year-old, I admit, and anyway I'd much rather he had some sort of relationship with his dad. But that doesn't stop it all being very disgruntling.

'I don't know why you don't push him for more money, you know, I really don't. Wanker. That car must be costing him a fucking fortune.'

'I know. But I've told you, I don't want his money. I know what he's like. If he was paying real money he'd feel he was off the hook and Alfie would never get to see him. Or he'd start throwing his weight around and asking to have him all weekend or something, to get his money's worth.'

'Well, that wouldn't be so bad, would it? I mean for you to have a weekend off occasionally?'

'Yes, it bloody would. I couldn't cope with a whole weekend without him, not yet. Maybe when he's bigger. If he wants to. He's too little now.'

God, there really must be something the matter with me – I'm actually feeling a bit tearful, just at the prospect of Alfie going away for the weekend. Maybe I should try to get out more.

'All right, don't start getting all wobbly. Blimey. Anyway, I think the chances of Mork and Mindy wanting our Alf round trashing the place for the whole weekend are pretty slim, don't you?'

'True.'

'But I still think you should screw him for every penny he's got.'

'I know. But I don't want to. Apart from anything else, this way I don't feel dependent on him. I'd hate that.'

'Fair enough. Well, come on then, little Miss Independence. If we're going shopping, let's get it over with. Although I'm warning you, five shops and that's my limit.'

'And what was all that about a hot date? It's just a tea party, you know.'

'I know. But he doesn't have to know that. Wanker.'

Ezra's party is in full swing when we arrive. Alfie's clutching his present as Lola opens the front door, draped in a beautiful dark-green silk dress, which she has inexplicably teamed up with fishnets and very high red suede shoes. I know fishnets are trendy, but I can't help thinking that the last time they've been seen round here was at the Vicars and Tarts party, and even then only on the men.

I'm wearing my best black trouser suit that I wear for client meetings. It's a bit boring but fairly flattering, with my new white shirt that I bought yesterday, after I'd tried on so many different outfits that I ended up feeling dizzy. I'll just have to hope nobody mistakes me for a waiter.

'Hello, welcome. Oh you've brought a present – how lovely.'

Alfie grips his present tightly to his chest and says it's for Ezra. He seems rather worried that Lola might claim it for herself, and then Ezra appears, grabs it and runs off, ripping paper as he runs.

'Ezra darling, come back and say thank you to Alfie.'

'No.'

'He's been up since five waiting for the magician to turn up. It's been hell.'

The noise inside the house is incredible. Hordes of people are standing around in groups drinking champagne and seem oblivious to the fact that their children are wreaking havoc.

Jim takes Alfie for a wander round, but really he's just checking out the women: he reckons his attractiveness rating goes up stratospherically whenever he's got Alfie with him. I just wish it worked so well for me.

The people from Lola's office all seem to be wearing designer clothing, and in one or two cases designer sunglasses as well, and most of the villagers have taken refuge in the dining room and are looking suspiciously at the trays of sushi, which are being circulated by a couple of young women wearing long white aprons over short black dresses.

The caterer, who has a ponytail, is busy in the kitchen, and when I go in to find some juice for Alfie he asks me if I have any idea how he can get his wok to work on the Aga. He says he's dreading the children's tea, and seems particularly offended by the birthday cake, which is a large blue dinosaur.

The magician, Barry, also known as Waldo the Wizard, is ready for the off and begins by making animal shapes with balloons, which goes down well, and rude noises with the balloons, which goes down even better, but then the disappearing rabbit reappears, thanks to a bit of over-enthusiasm from Ezra, and escapes and races round the room pursued by all the children screaming.

Barry tells me and Molly that he thinks he's going to buy a shotgun, because the same thing happens nearly every week, and shooting the rabbit as a sort of grand finale would go down really well, he thinks. He's probably right.

Finally Charles manages to sort things out by telling everyone the ice cream is melting, so they swarm into the dining room. Lola's moved all of the villagers out while the children have tea, and is now holding court in one of the sitting rooms, and she's Not Happy. I think she thought all the London people would be fascinated by her new rural friends, whereas in fact they're all standing round in groups not talking to each other. She says she's tried introducing people but it hasn't really been a success.

'I mean they're not making the slightest effort – it's pathetic. I'm starting to think this garden thing might not be such a good idea, you know. I mean if I want a load of sullen-looking people hanging around the place I can hire a few more nannies. And that old man over there keeps going on about his uncle who was taken prisoner by the Japanese. Like I care.'

'I think he's trying to make a point about the sushi, darling.'

Charles is smiling.

'Oh is he? Well, if he doesn't like it he can just bugger off home then, can't he? I'm sure we'll struggle on somehow, without his scintillating company. No, really, Charles, it's not funny. Alice – this can't really be the cream of the village, surely? Tell me there are some fascinating people who some-how got missed off the list. Local artists, something like that?'

'Um. Not really. I mean I don't know everybody, but this is pretty much it as far as I can see.'

'Bloody hell. Well, that's definite then. I thought this garden thing would be fun, but they're all so boring. I'm sure they can use someone else's garden. You wouldn't mind, would you, Alice?'

Christ. I can't believe she's really going to pull out now. I mean obviously part of me is rather glad because it will get me off the hook, but it does seem rather hard just because people aren't being very sparkling at her party.

Charles looks furious. Actually, he looks quite steely when he gets going.

'Don't be ridiculous, Lola – we've said yes now. We can't suddenly change our minds just because a few people turn out to be rather shy. Not everybody is as good at socialising as you are, you know.'

'You'd think they'd welcome a bit of glamour. It's ridi-culous.'

'We can't back out now – we've said they can have the land.'

'Well, don't expect me to sort it out when it's a total disaster.'

'Thank you for being so encouraging, darling.'

Lola flounces off.

Charles smiles at me apologetically.

'Sorry about that. Lola's enthusiasms tend to come and go, but I'm sure she didn't mean to be rude about your design.'

'Oh no, not at all. I mean she has got a point, you know – I haven't got the faintest idea about gardens.'

'I'm sure it will be lovely.'

Lola's parents have arrived, and The Great Composer is soon ensconced in a corner with a couple of trendy types dancing attendance and talking about tonal music. Lola's mother has given Ezra loads of classical CDs because it's never too early to start educating musical tastes, and then she hovers near her husband, looking anxious.

I'm introduced to Gerald and Lavinia, Charles's parents, who also seem slightly vague about their grandparently duties. Lavinia is drinking sherry and having a long conversation with a woman who breeds cocker spaniels, and Gerald appears to be having a light doze in an armchair. But they have at least brought a nice present, a beautiful rocking horse which Ezra seems to like, mainly because Mabel has already fallen off it.

Lavinia keeps barking out orders at Charles: no wonder he copes so well with Lola. Years of being bossed about by his mother must have been really good preparation.

The afternoon passes in a blur of cake and yelling. Thankfully it's dry so the children can play in the garden, although Bruno, a rather sturdy five-year-old, manages to get wedged into a bush behind the garage and has to be dragged out screaming. This doesn't seem to bother his father, who works in Lola's office and is wearing a mohair jumper, but his mother, Mimi, is worried that he might have developed claustrophobia and rings her homeopath on her mobile to book an emergency appointment.

Bruno appears to recover when Lola gives him a fun-size Mars Bar, which he crams into his mouth while his mother is busy explaining that he doesn't really like chocolate and prefers dried apricots. Molly and I exchange amused glances, because Bruno looks just like the kind of child who would bite you hard if you tried to fob him off with a dried apricot.

Ezra's busy marching round the garden telling everyone he's six now, and a big boy, not like silly Mabel, who's playing quite happily with Lily. They're both having a lovely time in their pink party frocks and Lily's teaching Mabel how to do ballet. Alfie and his new friend George are being dogs, and gradually Lily and Mabel get drawn in. Mabel might be the youngest but she can certainly hold her own. She refuses point blank to sit, but quite likes crawling round on all fours barking. They're all enjoying themselves immensely when Ezra tries to join them.

'I'm the biggest, so I'm in charge.'

George isn't keen.

'I'm the big dog. You can be a sheep.'

Oh dear. Somehow I don't think the birthday boy is going to see himself as a sheep.

'You can't be the big dog – you're just a baby. A baby like Mabel. Mabel table.'

Mabel is having none of this, and chucks a stick at him, and Alfie looks like he might be about to do the same and I'm just on the point of heading over to calm things down before someone gets impaled on something when Lily takes charge and announces that Ezra's being Very Horrible, and nobody is to play with him. She's very good at this sort of thing and likes to boss the little ones around at playgroup, but she does it so nicely that they mostly don't care.

Alfie and George are still rather keen on the stick-throwing thing, but fall into line when Lily says she and Mabel are now cats, and Alfie and George have to chase them. They race off squealing and poor old Ezra is left looking very miserable.

Molly tries to help him out by asking him to show us his brilliant new rocking horse, and he reluctantly agrees, but then wanders off while Lola is introducing us to a man from her office who I think is called Tray, but it might be Troy, who seems very pleased with himself, and begins telling us about his recent trip to Peru.

Molly manages to escape but I get stuck with Tray for what seems like hours until Dan comes over to rescue me, after I've been giving him frantic looks.

'Sorry, Alice, but Jim says he needs your help with Alfie.'

We move off towards the other side of the garden.

'Did he really say that?'

'No. He's having a blinding time, chatting up all the women. Have you seen Moll?'

'No. I think she's gone inside. Oh, and congratulations, by the way, I forgot to say earlier, about the baby.'

'Oh thanks. We're hoping the next one might be a good sleeper. Lily was awful. Well, she still is really. She was up at half-past five this morning. Dancing round in her ballet outfit. Did Moll tell you? Janice's signed her up for baby ballet, one afternoon a week. They all prance round in little skirts, hopping and stuff. She looks really sweet, but not at the crack of bloody dawn. I had to get up in the end – Moll needs her sleep at the moment.'

'I think second ones are supposed to be easier.'

Actually, I'm not sure this is strictly true. Jim was a really good sleeper according to Mum, whereas I was terrible. But I want to be encouraging.

'As long as it's all right, I don't care really. You forget, don't you, how nervous you get, before they're born, I mean. We've got the first scan in a few weeks, and I was thinking, maybe we should take Lily. Start getting her used to the idea. Moll thinks she'd be bored with all the hanging about, but I think she'd quite like it.'

I know what's really scaring Molly is the thought of there being something wrong, and if there was it would be awful if Lily was there. But she doesn't want to tell Dan because then he'll worry. She rang last night, and I'm under strict instructions to say I think they'd be better off going on their own.

'Maybe taking her to the next scan would be better – you know, the one where the baby's a bit bigger. It's hard to work out what's going on when they're so tiny, isn't it?'

'True, and I think Moll's worried there might be something the matter with it. She was convinced there'd be something wrong with Lily right up until she was born. She won't say anything, of course, but I know she is.'

'I did too, with Alfie. I think everyone does.'

'I just wish she'd slow down. She's always working on something, you know, for school. She was up really late last night covering loads of cards in that plastic stuff. And she's always got work to do at the weekends.'

'I know. But it's half-term coming up soon, isn't it?'

'Yes, we were going to try to get away for a few days, but I've got a big job on. Oh and I meant to say, just let me know if you need any help with the garden. Moll's been telling me all about it.'

'Oh thanks, Dan, that'd be great.'

We talk about the plans while we walk back to the house to get some tea. It might be sunny but it's still bloody freezing outside. He's so nice, Dan, and he seems really excited about the new baby, although he says he thinks Molly's got the idea he wants a boy, whereas in fact he'd prefer another girl because he thinks it would be nicer for Lily.

Molly seems to have got stuck in a long complicated conversation about the history of her cottage with an old man who's lived in the village for about three hundred years, and Jim's still roaming the house and seems especially keen on a rather gorgeous blonde woman called Nicky, who has fantastic legs, and works in Lola's office. He says Lola's been giving him the eye but he's trying to avoid her because he's been getting loads of good gossip, and apparently most of Lola's office, especially the juniors, really hate her. According to Nicky Lola fired her secretary and an account manager in the same afternoon, mainly because she'd been shopping for trousers at lunchtime and couldn't find any that fitted properly.

I wander back into the garden with my tea to check on Alfie but mainly to escape Tray again, who's been giving me a lecture on Bauhaus now he's discovered that I'm an architect.

Charles is outside too, trying to make sure none of the children end up in the pond.

'The party seems to be going well.'

'Yes, Lola's marvellous at organising parties – well, marvellous at organising everything really. Good job too, because it's not my strong point. Not a great multi-tasker – I think that's what Lola calls it. It's in the genes, I think. My mother's always saying my father's hopeless as well. Even the dogs ignore him. But if my mother so much as raises her eyebrows they all charge off to their baskets.'

'Perhaps she might like to come round one day and try raising her eyebrows at Alfie.'

Alfie's still running round in circles with George being a dog, but he doesn't seem to be annoying anyone so I decide to leave him to it. Lily and Mabel are back to doing ballet, with occasional bursts of being sheep, just to keep Alfie and George busy. Ezra's still circling on the outskirts trying to look disdainful, but obviously desperate to join in, poor thing, but in the end he goes back into the house. I've always thought it can be quite hard being the birthday boy.

Mr Channing comes over, and then someone called Frank, and Elsie Thomas, and we start talking about the plans for the new garden. Before I know it I'm being bombarded with information on soil types and herbs I've barely heard of. Mr Channing says he loves fennel, and Frank says he can highly recommend sage and then everybody gets rather overexcited, and starts talking about walled gardens and whether it's possible to grow a really good peach on a south-facing wall.

'If you're after fruit trees, Graham Poltney's your man. He

comes to the meetings usually, but he's had a terrible chest this winter. I saw his wife in the shop the other day and she said he's on the mend, but he's had a terrible time of it. He's had a cough to wake the dead.'

Before Elsie can get too involved in Mr Poltney's chest Charles steers her on to safer ground.

'It's so good of you all to help out like this.'

Mrs Thomas, who must be at least eighty, gives Charles a very flirty look.

'They'll be delighted, I'd say. Be nice to be taken a bit of notice of for a change. I was saying to old Frank, just the other day, wasn't I, Frank, it's as if you become invisible once you get your pension.'

Old Frank, who actually looks at least twenty years younger than Elsie, nods.

Elsie's really going into one now.

'It's like that girl in the shop. Do you know she asked me if I needed any help carrying my shopping home the other day. The cheek of it! Day I can't carry my own bit of supper home is a long way off yet, I hope. And when it does come I shan't be bothering anyone to carry my shopping for me, I can tell you. I'm getting one of those wheelie bins, like Mrs Norris.'

Nobody seems quite sure what she's talking about until Frank suddenly works it out.

'Oh, you mean her electric scooter.'

Elsie gives Frank a withering look.

'Yes, that's what I'm saying. Nearly flattened me, outside the shop. Daft woman, she can't control it, you know. They shouldn't have given it to her, if you ask me. But she's always been in with the doctor, that one. I've got a bad hip, and it's no joke, believe me. But I just carry on – I don't like a fuss. And I'm not having one of those home helps either. Waste of time and money, if you ask me. Snooping into all your things, and emptying out your cupboards. No thank you very much.'

Alfie chooses this moment to come over demanding more cake. Thankfully he says please, and gives Mrs Thomas one of his special pleading smiles, which she says reminds her of her grandson, and she wouldn't mind another tiny slice of cake herself, so we all troop back indoors.

Lola's in the kitchen making pasta sauce, and seems to have invited all her London friends to stay to supper, whilst making it fairly clear that the locals should be thinking about leaving.

Frank offers to drive Elsie home, and this seems to be a signal for most of the villagers to leave, so I invite Molly and Dan back to supper, and find Lola to say goodbye.

'Oh do stay to supper – I'm making my special sauce. It's fabulous.'

'I'm sure it is, but Alfie's really tired. We'd better get home before he starts kicking off. But thanks so much, it's been lovely.'

'Oh well, if you're sure. Charles, give Alice some cake. And do take a party bag – they're in the hall.'

It turns out we've all got party bags, and all the bags have names written on them. Mine's full of jelly babies, and mini bottles of posh bubble bath and some silver nail varnish. Molly gets chocolate buttons, and metallic-blue nail varnish, which I know she'll never wear. I must remember to ask her if I can swap it for some jelly babies. Alfie and Lily get whistles and sweets, and Jim and Dan get chocolate footballs and racing cars. Whoever did the research on the party bags did a brilliant job.

We try to persuade Alfie and Lily to wait until we get home before they start eating their sweets, but they're having none of it and begin blowing their whistles, and then Ezra and Mabel start getting very agitated because they don't have bags, and things get rather Tense. Lola tries explaining that the bags are for people who are leaving, so Ezra puts his coat on and says he's coming with us and he wants a bag too.

Still on a high from discovering I now own silver nail varnish and have a pretty good chance of adding metallic-blue to my collection, I say they can come home with us for a bit if they like, because Ezra seems so desperate. Of course I don't actually mean this, because nobody in their right mind would willingly take on a six-year-old at the end of his birthday party, especially not Ezra, but Lola seems delighted.

'Maybe they could just wander down the lane with you for a bit. What do you think, Charles? I know, why don't you go with them, get some fresh air, and see if you can't get Ezra to calm down.'

We all walk down the lane, which is crowded with BMWs and massive jeeps, and the children begin squabbling, and Lily drops her sweets. Dan begins singing 'Old Macdonald' before she can get completely distraught, and does a very realistic impression of a sheep, which Lily loves. Alfie and Mabel soon join in, and even Ezra can't resist. Jim gives me a pleading look, but I insist he sings too, and it turns out he can do a very good impression of a donkey, much to his horror.

When we get in Dan puts on a video while I open some wine and Jim lights the fire, and while I'm making pizzas Molly begins a story with a starring role for each child, and they all sit transfixed. Dan takes over, and then Charles has a go, although Molly has to take over again when Ezra climbs on Charles's back and begins jabbing him in the bottom while he's being a lion. I'm excused story-telling duty because I'm busy grating cheese and trying to work out who's likely to throw themselves on the floor screaming if I put olives on their pizza.

Charles says he'd better get the children home but seems rather reluctant to leave. I don't think he's really looking forward to an evening with Lola's smart friends. I've asked them to stay to supper but Ezra's definitely had enough of being the birthday boy. He's already whacked Mabel a couple of times and she's squirted juice all over him, and looks like she might be building up to more violent retribution any minute. Sure enough as they're leaving they start shoving each other and Charles ends up having to march them up the lane in disgrace.

The pizzas are a great success, and Jim and Dan talk about

football while Molly and I are reduced to talking about clothes and babies, until we realise we'd better call it a night before we start swapping recipes for Victoria sponge.

Lily's fast asleep as Dan carries her out to the car, and Alfie's gone into a sort of half-asleep, half-awake trance in front of the telly. He doesn't even murmur when Jim carries him up to bed.

All the talk about gardens and plants at the party has made me realise that I'm really going to have to start concentrating, and I fall asleep thinking about circular walls and water features, and end up dreaming about a huge wall, which falls down, and an enormous fountain that takes up the entire garden and for some reason is full of bright-pink water. Oh god.

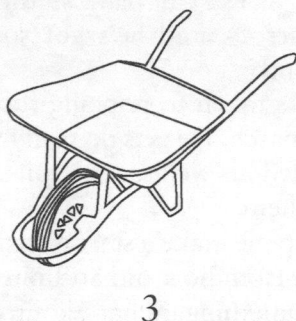

3

MARCH

Dig for Victory

Garden Diary

Lift and replant snowdrops, deadhead daffodils. Prune summer-flowering shrubs and check fruit trees. Dress lawn with spring fertiliser.

I've spent so long finishing off the plans for the new garden that I don't have time to do anything at home. Some daffodils have managed to come out in the front garden and look very jolly, but torrential rain and hail threaten to flatten them completely so I decide on a rescue mission and run outside in a torrential downpour clutching my umbrella and hoping that I'm not about to get hit by lightning: you'd feel so stupid being taken to hospital after having been electrified by your own umbrella while rescuing daffodils. They'd probably treat you like a complete nutter, and all the nurses would wander into your cubicle for a quick smirk. Just like they do if you accidentally Superglue a chunk of wicker to your arm when you're trying to renovate an old cane chair, which is much more painful than you'd think, and isn't actually funny at all. I still think that nurse shouldn't have laughed quite so much.

'M R CHANNING SAYS I can plant seed potatoes now, and peas and carrots, and he's got some seedlings he's going to bring round.'

Mr Channing has taken to popping round to help Molly with her vegetable patch. He gets on really well with Lily too, even though she filled his wellies with soil last week, while he was still wearing them.

'He says he'll help me make a start on my herb garden, and I'm to call him Bill from now on. So I must have passed the initiation test or something. What about you?'

'Well, nobody's asked me to call them Bill, but I've been getting loads of gossip. Old Elsie's a scream – she's been telling me all about Mrs Baxter, you know, the one who works in the shop sometimes. Apparently she had an affair with a flamenco dancer last year in Spain, and she's never been the same since.'

'Well, good for her. Is she the short one with dark hair?'

'Yes. I must get Alfie to take his castanets into the shop with us and see if she goes all funny.'

'I wonder if she knows how to do that stamping and clapping thing. Maybe she could teach me – it'd be really handy for school.'

'Yes, and I bet they'd love it at playgroup. Actually, Alfie's already quite good at the stamping. I know, we could start a class, Flamenco for the Under-Fives. It's got to be better than 'Here We Go Round the Bloody Mulberry Bush'.'

'Yes, and so multi-cultural – Ofsted would love it. I might suggest it to our head of music – she's completely hopeless. Last week she told one of my kids to practise a piece of music at home, on saucepans. Can you imagine the racket? I don't know what planet she lives on sometimes. His mum was furious.'

'I bet she was. God, I hope nobody sends Alfie home in a few years to practise 'Jingle Bells' on my saucepans. Actually, I'd better go. He's putting his cars into the washing machine again and if I don't take them out now I'll forget and they make a terrible noise on fast spin.'

'Have you finished the plans yet?'

'Not quite, but nearly. I've changed it round again and I think it works better now.'

'Well, ring me later if you need a hand. I can come round after school, if you like, and Dan says he'll have the kids tomorrow, when we're at the meeting.'

'Great.'

I spend most of the day working on the plans. I'm feeling extraordinarily nervous about presenting them to the Garden Society tomorrow. Alfie's had a busy morning too, and when I collect him from nursery he's covered in paint and glitter. He spends most of his afternoon watching videos and playing, and demanding snacks every five minutes, while I get increasingly frazzled trying to finish everything. By bedtime we're both pretty tired and grumpy, and I've got a sinking feeling that bath time is going to be a bit of a challenge.

'Can I have a biscuit in the bath, a chocolate one? I need a biscuit.'

He tends to need things rather badly when I'm trying to get him into the bath, especially if they involve going back downstairs.

'No, last time it fell in, remember? And then it went all soggy.'

He looks at me for a bit, and I try to look determined, but he launches into a massive wobbler, hurling himself round the bathroom, stamping and shrieking, and the fact that the bathroom's so tiny only seems to magnify the noise. I'm trying to do the positive-parenting-ignoring thing, where you stand by with a kindly smile on your face ready to reassure them when they've finished. But it's easier said than done when you're pressed up against a towel rail.

'Stop it, Alfie – you're being very silly. Get in the bath and you can play with your toys. Look, I've put all your boats in.'

He announces that he doesn't want boats, in fact he hates boats, and then he gets into the bath and chucks them out on to the floor, along with gallons of water.

'Stop that right now – the floor's getting wet.'

'Stupid Mummy.'

'Stupid Alfie.'

There's a shocked silence. The usual drill is that he calls me stupid at least six times a day, but I never retaliate.

'You can't call me stupid – you're horrible.'

'Oh yes I can. Stupid people wet the bathroom floor on purpose. That's a stupid thing to do. I'm not being stupid, I'm drying the floor. Look.'

Another boat comes flying out of the bath, only just missing my ear.

'Right. That's it. No more bath.'

I pull the plug out. He makes the kind of noise I imagine people used to make in the days before anaesthetics when the doctor got his saw out. I try to ignore it while he thrashes around in the bath. He's still got quite a lot of glitter on his knees, and now there's no chance of me having a quick dab with a flannel unless I can rig up some sort of restraint harness.

Actually, I've often thought some sort of mini straitjacket would be very handy, a sort of Naughty Coat. Something soft and fleecy, maybe with rabbits on it to make it look friendly, that you could fling on in meltdown moments. Never mind all that bollocks about Time Out and sitting on the Naughty Stair. I reckon if you've got the kind of child who'll actually sit on a stair at the bottom of the staircase and think about how naughty they've been, then they probably haven't been that naughty in the first place.

Whereas if you've got one like Alfie you'd have to lurk by the stairs and make sure they actually stayed sitting, and didn't grab the chance for a quick spot of *Peter Pan*, or have a go at dismantling the telephone. Some sort of Velcro garment would be really useful, and you could just pop it on, and then sit them on the sofa and watch them having a Houdini session while you had a nice cup of tea. I'm sure it would be illegal, but I bet Baby Gap would make a fortune. Maybe I could ask Mum to knit me something.

All the water's drained away now but he's still thrashing about. I wish I'd waited until I'd got him out of the bath before Making A Stand: last time I tried to get him out of the bath mid-meltdown I nearly dislocated my shoulder. He's soaking wet and slippery, and getting a grip is not going to be easy, but just when I think I'm going to have to give in and go and get the biscuit tin, I'm suddenly inspired. We watched a wildlife documentary at the weekend with some twit wrestling a crocodile by wrapping a sheet round it and then sitting on it and holding on tight while it bucked him round the swamp.

I drop a large bath towel on to Alfie, and then grab him, still wriggling, and stagger into his bedroom. At least his shouts are now slightly muffled. He emerges from the towel red-faced and outraged, with his hair all sticking up, but at least the glitter's come off his knees. He is speechless with fury, but before he can launch into another magic moment I nip in quickly and declare a truce.

'There you are, all lovely and dry. Let's put your pyjamas on and we can have a story. But no more silly shouting, OK?'

He gives me a filthy look, and flings the towel out of the door, just to make the point.

'Which book would you like, penguins or bears?'

'I nearly couldn't breathe all covered up.'

He shakes his head sadly and gives me a long woeful look as if to emphasise his point. I decide to ignore this because I'm rather impressed by my new emergency swaddling technique and I might be using it again; although taking a large bath towel round Sainsbury's might look a bit odd.

'Or we could read *Winnie the Pooh*?'

I know this will divert him, because yesterday he announced that he hates *Winnie the Pooh*.

'I could go and get you a drink of water if you put your pyjamas on nicely.'

I wonder if I can risk insisting on teeth-brushing. Returning to the scene of the crime might trigger him off again, but on the other hand there is another towel in the bathroom.

Perhaps I shouldn't overdo it, though. He might become phobic about towels, and that could get rather boring after a while. I'd have to dry him with a tea towel.

'I want juice.'

He puts his pyjamas on without too much trouble and is sitting up in bed looking angelic when I return with his drink. He settles down quite quickly, clearly exhausted after all the excitement. His breathing slows right down, and he's nearly asleep as I'm turning off the lights.

I notice that the towel rail is empty, and come to think of it the towel he chucked out of his door earlier has also disappeared. I finally find them under my bed, covered in dust. He must have run round trying to find somewhere to stash them while I got his juice, just in case I fancied another bit of swaddling.

As I get back downstairs Lola rings, which tends to mean she wants something. It turns out she's also had a fairly exhausting afternoon, and her PA Sophie screwed up her lunch booking, so she sent her some sort of email telling her exactly what would happen to her if she ever did it again, but she must have pressed the wrong button because she somehow managed to copy it to the entire office and most of her clients.

'And then ten minutes later I got a stroppy message from Penelope in human resources, asking me if I'd like a chat about the company's policy on bullying at work. Fucking cheek. Human resources, Jesus, they've got to be joking. Anyway I told her, if she thinks a simple little email counts as bullying then she's in for a big surprise. And the traffic was murder this evening – the sooner they bring in road-charging on every road in the entire country the better, if you ask me. Anything if it's going to force people back on to buses where they belong. And then when I got home Charles announced Mrs Bishop couldn't come in today, again, because her mother's knee is bad. I don't know why she doesn't just stick her in an old people's home or something. Or just leave her at the doctor's – she seems to spend most of her time there. We'll have to get someone else, I can't have the place looking like this. It's the exact opposite of calm when I come home. And I've just eaten a large tub of vanilla ice cream.'

'Oh.'

'Yes. And I've got my eye on a family-size bag of crisps. And Charles is no help at all. When he's not talking about fucking fennel with half the village he seems to spend his time making as much mess as possible. Anyway, I've just been reading about this fabulous herb place, and it's quite near here, so I thought we might go. I mean not for the village thing obviously, I'm still keeping well clear of that, but I thought a herb garden outside the kitchen might be nice. They can't be that tricky, can they?'

'I don't really know.'

God. I bet she's going to ask me to design her a herb garden next.

'Well, Charles is bound to pick up some tips. He's reading loads of books so there's bound to be something he can copy. Or you could do him a little drawing? How's the plan going, by the way?'

'Oh nearly finished, I think.'

'I saw a fabulous thing on Channel 4 last night, a sort of wooden pavilion suspended over water. Really stylish. Maybe you could do something like that.'

'I think that might be slightly over the Garden Society's budget.'

'Oh. Well, I hope it's not going to be too boring. I mean it is practically right next to our house. I'm sure your plan will be fabulous, but if they just fill it with boring suburban plants it's going to be dreadful. Let's go to this herb place and see if we can't find a few classy things you can slip in without them noticing. I'll find out where it is and let you know, shall I?'

And somehow I end up saying yes, that would be lovely, even though I really don't want to go herb shopping. Perhaps she'll forget, although somehow I've got a feeling she won't.

*   *   *

I arrive at the village hall with Molly to find half the village has turned up. People seem very excited, and Mrs Pomeroy's gone quite pink. Everyone gathers round the table as I lay out the plans, and then Mrs Pomeroy claps her hands and asks everyone to be quiet. Christ, talk about building up the tension.

I explain that I've gone for a fairly formal kitchen garden, with a sort of secret garden Alhambra theme, with a new curved wall which will enclose one corner of the existing garden, and we can use old bricks so it looks like it's been there for years, and it will be high enough to hide the garden completely. The doorway will be screened by trees and bushes so it'll feel like you're entering a whole new space.

The basic plan is pretty simple. There's a central circle with six paths running out from it, which all join the main path that runs round the entire garden. There'll be a border running all the way round, planted with fruit trees and lots of flowers and bushes to make it feel slightly overgrown. I want some of it to overhang the path slightly, and break up the lines. The paths will be a mixture of gravel and bricks, and all the beds will be edged with different things: I've seen pictures of lavender, and marigolds and nasturtiums, as well as the more traditional green stuff like box, and I want to try to persuade the Garden Society to use a mixture of all these, so it feels quite informal. Though obviously within limits, or it'll just look mad.

I've put a small summer house in one corner, and a children's play house in the other, and opposite the doorway we'll have a raised pond with a fountain, lined with slate and linked to two smaller pools on each of the other two corners, with a shallow rill of water running between them on a slight incline down from the main pond so the sound of trickling water fills the garden. The rills will be edged with brick and slate too, and I want the light from the water to reflect on the walls, and I've planned lights set into the paths and the water, just flat white ones to keep it simple, so it will look completely different in the dark. We might even go for some dramatic central lighting in amongst the plants if we can afford it.

I want to break up the garden with tunnels over the main pathways leading out from the centre, with arches covered with grapevines and climbing roses, or whatever else the Garden Society thinks will make the tunnels shady and cool. Basically, you won't be able to stand anywhere and see the whole garden, and as you walk round you'll keep finding new bits.

By the time I've finished everyone has gone rather quiet and I'm feeling rather sick until Charles says he thinks it's going to be fantastic, and he never imagined anything so wonderful, and then people start to clap and I go so red even my knees feel hot, and then everyone joins in with different ideas about what to plant where, and Mrs Pomeroy says she's sure we'll win the competition if the real thing looks anything like as good as the plan.

'Just think, we'll have an award-winning garden.'

Charles seems really excited.

'I wouldn't count your chickens, you know – them judges are famous for being daft. Last year one of them came down from London to give us a talk, and you've never seen such a sight. As I if needed telling about soft fruit by a man in leather trousers.'

Mrs Pomeroy gives Elsie a rather a pointed look, and seems to be hoping she might pick up the hint and be quiet.

'Oh I speak as I find, Mrs Pomalloy, as you well know. I don't have nothing against them – each to his own. My sister's boy was never a hundred per cent in the trouser department, but you couldn't find a nicer lad, you really couldn't. Moved in with her when she got a bit forgetful, and he took care of her lovely.'

'How nice.'

Charles is clearly trying not to laugh.

'Yes, it was. Nice to see children taking care of their parents, I mean with most of them you could be dead on the floor for weeks and they'd never know. My June's good though. She comes in every week, and always brings a bit of shopping, although she will keep getting me ham, and I've told her, I've gone off it. Mind you, it's how you bring them up. What goes around comes around, I always say. If you bother with them when they're little then they'll do the same for you later on. Not like men, less you bother with them the better, in my opinion.'

'Treat them mean and keep them keen, Elsie, is that it?'

Charles seems very relaxed around the rather formidable Elsie.

'That's right, Mr B, although I wouldn't treat you mean, oh no I wouldn't. If I was ten years younger I'd give you a run for your money, that I would.'

Everyone laughs, including Elsie.

'Oh yes, you can laugh now, but you should have seen me in my heyday. I was a heartbreaker all right.'

Charles tells her she still is, and she blushes.

I haven't really talked to anyone properly about the budget, although we can use different materials depending on how much they want to spend, and I also need to make sure we've got someone who can be around every day. I decide to start with Charles, who says he doesn't really care what it costs, and he and Mr Channing can share running the project, if Mr Channing will put up with working with a complete beginner. Mr Channing's obviously very pleased to be chosen as a project leader, and one by one people say they've been growing on little plantlets especially for the garden, so we'll only need to buy the bigger stuff.

I really want to put in some mature trees, which I imagine will cost a fortune, but they'll make a real difference to the feel of the whole garden. Mr Channing says he knows a good man who he thinks will be able to let us have the right sort of thing at reasonable prices, and we start talking about fruit trees. Charles says Lola's already told him she wants a quince, and one of those trendy medlar trees where the fruit looks like it's gone mouldy before you even pick it, because she's seen them in *Country Life*, and even though she's gone off the idea of the garden now we might as well get a few of the trees she likes, just in case she changes her mind.

I'm actually really happy as Molly drives us home. Even if the garden doesn't win any prizes, it's been great to be working on plans that don't involve fridges.

'Well done – it's going to be fantastic.'

'Thanks. I was so nervous about it.'

'I thought you were a bit quiet in the car. Can we go to your place for a coffee before you collect Alfie? I'm not sure I'm up to going straight back just yet.'

'Sounds great, if you don't think Dan will mind.'

'Oh he'll be fine. He loves Alfie – I think he'd really like this one to be a boy.'

We get back to my cottage and I put the kettle on. Molly seems very quiet.

'Are you all right?'

'Fine, I'm just knackered.'

'How's work?'

'Bloody awful. One of the PE teachers was dragging one of my boys along by his ear the other day and when I tried to have a quiet word with him he wouldn't have it. Kept going on about how any boy in his class who refused to climb up the wall bars knew what to expect.'

'Charming.'

'He's a complete bastard. And then he said the only thing these kids understand is a good hiding, and I lost it, and told him to piss off.'

'Good for you.'

'Yes, but not terribly professional. Anyway I don't care – I'm fed up with trying to talk to old gits like him. He should have retired years ago.'

'Well, when you're the deputy head you can sort it out.'

'If I get it. And even if I do I'm not sure how I'll manage it all. Lily's been really annoying me the last few days, refusing to get dressed and all that kind of thing, and it's reminded me how much work babies are. Sometimes she really drives me crazy.'

'Oh, I know what you mean. Alfie gets so annoying sometimes I just want to shut myself in a cupboard or something.'

'Dan's great with her. He just stands there chatting. He's so much nicer than I am.'

'That's not true. You're just tired.'

'No, I think he is. Really. He'll do the same thing again and again, for hours.'

'Sounds a bit retarded, if you ask me. Oh sorry.'

Molly laughs.

'He's just so much more patient than me.'

'Don't be so hard on yourself – it's really tough working full-time. I get so tired sometimes, even now I'm part-time. I'd do anything for a couple of extra hours in bed. And I'm not pregnant. You're great with Lily. And you'll be a great deputy head.'

'I just wish it wasn't so tough. You know, I was thinking the other day I really envy you, the way your family all help out. Mine are so far away, and Dan's mum hates me.'

'She does not.'

'She bloody well does. She's still furious we're not married, and we haven't had Lily christened. She thinks I'm terrible, I know she does.'

'Why didn't you, I mean have a christening?'

'Oh mainly because my mum would have a fit if we didn't go Catholic, and then we'd have had to be married, and I don't want to have to get married just to keep my mum happy.'

'Did Dan ask you then?'

'No, he did that boy thing: I don't mind if you want to, whatever you want is fine by me.'

'Oh, that's *so* annoying.'

'I know. But his mum thinks he really wants to, so it's all down to me. Did you have a proper christening?'

'No, Patric thinks they're bourgeois. We had a tea party

though. It was quite sweet really. Alfie got loads of presents and Dad made a speech, and he went bright red. Mum thought he was having a heart attack. And my friend Em was Alfie's Fairy Godmother and Jim was the Godfather. He spent half the afternoon with a chunk of orange in his mouth pretending to be Marlon Brando. Mum got really cross with him.'

'Oh it sounds great. I'd have one too if Doreen would spend the afternoon with an orange in her mouth. Or maybe a pineapple, she's got such a gob on her. I must tell Dan.'

'I'd leave out the bit about the pineapple, if I were you.'

'But you see what I mean? Somehow you managed to do what you wanted. And people help you out, because you're on your own. I mean that's right, obviously, don't get me wrong. It must be really hard coping with everything on your own, and I know I should be grateful, and I'd never cope without Dan, I really wouldn't. But just sometimes I wish we got more help. It's like because there's two of us we're bound to be fine: my mum wouldn't dream of coming down to give me a hand, but if I was on my own she'd be round like a shot. She'd probably make my dad move somewhere nearer so she could keep an eye on me. I bet your mum wouldn't help out nearly so much if you had a man lurking about.'

'No, you're right, she wouldn't. She'd worry she was intruding.'

'Yes. And while I'm having a moan I'd just like to say I'm completely pissed off with being grateful to Dan for being so good with Lily. I mean I am, obviously, but sometimes it really annoys me the way people think he's some sort of saint just because he's interested in his daughter. Nobody says oh what a lovely woman when I get up in the middle of the night, but when he does it it's like he's being some sort of hero. It really pisses me off.'

'Well, I think you're a lovely woman, and it really pisses me off too. And I'll tell you something else that's crap. If I was a man bringing up Alfie on my own I'd practically be guaranteed sainthood. I'd probably get a medal, or I'd be on telly, and everyone would go oh how lovely. What a nice man. But a woman bringing up her kids on her own isn't quite so special. In fact it's probably all her own fault.'

'Exactly. Bastards. And Dan's gone all silent again. I think he's finding it hard-going too and he's got this big new job on. And then he said last night he wasn't sure I should be taking on more responsibility at work, and I lost it and told him not to be so pathetic. And he hates it when I say that. It's nothing serious, and he was fine this morning, but it just feels like everything's uphill at the moment.'

Molly actually looks quite close to tears, and really tired, and sort of washed out.

'Maybe you should try to get a night off, the two of you. Go out somewhere or something. I'll have Lily, if you like.'

'Oh would you? That would be great. I'll ask Dan. He's working all hours on this bloody conversion at the moment, but maybe next weekend.'

'Fine. Whenever, just let me know. Oh, and I've definitely got something to cheer you up. Just wait till I show you.'

I pass her the loaf of bread I made yesterday, as a displacement activity when I was meant to be working.

'Look. I've tried to cut a slice but I think you'd need some sort of drill.'

Molly starts to laugh.

'I'm sorry.'

'I followed the bloody book and everything. I don't under-stand it.'

'How much yeast did you use?'

'Yeast? Sounds a bit technical to me.'

'Alice, you must have used yeast.'

'Well, yes, but it said on the packet it was supposed to froth up, and it didn't, so I chucked it all in anyway. I thought it might froth up when nobody was looking. If I have another go, do you fancy supervising? See if you can spot the vital stage I'm missing out?'

'OK. And thanks, I feel much better now.'

*   *   *

The work on the new garden starts almost immediately, and it turns out Frank used to be a builder, so he marks out the position of the wall with sticks and string, and then starts work with Dan on the foundations. Various old codgers turn up to help and most of them look too old to lift a spade, but turn out to be terrifically hard workers who get loads more done than half the builders I work with. It's amazing to think of all that talent just going to waste, and they all seem really pleased to be involved.

We have to do lots of digging because Mr Channing says the soil is very compacted or something, and needs stacks of compost working in. Most of the village donates a barrow-load or two of their favourite mixture, and Frank attaches a trailer to the back of his ancient mini, which has a cruising speed of about fifteen miles an hour, and he and Elsie drive up and down the village in it collecting compost. Elsie has a lovely time waving at everyone they pass, like she was in some sort of agricultural royal motorcade. Even Lola turns up briefly, but disappears when she realises how much digging's involved.

Molly says Dan is spending ages working on the foundations, and she's hoping he might get a bit more interested in their garden now, so she's trying to think of projects that involve bricks to capture his interest.

Graham Poltney turns up to advise on the position of the fruit trees, and Frank brings old George Dawes, who was some sort of master builder before he retired. He's rather keen on what he refers to as 'the ladies', and greets anyone under fifty with a rather alarming grin and a Leslie Phillips-type 'Hello', but he promises to send his sons round to help build the wall if we get the bricks.

He insists on talking to Dan about the kind of bricks we want, so I go all technical on him, which gives him a bit of a shock, but he recovers quite well, and we end up having a really great conversation about what we might be able to get where, and at what price. He knows all the local suppliers, and promises to get us a big discount.

*   *   *

The day the bricks arrive quite a little procession turns up. Alfie has a lovely afternoon getting in everybody's way and eating too much of Mrs Bishop's special walnut cake. The bulk of the wall goes up remarkably quickly, with most of us acting as navvies, and everyone gets the chance to lay a brick or two, even if they then have to be surreptitiously repositioned.

Even Alfie has a go, but soon gets bored and spends most of his time running round with one of Ezra's swords, much to Ezra's irritation. There's a great deal of tapping bricks with trowels, and Charles has to take the children indoors to watch cartoons.

The new nanny has arrived. She's called Kimberley and seems very nice, if a bit downtrodden and silent. But she seems happy enough and Charles says Mabel adores her, although Ezra still hasn't made up his mind.

The wall really is starting to look great, and Mr Dawes and his boys clearly know their stuff. It's nearly dark by the time we decide to call it a day. Mrs Pomeroy has taken loads of photographs, which she's going to put into a special album to show to the judges. Our entry has been accepted and they're due to visit at some point in the summer. It's just a sea of mud at the moment, but if you imagine it with plants climbing up the walls and filling all the beds you can see how it might actually work.

Charles has arranged a shopping trip with Mr Channing as expert back-up, to try to make a start on buying all the plants we need, and at the last minute Lola announces she's coming too. I think she's been feeling a bit left out. Charles and Mr Channing set off in the Range Rover, and Lola brings Mabel with us in her car, because it's Kimberley's morning off.

She drives extremely fast down the lanes between the nurseries on the list and I'm slightly rattled at finding myself hurtled through the countryside at such speed. It ends up as a sort of horticultural Grand Prix, with us getting to each nursery ages before Charles and Mr Channing, and Lola asking Charles where on earth he's been when they arrive.

Mabel seems quite happy, and is busy chewing away at a baguette in her car seat, but every time Lola lifts her out she puts the half-chewed bread on the roof of the car, and then gives it back to Mabel half an hour later when she puts her back in the seat, which strikes me as highly unhygienic and just the kind of thing that would make Mum reach for the emergency Dettox wipes.

It's always nice to feel smug about your mothering skills, and I did fob Alfie off with a slightly fluffy Chewitt from the bottom of my handbag last week, but at least I don't pick food off the top of cars to give to him.

We buy trays of lavender plants and all sorts of herbs at one place, and fruit bushes at another, and our final stop is the specialist nursery Mr Poltney has recommended for apple trees. While Mr Channing talks to the owner and dithers between Epicure and Egremont Russet, Lola and I wander off and get carried away with damsons and cherries, even though they're not actually on our list, and then Lola spots a medlar tree.

They all look like sticks in pots at the moment, but the pictures on the labels are lovely. We end up with far too many, and then Lola starts bargaining for free delivery and a discount, which embarrasses Charles so much he has to go and sit in the car.

By the time we've got back to Charles and Lola's and unloaded all the plants, we're exhausted, and we end up in the living room by the fire drinking gin and tonics. Lola seems to go in for large doubles with very little tonic, so I have to make a superwoman effort to sit up straight and not fall asleep.

'I must get home – Mum will want to be off. But thanks for a lovely afternoon. I never thought shopping for plants would be so great.'

'Oh, before you go – Charles, go and get that thing.'

'What thing?'

'The thing for Alice. You know.'

Charles looks blank.

'Oh for god's sake, sometimes I wonder if you ever listen to me at all. The bag, in the hall, the one I told you is for Alice. To say thank you. Ring any bells?'

'Oh that thing. Yes, of course.'

'Honestly. I sometimes think flash cards might be a good idea.'

Charles brings in a Liberty bag, and makes a face behind Lola's back as he hands me the bag.

'I heard that crack about flash cards, Lola. Alice, this is a little present from us both, just to say thank you, for doing the garden.'

The bag contains a fabulous grey embroidered shawl, like a pashmina, only much nicer, in some sort of velvet material, but soft so it drapes beautifully.

'Oh god, it's beautiful. Thank you so much.'

Lola gets up and adjusts the shawl over my shoulders.

'There, like that, it really suits you. I thought the colour would be perfect for you. I bought one for myself too, I couldn't resist. Mine's blue.'

'Well, thank you, it's lovely.'

I wander off up the lane swinging my carrier bag, feeling very pleased with myself. Mum and Alfie have been making cakes, so most of the kitchen is covered in flour. I show them both my new shawl.

'Lovely, dear. It's almost big enough for a blanket, isn't it?'

'Yes, but that's the way they're meant to be. I can't wait to wear it somewhere.'

Alfie wants a go on my blanket, but he's covered in flour so I take it upstairs while Mum distracts him with the prospect of making icing. By the time I get back downstairs they're mixing up a bowl of chocolate, with Alfie perched on a kitchen chair bashing his wooden spoon on the table and singing a medley of songs from *Jungle Book*. 'Up Two Three

Four, Keep It Up, Bare Necessities', with a bit of 'King of the Swingers' mixed in.

The icing goes everywhere and we all eat far too many cakes, and then Alfie very solemnly gets up and finds a bowl and puts a cake in it for Mum to take home to Grandad. Sometimes he does the sweetest things. Sadly he then proceeds to eat it, but it's the thought that counts, and anyway Dad's not really that keen on cakes.

Finally we all start to feel sick and stop eating, and I promise Mum I'll clean the kitchen later. We both know she'll do it properly tomorrow morning, but at least it means she can go home now.

Alfie and I sit by the fire and watch telly, and he falls asleep mid-cuddle, but the combination of gin and cake, one which I'd never tried before but now realise is a very good combination indeed, means I don't really care.

The weather finally clears up and we have a mass planting afternoon in the new garden. We're putting cordons of apples along the inside of the new wall, along with pears, espaliered peach trees and a fig tree. If everything grows properly we'll be able to open a greengrocer's. Mr Channing reckons that with a bit of protection in the winter the trees will be fine, although it's hard to believe that these spindly little sticks will ever grow leaves, let alone fruit.

Around the outside of the wall Mr Poltney and Mrs Pomeroy are planting apples, damsons, plums and cherries. Inside all the beds are a mixture of herbs and vegetables. They've decided on a fruit area in one corner, with a fruit cage where we can drape green netting over the plants to thwart the birds. We plant blackcurrants, redcurrants, gooseberries and raspberries, which makes me feel hungry, and Mrs Pomeroy says she's growing some strawberry plants in her greenhouse, which we can put in later once the weather warms up.

Frank has brought some herbs he's been growing, and Mrs Pomeroy has brought her husband who's making a video so we can include it in our submission to the judges. Elsie arrives, and is very pleased when Charles insists she help plant the walnut tree in the centre of the garden. She puts a small shovel of earth into the hole and then Mrs Pomeroy persuades Mabel to tip a handful of earth in too, so the oldest and the youngest villagers have both taken part. Mrs Pomeroy says she thinks the judges will like that. Then she realises her husband had recorded her saying this, so she tells him off and makes Elsie and Mabel do it again.

Graham Poltney has brought some of his special planting mixture along, which he says never fails to give things a head start. It smells disgusting, whatever it is. Then we move on to vegetables, and plant cabbages and leeks, onions, runner beans, and garlic. The courgettes and peas have to wait until the ground warms up a bit.

Molly and I are busy planting herbs, and Frank tells us to put the mint inside a large bucket because he says it goes like the clappers and will take over the entire garden, given half a chance, and then we plant some fennel, thyme, and dill. Frank says we have to plant the dill as far away as possible from the fennel, otherwise they cross-pollinate or something. Herbs are obviously a rather lively lot.

Lola is looking glamorous as usual in very tight black jeans and a tiny lilac vest with a matching cardigan. Even with wellies on she looks fabulous, and she spends most of her time flirting like mad, which seems to go down well with everyone except Mrs Pomeroy, who sends Mr Pomeroy home in disgrace when she notices he's spending most of his time videoing Lola rather than concentrating on the rest of us digging holes for plants.

One of the beds is going to be a garden for the children, and they all get engrossed digging and planting – they're going to grow sunflowers and tomatoes later, but for now they're starting off with runner beans and potatoes. Charles helps them with the planting, and Mabel enjoys herself so much she begins digging up newly planted herbs to add to her garden until Lola takes her indoors for a biscuit.

Then Charles gives Lily a ride in his wheelbarrow, which turns out to be a bit of a mistake because he then has to wheel Alfie and Ezra up and down too. But it's really starting to look like a garden now, and while the children play upstairs we all sit in the kitchen, and eat bowls of Mrs Bishop's home-made pea-and-ham soup.

Charles makes sure everyone has a glass of wine and then goes bright red and says he wants to make a toast.

'To all of you, and to the beautiful garden. May it win every prize, and make the Village Garden Society famous.'

We all raise our glasses.

'Here's to victory.'

'To victory.'

And then Frank adds, 'And a warm spring. But not too warm, and not too much rain.'

He'll probably start going on about greenfly in a minute.

'Here's to victory, and a warm spring.'

4

APRIL

The Long Good Friday

Garden Diary

Plant aquatics and marginals and clear blanketweed from ponds. Place supports over flowering perennials, particularly delphiniums. Establish and maintain a strict regime for weeding. Prune back gooseberries and spray against mildew.

I try to clean up the small filthy pond in the corner of the back garden and get covered in black slime, which smells revolting. I think it might be easier to fill it in and start again, but Alfie's certain he's seen a frog. It must be a very stupid frog to have chosen such a tiny pond. I put canes around a plant that looks like it might be a delphinium at some point in the future, and then nearly poke my eye out on the cane when I lean down to pick up the trowel. Go to the garden centre to buy rubber tops for canes, and see trays of delphiniums. Realise plant cannot be a delphinium. May in fact be a very large weed.

'YOU'LL NEVER GUESS WHAT Dan's done now.'
    'What?'
'Invited his mother down for Easter, the idiot. She rang up and said she'd got an Easter egg for Lily and he just caved.'
'Oh dear.'
'The last time she came she nearly drove me round the bend, and that was only for the day. She offered to hoover – did I tell you?'
'What a cow.'
'I know. And the house is a complete tip, and we'll need new curtains for the spare room – the ones we've got are too short. I've tried telling him, and do you know what he said?'
'No, but I'm guessing he didn't handle it well.'
'He said he couldn't talk to me when I was being hysterical.'
'That was clever. I bet that calmed you down.'
'Oh definitely. I said I was going upstairs for a bath, and then he said well, go easy, because the new floorboards under the bath aren't finished yet and he's not sure how much weight the old ones can take. Anyway I've told him, he'd better sort them out before his mother turns up, or she'll be sitting in the bath and find herself downstairs in the kitchen. That'll show her. He won't be such a golden boy then, will he?'
'Probably not.'
'And we don't break up at school until the Thursday before Good Friday, so I won't have time to get anything ready.'
'You can borrow the curtains from my spare room, if you like. My Aunty Shirley bought them for a housewarming present. They're a bit floral, but they'll be long enough.'
'Oh that's great. Can I come round now and collect them? Only Dan's taken Lily off to Tesco's as a penance, so I've got half an hour spare.'
'Sure. Was she tired before they left, by any chance?'
'Completely knackered. She'll be throwing an epi any minute now.'
'Shame.'

*   *   *

91

At least my Easter's going to be easier than Molly's. But somehow my plan of us all going to Mum's, and covering her soft furnishings with chocolate, has mysteriously mutated into an arrangement whereby everyone comes to me for Easter Sunday lunch. Which is a bit of a blow really, because I'm not sure pizza's quite what she's got in mind.

I'm trying to persuade her not to get Alfie a record-breaking Easter egg like she did last year, but I know I'm fighting a losing battle, so he'll be having a massive sugar high on Easter Sunday, just when I'm trying to cook lunch.

And I'm frantically busy at work, and Janet's sulking about my doing the design for the Garden Society. I've told her I did all the work in my free time, and Malcolm's fine about it, but she seems to think I'm somehow cheating the firm. Last night I had a dream about punching her, which isn't good, whichever way you look at it. But at least Alfie's having a lovely time at nursery at the moment: they're making eggs and chicks and he's either covered in glitter when he comes home, or tufts of cotton wool and yellow paint.

Molly collects the curtains, and I spend the afternoon trying to work while Alfie gets all of his jigsaws out, spreads them all over the floor, and then decides he can't be bothered to actually do them. Supper goes fairly well because it's one of his favourites, fish pie with lots of cheese, and then Lola rings just after I've got him into bed.

'I hate my children, I've decided. Tell me Alfie's being appalling too – I need a bit of solidarity.'

'Oh pretty revolting. And very sparkly at the moment. They're doing Easter at nursery, with glitter. It's a bugger to get off the bottom of the bath.'

'Oh sweet. I wouldn't mind a sparkly bath. It sounds rather nice. Maybe if I sprinkled glitter on Ezra and Mabel they wouldn't annoy me so much. I made a fantastic minestrone for supper tonight but Ezra spent the entire time trying to pick out all the pasta, and then Mabel refused to eat any at all. Christ. I don't cook very often, and now I know why. And bedtime was a total nightmare. Ezra tried to drown Mabel in the bath, and she squirted him with shampoo, and then she wouldn't settle and kept clinging on screaming when I tried to get her into bed. In the end I just left her to it. Honestly, you'd think I was abandoning her in an orphanage or something. Which I bloody well might if she carries on like this. What's Alfie like at bedtime?'

'Pretty lethal. You have to do the whole routine – story, drink, another story, drink. It can go on for hours.'

'Oh I can't be doing with all that. I try to ignore them if they shout. I think you need to establish proper boundaries, I read it in this marvellous book. But Charles always gives in and goes back up to them, which is useless. I think we need a proper bedtime routine. We sort of play it by ear at the moment and it's not bloody working.'

I've always thought it was pretty important for kids to know someone will come when they shout. But maybe that's why it takes me so long to get Alfie into bed.

'Star charts are supposed to be good.'

'Oh we tried that ages ago. We had a star chart for practically everything, but Ezra's so Machiavellian he got all the stars he needed by Wednesday and then he went tonto, and anyway I really resent having to bribe them to behave well, don't you? I think they should just do it anyway.'

'Maybe, but I'd be totally buggered without a bit of bribery and corruption.'

'But Alfie's so sweet.'

'Other people's children are always sweet. Haven't you noticed?'

'Not always. My friend Hermione's little boy Moby is appalling.'

'Is he?'

'Yes. And he's got a terrible lisp. But I think he just does that to annoy her.'

Poor little thing. I bet some bright spark at school calls him

Moby Dick, and that's just what you need, on top of a lisp, a name that makes everyone laugh.

'Honestly, sometimes I think boarding schools might be a good idea. I really do.'

I hate the idea of boarding schools, but know it's a tricky subject, especially if you were packed off to one yourself, which I think Lola was.

'I think they all go through phases – I mean I know I did. Some of the stories about me and Jim fighting are terrible. I shut his hand in the kitchen door once, and he locked me in the shed for hours, while the lady next door was meant to be looking after us, and I got covered in creosote.'

'You seem so close now, and he's rather gorgeous, if you don't mind me saying. Lovely eyes.'

'Oh yes, we get on now, but when we were little it was like World War Three. And he uses those lovely eyes to transfix all sorts of women, so don't be taken in by his butter-wouldn't-melt routine. He causes all sorts of havoc.'

'Oh I adore havoc. A nice little diversion to take my mind off my horrible children would be perfect. Send him round next time he's down. With glitter if you've got some spare.'

I'm sure she's joking. God, I hope she's joking.

'Anyway, I should go, I've got tons of calls to make. We're doing a work–life balance thing at work next week, and half our clients are coming. And some idiot's completely screwed up the invitation list, so I've got to ring round and make sure everyone's been invited, which has completely fucked up my work–life balance for this week, I can tell you. Oh but I meant to say – I've found out the name of that herb place, and they sell all sorts of amazing stuff you can't get anywhere else, apparently – shall we go? I think it's run by some eccentric. It might be fun.'

'OK, but it'll have to be Friday morning. I'll ask Mr Channing if there's anything else we need for the new garden.'

'Great, Friday's good for me too.'

* * *

I ponder my work–life balance and wonder if I actually have one, but I think they're meant for people earning a fortune who take themselves very seriously indeed, not people with part-time jobs who just get on with it.

I hope Lola's not really interested in Jim. I've had friends in the past who thought he was lovely, and it always ended in tears. And none of them were married. I'm sure she doesn't really mean it, and even if she does I'm sure she won't do anything about it, unless of course she and Charles are what my Aunty Shirley calls swingers, which always makes me think of Tupperware parties and fondue sets.

There was a couple in her road who turned out to be swinging away like mad with half the neighbourhood, and poor old Shirley was furious. She said it was bound to affect house prices, but I think she was just a bit miffed that they didn't ask her and Uncle Bernard to join in.

The eccentric herb-grower lives about half an hour's drive away, in the middle of nowhere in a totally ramshackle house. It must have once been the gatehouse to the enormous mansion you can just glimpse behind the gates, and although the house has clearly seen better days the garden's amazing. There are all sorts of plants, some of which are huge, and they all smell wonderful, and there are rows and rows of black plastic pots with seedlings in them all over what used to be the lawn, and lines of polystyrene plant trays.

We bang on the front door for a bit and then give up and go round the back, which is easier said than done because we have to fight our way through a jungle of some sort of creeper, which smells gorgeous and has stacks of tiny white flowers.

'You total bastards. Right, well, that's it. I'm getting the poison out.'

Someone who looks like an old tramp is crouched down by the back wall shouting at a plant pot, but when he stands up he turns out to be a man in his mid-thirties, with nice green eyes and short dark hair that is hidden under a tragic old woolly hat, which he takes off as soon as he sees us.

'Oh hello, sorry, I didn't hear you. I hate slugs, don't you? And beer doesn't always work, you know. I think mine are teetotal. And I've tried coffee, I heard it on the radio, but it didn't work either. So I'm reduced to those disgusting blue pellets. But it's either that or lose half my plants.'

Lola recovers first.

'Yes, well, quite. What a nightmare. We've come to buy some herbs. I gather you sell things. Is that right?'

'Oh yes, well, sometimes. I do the odd market, or people come here. Would you like some coffee? I was just about to make some.'

We follow him into the house, which is a complete tip. A mixture of rather serious antique furniture that would probably be worth a fortune if you cleaned it up, and piles of catalogues, bits of string, plant pots and lethal-looking saws, and a huge scythe in the middle of the kitchen table. It looks like the floor hasn't been cleaned in decades. Mum would have a heart attack.

'Sorry about the mess. Now, where's the coffee pot? It's silver, sort of battered-looking. Can anyone spot it?'

'Is this it?'

Lola has found it on the floor, on a cushion, for some reason.

'That's it. OK, coffee coming up. I like mine strong – I hope you do too.'

He starts whistling while he fills the pot up with water and puts it on an ancient-looking Aga. He's wearing really muddy jeans and a checked flannel shirt with a rip on one sleeve, but he's got nice hands, even if they are filthy.

A very muddy black Labrador wanders in, looks at us for a bit, and then lies down in a basket under the table. It smells revolting and has presumably been on some sort of forensic mission in the garden.

We sit down at the table, trying to avoid getting too close to the dog.

'What plants are you looking for?'

Before I get a chance to read out the list from Mr Channing Lola says she wants something fabulous to put in pots outside the kitchen.

'And preferably easy to grow, because I'm a complete beginner.'

She raises her eyebrows at him in a very suggestive way. Oh god. How embarrassing. The poor man's gone beetroot-red.

'Right. Well, I've got some lovely rosemary, and it's practically impossible to kill that, unless you're really determined. I'll show you round after we have our coffee and you can see if you like the look of anything. Damn.'

The telephone is ringing and as he gets up to answer it we both notice his trousers are split at the back, revealing a large expanse of white underpants. We both try to look away, and are dangerously close to sniggering.

'Yes, Ma, I do remember. Yes. I said yes, didn't I? I've got to go, I've got customers here. Bye. Good god, she's getting worse, she really is. As if I haven't got enough to do without taking people to Waitrose. Sorry, do excuse me. My mother tends to bring out the worst in me.'

'Oh mine too. Do you live alone then?'

I can't quite believe Lola has said this.

'Oh yes. Well, my mother's just up the lane, but I try to stay out of her way.'

'And who lives in that fabulous big house – the local squire? Lord and Lady Somebody?'

'Something like that. Lady Boughton. The old man died a few years ago.'

'Are they nice or mad? Aristocrats are usually a bit of both.'

'Oh mostly mad. She keeps ringing me up and asking me to take her to Waitrose.'

He's smiling now, and doesn't seem at all bothered that Lola's just suggested his mother is round the twist. I'd be mortified, but Lola just gives him one of her dazzling smiles.

'Oh, so you're the local gentry. Good. Well, you must come to dinner – I need some more ruling classes to balance things up a bit. Don't look so appalled – you might enjoy yourself. I'm Lola, by the way, Lola Barker, and I give fantastic dinner parties, if I say so myself.'

'Harry Broughton, and I'm sure you do. But I'm allergic to that kind of thing.'

'Lord Harry to your friends?'

'Good god, no. My father was the Lord. He was in the Foreign Office. It was a sort of retirement present. They all get one, I think.'

I'd bet serious money the cleaners don't get one when they retire, but I don't actually say this, mainly because Lola is on some sort of one-woman fact-finding mission and is not going to give up until she's got all the information she requires.

'So have you always lived round here then, or is the house a new acquisition?'

'Oh no, my mother's the gentry in our family. The house has been in her family for years.'

Lola prods with more questions and discovers that his parents kept the house as a base while they were abroad, and then retired down here. I can't believe she's being so nosy.

'Well, good for you. I love London, but I like the country life too. Couldn't do it full-time, though, I'd go mad.'

'Oh I think that helps.'

Lola continues her cross-examination and he says he used to be in the City like his brother, at some posh firm Lola knows, but he got fed up with it and gave it all up to grow herbs. He's got lovely eyes, actually, and a really nice smile. Lola's flirting like mad with him.

We walk round the garden being given amazing facts about all sorts of plants, most of which I barely recognise. He clearly knows his stuff. I tell him about the new garden and show him Mr Channing's list, and he seems to have most of the things on it, and then Lola buys some rosemary bushes, and asks him if he can deliver them tomorrow, because we're in a bit of a rush and need to get back. He seems fine about this, and she gives him her number and address. As we drive off she waves out of the window, and toots.

'Well, what a find. Gorgeous. I must invite him to dinner. I mean what's the point if you can't have a bit of a frisson now and then with a handsome stranger?'

I don't really know what to say to this, but I feel I'm somehow being disloyal to Charles.

'Lovely plants, weren't they? I bet Charles will be pleased. Mr Channing thinks he's got a real talent for gardens, you know.'

'Nice to know he's got a talent for something.'

Oh. Well that worked really well then.

'I'll look through the diary and see what I've got coming up that I can invite him to. Or I could ask Tina down for the weekend. He might do for her – she's completely desperate at the moment. He had lovely hands – did you notice? I love men who work with their hands, don't you?' And she sniggers in a very suggestive way.

I spend half the afternoon thinking about passionate moments with handsome strangers who've got nice hands. But my track record with passion isn't exactly inspiring, although I did once have a brilliant weekend in Brighton with Patric, in the early days before he went all boring. Actually, a weekend away might be nice. But then I'd have to explain to Mum why I want her to have Alfie and she'd go all Spanish Inquisition on me, and anyway the last thing I need is to get entangled with some barking herb grower who lives with his mother. Even if he does have lovely eyes.

Alfie watches cartoons for most of Saturday morning, so he's especially lively during lunch. He's still leaping about when Patric arrives, nearly three-quarters of an hour late, complaining that the traffic was murder and he got stuck behind a police car on the motorway so he couldn't make up time by speeding. Somehow he manages to say this in a tone of voice that suggests that it's all my fault.

Then he announces that one of Alfie's armbands has got a slow puncture.

'Have you got a puncture kit?'

'Funnily enough, not on me, no. If you'd told me last time you took him swimming I'd have got one, but at this precise moment, no.'

'Oh. Well, I'll have to get him some new armbands then, won't I?'

'Yes. Unless you want him swimming round in circles all afternoon.'

'You might try to be a little less aggressive, you know, Alice. I was only asking.'

Christ, he's annoying.

'His swimming bag's by the door, and I've put some juice in, in case he gets thirsty.'

This is me trying to be subtle and non-aggressive, but still make sure he gets the message that I'd rather Alfie had juice to drink than Coke. I know he wants to give him treats when he sees him, but it's me that has him bouncing off the walls when he gets home, full of sweets and Coke.

About half an hour after they've left I hear the sound of a car pulling up outside. They can't be back already, unless Alfie's managed to throw up all over Patric's new car. A black Labrador bounds up the path as I open the door.

'Christ, I'm sorry. Basil. Sit. *Basil.*'

It's Harry, carrying a tray of plants. He's looking marginally less tramp-like than yesterday, and has a clean pair of jeans on, and a fairly clean navy-blue jumper. Basil's running round in circles wagging his tail and barking.

'Have I got the right place?'

'Yes, but it's the house just up the lane.'

'Basil. Shut up. *Sit.* Oh, right, only I've been up there and there's nobody around. I'm a bit late actually – I got stuck with customers all morning. Where's the new garden, by the way? The one you were telling me about – I'd love to see it.'

'You mean the Garden Society one?'

'Yes, I've brought a few extra things, as my contribution. I hope they're all right – just some lavenders – I'm very pro garden societies. I get lots of my customers through them.'

'Oh thank you, really, that's very kind. You must come up and have a look round. I'm sure Lola and Charles won't mind.'

'I take it you're not a mad keen plantswoman?'

He looks round my garden and shakes his head.

'I like it like this.'

'Really? Sorry, I didn't mean to be rude.'

'No, actually, I've been trying to sort it out. I've got a book and everything, but it doesn't seem to have made much difference. I was thinking about a flamethrower.'

He laughs.

'Actually, there are some decent plants under this lot. It wouldn't take long, you know.'

'The trouble is, I'm not really sure where to start.'

'I could get you started.'

He blushes. And so do I. Christ. This is turning into a *Carry On* film. All we need now is Sid James.

'I mean, I'd be happy to help, if you like. I love rescuing gardens.'

I thank him, but say I think I'd better finish the other garden first, and we drive back up the lane in his jeep. There's no sign of Lola or Charles at the house, so we put the plants in the garage out of the sun, and go through the side gate and across the lawns.

I'm surprised at how proud I feel when we walk through the doorway into the new garden. Dan spent ages last week fiddling with the water, and it now flows down from the main pond into the two smaller ones, with lovely trickling noises. Harry's very impressed.

'I think we might need some water plants. Tall thin ones, so they move a bit, but nothing flowery. But the slate looks great, doesn't it?'

'Fabulous. Are you sure you haven't done gardens before? This really is terrific.'

'No, but I didn't do the plants – they're all down to the Garden Society. The structure's fairly simple, it's the plants that really make it.'

'Mmm. Well, I love the water, and the brick paths. They can look really awful, you know, if you get them wrong. You've obviously got the knack. What's going in here?'

'A play house, so the children have somewhere of their own. They've planted things too, look. Potatoes and um, I've forgotten what these are, actually.'

'Runner beans, by the look of it. They'll be up those canes in no time.'

'Alfie wants to grow bananas.'

'He'll have a hard job round here.'

We walk round once more and he asks me who Alfie is, and I explain, and tell him he's off swimming with Patric who comes down most weekends to see him since we split up. Which I think is a rather neat way of avoiding giving him the impression that I'm happily ensconced in couple land, not that it really matters, but well, you never know.

We drive back down the lane and I offer him tea, and we're in the middle of investigating the front garden with him telling me about the plants I've already got, and what new ones would do well, when Patric and Alfie come back from swimming. Basil leaps up at them and plants a thin line of dribble on Patric's left leg. He's not terribly pleased, but Alfie's delighted: he adores dogs, and has been campaigning sporadically to be allowed to adopt a St Bernard like the one in *Peter Pan*.

'Sorry. I'm trying to get him to stop doing that. Basil. Sit. *Sit*.'

Basil totally ignores him, and Harry looks mortified, but it's mainly Alfie's fault because he's running round in circles squealing.

'Alfie. Stop it. Patric, this is Harry. Harry, Patric.'

Patric glares at Harry, who doesn't seem to notice.

'Why's he called Basil?'

Harry explains to Alfie that he named him after Basil Fawlty, who used to be in a television programme he liked when he was little. Although I bet it was herbs that finally decided him.

'I need a dog, but Mummy won't let me have one.'

Alfie pauses, hoping Harry will pass out with shock at my cruelty.

'Oh right, well, they are a great deal of work, you know, and they're very stupid. Basil in particular, actually. He gets completely filthy, and brings things in from the garden. He put a field mouse in my slippers last week.'

I can tell the idea of having a large muddy dog put mice in your slippers strikes Alfie as completely marvellous.

'Thanks, Harry, that's really put him off. Look, Alfie, when you're big enough to take it for a walk in the pouring rain every night, then you can have one, all right?'

'I can walk in the rain now, I can. I've got my wellies. Daddy, you can get a dog, can't you? And then it can come swimming with us, can't it?'

'No, not really. Look, I'd better be off, Alice. I'll call, but next weekend might be tricky. I'll let you know, all right?'

'Fine.'

He glares at Harry again, and then stomps off down the path towards Alfie, who gives him a quick kiss goodbye and then runs off after Basil again.

He's still looking pretty furious when he drives off. Excellent.

'Well, I'd better be off too. But thank you, for showing me the garden.'

'You're welcome. Are you sure you wouldn't like that tea I promised you? Only I think we might have a bit of a riot on our hands trying to separate them at the moment.'

Alfie and Basil are now rolling around on the grass, having a brilliant time.

'I see what you mean. Well, yes please then – tea would be lovely. Basil. Stop that. *Basil*.'

* * *

103

When I bring the tea outside Alfie's showing off his toys, and Harry seems particularly taken with a bright-yellow digger. He says he never had toys as nice as this when he was little. Alfie says he can borrow it if he likes, and Harry very solemnly says thank you, he would like that very much.

We drink our tea and Harry throws sticks for Basil to catch, which Alfie thinks is fabulous. Then they run round and round the garden again. Basil's wagging his tail so hard he looks like he might wag it right off, and then he starts leaping up at Alfie, who looks like he's about to get flattened at any minute. But he doesn't seem to care.

'Stop that, Basil. Sit.'

Basil completely ignores him.

'Sorry about this. I never really trained him properly – he's too stupid. *Basil*. Stop it.'

Actually, he sounds quite sexy when he shouts.

Alfie is now lying in the mud with Basil licking his face.

'God, I'm so sorry.'

'Don't worry about it. Alfie's in bliss.'

He is. He's giggling like mad, and even though I'm not that keen on the idea of dogs licking his face I'm certainly not going to be the one to try to separate them. Harry grabs Basil's collar and pulls him off, and gets a filthy look from Alfie for his trouble.

'We were playing and Basil's being the bear cub and I'm the big bear.'

It looked very much like the other way round to me, but I'm staying out of it.

'Sorry, but he can't go about licking people's faces. Some people don't like it.'

'Stupid people.'

'Well, yes, maybe, but some dogs might bite, you see, and people wouldn't know, would they? I could get into trouble.'

Basil is now leaping up at Harry and licking his hands.

'Get off. Stop it.'

Harry ends up leaning over and pressing Basil on to the ground to make him sit. Basil seems to think this is a cue to roll over and wave his legs in the air, clearly hoping for a bit of stroking. Alfie obliges and before we know it they're back to the licking thing again.

Harry finally manages to untangle them and drags Basil off towards his jeep. Alfie thinks this is outrageous and bursts into tears.

'We were playing. Can Basil come to play another day? Can he?'

'Yes, I'm sure he can. One day.'

One day when we're out, preferably. This little episode is not going to help me maintain our pet-free status. I've been hoping he'll move off dogs and on to something more relaxing, like goldfish. Or possibly a hamster.

'Alfie, get up now, sweetheart – you're getting all muddy.'

Alfie ignores me.

Harry comes back up the path.

'I'm sorry about that. And thank you very much for the loan of the digger, Alfie.'

Alfie makes a run for the garden gate and I have to race after him. It's amazing how fast small boys can move when they want to. I begin another instalment of my road-safety lecture and hold Alfie's hand very tightly while Harry nods and says I'm quite right, he knew a boy at school who nearly got squashed by a lorry.

But then Alfie wants to know if he was squashed completely flat or only nearly flat, and Harry tries to change the subject. I'm not sure if he's about to say anything else, when Alfie remembers the yellow digger, and retrieves it from the front step.

'Here you are, you nearly forgeted.'

'Oh thanks, marvellous.'

Harry looks rather blank.

'You can borrow it, and when you come back you can bring Basil.'

'Oh. Right. Um, well, thank you again, and for the digger – marvellous.'

And then he whispers to me should he really take it.

'Oh yes, it'll be fine. Just drop it in next time you're passing.'

Alfie's looking longingly towards the jeep, which is now rocking from side to side while Basil presumably settles himself down.

'I'd better be off then.'

The jeep is really rocking now and Basil has started barking.

'Well, thanks again. For the digger, I mean.'

Alfie's trying to sneak past me again, and as I grab him Harry walks backwards down the path, nearly trips over a bucket, and then waves and gets into the jeep and drives off.

Damn. I thought he might be going to ask me out for a drink or something. I'm not sure whether to be disappointed or not. I mean on the one hand I really don't need someone with a mad dog popping round all the time. On the other hand he does have lovely eyes, and well, maybe I'll just wait and see if he rings, and if he doesn't perhaps we might need to buy some more herbs for the garden. I could just drop in, in a casual sort of way, to buy something. Maybe after Easter, so it doesn't seem too obvious.

Lola rings in the evening and is rather put out that she missed Harry.

'I showed him round the new garden.'

'And was he impressed?'

'Very. And then he came back for tea and Patric came back.'

'Oh good. I bet that put his nose out of joint. I still haven't met him, you know. You must bring him up next time – from what you've said he's a complete prick, and I'm rather good with them. I get loads of practice at work. Actually, you know, I've just thought, Harry might be perfect for you – just what you need to liven up your summer.'

'Oh no, he's not my type really.'

Actually, I don't really know what my type is, but I don't want Lola getting the idea that I might be interested. She'd be bound to take over and organise some sort of hideous dinner party or something. And I still haven't made up my mind. Well, not completely, anyway.

'Oh well, if you're sure. I must ring him up and get him round for supper when Tina's down.'

Bugger. Well, that serves me right for not being more assertive, I suppose. Mind you, I'm not completely sure Lola would take much notice even if I was.

We talk about Molly's surprise Easter present, which Dan's arranging to say sorry about his mother visiting. He's getting her some chickens, because she's always wanted some, and he's made a hen house round at Frank's.

'It's so sweet. He's painted it white, with a blue roof.'

'How lovely. Very *Little House on the Prairie*. Well, I hope the foxes don't get them. Isn't that meant to be why everyone goes hunting in the country?'

Actually, I don't know anyone who goes hunting, and neither does Lola, as far as I know, but I think she's just feeling rather grumpy. I think she's still irritated by the new garden: she was pretty sarcastic about the lack of anything really trendy in it, like the zinc pavilion she was campaigning for at one point. She even showed me some pictures of a hideous-looking giant glass ball that you move around the garden, and then sit in, once you've anchored it, presumably. Unless you want to roll around like a hamster. And she keeps telling me shrubs are bourgeois, and I must make sure nobody sneaks any in. I don't know who decided that shrubs are bourgeois, probably someone in one of those magazines that cost eight quid and are full of adverts for leather fruit bowls and villas in Tuscany. But I think she's rather torn now the garden's starting to take shape, and seems to be so popular.

'What are you doing for Easter?'

'Nothing. It's going to be awful. I wanted to go away but I'm too busy at work, so we'll just have people for lunch or something. And Charles's parents are coming, for some reason, which is bloody annoying. God, they're boring. I'll have to get some more people down, or I'll go mad.'

Lola seems to collect people like other people collect teapots – she's always having dinner parties or people for lunch or the weekend. Actually, I'm not sure she's that keen on spending too much time on her own with Charles and the kids.

'If I'm desperate I'll just come down to you and hide. You're not doing anything, are you?'

'Not really. I've got everyone for lunch on Sunday, but apart from that, no.'

'Good. Well, pencil me in then. I'll bring the vodka.'

Molly's invited us to tea on Good Friday, to meet the new chickens. She says they're Buff Orpingtons, which makes them sound like retired army colonels. They're a pretty caramel colour and completely mad, and the chicks are really sweet, like little balls of cheeping fluff. They swarm all over Alfie when he lies down inside the chicken coop, even though I ask him not to, and peck at his knees, which he loves. The cockerel is called Bernard, after Bernard Matthews, and Lily's christened the hens Hoppy, Poppy and Loppy, and her chick Tigger. Molly says Alfie can have a chick too, so he spends ages choosing a name and then finally christens it Edward, after his best friend at nursery.

Harry hasn't rung, which is a bit disappointing if I'm honest, although I'm trying to pretend I don't care. Molly says everyone knows men have a completely different timescale to women, and he's probably just trying to make sure he doesn't look too keen. I'm not sure she's right, I think it's far more likely that he's not interested in the slightest, but my mission to cook lunch for the entire family is looming, and I'm in enough of a panic about that without adding Harry into the mix.

Dan's mum Doreen's already driving Molly round the bend. She really is awful. Molly's made three different sorts of cake for tea but Doreen says she can only eat plain Madeira, and then criticises Lily's table manners, which are fine, but ignores Alfie's, which are appalling. He actually floats a bit of his flapjack in my tea, just to see what will happen, and when I fish it out and tell him to stop it she says bless him, he's just being inquisitive.

Dan takes the children for a walk after tea, mainly to escape Doreen, I think. She settles herself in an armchair and begins a long speech about how marvellous he is.

'It's so different nowadays. I mean men didn't really used to bother with children, but then we didn't ask them to, we just got on with it. I don't know how you modern women do it, I really don't, going out to work and every-thing.'

What she means is she doesn't know *why* we do it, and she thinks it's a scandal.

'He does seem tired, though. He was telling me you take it in turns to make supper. Do you think going for this new job Dan was telling me about is really a good idea, dear? Only I should think you'd find it hard enough just coping with things as they are without taking on more. I think it's wonderful that you devote so much of your time to your children at school, I really do, but Lily and the new baby will need you too, you know.'

Jesus, she's actually accusing Molly of being a bad mother now.

'Still, I'm sure between the two of you it'll be fine. And at least you're in a nice warm school, not outdoors on a building site. He's out in all weathers, you know.'

I can't let her get away with this.

'Oh, I don't know about that. I spend quite a lot of time on building sites, and there's a lot of sitting about in huts drinking tea, reading the paper and making rude jokes.'

She completely ignores me.

'I think it's wonderful the way men today do their share. When I think of how much harder it was for us. I mean I didn't have a washing machine until Danny was four, you

109

know. I did it all by hand. Mind you, I still do a fair bit by hand – I find it's kinder on delicates.'

Old bag. She'd probably have us down by a river bashing stuff on stones if she could. Now Molly has to feel like a failure because she doesn't do all the washing by hand.

'Actually, I'm not sure men today really are that wonderful. I was reading something about it in the paper the other day, and apparently one in three men don't even wake up if their babies cry in the night, let alone get up to them. Patric definitely never got up for Alfie, before he buggered off completely, I mean.'

Molly gives me a grateful sort of look.

'Yes, and if they do wake up they just poke you in the back and say she's crying again. Dan does get up sometimes, but I still do most of it.'

'I never minded getting up to my babies.'

Bloody hell, she's annoying.

'Didn't you? Oh I do. As much as I love Alfie I swear I'd swap him for a nice cup of tea and an extra hour in bed most mornings. But I suppose some things have changed for the better. Mum was just saying the other day how much better it is now people realise that having a baby doesn't mean you have to stay at home for the rest of your life. She said she thought she was going to go round the bend when we were little. She was worried she was going to turn into one of those mad women who can recite recipes off by heart.'

Doreen has a habit of cutting recipes out of magazines and sending them to Molly. Quick suppers, nourishing soups, that kind of thing. Poor Molly looks close to tears. Time for my emergency escape plan.

'Talking of brilliant cooks, I need to borrow Molly later, if that's all right, only I've got to make a cake for Sunday, and I need her help. You don't mind, do you? She's so fabulous with cakes and I'm sure Dan will make supper. He can make you one of his special omelettes.'

Dan makes the worst omelette you've ever tasted. He manages to burn it and not cook it in the middle at the same time, which as Molly says is quite a special talent really. Serve the old bag right, eating one of the golden boy's cheese-omelette specials.

'Let's go and look at the chicks again.'

'I'll stay by the fire, if you don't mind, dear. I've got a bit of a headache coming on.'

We find her some headache tablets, which I notice she doesn't take, and then go out to look at the chickens.

'God, she's awful.'

'I know. I feel she's judging my every move, and even though I know she's wrong, and there's more to life than cleaning the kitchen floor every day, I still hate it. It's like she's catching me out all the time.'

'Who cleans their kitchen floor every day? God, don't tell Mum.'

'She does. She's got timetables inside the cupboard doors in the kitchen. She ticks off the jobs as she does them.'

'Maybe we should sneak round and write things on them.'

'What, like Tuesday. Get A Life.'

'Yes, or Friday. Get Over It.'

'Thanks for rescuing me – you're an angel.'

'There is a catch, you know.'

'I don't care.'

'You might. I really do want you to help me with the cake – I've made one, but it's gone all lopsided. I've got some decorations, some little chickens, but I need you to help me with the icing so it doesn't look like they're trying to commit suicide by hurling themselves off a cliff.'

'It's a deal. Anything, as long as I can stay until past Lily's bedtime.'

'Stay all night, if you like. We can make wax models of Doreen and stick pins in them. That'll sort out her headache.'

Easter Sunday is not going well, and it's only half-past ten. Molly has rung to say that Doreen is still being awful, and got up at 7 a.m. to make breakfast for Dan, and used the last

111

of the eggs, but she didn't make anything for Molly because she said she didn't know what she liked. And then the chickens got out, and it took them ages to get them back in, and apparently Edward was especially hard to track down and has now been rechristened Fast Eddie.

Mum rings after Molly, to remind me that it's important to cook meat all the way through, and then Jim calls to say he'll be late, and Alfie says he wants to go and see the chickens again, and he's already eaten two Easter eggs. He's got a manic grin on his face, and is busy being a chicken, which involves making a nest with all the cushions and lots of elbow-flapping.

I feel very tempted to go back to bed and pretend to be ill when Mum and Dad arrive, but instead I have to wrestle a giant ham into the roasting tin, and then coat it with honey. I start off with a spoon but end up using my hands. Actually it's quite therapeutic, massaging away making lovely squelching noises. Until the phone rings. I forget I'm covered in honey and grab it, but it shoots out of my hands and skids across the floor. I shout 'Bollocks' very loudly, grab a tea towel and retrieve the phone, but whoever was calling has rung off. Bloody typical. It was probably some flaming double-glazing salesman thinking that Easter Sunday was the perfect time to catch people in and ask them how many windows they wanted replaced free of charge.

The phone is now covered in very unpleasant-looking brown marks, and I'm busy trying to wash them off when it starts ringing again. It's Harry.

'Was that you just then?'

'What?'

'Answering the phone by yelling "Bollocks".'

'Oh yes, sorry. I dropped the phone – I'm cooking.'

'Right.'

'And I'm covered in honey.'

'Nice.'

Oh god, he must think I'm completely mad.

'I'm doing a ham, and you have to put honey on it. It helps the flavour.'

'Sounds delicious.'

Thank god I haven't got one of those video-phones where the person you're talking to can see you. Come to think of it I can't work out who'd want a phone like that: you'd never be able to get in the bath in case someone rang up.

'Anyway, the thing is, I was just wondering, if you're not busy or anything, if you'd like to come out for dinner one night? There's a new Italian place in Tonbridge that's supposed to be all right. We could talk about your garden. I've been thinking, it wouldn't take much to get it sorted out, you know, and I think it would be fun.'

'What, dinner or the garden?'

Bugger. I wish I hadn't said that.

'Both, I hope. Any night really, except Thursdays. My mother has all her old bags round for bridge and I have to lurk with drinks and sort out any major disputes. It can get quite nasty.'

'Friday might be all right.'

'Great. Friday it is. Shall I pick you up, around seven? Or is that too early?'

'No, seven should be fine. I should have got the honey off by then.'

Oh god. I wish I hadn't said that too.

'Shame. Well, until Friday then. Oh and by the way, I haven't forgotten about Alfie's digger – I don't want him to think I've stolen it. I'll bring it on Friday. Bye.'

Bloody hell. I call Molly, who's delighted, but she can't really chat because Lily's just poured lemonade all over the sofa.

'What are you going to wear?'

'God knows.'

'I'll come round if you like and we can have a dressing-up session.'

'Brilliant.'

At least Molly knows just how limited my wardrobe is, and won't make me throw away things that aren't fashionable any more like they do on those television programmes where people's special old jumpers are slung into skips.

Jim arrives with a terrible hangover, and a huge Easter egg for Alfie, which I grab and try to hide on a top shelf in the kitchen. Alfie thinks I'm being very unreasonable, and Jim agrees.

'Fine. He's already eaten two this morning, and a load of mini eggs, but if you want to give him another one and explain to Mum why he won't eat his lunch then that'll be fine. Oh and he might get a bit lively with all the extra sugar and then he'll probably be sick. But he can sit near you, and you'll take care of it, won't you?'

'Actually, Alf, you know, she might have a point. I mean maybe you should save it for tea. Or maybe for tomorrow. Then you'll have something to look forward to. What do you think?'

'Bollocks'.

Jim and I look at each other. He can't really have said 'Bollocks.'

'Bollocks. I want my egg. Now.'

'Alfie, that's a very rude thing to say.'

'You said it, you did, when the phone fell down, and you say it in the car when there's a bus.'

'Well, I shouldn't say it, but sometimes grown-ups are allowed to do things they shouldn't. But little boys aren't – it's very rude when little boys do it, much ruder than for grown-ups.'

'Bollocks.'

I have to admit he's got a point. But I also know it's pretty crucial we clear this up before Mum and Dad arrive, or lunch could be tricky. I decide to try one of the most reliable ways of putting him off something, even though it drives me crazy.

'Jim never says it. It's quite a girly thing to say, actually.'

Thankfully, Jim works out what I'm up to and plays along.

'Oh yes, very girly. Only mummies and girls say it really. I'd never say it.'

114

'Would the big boys in your office laugh at you?'

'Oh yes, they'd laugh themselves sick.'

Alfie considers this for a moment.

'I want my egg. Now.'

I think he knows he's being fobbed off, but he's just not willing to risk adopting a word that might make the big boys laugh.

'All right, but only have one piece?'

'A big piece?'

'OK.'

Mum and Dad arrive with another giant Easter egg. Great.

'Hello, my little chicken, look what Nana's brought you, a lovely big egg, but you've got to wait until after lunch, all right, sweetheart?'

'All right, Nana. I love you, Nana. And I've got a chicken. He's called Eddie. He lives at Aunty Molly's house but he's mine, he really is.'

How very bloody annoying. If I'd said he couldn't start eating his egg he'd be on the floor having a fit, but when Nana says it it's somehow completely fine.

'How lovely, your very own chick. What a clever boy you are – come and sit down and tell me all about it. Bob, go and get my bag. I've got a new book for you, sweetheart, and it's all about chickens. We can see if there's one like yours in it, can't we? Hello, James, why haven't you shaved this morning? You look as if you've slept all night in that jumper.'

Mum insists on calling him James, for some reason best known to herself. Mainly because it annoys him, I think.

'Lovely to see you too, Mum. Alf, enjoy it while you can. She'll be telling you off about your jumpers soon.'

'No I won't, poppet. You won't come to see your Nana in a scruffy jumper, will you?'

'No. I like sweatshirts. I've got one with a dog on.'

'I know you have. We should get you one with a chicken, shouldn't we?'

'Do you want a coffee, Mum?'

'Oh yes please. And one for your father. Where's he got to with that bag? Honestly, you can't let him out of your sight for a minute. James, go and see what he's doing, and if he's heading off towards the pub just you turn him right back round again.'

Dad once stopped off at the pub on his way home from buying the Sunday papers about fifteen years ago, and she's never let him forget it.

Lunch is a triumph: the ham looks rather black with the special honey coating, and Jim makes all sorts of comments about it until I explain it's meant to look like this. It tastes fabulous, and the cake is nice too although Jim is very sarcastic about my chickens looking like they're going skiing, and this reminds Dad of the skiing holiday we all went on when we were little when Jim skied straight into a tree and got concussion.

Mum makes Dad and Jim do the washing up, while we drink coffee and Alfie continues work on his entry into *The Guiness Book of Records* as the boy who ate the most chocolate in one day.

Dad and Jim are laughing in the kitchen, which is too much for Mum so she goes in to investigate. I just hope they're not talking about Alfie saying 'Bollocks'.

We go for a walk before tea to visit Molly and the chickens. Doreen tries to bond with Mum as soon as we arrive and says doesn't she think children today are very badly behaved and noisy, and Mum says no, not really, and Doreen sulks.

I grab a quick five minutes with Molly in the kitchen. She's looking tired.

'Why don't you ask Doreen to babysit? She might as well do something useful. Go out for the night, just you and Dan.'

'Oh no, I'd spend the whole time worrying about her going through all the cupboards and looking at our bank statements.'

'True. But at least the place would be nice and tidy when you got home.'

'Actually, that's not a bad idea, you know – the airing cupboard's in a right state. Every time I open the door something falls out. I keep meaning to tidy it but I never get round to it, but she'd be bound to have a snoop, and then she'd just have to sort it out – she'd say she needed a towel or something. I might see what Dan thinks.'

But Dan says he's knackered and anyway he thinks Doreen would sulk if they asked her to babysit, because she keeps saying she doesn't see enough of him, which is fair enough, I suppose.

Mum says she thinks we'd better leave soon because Alfie is trying to work out how he can smuggle Eddie back to our house, so we walk home and have more sloping cake, and then just as Mum and Dad are leaving Mum says it's been lovely having someone else do lunch, and she knew I could cook properly if I just concentrated. And maybe we should have Christmas at my house this year, because it's all been so nice. I'm half pleased with this, and half appalled.

Alfie has now eaten so much he can barely move, and he watches telly lying flat out on the sofa, while Jim and I sort out the tea things.

'I meant to ask you – you don't fancy coming down again next weekend, do you? On Friday, so I can go out?'

'What for?'

'Oh just a meal, with one of the garden people.'

'Single?'

'Yes.'

'Male and under eighty?'

'Yes.'

'Ooh. A real live man on the horizon. Which is why you don't want Mum babysitting, I take it?'

'Yes.'

'What does he do, then?'

'He's a herb-dealer.'

'Round my way that's a euphemism for the stuff you don't inhale if you want to be President.'

'Well, round here it means real herbs. He's called Harry, and he's got a dog called Basil.'

'Sounds like a right wally to me. Harry the Herb Man. What car does he drive?'

'You are *such* a boy. An old jeep. And anyway I'm not sure if he's really my type. It's just dinner.'

'And what's that then, your type? A total wanker like Mork?'

'It's only dinner. Honestly, I wish I hadn't asked you now.'

'All right, all right, keep your hair on. I'm sure I can do it, but I'll call you tomorrow when I'm in the office and I can check the diary. And I won't breathe a word to Mum. I just want you to have a bit of fun, you know. I was only teasing.'

'I do have fun. Just because I'm not shagging my way round the village doesn't mean I'm not having fun. Talking of which, did you ever see that woman from Lola's office?'

'Yes. Bit of a handful really, but I got loads of info on your Lola: and she sounds a total nightmare. Did you know she actually drew round one of her kids' feet, and then faxed it through to the office so her PA could go and get him some new shoes? The poor girl had to take the fax into John Lewis and get them to measure it, and then she threw a fit apparently because the shoes weren't trendy enough.'

'Blimey.'

'Yes. I'd watch her, if I were you. I thought she seemed a bit high-maintenance at that party.'

'And you'd know, of course.'

'I'm only saying. Anyway, Stella's back in town now, so I'm seeing quite a lot of her, sort of exclusively really. I was thinking I might bring her down, if that's OK. She keeps going on about a weekend in the country.'

'I bet she doesn't mean a weekend with your sister.'

'Oh yes she does. She really wants to meet you. And Alfie.'

Jim doesn't usually bring his women home: he must really like her.

'Actually, I might bring her down on Friday, if that's OK.'

'Fine by me. Do you fancy a drink? There's a bottle of wine in the fridge.'

'I was thinking of ringing Dan, having an hour down the pub. He's probably desperate to get out. Is it all right if I stay over?'

'Sure. But don't you dare ring Dan. He's supposed to be staying in with his mother.'

'Oh well, in that case I'm definitely going to ring him. Rescue him from all those women.'

I poke my tongue out at him and he laughs.

'Oh go on then.'

'Great. Now I have permission from ground control I'll give him a call.'

'But you have to promise, no singing when you come home. You sound nothing like Frank Sinatra – you know that, don't you?'

'And now, the end is near . . .'

'Stop it. Quick, Alfie, sit on Uncle Jim. He's trying to sing again.'

'Boss, boss, boss. You're a very bossy girl, Alice Mayhew. Harry the Herb Man is in for a big surprise, if you ask me. Come on, Alf, help your Uncle Jim stop Mummy being such a bossy boots. Let's tickle her feet – she hates that.'

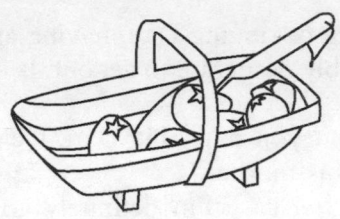

5

MAY

Parsley, Sage, Rosemary and Thyme

Garden Diary

Water and feed all newly planted beds, and continue strict weeding programme. When weather allows plant strawberry runners, and pinch out and disbud new vine shoots. Sow lettuce, spinach and carrots.

I have a go at establishing a strict weeding regime, and cut back the creeper, which keeps trying to poke itself through the kitchen window. I end up with loads of garden rubbish, which Mr Channing says you can't put in your wheelie bin unless you give the bin men a substantial bribe. Otherwise they'll tip it all over your front garden. After hours of grubbing about with a trowel I now have one relatively clear flowerbed, with a few roses and a couple of knackered-looking plants. I think I preferred it with the weeds. Alfie's been busy too, and has dug a small but significant hole in the middle of the lawn. He says it's for rabbits, in case they would like to live in our garden but need a hole to start them off. He's very keen to put some food in to encourage them, and ends up putting in some salad left over from lunch. I wonder if rabbits actually like tuna.

MOLLY COMES ROUND AND helps me choose what to wear for my dinner with Harry. We finally settle on black trousers and a grey silk shirt, and I can wear my new shawl to add a bit of glamour. Molly's got her interview for the deputy-head job on Friday, and she's dreading it. She's got to meet all the governors, and she's worried that being five months pregnant isn't exactly going to help.

'The head says it's fine, and the post can wait until I get back from maternity leave, but I bet they won't be keen.'

'Can't they get some sort of temporary one in then?'

'Yes, and Mr Marchent says he'll stay on for a bit if they want him to. He doesn't really want to go, but his wife wants him to take early retirement: she wants to move nearer her mother. But I still think it's going to count against me.'

'What are you wearing?'

'That's another thing. Nothing fits me any more, and I can't really afford a new suit. I'm wearing the stuff I wore when I was pregnant with Lily, but that's not really right for an interview. And my jacket won't do up.'

'What about a big scarf, and you could just leave your jacket undone.'

'Actually, I don't know why I'm bothering. I can't cope as it is. Dan's been sulking all week – we seem to keep bickering about nothing at the moment, and I'm starting to get slightly breathless now, walking up stairs.'

'I remember that bit, I got really fed up too. It feels like for ever.'

'Yes, it bloody does. Oh, but it was good yesterday. Lily seems to have finally got her head round the idea of the new baby. She fed it some of her spaghetti, well, actually, she poked me in the stomach with her spoon, and asked me if the baby was hungry. It was really sweet.'

'And did the baby like spaghetti?'

'Loved it. Made a hell of a mess of my jumper, though.'

'Let's hope she doesn't feed it the real thing when it arrives. Well, not for a while anyway. Jim used to stuff all sorts in my mouth. He gave me coal once.'

'I know, I'm really worried about her feeling jealous. It feels like we're betraying her in a way, like she's not enough.'

'I'm sure she'll be fine. I know you'll be careful, and you can dump the baby on me, you know, so you can have special Lily time.'

'I'll be taking you up on that, definitely, as long as you think Alfie won't mind.'

'He likes babies – he loves anything he can feel superior to. Mind you, that includes just about everybody at the moment. He told me I was very stupid this morning, just because I couldn't find his shoes. And when I said he should find his own shoes he gave me that look they do, like you're an idiot and it's a miracle that you're actually allowed out without a special sign on your coat to warn people.'

'Oh Lily goes in for that quite a lot too. I wonder when they grow out of it.'

'About thirty-five, probably. Although I've got a horrible feeling I still do it to Mum. In fact I know I do. She was saying something about it the other day – she said she wondered how she'd ever coped without me to tell her how to do things properly.'

I'm getting nervous about dinner with Harry, and feel faintly sick by the time Jim and Stella arrive, rather late and breathless because they've been stuck in horrendous traffic.

'It's getting ridiculous – we left the office really early. Where's Alfie?'

'Out in the back garden digging holes for rabbits. It's driving me mad – the lawn looks like we've got giant moles.'

'Isn't it getting a bit dark?'

'Yes, but he's having such a great time I'm letting him have five more minutes.'

'You mean you've tried to get him in and he threw a fit.'

'Yes.'

'Come and meet him, Stella, he's pretty cool. Takes after his uncle, of course.'

Stella seems very nice, and is wearing a really pretty skirt, which I would be tempted to covet if it wasn't about three sizes too small for me, and a tiny white T-shirt, which I don't covet in the slightest because I could barely get it over my head, let alone anything else. And she seems capable of normal conversation, which is unusual, because Jim usually goes for slightly dim, fawning types.

I can hear them laughing in the garden while I'm getting dressed, but when I come back downstairs they're all sitting on the sofa watching *Peter Pan*. Alfie's explaining the plot to Stella, who's doing a very good impression of someone who's totally gripped.

'You can be Wendy. You look a bit like her.'

I hope she realises this is very high praise indeed.

'Did you have a dog when you were little?'

'No, but I had a cat.'

'I don't want a cat, I want a dog, but Mummy won't let me. And I'm going to have rabbits. But I've got a nana, like Wendy and Michael, only mine's not a dog.'

Jim seems to find the idea of Mum being compared to the St Bernard called Nana in *Peter Pan* most amusing. In fact he chokes on his coffee.

'Uncle Jim's spitted on my leg. Look.'

Stella tuts and says, 'Yes, isn't he revolting? Let's ignore him – that usually works. You look fabulous, Alice. That scarf is lovely.'

I think I could get quite fond of Stella.

By the time Harry actually arrives I'm so nervous I can hardly open the door. He's wearing brown corduroy trousers and a pale-green shirt, and seems taller than I remember. Jim makes faces behind his back, which doesn't really help, but we leave without any major incidents apart from when Alfie declares he's starving when I explain that I'm going out for supper.

He's just about to start asking if he can come too when Stella says she's seen a big bag of crisps in the kitchen and maybe they could all have a crisp-eating competition, which of course he thinks is an excellent plan.

We drive to the restaurant talking about gardens and the weather, and how Harry got into herbs. He drives really well, not so fast that you're clinging on to your seatbelt, but not doddering along either, and it's very nice having someone else doing the driving for a change.

'I've always liked growing things. I had my own bit of garden at school. I used to do it instead of rugby; I mean they tried, they really did, but in the end they gave up and said as long as I was outdoors and not causing trouble I could do the garden. My father was furious.'

'Was he keen on rugby then?'

'Oh yes. He'd been in the first team, and of course my brother was red hot. Just another example of how disappointing I could be.'

'I'm sure he didn't really think that.'

'Oh yes he did – he told me. We didn't get on, but I was away at school so much it didn't really matter. He was keen on me going into the City though, so that was all right. Until I chucked it all in to grow herbs.'

'I'm guessing he wasn't pleased.'

'Incandescent. My mother said I could have the gatehouse, but I think that was only to spite him. I think she's still hoping I'll come to my senses and go back.'

'And will you?'

'Oh no. Never. I'd rather work in an abattoir.'

'Did you make it up – before he died, I mean? Oh I'm sorry. You don't have to talk about it if you don't want to.'

'No, it's OK. We did a bit, I suppose. He said he thought I was a damn fool but at least I'd stuck to my guns, so he wasn't going to cut me out of the will like he'd said he would. Which is probably a good thing really, because at least I don't have to worry about money for a while. Growing herbs doesn't exactly pay well. Well, not the way I do it, anyway.'

I didn't actually want to know about his father's will. God, I hope he didn't think that's what I meant.

The meal is lovely: especially with no Alfie wanting things off my plate, and getting sauce in his hair. I'd forgotten how nice it is to eat in restaurants with someone whose main topic of conversation is not Pets I Am Dying To Own. But weirdly I sort of miss him too, and find myself ordering garlic bread because I know he likes it, which is pathetic. I really must try to get out more.

We talk about the City and investment brokers, and Harry makes me laugh about some of his mad ex-clients.

'So how did you get them then, your clients? Did you have to do pitches like we do at work, give them an idea of what you can do for them, that kind of thing? I hate it. Half the time they just nick your ideas and then say you're too expensive.'

'No, although it might have been a good idea. We could have weeded out the most psychotic ones. No, I did mostly corporate stuff, and they tend to come to you, especially if you're one of the big firms like we were, one of the top five. They like to use the big firms – it makes them look good.'

'Sort of who's got the biggest willy kind of thing?'

Bugger. I wish I hadn't said the willy word. He looks mildly startled, but recovers quite well.

'Oh yes, there's quite a lot of that.'

'Great career for a woman then.'

'Well, some of them seem to like it, but there weren't many women partners at my firm. Too sensible to spend every waking moment at work.'

'How long was it before you realised you had to get out?'

'Oh about ten years. I loved it at first – I'm very competitive in my own weird way, but in the end it gets you down. I mean there are a few decent blokes – I still see a couple of them, actually – but on the whole they're a boring bunch of bastards. Totally obsessed with money.'

'How do people cope when they have kids? They must never see them.'

'I think they call them boarding schools, don't they?'

'Oh, right.'

We order coffee, and I decide not to have a pudding because it seems more grown-up and restrained. And snorking through a big bowl of trifle doesn't really go with the new adult image I'm trying for.

Harry gets a bit of paper out of his jacket while we're waiting for the coffee to arrive, and goes a bit red.

'I've done this for you, I hope you don't mind, just a few rough ideas.'

It's a sketch of my garden, covered in lots of scribbled plant names, which is really sweet of him, although if he ever wants to be a designer he's going to have to learn to draw. He's managed to include a weird combination of straight and wiggly lines that are pretty mystifying.

'Oh how lovely. Talk me through it then.'

And he does. Three cups of coffee later I'm having a caffeine high of such major proportions that my hands are starting to shake, but that might also be because I'm itching to redraw the plan. He says he started just working on a rough idea but he's ended up with a whole new garden.

Instead of going straight up to the front door the path now winds around the front garden. The postman will be thrilled, because it'll take him at least twenty minutes to get to the front door. The back garden now has a new terrace, a gazebo, a vegetable garden, a herb garden and a formal knot garden. And about fifteen tons of gravel, from what I can make out. I'm going to need about three more acres to fit everything in.

I point this out as gently as I can, and he says oh yes, he realises he has no idea of the proportions but it's the general idea, and don't I think it would be wonderful, and he'd be more than happy to help. We could just do the things that would fit in.

We end up drawing all over his plan and come up with a new, more realistic version. But when it comes to the plants he's in his element, and gives me all sorts of fantastic information about what things smell like, and the colour of their flowers, which really makes me want every single one of them. I end up getting really keen on the idea.

On the drive home we talk more about the garden and a bit about my work, and he says if he ever needs a new bathroom he knows where to come, and actually his mother does need the big house sorting out, but she'll never do it because she likes it the way it is. But one day it could be fabulous.

And then we talk a bit about Alfie, and I do that English thing of being very dismissive about him, which I only manage because I don't have to do it for too long, and anyway he doesn't seem that interested.

We arrive back at the cottage and I start to feel slightly sick again. I can't remember what the form is: do you just say thanks and leap out of the car, or what?

'Thanks for dinner, it was lovely.'

'Yes, it was, wasn't it? And thank you. We must do it again. I'll ring you about the garden, shall I? I mean it, you know – I'd like to help.'

'Great.'

There's an awkward silence. And I've got a horrible feeling Jim is peeping out from behind the curtains, because I'm sure they've just moved.

'I'd better get in. I wouldn't be surprised if Alfie's still up and Jim and Stella will need a break.'

'Oh yes, sorry, of course.'

And then just as I'm about to open my door he gets out and walks round to do it for me. Blimey. It's been a long time since anyone opened a car door for me. As I get out of the car he leans forward and kisses me on the cheek.

'Well, goodnight. I'll call you.'

'Night.'

I bolt up the path and open the door, and turn to wave as he drives off. Luckily the jeep is really noisy, so I don't think he hears Jim yelling 'He kissed her', 'He kissed her', and running round the living room with his T-shirt over his head like footballers do when they've just scored a goal.

'Just ignore him. Stop it, Jim, you're being a pig. How would you like it if Alice did a peeping-Tom number on you?'

'Oh, I wouldn't mind. There's nothing I do that I wouldn't want my sister seeing.'

'Oh really?'

Stella gives him a very hard stare and he goes bright red.

We make coffee, and Jim says Alfie went to bed fairly late. They had to watch *Peter Pan* twice and then play horsey for hours. Stella says he was a little sweetheart, but she's feeling pretty tired and she's going up to bed, if it's all right with us, which I think is just her being subtle because she knows Jim is dying to cross-examine me about dinner.

The minute she goes upstairs he starts.

'So how did it go then?'

'Fine. Really nice.'

'Nice. Oh dear. Nice isn't good.'

'Jim, I'm knackered. Can we do this in the morning?'

'No. I promised Alfie we'd dig a really big hole, and anyway I want to know. My little sister has her first proper date in ages – I need all the info, stands to reason. Did he chance his arm? Do I need to go round there and punch him on the nose? Or didn't he, in which case I'm definitely going to go round there and punch him.'

'No, it was lovely. The meal was great and we talked about all sorts. He's going to help me with the garden, he's done a plan and everything, and we just sort of got on. Nice. Bit scary, though.'

'Oh it's always scary. That moment before you take the plunge. Did he ask you lots of questions, about you and Alfie, that sort of thing?'

'No, not really. We talked about my work though. I like him – it was a nice evening.'

'Like. You don't want to like him. You want to shag him

senseless. Have a bit of fun. I'm not watching sodding *Peter Pan* and being a horse for bloody hours so you can just like somebody.'

'Don't you like Stella then?'

'Oh yes, of course I do, I adore her, but what I really like about her, well, one of the main things, well, I can't say it, it's no good, you just can't have this kind of conversation with women. They go all huffy.'

'You've gone red.'

'Shut up.'

'You have. Bright red. I bet it was something to do with her chest.'

'Stop it, or I'll have to give you a Chinese burn.'

He used to give me Chinese burns all the time when we were little. Sometimes he'd wake me up in the morning by sneaking into my room and giving me a Chinese burn.

'Look, it was nice, and we might even get to the bit where we do more kissing. Especially if nobody's looking out the window. That do you?'

'Yes, I suppose so.'

'Thank god for that.'

Harry rings up the next morning, which Jim says is a sure sign of being a stalker, and everyone knows you don't ring up the next day. We arrange to meet up next Saturday when he'll come round and help me make a start on the garden.

Jim and Stella leave after lunch, and Alfie and I walk up to see how the new garden's getting on. Charles is busy weeding.

'It's so easy weeding veg – they're all in straight lines so you can easily spot what's a weed and what's a courgette.'

'That's handy.'

'I must say I'm really enjoying this gardening lark. I come out here for a bit of peace sometimes, and it's just marvellous. I find myself quite looking forward to gardening programmes – it's quite worrying. I even came out in the rain last week.'

He's smiling, and he does look much more relaxed than he usually does.

'I know. There's something very calming about it, isn't there?'

'Yes. And it makes you feel connected to things, like you're more part of it all, somehow.'

'Do you think we'll end up completely barmy, obsessing about seed catalogues?'

'Probably. Personally I can't wait.'

'I'm making a start on my garden next weekend – I just can't bear it in such a mess any more – so I must have got the bug. Oh, and that reminds me – would you mind if I borrowed your wheelbarrow next Saturday, only I haven't got one and it seems daft to buy one until I know what I'm really going to need.'

'Sure, no problem, I'll bring it round if you like, and give you a hand for a couple of hours. Let me know if you need anything else.'

Molly rings up to say she's got her deputy-head job. They told her today, and they want her to start when she's back from maternity leave, so it's all worked out really well.

'They said they really liked my ideas about inclusion programmes.'

'Oh that's great, well done. I knew you'd do it.'

'Thanks. I really didn't think I would. Some of the other people who came for interview were terrifying. One woman brought her laptop and looked like she could run a multinational. Oh it's so great, and it'll mean more money, and obviously the job will be huge and I know I'll feel like I can't cope, but it's what I want, it really is. I really think I can make a difference.'

'I'm so pleased. I bet Dan is too.'

'Yes. Kind of. No, that's not fair. He was really pleased but then he sort of got over it quite quickly. One minute he was all "That's brilliant" and the next he was asking what was for tea. I think he's just too tired to get really enthusiastic about anything at the moment. He's working so hard and he's out until late, so when he does get home he's just exhausted.'

I can tell she's trying really hard not to mind that he didn't go overboard about her getting the job.

'But I think everything's finally turning the corner and it's going to be great. And Lola's invited us to your garden party on Saturday, so I'll get to meet Harry.'

'Bloody hell, what garden party?'

'Lola said you're having a party to sort out your garden. Don't you want us then?'

'Oh sorry, Moll, of course I do. But I've only just met him and I'd sort of like to keep it low-key. And it wasn't meant to be a party or anything. I only mentioned it to Charles because I wanted to borrow his wheelbarrow.'

'Not according to Lola. She says we've all got to bring stuff. I thought it was a nice idea. I mean I know she's a terrible snob and bossy and everything, but I thought it was quite sweet of her.'

'Well, yes, it is, of course it is. I just wish she'd asked.'

'Oh sod it – maybe she meant it to be a surprise, and I've gone and ruined it. Sod it.'

'Don't be daft – I'm really glad you did. At least I won't get such a shock on Saturday. I wonder if I should warn Harry?'

'He'll just think you've got loads of friends. Which you have, so it'll be fine.'

Of course it's raining first thing on Saturday morning, but it soon stops and even though everything's a bit wet I don't suppose it will really matter. Charles arrives early with the wheelbarrow and Molly prunes the bushes in the front garden with the special lethal-looking loppers that Charles has brought with him.

When Harry arrives he doesn't seem at all put out to find the garden full of people he's never met: Frank's turned up with Mr Channing and they've brought a few tomato plants and a big pot of chives. I feel almost tearful when I come out

131

of the kitchen with coffees for everyone and see them all beavering away.

And then Elsie turns up with Mrs Pomeroy.

'I heard you were sorting out your garden, so I brought you this. I've got it in my front and it smells lovely. It's winter jasmine so I've took some cuttings. Lovely colour.'

'Oh thank you, Elsie, that's really kind.'

Mrs Pomeroy hands me a polystyrene tray of plants.

'Yes, and I've brought you some marigolds. Now what would you like me to do? I can spare you an hour, but then I must get back. I'm doing the church flowers tomorrow and I need to pop in and see what's what. Miss Garnett has a terrible habit of taking the vases home and forgetting to return them.'

Elsie tuts.

'I hope you're not going in for them twig things – they look ridiculous, if you ask me. Nice bunch of flowers, that's what you need in church. Not silver twigs and a few berries.'

'That was a winter arrangement, Mrs Thomas, and it won Highly Commended. The judge said it was a very creative use of winter foliage.'

'Load of old twigs. Miss Garnett always does something lovely. She did lovely flowers for my June's wedding, really lovely.'

Elsie settles down in a chair and gives handy hints to anyone passing, and makes a great fuss of Charles as always. She seems to take a bit of a shine to Harry too. She tells him all about the old remedies her mother taught her, and recommends nettle tea.

'And if you're feeling nervy camomile's a good tonic, and comfrey's good for healing. My mum used to swear by it. I prefer a bit of Savlon myself – all that boiling up leaves gets on my wick. But you can't beat dandelion if you need flushing out.'

Harry smiles.

'I'll try to remember that.'

The front garden's starting to look much better and you can actually see some plants now. Molly has planted the marigolds in two old pots she found in the garage, and they're now standing on either side of the front door, and Frank and Charles have shaped the lawn in the back into more of an oval, and have filled in all the rabbit holes. They're weeding the flowerbeds while Mr Channing digs a new bed for vegetables and herbs just in front of the terrace by the back door.

Frank and Mr Channing leave just before lunch, but offer to come back any time if I need a hand, which is really sweet of them, and Mrs Pomeroy heads off to do her flowers with Elsie.

Lola arrives with one of Mrs Bishop's walnut cakes, so we sit outside eating sandwiches and cake, and I can't really believe the transformation. It's been such a lovely morning, apart from being hyper-conscious of Harry all the time, but in a way having so many people around has made it more relaxing. Molly says she thinks he's lovely, and he keeps looking at me when he thinks I can't see.

'Now everybody, time for the surprise.'

Oh God, what's Lola up to now? I just hope it doesn't involve more bloody digging because I'm knackered.

Charles gets up and disappears round to the front of the house with his wheelbarrow, and then comes back with it full of plants.

'These are from us and Molly, just a few things we thought you might like.'

Charles starts unloading the plants. There's a rose bush, and some poppies, and all sorts of things I vaguely recognise but don't know the names of.

'Oh thank you. Really. Thank you so much, they're all fantastic.'

I actually really do feel close to tears now, which is embarrassing, but I manage to pull myself together. Molly says she'll take Alfie and Lily home to play because they're starting to get bored and we've still got loads of planting to do, and Lola says she'd better be off too.

'I should go and rescue Kimberley really – she wants to go shopping. I know, why don't you all come to supper? Just us, and Marissa and her husband, around eight? Bring Alfie – Kimberley will be around. Oh and you too, Molly, and Dan, the more the merrier, and Mabel adores Lily. Nothing formal, just come as you are. Harry, are you free for supper?'

'Oh well, yes, that would be lovely.'

Before we know where we are Lola's organised a supper party, and Molly says she'll give Alfie some tea and then bring him to Lola's later with Lily. I'm not really sure I'm up for an evening out. I mean apart from being knackered I'm filthy, but there's no stopping Lola when she has one of her good ideas, and she's been so kind I can't really say no.

We spend ages working out where to plant things. It really looks like a proper garden now although it's getting quite cold by the time we finish. Charles says he'd better go and help with supper, and I give him a hug to say thank you and he goes pink, and then Harry makes more tea and we sit out and admire the new plants. I can't quite believe it's the same place as this morning. It's amazing.

Actually, I'm feeling a bit nervous now everybody's gone and it's just me and Harry. There are awkward silences, and I'm suddenly aware that my jeans have got very muddy, and my hands are filthy.

Harry's obviously thinking along the same lines.

'Would you mind awfully if I had a bath, only it's a bit too far to get home and back, and I can't go to supper looking like this, can I?'

'No, of course not. The water's on – put the hot in first, though. It runs out quite quickly, and suddenly it'll go freezing.'

'Will you want one?'

'What?'

'A bath.'

I hope he's not going to offer to share, because I don't

134

think I'm quite ready for that. In fact I don't think I ever will be, because apart from anything else our bath's not really that big. In films the baths are always huge. I'd like to see Richard Gere and Julia Roberts try to fit into my old bath and still look gorgeous: one of them would be bound to get cramp.

'Um, yes, I suppose so.'

'Righty ho, well, I won't be long.'

'There are clean towels in the airing cupboard, next to the bathroom.'

He goes off upstairs whistling.

I'd quite like to go up too and start trying to work out what to wear, but I can't quite cope with the idea of being upstairs when he's in the bath, so I wander round the garden for a bit and then decide to light the fire so the house won't be freezing when we come home. Alfie will be exhausted, and getting him into pyjamas isn't easy at the best of times.

I'm just lighting the kindling when Harry comes back downstairs, with his hair all damp from the bath. Somehow the sight of his bare feet really gets to me.

'Fabulous bath toys. I might have to borrow that submarine, but it doesn't really dive terribly well.'

'It used to, but Alfie bent the tube.'

'I noticed. The frog's good too.'

'Glad you approve. I suppose I'd better go up and get ready too. Do you want a coffee or anything? I think there's some wine in the fridge. Put the telly on, if you like. I won't be long.

'The water won't be hot again yet, will it? Have a drink with me first.'

Oh god. Oh god. We have a drink, a small glass of wine each because there isn't as much left in the bottle as I thought, and then we sit chatting on the sofa and he leans over and kisses me and says he's had a lovely day, and he's been wanting to do this since practically the moment he arrived, and he hopes I don't mind but he might have to do it again. And he does. And then it all gets a bit tricky. Nice tricky, but tricky. We're due at Lola and Charles's for supper in about half an hour and actually this kissing business is rather nice and I'm not entirely sure I want to get myself off the sofa and upstairs to get changed.

Eventually I manage to surface and he gives me a very smouldering look and says he'll wait down here but I'd better hurry up. I go upstairs and have a mini crisis about what to wear. I wish I had something casual but gorgeous. But I don't, so I find some clean jeans and a clean shirt, and put on the earrings that Molly bought me for Christmas, and squirt on some perfume. I go back downstairs feeling slightly shaky.

'We should go really. Sorry I was so long.'

'Righty-ho, I'll just find my shoes.'

'Do you say righty-ho a lot?'

'Yes, I suppose I do. Why, is it a problem?'

'No, of course not, sorry. It's a bit *Just William*, that's all, in a nice way though.'

'Well, I am a bit *Just William*. Except I don't hate girls. Well, not all girls anyway.'

Blimey, he's at it again. Twinkling away, and holding my jacket for me while I try to find my door keys. Maybe we could just stay here and forget about supper. But I've got to collect Alfie, and anyway I'm starving.

We're the last to arrive, but we're not exactly late so nobody seems to mind. Alfie leaps on me the minute I walk through the door and begins telling me all about his lovely tea, and Eddie, and how much bigger he is today and how he can peck you on the hand now, and then he spots Harry.

'Where's Basil?'

I think he's hoping Harry will have gone home to fetch the dog. He gave him strict instructions to do so earlier, before he left with Lily and Molly.

'At home. He doesn't really like parties.'

'Are you sure? He might. You could go and get him. And if he didn't like it he could come upstairs with me and watch cartoons.'

Harry laughs and says dogs don't really watch a lot of

cartoons, and then Lola introduces us to Campbell and Marissa, who are friends of hers from London.

Marissa's wearing the most extraordinary see-through dress in a sort of navy wispy material, with a tiny slip underneath, and very high-heeled sandals, and I'm not at all surprised when Lola says she used to work for *Vogue*. I just hope nobody offers to show her round the new garden in those heels or she'll get stuck in the gravel and have to be lifted out. Lola doesn't say what Campbell does, but he looks very grumpy. He barely nods when we're introduced, and seems to think he's very special. Molly looks tired and Dan's nowhere to be seen.

'Where's Dan? Checking out his handiwork in the garden?'

'No, he's on some emergency job with John, some sort of burst pipe, I think, and the ceiling's come down, so he can't make it.'

'Oh Molly, you should have rung. I could have picked Alfie up ages ago.'

'Don't be silly, he was fine. They watched telly and played with the chickens. It was better than having Lily by herself, actually. She loves having Alfie around – it's less boring.'

'Where is she?'

'Upstairs.'

'I'll come up with you and see if she's all right, if you like.'

I give her what I hope is a meaningful look, and even though she seems rather puzzled she gets up and follows me upstairs.

'What's up?'

'Oh not much, only that things are hotting up with Harry, and it's all a bit scary.'

'Well, he seems nice to me. Just give him a go and see how you feel.'

'Give him a go? He's not a new brand of shampoo, you know. It could get really complicated.'

'Yes, but complicated is fun.'

'True.'

'So you might as well relax and enjoy yourself. Look, we'd better go back down, but you'll be fine, I'm sure you will, and if you change your mind just let me know and I'll come back with you, with Lily. That'll slow him down.'

We check on Lily, who's playing Barbies with Mabel, and then we go back downstairs.

Harry is talking to Campbell.

'So do you and Marissa have children then?'

'Oh no, god forbid. I find children terribly boring. So attention-seeking. I mean I'm sure it doesn't feel that way if they're yours, but I've never seen the point, myself.'

Lola laughs.

'Campbell, honestly.'

Oh lovely. What a nice man. I just hope Alfie leaves him alone, because he tends to be strangely drawn to people who aren't keen on children, a bit like the way cats always make a beeline for anyone who's allergic. Oh, here we go. He's gone straight over to Campbell.

'I've got a chicken.'

'I beg your pardon?'

'I've got a chicken. He's called Eddie. He can jump, and he pecks your hand.'

'How marvellous.'

It's a good job sarcasm is completely wasted on Alfie.

'Have you got a dog?'

Campbell looks extremely annoyed at being asked so many questions, but Alfie doesn't seem to have noticed. And to be truthful even if he had he'd probably ignore it.

'No.'

'Do you want one?'

'No.'

'Alfie, why don't you go and see if there are any films you want to watch upstairs. I think Ezra's got some crisps, but you'd better be quick because he'll have eaten them all in a minute.'

Well done, Charles. Alfie rushes off.

Molly and I exchange glances, and Charles offers everyone

138

a drink while Lola goes into the kitchen to make her special salad dressing.

'So, Campbell, what do you do then, apart from not liking children, that is?'

Charles says this with such a charming smile that Campbell can't really take offence.

'Oh this and that – I'm in television.'

'What, selling them, or repairs?'

'Producing, actually, I produce documentaries.'

'Anything we might have seen?'

Campbell looks really furious now.

'Probably not. I can't bear all that dumbing-down crap.'

'Campbell's a genius, aren't you, darling? He specialises in opera, but his series on the Royal Ballet won stacks of awards.'

Marissa seems very proud of him.

'Yes, the ballet thing did work rather well, if I say so myself.'

Charles gives him an amused and half-horrified look, the kind of look eleven-year-old boys would give you if you said you were mad about ballet. Well, most eleven-year-old boys: not Billy Elliot, obviously.

'Ballet. Right. How marvellous.'

The food is wonderful. Mrs Bishop's salmon is delicious and there's posh apple tart for pudding, and ice cream for the children. Lola's wearing a fabulous black-lace dress and flirting like mad with Harry, and I'm feeling rather under-dressed and lumpen in my jeans and shirt: I thought she really meant it when she said just come as you are. But at least Harry isn't flirting back. In fact he winks at me at one point and I choke slightly, which makes him laugh.

We all drink too much wine apart from Molly, who has two helpings of apple tart to make up. Lily's very sweet and gives some imaginary ice cream to the baby, which Campbell seems to find particularly nauseating. Marissa's only eaten about two mouthfuls of salmon and a small piece of cucumber, and goes visibly pale at the sight of pudding.

We're drinking coffee while the children run around yelling, when Charles suddenly has the genius idea of playing charades. I usually hate party games that involve making a complete fool of yourself in front of total strangers, but this time it turns out to be rather good fun. We're in two teams, with Lola, Marissa and Harry on one, and me and Charles and Campbell on the other. Molly says pregnant women can't play charades, it's a well-known medical fact, so she'll be the judge and choose the titles we have to act.

I get *Crouching Tiger Hidden Dragon*, which is fairly easy, and *The Magic Roundabout*, which is not, and Harry does a brilliant job on *The Big Easy*, which is a bit cheeky of Molly because she knows I love that film, but it's Charles who turns out to be the real genius, and hurls himself into *Last Tango In Paris* with great gusto and doesn't seem to mind making a total fool of himself. Marissa gets *Moby Dick*, and goes for trying to be a whale, and I can't say I blame her, but the best bit is Campbell trying to do *101 Dalmatians*. He must have decided it was beneath his dignity to be a dog, so he tries some complicated sounds-like routine, which we can't guess, so he sulks. We all end up in hysterics and even Marissa laughs at him, which is not something he's terribly used to as far as I can see.

It's getting quite late, and I say I'd better be going before Alfie conks out completely. Harry carries a fast-asleep Lily out to Molly's car, and says he'll come back with us to collect his jeep. Molly drops us off, and winks at me when I get out of the car, which makes me laugh, and Harry offers to make some more coffee while I take Alfie up to bed. He's so knackered he settles down without a peep. Yes, there is a God.

Harry's put some logs on the fire and the coffee's almost ready when I get back downstairs.

'Good evening that. Well, apart from that ghastly man. She's quite a livewire, your friend Lola, isn't she? And her husband seemed nice.'

'Oh yes, Charles is lovely.'

'I thought your *Tiger* was brilliant, though your *Magic Roundabout* could do with some work.'

'Oh really. Do your *Big Easy* again then. It wasn't that good, you know.'

'I thought you'd never ask.'

We stay in the living room, but end up on the floor on the rug in front of the fire, which isn't as nice as it sounds, until Harry has the brilliant idea of taking the sofa apart and chucking the cushions all over the floor. I make some tea at some point, feeling very pleased with myself. I've forgotten how chirpy a nice bit of lust can make you feel.

'Well, that was nice. Makes a change from wondering what Basil is going to put in my slippers for the morning.'

'Nice. Nice?'

'Extremely nice then – that do you? Exceptionally nice.'

I hit him with a cushion.

'Look, don't start that again, I'm knackered. I've been doing your bloody garden all day, you know. My back's just not up to it.'

'Oh dear. And I had such high hopes.'

'Oh did you?'

'Yes. Just my luck, I always pick the weaklings.'

He laughs and I realise that I've just given him the perfect opener to say the magic line from *The Big Easy*, the one when Dennis Quaid and Ellen Barkin have finally made it into bed and are just getting going when his bleeper goes, and he's called out on a case. She says she's never had much luck with men, and he gets back into bed and says, 'Well, your luck's about to change.' I really hope Harry doesn't say it, or if he does, he gets it right. This would not be a good moment for him to reveal that he doesn't get it.

'Well, your luck's about to change, sweetheart.'

Bingo. And even though he doesn't say it in Dennis Quaid's fantastic Cajun accent, and in fact he goes a bit Humphrey Bogart, it doesn't matter. It's still magic. Works every time.

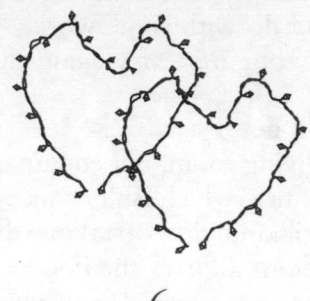

6

JUNE

Singing in the Rain

Garden Diary

Plant lettuce and other salad crops for late harvesting, divide water lilies, plant annuals, maintain rigorous weeding regime, attend to lawn.

My birthday present from Mum and Dad turns out to be a willow gate for the front garden, which arrives in bits, takes ages to assemble but looks great: although I think what it really needs are some fairy lights as a sort of post-modern take on rural gateways. I spend hours threading white fairy lights through the wicker and then poke the cable into a hosepipe and bury it in the flowerbeds. I hope no small animals will be able to chew through it and shoot themselves across the garden in an unexpected flame-grilled fashion. I've put a circuit breaker on the socket in the garage, so at least Alfie won't end up with a new hairstyle the next time he does a spot of digging. We have a mini switching-the-lights-on ceremony, and Alfie is delighted, but Mum says it looks like the entrance to a fairground and will I be selling candyfloss? I pretend

*to ignore her but secretly worry I am lowering the
tone of the entire village.*

'HOW DID IT GO with Harry then?'
'Very well, thanks.'
'What time did he leave?'
'About four.'
'Blimey, lucky you. Lily woke me up at five, I could have
come round. Have you got an action replay booked?'
'No. He did that thing where they suddenly get all keen to
be off and say they'll call you. Which was fine, because I
didn't really want him there when Alfie woke up.'
'But you'll see him again, when he calls?'
'Oh yes. Definitely. Although I'd forgotten how knackered
you get.'
'Oh stop it. The only thing that's making me knackered at
the moment is trying to get up the stairs. And I've run out of
clothes that fit again. Will you come shopping with me later?
Come round all the pregnant-lady shops and help me
choose?'
'Sure.'
Molly hates maternity departments.
'Thanks. And I'm really pleased for you, about Harry, I
mean. It's about time you had some fun.'

I'm feeling rather pleased with myself too, if I'm honest, and
it's definitely been a nice way of sorting out some of the
echoes left over from Patric. I mean it's early days, obviously,
but I really hope he's not about to produce a hidden wife, or
confess that he likes dressing up as a traffic warden or
something, because it would be very annoying if he turned
out to be another nutter.

And the really great thing about it is that so far I don't feel
totally obsessed by it all – in the past a new man on the
horizon would sort of push everything else out of focus, and
I'd spend hours fretting about when he'd call, if he'd call,
what I'd be wearing if he called. I'd end up feeling totally out

of my depth. But I don't feel like that with Harry, and not because he's boring or anything. I mean obviously things might change and I might end up going all *Fatal Attraction*, and start stalking him, but somehow I don't think so. Maybe it's down to Alfie; perhaps loving him so much has used up all my spare stalker-type energies. Maybe I've turned into a grown-up without realising it. God, how brilliant.

Lola comes round for tea on Sunday with Mabel and Ezra. Mabel's wearing her fairy wings, which are white and sparkly and wobble when she walks. She's very proud of them.

Lola loves the lights round the new gate, and says she wants fairy lights for the new garden, in fact she wants the whole garden filled with them. It takes me ages to persuade her that the elegant lighting we've already got is far more suitable; and anyway Mr Channing would probably have some sort of cardiac moment if he found the garden filled with fairy lights.

Mabel suddenly starts shrieking and it turns out that Ezra's bent one of her wings, and is just about to try and bend the other one, so Lola yells at him and then we have tea before any more damage can be done.

Mabel glares at Ezra, and Ezra kicks her under the table, and then Alfie joins in, and Lola says they've been driving her crazy all day.

'Charles is off buying paintings. God knows why he had to choose today, probably just to spite me. And Kimberley's just resigned.'

'Oh dear, why?'

'God knows. She was always late – I think live-ins are better. At least you know where they are most of the time. So I told her if she was late again I'd have to deduct it from her salary and she came in the next day and handed in her notice. She was quite rude, actually.'

I thought she was quite sweet: not exactly Brain of Britain, and she did sort of jump slightly whenever Lola came into the room, but she seemed really nice with the children.

'Charles keeps saying we don't need a nanny, and with both of us and Mrs Bishop we can cope, and then he disappears for the entire fucking day. It's hopeless – I've got too much else going on. I'll have to ring round those bloody agencies again.'

'But Mabel will be starting nursery soon, won't she?'

'Yes.'

'And with Ezra at school he might have a point, you know. It would save you a fortune.'

'Not if I'm going to get stuck with them all day, it won't. I've got a terrible headache. Actually, what I really need is a little sleep, just for half an hour. You wouldn't mind, would you, darling? Oh thanks, you're an angel.'

And before I can stop her she's belted upstairs to my bedroom and I'm left downstairs with all the kids. She doesn't emerge for nearly an hour, by which time I'm ready to choke Ezra who's spilled his juice twice, on purpose, and launched countless assaults on his sister.

'Thank you so much, darling, I feel almost human now. I'll take them home – you're probably dying to get rid of us, but I meant to say, I'm organising a party for Glyndebourne – we've got loads of tickets at work. I can't remember which opera it is, but we can sort out the details later. I need as many people as possible, anything so I don't have to talk to fucking clients all night. I thought you and Molly and Dan. What do you think?'

'Oh, I don't know, Lola. It's very kind, but I'm not really an opera fan.'

'Oh, you'll love Glyndebourne, it's always fabulous. I might ask Harry too. What do you think?'

Bugger.

'That might be a bit complicated, actually. I meant to tell you, he sort of stayed last night.'

'What?'

'After we got home, he stayed here, and, well, if you ring him up and ask him to the opera it'll look like I've asked you to call him, won't it? Which I really don't want.'

Lola's slightly chilly about my not ringing her up the minute Harry left and giving her all the details, but she recovers fairly quickly and says we must both come to dinner, which is exactly the kind of catapulting into couple-dom that I wanted to avoid.

'I think I'd rather take it slowly, for now.'

'Oh you don't want to do that. Ring him up and go for it. I think you're allowed to ring them now – it's post-feminist, I think. Or maybe that means you can't ring. I'm not sure. High heels are definitely back in, but I'm not sure about the phone thing. Shall I ask one of the girls at work what the latest form is in *Dating Wars*?'

'No thanks. I'm feeling pretty relaxed about it all. I think I'll just see what happens.'

'Well, if you crack by Wednesday let me know.'

Em calls in the evening and says she's coming over from Italy for a few days, and will come and stay for the weekend, which is brilliant because I haven't seen her since Christmas and I really miss her. We shared a flat when we first lived in London, and she was great when Patric left. She came straight down and helped me get through the first few days when I felt like I'd been run over.

Jim's coming down this weekend too, because Stella's away on some course and I don't think he wants to stay in town without her, which is quite sweet. Although he'll have to sleep on the sofa, and Em can have Alfie's room. She's going to leave Luca in charge of the hotel for a few days, and I tell her about Harry and she's very impressed at how calm I'm being and says that she thinks it's a very good sign, and means I'm totally over Patric, which she thinks is brilliant because she always hated him.

Harry rings on Tuesday night and we end up arranging to meet on Friday, and he stays until four in the morning, which is lovely. It's just starting to get light as he's leaving. I've asked him to supper with Em and Jim, assuming he'd say no but he's said he'd love to come, although he'll have to leave early because he's taking his mother up to London for lunch with his brother on Sunday, which he's dreading.

'So, I'll see you later then?'

He's doing that twinkly smiling thing again. I love it when he does that.

'Yes.'

'Around eight?'

'Fine.'

'I think I'll go home for a quick kip before I start on the orders. I'm completely knackered.'

'Good idea.'

'Or I could stay for another cup of tea?'

'Even better.'

He finally leaves just before five. God, I'm not sure if I can cope with all this action. I'm completely knackered, but in a very nice, smiley sort of way, and Alfie's pretty pleased with himself too, because I let him watch cartoons all morning. Patric's cancelled swimming, again, so at least I won't have to cope with him turning up. Although actually that might not be so bad, if next time he turns up Harry's here again. He's never mentioned meeting him, but I know he was narked about it. He was even more clipped on the phone than usual when he rang to cancel this weekend.

Em arrives on Saturday morning to a rapturous reception from Alfie, mainly because she's brought him an enormous tube of Smarties and a children's book in Italian, with lots of pictures of a dog doing all sorts of naughty things like stealing salami and running round the town being chased by irate shopkeepers.

She thinks my newfound passion for gardening is very amusing, but when we walk up the lane and I show her round the new garden I can tell she's really impressed.

'You should do this, you know. Full-time. It's brilliant.'

'Thanks. I'm really enjoying it. I mean I hated it at first, but now I'm really getting into it.'

'So tell me more about Harry then. Is he a grown-up?'

Em has this theory that most men are stuck at about eight years of age, which is why they go in for so many annoying stunts. She reckons there are a few grown-up ones, but you have to look very carefully.

'Oh yes. I think so. I mean it's early days, but so far, so good.'

'Good in bed?'

'Very good on cushions on the floor.'

'Ooh Alice, what would your mum say?'

'God knows. But I bet she'd get the mop out.'

'And is he nice with Alfie?'

'Yes. Well, he hasn't actually spent that much time with him so far – I mean up to now he's left before Alfie wakes up, which I think I prefer at the moment really, when it's all so new. But when he first came round he brought his dog, so Alfie thinks he's great. And he was quite sweet with him. He borrowed his digger.'

We watch Alfie, who is hopping around the path, bashing things with his stick.

'Stop that, Alfie, you'll hurt the plants.'

He pretends he hasn't heard me, but stops and starts bashing the path instead.

'He's getting so big. Every time I see him he's grown so much – it's going too quickly.'

'I know. He needs new shoes again, and he'll be four next month, you know; he's got to start school in September. It doesn't seem possible, does it?'

'No. God, I remember the night he was born.'

'So do I, funnily enough.'

'He seemed so tiny.'

'I know. Molly's having another one – did I tell you?'

'Yes, I'd love to see her.'

'Oh good. I said we'd go round for tea tomorrow, if that's OK with you.'

'Great.'

'And it's still going all right then, with the hotel and everything?'

'Oh yes, the business is fine. We're booked solid, and Luca's wonderful. Actually, that's one of the reasons I came over, to tell you, I mean, to ask you, will you be my brides-maid?'

It takes me a minute to work out what she's just said, and then we both end up shrieking and hugging, and Alfie comes running over, and she asks him to be her page boy and he says yes, even though he has no idea what a page boy is. Actually, that bit might be slightly tricky – he's bound to stand on her dress or something. But she seems so happy: I knew it was going well with Luca, but she says the last few months have been perfect, and she knows he's The One.

'I mean not that he doesn't drive me mad sometimes, and his mother's crazy – I think she'd still dress him in the mornings if she could – the way she fusses round him is unbelievable. But I love him, and I want to have babies with him, lots of bilingual babies. We want the wedding to be fairly low-key, but my mum's gone into overdrive already, so you'll have to help me with her. And it's in six weeks. I know it's all a rush but I think his mother wants to get on with it in case we change our minds. Half the island thinks I'm preg-nant.'

'But you're not, right?'

'No, but I want to be. That's what finally decided me. You can't have children and not get married – they'd probably parade you round the harbour on a special boat or some-thing.'

How sweet. She looks so happy, and I'm really pleased for her. I promise to help her handle her mum, and say I think the hotel sounds perfect, and then we go into serious dress talk. She's thinking of a veil and everything, but she's also quite keen on a trouser suit, mainly to annoy her mother. I make her promise not to kit me out in anything too reminiscent of

Little Bo Peep, and god knows what Alfie will wear, but if it involves kilts she won't stand a chance.

Supper on Saturday goes very well, and I've told Jim about Em getting engaged so he arrives early with two bottles of champagne and we all get rather drunk while Em cooks, which is great because living in Italy has only improved her cooking, which was pretty good to begin with. She does something very clever to the joint of lamb with rosemary from the garden, and Jim pretends to be devastated that she's got engaged and says he's been saving himself for her, and she's the only girl he ever wanted to marry and now she's broken his heart.

Em ignores him, and concentrates on Harry. They talk about herbs, and cooking, and then they talk about wine and Em tells him all about the local wines on the island, which apparently taste fantastic when you're there but if you bring them back with you to England they taste just like syrup.

Jim puts Alfie to bed, which takes hours, so we eat quite late, and we end up having a competition to see who's had the most annoying client, which Em wins with a woman who turned up at the hotel and handed her a huge pile of clothes to iron, and then rang room service in the middle of the night to complain that her mineral water had gone flat. In the end she drove them all so crazy that when she rang up a few months later to make another booking Em says she kept pressing buttons on the phone and pretended the line was breaking up.

Jim is very impressed with this, and says he once tried something similar with his managing director, but unfortunately he was on his mobile, and only managed to activate some traffic-update service, which meant his phone rang every thirty seconds with an update on tailbacks on the M25.

Harry helps me make coffee, which is a good job because I've drunk rather a lot, whereas he hasn't. He's really dreading his lunch tomorrow, and says his brother is very dismissive of rural life and makes lots of jokes about compost.

'He's probably jealous.'

'I don't think so.'

'Well, you never know.'

'Trust me. Actually, I really must be making a move soon, or I'm going to be tempted to stay until dawn again, and I'm knackered enough already.'

'Charming.'

'Sorry, I didn't mean it like that, but I was really busy with deliveries this afternoon, and it's been a long day. And tomorrow's going to be even longer.'

Jim starts shouting from the living room.

'Come on you two, where's that coffee? Honestly, what are you doing in there? I hope you're not snogging.'

We hear Em hit him with something that sounds like a cushion because he suddenly goes all muffled.

Harry smiles.

'What a good idea.'

After Harry leaves we open another bottle of wine. I'm relieved he's gone in a weird sort of way. I mean apart from anything else, with Alfie in my bed and Jim on the sofa we'd have ended up in a tent in the garden if he'd been able to stay. And I haven't actually got a tent. But also it's nice just to be able to relax with Em and Jim and not have to be on my best behaviour, which I know technically I don't have to be with Harry, but I'm still at the stage where I hold my stomach in if I think he's looking at me, and it's pretty exhausting.

'So what's the verdict then?'

'He's all right, I suppose, although I still think herbs are girly. At least he could grow something a bit more macho. Killer vines or something. And his mother sounds like a nightmare. But he seems all right, if you like that kind of thing.'

'I wasn't asking you, actually.'

Em says she thinks he's a grown-up, and he seems really keen.

'And he doesn't seem like he'll suddenly announce he needs "space", or anything crap like that. God, this wine is delicious.'

'Blimey, he's certainly taught you how to knock it back, this Captain Kirk of yours.'

Jim has decided, for reasons best known to himself, to refer to Luca as Captain Kirk. Something to do with Jean Luc Picard and *Star Trek* I think.

'Shut up.'

'To boldly go where no man has gone before. But are you sure he's The One, Em? That's the thing. You could be making a terrible mistake.'

'Just ignore him.'

'Mock me now but you'll see. When his mother turns out to be a klingon, you'll wish you listened.'

'You might have a point there. I could really do with one of those transporter-beam thingies – that would be a really great wedding present. I could beam her off somewhere useful when she gets too annoying.'

'We might need one for Alfie, you know. I'm still not completely sure about this page-boy idea – he's quite likely to start singing or something, you know.'

Jim seems delighted at the prospect of Alfie bursting into song in the middle of the service.

'I'll teach him a few useful tunes, if you like. "My Old Man's a Dustman", "Rule Britannia". That kind of thing. Liven things up a bit for you.'

I'm so looking forward to this wedding.

We spend Sunday reading the papers and trying to stop Jim teaching Alfie 'Rule Britannia'. Luckily he's not that interested, and is concentrating on getting us round to Molly's to meet Eddie and the other chickens.

Jim leaves after lunch and Alfie drags us straight to Molly's. Eddie's got much bigger, and all the chicks run round in hysterics pecking and flapping, while Em makes suitably impressed noises and says she thinks Eddie is the best chicken she's ever seen.

'But isn't Eddie short for Edward? That's a boy's name, and Eddie's a chicken and they're all girls, aren't they?'

'I know that, silly. Boy chickens are called cockenels. But I want her to be called Edward. Girls can have boys' names. There's a girl at my playgroup called Sydney.'

'Fair enough.'

We sit in the kitchen watching Alfie and Lily to make sure they're not rounding up the chickens too enthusiastically.

'You're looking very pregnant all of a sudden, you know, Molly.'

'I know. If I go on like this I won't be able to get in the car. Dan says he'll rig up a roof rack for me, but I don't really fancy it.'

'I think you look fabulous. I used to love the feel of Alice's tummy with Alfie.'

Em gets a dreamy look on her face.

'Oh yes, it's marvellous. I can't sleep for more than an hour because the baby's lying on something vital, and then Lily wakes up at the crack of dawn. And even if she sleeps in, bloody Bernard's up doing his cock-a-doodle-do thing. It's bloody getting on my nerves, I can tell you. I think we might have to go in for some *coq au vin* soon.'

'I thought you were a vegetarian.'

'I am. But I'll make an exception for Bernard.'

'I really envy you, though. It must be lovely being pregnant.'

'Feeling broody, are we?'

'Definitely. Ever since Alfie was born, to be honest.'

I'm rather touched by this.

'I remember feeling like that.'

'Me too. It soon wears off – trust me.'

'Oh don't be so horrible – you adore Alfie.'

'Yes, of course I do, but I never realised just how big a deal it is. I mean everything changes, you know. Everything. I really can't remember what it was like before I had him: it's like I've had some sort of operation and that bit of my brain has gone for ever, the bit that could read for hours, or really

153

get engrossed in something. And your memory goes too. I used to be able to plan out all sorts of things in my head, but now I have to write it all down. They say it comes back, but mine bloody hasn't.'

'Neither has mine, and it's getting worse. I nearly got lost driving home the other day – I went right past our turning. God knows why.'

'Oh I get it. This is the put-me-off-having-babies talk. OK, what else?'

Molly laughs.

'Sorry, it's lovely, it really is, but it does change you. You can't ever be totally selfish again. They come first. For ever.'

'And you love them so much, it's scary. Terrifying, actually. I used to look at Alfie sometimes when he was tiny and I loved him so much it hurt. Actually physically hurt. They're so fragile and it's all down to you. I have nightmares sometimes where I can't get to him, and it's awful. It's like you've got a layer of skin missing. You look the same, but everything's changed.'

'That sounds quite nice, actually. Well, apart from the skin thing.'

'It is, but Alice's right, that's just how it feels. And then there's your pelvic floor, of course.'

'I beg your pardon?'

We explain about pelvic floors and the dire warnings you get about not being able to sneeze in public if you don't do your exercises every ten seconds for the rest of your life. We all sit in silence for a bit, having a pelvic-floor moment. Clenching and unclenching with rather strained looks on our faces.

'God, it's really hard, isn't it?'

'The woman who runs the classes at the hospital says you have to imagine it's a lift. And you go from the ground floor up to the tenth, and then back.'

We all consider this.

'I can only get to the third.'

'So can I.'

'Fuck.'

Mum's made me promise to get home from work early if I can, for my birthday tea. The tradition in the office is that you buy cakes for everyone, and then we all stand round at teatime in an awkward silence while Janet presents you with a really cheap card. But since I want to leave early I produce a selection of cakes at lunchtime.

Janet's not pleased.

'Oh well, if you insist, maybe I could just have a little smidgen of this one here.'

I really hate people who cut a chocolate éclair into three pieces, and then only eat the smallest piece.

Malcolm wanders over and grabs a large cream horn, and licks his lips in a rather unattractive manner.

'Happy Birthday, and many more. You seem to look younger by the day, you know, Alice – you must tell us your secret.'

'Gin, mostly.'

Malcolm laughs, but Janet's not amused.

Brenda has organised my card herself this time, which has been signed by everyone and is along whisky-makes-you-frisky-brandy-makes-you-randy lines. There's a special badge with the card, which says 'Make Mine A Large One'.

Brenda's asking me about the latest on Em's wedding. I've shown her the email from Em with a selection of hideous frocks in various shades of what Em calls aubergine but is actually purple. I think she's joking, but I'm not sure.

'She's only got two more weeks to get everything organised, so she'll have to get a move on. And her mother's driving her demented.'

'Oh mine did that too. I almost called the whole thing off. And then my Brian got drunk at the reception and told her to piss off.'

'What about you, Janet? Any last-minute wedding dramas?'

'Oh no, it was all perfect.'

'Well, apart from the fact that it poured with rain, and half the guests got food poisoning, that is.'

Janet's looking really furious now. I don't think she was expecting Malcolm to be quite so forthcoming.

'Actually, I was meaning to have a little word, Alice. I notice you've been getting rather a lot of emails lately from your friend, and we don't really encourage people to use the office computers for personal communications, you know. It's not really appropriate.'

'Sorry, she normally emails me at home, Janet, but my modem's gone on the blink so I asked her to send it here. I use my computer at home quite a bit for work, actually, so I'm sure it all balances out.'

Mean cow. That should shut her up.

'I'm sure it does, Alice, and I'm sure Janet wouldn't want you to think we were being petty, would you, darling?'

Oh dear. Janet's really going to hate me now. Public criticism from the great man himself.

'And if we do owe you anything, for the work you do at home, Alice, please do let us know. I don't want you subsidising your work for us – far from it.'

This just gets better and better.

I drive home and the man behind the till in the petrol station gives me a very strange look and winks, which alerts me to the fact that I'm still wearing my 'Make Mine A Large One' badge. I take it off before I get home because I don't think Mum would think it was funny: 'Make Mine A Large One' badges aren't really her style, unless Domestos have started issuing them.

Alfie's standing in the front garden keeping watch, and I promise to close my eyes as he leads me into the living room rather fast, so I walk straight into the door. I manage not to swear, but only just, and then he says I can open my eyes, and presents me with a large box of Maltesers. He thinks Maltesers are the height of sophistication because I told him we couldn't buy a big box in the village shop once because they're only for grown-ups.

'Oh thank you, darling, how lovely.'

'Yes, and you can eat them all yourself. Although sharing is good, you know, Mummy. Very good. Nice people share.'

Mum's done a proper birthday tea, with sausages on sticks, crisps, and jelly. And balloons, which unfortunately Alfie decides to pop just as we're having our second cup of tea. She draws the curtains and turns the lights out, just like she used to do when we were little, and carries in the birthday cake, with Alfie doing a faintly Nazi-type military march and what look suspiciously like kung fu kicking actions. The icing is bubble-gum pink, and there's a great deal of it, and in chocolate letters it says 'HAPPY BIRTHDAY MAM', which strikes me as a bit Catherine Cookson until Mum explains that she bought the letters in the special cake shop in town, and it was meant to say MAMA, but Alfie ate the other A.

We blow out the candles, and I make a wish, and then we light them again so Alfie can make a wish. I know he's wished for a dog, mainly because he tells me, and I wish for more birthdays just like this one, although maybe without quite so much balloon-popping.

Mum goes off home with a slice of cake for Dad, and as she's leaving I give her a hug.

'Thanks, Mum. Really.'

'What for? It was just a little cake.'

'Yes, but the tea and everything. I don't know what I'd do without you. You know that, don't you?'

'Oh stop it and get back inside – it's getting quite chilly.'

Alfie and I wave her off, and then go back inside to watch telly and eat all my Maltesers. Bliss.

Harry calls to wish me Happy Birthday and we arrange to meet up at the weekend. We're sort of developing a little Friday-night routine, which suits us both, I think. He comes round for supper and stays until four or five, and then he leaves before Alfie wakes up. He doesn't seem that bothered about us going out anywhere, and neither am I, to be honest. I'm happy keeping things fairly low-key: it makes it more manageable, somehow.

'So, I'll see you Friday then?'

'Sure. Around eight. Oh, and by the way, your friend Lola rang and asked me along to Glyndebourne, but I said I couldn't make it. I hope that's all right, only I had enough of that kind of thing when I was working. Corporate entertainment and all that – I always hated it.'

I'm sure I asked Lola not to call him. Bugger. He's bound to think I put her up to inviting him.

'That's fine. I didn't know she was calling you, actually, or I'd have warned you.'

'Well, I just hope it's not Wagner, for your sake – they're all about three weeks long. Oh and take an umbrella. In my experience it's always pouring with rain at Glyndebourne.'

Great.

Lola's sorted everything out perfectly for the Glyndebourne extravaganza, and she says she forgot she wasn't supposed to ring Harry, and she's pretty miffed he turned her down. She makes me promise to wear a dress, and no wellies, and not mention gardens all night because she says Charles is really annoying her talking about the garden all the time and he doesn't need encouraging.

Since I don't really have a dress that's posh enough I race round all the shops at lunchtime, and find one in pale-blue silky stuff, with little beads round the hem, in a new shop that has just opened, and I've got a pair of pale-blue girly mules, which I bought last summer, that will go with it perfectly.

Mum says I look lovely and she and Alfie stand waving me off as I walk up the lane. The only real problem is that Molly's just rung to say she's too tired and did I think Lola would kill her if she stayed at home and had an early night, only she really couldn't face sitting for hours on end listening to some woman yelling her head off. So it's just going to be me and Dan, which is a shame. Molly's insisting he still comes, because he's rented a dinner jacket and everything, and she thinks he's been really looking forward to it.

Charles opens the door.

'Crikey. You look wonderful. Oh sorry, I didn't mean it to sound like that, it's just, well, you look lovely.'

Lola appears looking amazing in a long violet swishy silk skirt, with a tight black-silk bodice which has produced a rather impressive cleavage. She looks like something out of *Gone With the Wind*.

'Champagne, I think, before we leave, don't you?'

Charles goes off to get the champagne as Dan arrives. He's looking fabulous too, like he's in an ad for aftershave or something. I've never seen him all dressed up before; it's such a shame Molly couldn't make it. Lola's impressed too, and keeps going all giggly and flirty, which is making Dan nervous, I think: he's knocking back the champagne like his life depended on it.

'Bring your glass out to the car, Alice, and we can have another drink on the way. We might as well start as we mean to go on. You too, Dan.'

It feels rather odd to be sitting in a Range Rover knocking back champagne while it's still light outside, but we have to get there by three because the whole thing kicks off really early, and then there are two intervals so everyone can have their picnics; apparently the picnic is a major part of the Glyndebourne experience, and people get very competitive.

We arrive and join a long queue of posh cars, full of jabbering Sloanes trying to unload picnic hampers. I've never seen so many BMWs and Range Rovers in one place – it's like some sort of *über*-rally. Lola starts telling us all about the opera, which is by Gluck apparently, who I've never heard of, but Lola says he's wonderful, and by the time we've found a parking space it's getting quite late, but Lola doesn't seem bothered.

We wander round the gardens and meet up with loads of her friends, who all seem to know each other, and then a rather flustered-looking woman from Lola's office rushes up with tickets and programmes, and says the clients have all arrived, apart from Graham, and shall she unload our picnic, only she's put tables and chairs on the balcony in case it rains. Lola hands her the car keys and tells her the hamper's in the boot, and on no account must she let Bernard know where we're sitting, and then she marches off and we all run along behind her.

She seems to know half the audience and it takes us ages to actually get in, because she has to keep stopping to kiss people hello. When we get inside we're ushered into a box, which is fantastic although the seats are arranged one in front of each other, so it's a bit like sitting on a bus. Whoever designed this place definitely cared more about acoustics than designing boxes for the snooters. But we've got a fantastic view, and the tickets must have cost a fortune. I suppose it just goes to show how much people will pay for a posh picnic and the chance to look at other people's frocks. Actually, it's all making me feel slightly guilty; there are probably opera nuts out there who'd give you their last Rolo to be sitting here right now, and I don't even know what opera we're going to be seeing.

The building's wonderful. I remember reading about how they built it to replace the old one, which everyone loved, and it's so fabulous I'm really looking forward to the opera until about ten minutes after the curtain rises. The set is completely dreadful: loads of white space, black-and-white lines, and awful flat lighting, and everyone's in modern suits and moves in slow motion like they're on castors.

For some reason the entire chorus enters the stage on all fours. I think it's meant to be something to do with Greek tragedy, and people being moved about by the gods like pawns, but it doesn't work, and the sword fights are especially comic.

The music seems fine at first but gradually you realise

you're just longing for it to end. Charles appears to have gone to sleep, and I'm tempted to try something similar, but Lola seems engrossed and Dan looks vaguely worried, as if he's somehow missing something. He keeps looking at his programme, and then leaning forward in his seat, as if concentrating a little bit harder might make it less impenetrable.

Finally it's the interval and we belt out to our picnic. It's pouring with rain, so nobody ventures off the balconies, which are now so crowded it's like being in an upper-class refugee camp. The woman who met us with the tickets has appeared like magic again, and asks Lola if she needs anything, otherwise she'd better go and see how the rest of the guests are doing in the restaurant – where all the corporates go, apparently, which is why Lola's insisted on us having a picnic.

'I'll have to say hello to people in a minute. Oh Christ, there's Bernard. He always turns up at company things, and he always does something annoying. Last year at Henley he fell out of a boat. Oh look, there's Tony, Tony Howard, you know, the film director.'

She stands up and waves at him repeatedly until he walks towards us, looking slightly puzzled as if he can't quite remember her name. She's giving him one of her special big smiles, where she shows off all her teeth.

'Tony, Lola Barker. I worked with you on that BT job last year, remember?'

'Oh yes, lovely to see you again. We're just on our way to dinner, actually. Chloe darling, come and say hello.'

A stunning young woman appears from behind his back. She's wearing a tiny shift dress in a sort of pale aqua-green silk.

Lola doesn't look pleased.

'What a sweet little dress. Is it from Ghost?'

'No. Top Shop.'

'Oh. How clever of you.'

Actually, that is quite annoying. At least if she'd spent five hundred quid on it you wouldn't mind so much.

Mr Howard is giving Lola a rather threatening sort of smile.

'So, what do you think of the opera then?'

Lola says something about Gluck always being marvellous, and then the great man turns to me.

'And what about you?'

Bugger. Even though I know I should just say something polite and vague I just can't bring myself to.

'I don't really know much about opera, but I think whoever did the sets should be shot.'

'I'd quite like to meet him, actually.'

Now he's giving me the threatening-smile routine. Oh dear.

Chloe smirks, and Lola jumps in and says she's sure she can arrange it – her father's an honorary member.

Mr Howard seems to find this rather amusing. 'Your father, he's the composer, isn't he?'

'Yes.'

Lola looks very pleased with herself.

'Well, please don't go to any trouble on my account. I only wanted to ask him what those bloody cubes were meant to be. But getting his guide dog through these crowds might be tricky.'

Charles laughs, which Mr Howard seems to like.

'Not a fan, I take it?'

'Not really. I'm with Alice, although I think shooting him might be going a bit far.'

'Oh I don't know. There are limits.'

Lola has recovered and says, 'Oh yes, well, quite. I was thinking the same thing, actually. The sets are a bit drab.'

'Drab? They're a fucking disgrace.'

Chloe is starting to look very bored.

'Darling, we should be going. They'll be waiting for us.'

'Yes, yes, of course. Sorry, we must go. But it was lovely seeing you again, Lola, and lovely to meet your friends. Good to know it's not just old bastards like me who hate this kind of bollocks.'

Lola's delighted.

'Maybe I could invite him for dinner one night, and you could come too, Alice. I'm sure he'd like that – he seemed quite keen on you.'

'Or you could ask Chloe.'

'Don't be stupid, Charles – I don't want her. She's just a girlfriend, I think, one of many.'

Charles smiles.

'Yes, I'm sure, and anyway she's a bit too gorgeous to be the ideal dinner party guest, isn't she?'

Lola looks annoyed, but Charles snorts with laughter and says if she's quite finished meeting and greeting could we please start eating because he's absolutely starving.

All sorts of lovely food emerges from the hamper. Lobster, little pots of shrimp, strawberries, chicken salad, and lots of fabulous cheeses. There's also a delicious-looking game pie, and all sorts of salads with little bottles of dressing.

'God, Lola, this is wonderful. Thank you so much, for asking us and organising everything. It's such a treat.'

'My pleasure, darling. Although I still think you should have brought Harry along.'

'He's not keen on opera.'

'Shame. I always think you can tell a great deal by how a man reacts to opera. It's very revealing.'

I don't think I want to ask her what she means by that – I think I'll just ignore it.

But she's not giving up.

'I'd have thought he'd welcome the chance of a glamorous night out – make a nice change from being surrounded by plant pots. Anyway, what about you, Dan? It's your first time, isn't it? And you know what they say about the first time.'

Christ. Dan goes bright red. Honestly. He's behaving like a rabbit caught in headlights.

'It's such a shame Molly couldn't make it.'

Good for Charles.

'We'll have to think of a nice treat for her, to make up. What do you think, Dan? I'll babysit, if you like, as long as you don't mind Alfie rearranging the chickens all night.'

'I've been trying to persuade her to slow down a bit, but she won't have it.'

'What about booking her a massage or something? Lola loved them when she was pregnant, didn't you, darling? And I've always thought being pregnant must be bloody hard work.'

Lola glares at Charles.

'I adore all that kind of thing. Book me one too, would you, darling, if you find somewhere local. Full body, with all the extras.'

Dan goes bright red again. God, Lola's really excelling herself tonight.

'Alice, would you like some strawberries?'

I think Charles is trying to change the subject.

'Yes please – they look lovely.'

'We'll have our own soon, from the garden. I can't wait. I was up there this morning and everything's coming on brilliantly. It's amazing how quickly things grow. I never realised.'

'I know. It's extraordinary, isn't it? One minute it's all floppy little seedlings and then suddenly you've got proper plants. I never knew how exciting it could be.'

Lola laughs.

'I can think of more exciting things.'

'Yes, I'm sure you can, darling, but the thing about gardening is you don't need an audience.'

Lola ignores him, but she's obviously rattled.

'Oh look, there's Melvyn. I must go and say hello.'

We all eat far too much, but at least the champagne makes the second half slightly less of an ordeal. Charles really falls asleep this time and has to be nudged awake when he starts snoring. The applause at the end isn't exactly thunderous, and I think the cast are quite relieved it's over too.

When we do finally get back to the car park, after Lola has

stopped to say goodbye to hundreds of people, we can't actually find the car. Lots of other people seem to be having the same problem and are walking up and down clicking their remote-control keys to see which BMW lights up. We eventually find it on almost the opposite side of the car park to where we started looking, and then it takes ages to get out because of the queues.

The drive home is nice and quiet, mainly because Lola falls asleep. Charles drops Dan off and then we're at the cottage.

'Thanks, Charles, and thank Lola for me, will you – it was lovely.'

'No, thank you, really, it was nice to have someone to talk to. I'm just sorry the opera was so awful.'

'Night then. Sweet dreams.'

God. I don't know why I said that. It sounded a bit flirty, which I really didn't mean, but he sounded so sad, and he's so lovely. I must have drunk more champagne than I thought.

'Goodnight, Alice.'

Mum says Alfie's fast asleep when I get in. He conked out quite early, which he never does with me, presumably as part of his strict adherence to the sod's-law rule of parenting. We have a cup of tea and I tell her all about the evening, and she says it sounds lovely, although she thinks Lola sounds like a bit of a madam.

She's been listening to one of my Frank Sinatra CDs while she's been doing the ironing, bless her, and as she leaves Frank starts telling us all to take it nice and easy. If they went in for a bit more of a big-band sound at Glyndebourne they'd probably be packed out every night. But somehow I just can't see old Frank putting up with those sets. I mean apart from the fact that he's dead, of course. But when he was still packing them in in Vegas, I just don't think he'd ever have entered the stage on all fours singing 'I Did It My Way' balanced on a cube. And even if he had, at least you'd have been able to sing along. Actually, I think I probably have had too much champagne.

7

JULY

La Dolce Vita

Garden Diary

Lay new turf in any bare patches in lawns. If sowing seed keep the ground well watered. Divide irises and plant bulbs. Trim hedges.

I have a go at digging out all the moss and weeds from the front lawn but get a bit carried away and end up with huge bare patches. I scatter a box of miracle grass seed which promises an emerald-green lawn up to your waist in two weeks, but every bloody bird within a five-mile radius then descends and takes its place in the formation pecking-team hoovering up the seed. Alfie and I make a scarecrow using a pair of his old pyjamas, but the flaming birds are delighted, and adopt it as their new team mascot, perching on it for rests in between meals. I end up buying black netting and pegging it all over the garden, while the birds sit on the fence and sulk, but it works. Now all I need to do is remember to water it, and we might have a new lawn one day.

MOLLY AND I HAVE decided to have a joint fourth birthday party for Alfie and Lily, and we can use her back garden if the weather holds, since they've got more room than me, and Dan's going to rent a mini bouncy castle. We've invited ten kids from nursery, and Ezra and Mabel are coming too so we'll have fourteen of them to contend with.

Alfie's spending ages looking at toy catalogues, and so far the list of things he's got his eye on comes to just under seven hundred quid. Jim's planning on getting him a bow and arrow, with those rubber sucker things on the arrows so they stick to walls and furniture, and people's heads, no doubt.

So I'm really glad when Stella rings. Hopefully I can get her to persuade Jim to find him something less annoying.

'So what time should we arrive then?'

'Around twelve-thirty, but don't worry if you're late – it'll just be salads and stuff for lunch. Is Jim really getting a bow and arrow?'

'Sorry. I did try. Anyway I'm not really speaking to him at the moment, to be honest – he keeps going all distant. He can be such a wanker, your brother. I don't know why I put up with it really. Well, I do.'

Oh God. I hope she's not going to tell me what a great shag he is or something.

'He can be so sweet sometimes.'

'Blimey. Can he? I'd never noticed.'

'Yes. But then he goes all cool and distant. It's like he's read some book that says if you've been warm and emotional you have to follow it up by being a prick. So if we have a really good weekend he goes all funny and charges back to his flat and says he's busy. It's really annoying.'

'A lot of them seem to have read that book. I wonder if they give it to them at Scouts or something. Dib dib dob, always play it cool with the girls.'

Stella laughs.

'They'd probably call them the ladies. Well, I'm going to snap his woggle for him if he keeps it up – it's really driving me crazy. Was he actually in the Scouts then?'

167

'No. Mum said he got into enough trouble, without learning how to start fires.'

'Does Harry do it too?'

'Not really. But we've sort of got a bit of a pattern going at the moment. I see him once a week and that's it really. But the thing is I quite like it that way. Do you think that's awful?'

'What?'

'That I don't want to move things on, spend weekends together, that kind of thing.'

'I think if you're both happy with it the way it is, then it's fine.'

'Yes, I suppose so, and I think we are. Well, I am anyway. Oh, and by the way, you do know Mum will be giving you the third degree at lunch, don't you? It might be an idea to bring your passport and a CV, because she likes as much info as possible. School reports, letter from your doctor. That kind of thing.'

'Jim did warn me. I just hope she likes me.'

'I'm only joking – she'll be fine. And I've already told her how nice you are.'

'Thanks, Alice.'

'My pleasure.'

'And Alice –'

'Yes?'

'I don't really think Jim's a wanker.'

'I know.'

Patric and Cindy turn up around eleven on the morning of Alfie's party day, loaded with perfectly wrapped presents, with ribbon and shiny bows. Cindy's even made him a little cake, which is very nice of her although I can't help thinking she's done it to impress Patric more than Alfie. But still, at least she's made the effort, which is more than you can say for Patric, who clearly has absolutely no idea what the presents are because Cindy's the one that's actually spent ages trailing round the shops. But he's very taken with the foam rocket launcher, and takes Alfie out into the garden to show him how to use it 'properly'.

Cindy's looking especially pink today, a bit like a Barbie but without the glitter, or Ken. But I'm determined to try to be nice, because she's obviously been trying really hard. I offer her a cup of tea but she says she's only drinking water at the moment, with a slice of lemon if I've got it, because it's so good for the skin.

'You should try it, you know, Alice. I detox every few weeks now, and it's amazing. And it really helps keep the pounds off too.'

'Great.'

Jesus. She'll be telling me how to put my lipstick on next.

'So, you're off to Italy next week, Patric was saying. How lovely.'

'Yes. I'm really looking forward to it.'

'I keep telling him, we must get away soon. He works so hard, poor lamb. But he won't let me book anything, he always says he's too busy.'

I could tell her that the reason he won't let her book anything is because he hates wasting money on holidays, and even if she does manage to drag him off somewhere he'll spend the whole time getting paranoid about work. But I won't. I'm going to be nice.

'Just book somewhere – that's my advice.'

I did that one year and he sulked for the entire fortnight, but you never know, he might have changed.

'I thought somewhere lovely and hot. I love the sun, don't you?'

'Yes.'

I wonder if I should tell her about his heat rash. It got so bad in Greece we had to go to a doctor and get special ointment.

'There's a lovely new hotel in Majorca I was reading about at the hairdresser's, all five star and everything and the suites have their own pools. And we'd definitely need a suite. I mean there's no point in going if you don't do it properly, is there?'

I don't think I'll mention the heat rash after all; she's bound to be much more sympathetic than me, and anyway a five-star hotel probably has its own clinic.

They leave just before Mum and Dad arrive, which is probably a good thing, and then Jim and Stella arrive, with the bow and arrow, so Alfie's back out in the garden again getting in some more target practice while I get the lunch ready.

Lunch goes fairly well, although Alfie's so excited about his party he can hardly sit still long enough to eat, and Mum puts Stella under the spotlight, which makes Jim nervous. He's made me promise to try to head her off from telling her favourite stories about him when he was little, especially the one about him when he was five, and he got what she still refers to as his winkle stuck in the zip of his shorts.

I do my best, but she still manages to remember about him dancing round the lawn stark naked in his Red Indian headdress when the Avon lady came round. Before she can get too carried away I confess that I've always wanted a turquoise zip-up bag like the one our Avon lady had, full of lipsticks and body lotion, and we move on to talking about handbags.

Mum and Dad have bought Alfie his first bike for his birthday, with stabiliser wheels, which Dad has fixed on, and a Dennis the Menace bell. He loves it, and we all take it in turns to jog up and down the lane with him while he pedals away like fury and rings his new bell, and then Dad goes off to play golf while we load up my car with all the party food.

I've got crisps and sausages on sticks and I've also made some fairy cakes, which look a bit flat but I'm sure nobody will mind. I tried to go a bit Nigella and went for lilac icing, but it's more of a nasty shade of purple and looks rather horrible. I've stuck lots of little silver balls on but they haven't really helped.

Mum's made stacks of mini sausage rolls and she's done some cheese on sticks, with pineapple, because she says we always loved them when we were little. Actually, I can remember thinking that the pineapple was rather horrible, but I'm hoping Alfie won't feel the same or he's quite likely to drop it on Molly's carpet when he thinks nobody's looking.

By the time we get to Molly's and start unpacking the food children are starting to arrive. Doreen's down for the afternoon, and is in charge of keeping the presents unopened and in separate piles, while the rest of us lay the table and try to work out what to do with the jelly, which hasn't quite set.

Molly says Dan's sulking because they've had a row: she forgot to buy birthday candles, so he had to go out and get some, and then he was away ages because he decided to go to the supermarket for special ones, so she had to cope with Doreen all on her own for nearly two hours. They're still not speaking really, and Doreen is loving it, you can just tell.

Dan goes outside with Jim to try to stop people bouncing off the bouncy castle into next door's garden and then Ezra lets the chickens out, and Frank and Bill and Elsie turn up, with little presents, which is really sweet of them. They stay for a cup of tea and a fairy cake, and are very polite and don't ask me why on earth I went for such revoltingly coloured icing, and then it starts to rain and all the children scream and stampede back into the house.

We make them all sit down for pass the parcel and Stella turns out to have a real knack for turning the CD player on and off at just the right moment so each child gets to tear off a piece of newspaper. For some mad reason Molly has put a small toy whistle in each layer, so Doreen goes upstairs with one of her heads.

Dan comes into the kitchen and says shall he make a cup of tea for her, or would Molly prefer to do it, because he's bound to do it wrong, or take too long or something.

'Oh stop it, Dan – just make the old bag some tea.'

'That's my mother you're talking about.'

'I know.'

'She'll hear you.'

'No she won't, not over all this noise.'

171

I'm trying to pile crisps on to a plate and keep a low profile. Dan reaches into the cupboard above my head and passes me a bowl.

'Here.'

'Thanks, Dan. Don't Molly's cakes look brilliant?'

'Yeah.'

'Could you take these in for me and put them on the table, and I'll put the kettle on for the tea for your mum.'

Molly hands him a plate of little sandwiches with all the crusts cut off, not that the children will care.

'I think I could manage that. Just about.'

But he sort of smiles as he goes out, and I think he's getting over whatever it was he was sulking about.

'Shall I put something in her tea?'

'What, like deadly nightshade or something?'

'If you've got some handy.'

The birthday tea is a big success, although Sydney eats a whole plate of sausage rolls and then says her mummy has told her to remind us she's a vegetarium. The birthday boy and girl both go very pink when it's their turn to have 'Happy Birthday' sung to them, and then we play musical statues and sleeping lions until people start turning up for home time, and Molly hands out the party bags. When only Ezra and Mabel are left we realise we've completely forgotten about the jelly, so we all have a bowlful.

The house is a complete shambles, but Molly says she doesn't mind, and what she really wants is a cup of tea and a little rest. Lola arrives and says she's been stuck in traffic behind a combine harvester, and we all sit around and end up talking about giving birth, which makes Jim and Dan go out into the garden to start deflating the bouncy castle.

'I'm not exactly looking forward to it, that's for sure.'

Molly looks tired all of a sudden. I hope she hasn't overdone it.

'I don't blame you – it was murder with Ezra. And Mabel wasn't much better.'

'Oh, but second babies are always quicker, aren't they? My sister says after the first it's a doddle. You'll be fine, I'm sure you will.'

Good old Stella. At least she's trying to be reassuring. Lola gives her a rather irritated look, but Stella is either oblivious or is made of sterner stuff than I thought.

'You seem to know a lot about babies.'

'Oh my sister's got three, and my yoga class is full of pregnant women. I think I might be in the wrong group, actually, but they make me feel so thin, I love it.'

'Oh I did all that yoga rubbish, sat around for hours in a white leotard visualising my cervix dilating like a petal. But it's bollocks: when it came to it I had all the drugs they could give me, and then they couldn't get him out and had to use that hoover thing they put on their heads and he had a pointy head for days. And with Mabel it was the same really. God.

'And as for all that breastfeeding crap, Jesus, nobody tells you how boring it is. I got fed up after a couple of months – I think that's long enough for anybody. I used to prop her up with a cushion and a bottle, and she soon got the hang of it. It saves you hours of faffing about.'

I can tell Molly doesn't approve, and neither do I really, but I'm sure she's exaggerating.

Stella says she thinks she'll start tidying up a bit and hands Lola a large black bin bag, but she simply puts it down on the floor and says she has to get the children home because it's getting really late, and then Ezra and Mabel start hitting each other with their party bags as they're leaving.

'What a horrible woman. Sorry, I mean I know she's a friend of yours, but I used to work for someone like that once, all fake smiles, and wanting to be the centre of attention all the time. She was a total bitch.'

Molly smiles.

'Oh she's all right really. She doesn't mean half of it, you know.'

Doreen's still sulking when we leave, for some reason

nobody can quite work out, and Mum's completely exhausted when we get home. Jim and Stella are heading off back to town for another party, although probably not one with so much jelly.

'So, this time next week you'll be in Italy.'

'I know. I can't wait. If you're still sure about driving us to the airport we should fix up times and everything, because we have to be there really early.'

'You've already told me that. Stop panicking. I might come down the night before, have another go with that bow and arrow.'

We watch them drive off, and Alfie shoots a few arrows after the car, which I have to retrieve from the lane, and then I make Mum a cup of tea while Alfie collapses in front of the telly completely exhausted.

'Thanks, love, I needed this. He had a lovely party, didn't he, bless him.'

'Yes, he did. And thanks, Mum, really, for the food and everything.'

'He loves his bike, doesn't he?'

'Loves it.'

'It all goes so quickly. I was thinking this afternoon, I can remember you both at that age, like it was yesterday. And now look at you.'

'What, still covered in jelly?'

'Stella seems nice, though. He could do a lot worse.'

'Yes, Mum, but don't say anything to him – you know how he gets.'

'He's always been the same. Secretive, like your father. And where's he got to now, I wonder? He was supposed to be here half an hour ago. Probably still in the bar at that silly golf club.'

But I can tell she's starting to worry. He arrives about five minutes later, and says someone had a puncture, so he stopped to help, which is just like him, and they go off bickering about what to have for supper.

'I've got kippers, and they won't keep.'

'I'm not really that keen on kippers – you know that.'

'Well, you might have said.'

'I have. For the last thirty years I've been telling you. I don't like kippers.'

'Well, it's the first I've heard of it. What about if I do them with some scrambled eggs?'

Jim arrives to drive us to Gatwick at the crack of dawn, and takes one look at my suit and says, 'Cabin crew, doors to manual.'

'Are you trying to tell me I look like an air hostess?'

'No.'

'Good, because I'm not in the mood, I'm completely knackered. I was up half the night packing and then I couldn't sleep.'

'It's a bit blue, isn't it?'

'That's because it's a navy suit. It's only for the journey. I read somewhere you have to dress up when you're flying, so you get an upgrade if the flight's full.'

'Good thinking, Batgirl, except for one teeny problem.'

'What?'

'Alfie. They're not likely to stick you in business class with Alfie, are they? The boys in suits wouldn't like it.'

'True, but at least they might not sit us right by the toilets.'

Actually, I bet they will. It's amazing how many people still seem to think it's fine to treat children like toxic waste. Usually exactly the same people who think it's perfectly all right to let their pets crap all over your garden. I mean obviously there are children who behave so appallingly that you want to give their parents a lethal injection, but Alfie's pretty good most of the time. Well, apart from a bit of low-level whining and the occasional juice-squirting moment. Actually, on second thoughts maybe the back of the plane will be fine.

By the time we finally get on the plane Alfie's so excited he's jiggling up and down in his seat. It's his first flight, and I'm half looking forward to it and half dreading it. The air steward, a man with an almost orange tan and very white teeth, is demonstrating the life jacket and has reached the bit about blowing your whistle to attract attention. Alfie's peering out of the window, which is a good job really, or he'd definitely be trying to find his life jacket.

I wish they wouldn't say that bit about the whistle. I mean if we're going to end up in the sea I'd kind of hope air-traffic control knew all about it, and it wouldn't be up to me to blow my whistle to attract attention. Although I suppose it would give you something to do while you bobbed up and down in the water.

To be honest, I think they should just leave out the chat about the life jacket completely, because it only makes you nervous, and I'm worried enough already, especially about hijackers. Jim reckons nobody in their right mind would hijack a flight to Sicily. And there were quite a few men in dark glasses and suits getting on who looked like they might be Mafia Dons. Or they could just be businessmen who like the Vinnie Jones look. But I keep having visions of having to get Alfie out of the plane and down that yellow plastic slide thing. Actually, he'd probably love that. It's probably a good thing we're not near the door where the slide is or he might have a go when we're cruising at fifty thousand feet.

At Sicily we have to change airports, which involves a rather epic taxi journey across the island to Trapani, and then we have to catch a flight to Pantelleria, which is the tiny island where Em and Luca have their hotel. It looks like we're about to descend straight into the sea, but at the last minute I catch a glimpse of some tarmac and then we see Em waving at us as we walk down the steps.

The airport's tiny, and Em runs across and picks Alfie up for a cuddle. Nobody shoots her or tells her to get back behind the barrier or anything, and she says we can leave our luggage and someone will come down to collect it later, which is a bit different to Gatwick, where they'd probably blow your suitcase into smithereens if you left it alone for more than ten seconds, or get a sniffer dog to wee on it.

The heat's staggering and the island seems quite barren and rocky, but very beautiful. Tunisia's only a few miles away and it feels more like Africa than Italy, not that I've actually been to Africa, of course. As we drive to the hotel in Em's old battered Fiat it all looks very Moorish. The houses, which Em says are called *dammusi*, have white-domed roofs and walls of black basalt, about three foot thick so it's cool inside. They're fabulous. In fact the whole island is fabulous, sort of magical and wild, with its black rocks looking like they've been thrown into the sea.

No wonder Armani has one of his villas here. Em's told me all about the jet set descending every summer. The local fishermen are all making fortunes renting out their houses, and apparently you can't move round the main town without bumping into some famous film star draped in cream linen. Which must be a bit of a nightmare: no wandering around in baggy old shorts and flip-flops, unless you want to feel like a total loser having your morning espresso as Armani and his guests float by on kitten heels.

As soon as we arrive at the hotel Em's mother comes barrelling out and says she's pleased we've arrived, because maybe I can talk some sense into Emily, and don't I think a proper sit-down buffet would be nicer than letting Luca's mother cook. Luca is gorgeous and obviously besotted with Em, and his brother Marco has turned up, and says he's very glad I've arrived because the two mothers are driving them all round the corner.

The hotel is stunning. It's a collection of *dammusi*, all done up with beautiful beds and rugs, with the biggest one turned into the main hotel building, with a terrace overlooking the sea. There's bougainvillea everywhere, and vines and lemon trees and pine and what look like wild rosemary bushes, and sage. It's like an alfresco aromatherapy session.

There's even a small pool. Em says they would have chosen a bigger one but water's very scarce and if you run out you have to get a tanker over on the ferry from Sicily, which costs a fortune, and is a major drama because the tanker only just fits down the track to the hotel. So they go in for a lot of recycling and filtering, and store water during the winter in huge stone wells in the gardens.

Just before I can start obsessing about Alfie falling down a well she shows me the massive boulders on the lids and says it takes two people to move them so I'm not to worry, which just shows how well she knows me, because that's just the kind of thing that would have me sitting bolt upright at midnight, looking up resuscitation in the first-aid book Mum put in my bag just as we were leaving.

Our little house has a terrace overlooking the sea and is basically a large bedroom and a huge bathroom, and they're both very beautiful. I always knew Em had brilliant taste but this is truly stunning. She helps me unpack and get ready for supper which is going to be a mega family affair at a local restaurant.

Em's mum is already sulking, because she isn't terribly good with large groups of Italians. Or large groups of anyone really. She usually eats her evening meal by seven, and likes to be in bed by ten at the absolute latest. The meal tonight won't start until nine at the earliest and is likely to go on for hours according to Em.

'We're so packed out with Luca's family and Mum, and we've got people staying all over the island, so I thought the restaurant was a good idea for tonight, but Mum thinks we should have a quiet supper just with her, and I still haven't sorted out the flowers and –'

She starts to cry. After a bit of heaving and sobbing she says it's all too much, and Luca just keeps saying he loves her, and nothing else matters. And it doesn't really, only she wants it to be perfect. It takes me almost ten minutes to calm her down, and I end up promising that I'll help her make everything just how she wants it, and I'll even push her mother off the terrace into the sea if necessary, and this cheers her up and she says she'd better go and get ready.

Supper's lovely although I lose track completely of exactly who everybody is – they all seem to be related to Luca in some complicated way, even the people who run the restaurant. Marco keeps trying to explain to me who people are, but after a couple of glasses of wine I don't really care. Everything is very relaxed and there are lots of children wandering about, and Alfie makes friends with a little boy called Giovanni and his sister Gabriella, who I think are one of Luca's sisters' children but I'm not sure.

Everyone seems mad about children here. I noticed it at the airport earlier, when even the policeman with a machine-gun slung over his shoulders came over to say hello to Em and made a fuss of Alfie. The idea of a restaurant putting up a 'Children Welcome' sign here would be a complete mystery to everyone.

There's a tiny baby who's come to supper tonight, but it takes me ages to work out who her mum is because everyone makes such a fuss of her. They seem to know it's a Herculean task to amuse a baby for hours, and nobody would dream of expecting one person to do it for the entire evening. She's passed up and down the table, and it's a bit like pass the parcel, without the music, and without anybody getting stuck with the parcel for too long.

A very smartly dressed man gets up when it's his turn and walks about jiggling her and sort of bobbing, singing in a very comical fashion, and she's totally enchanted. But nobody else takes any notice of him at all. Then he sits back down, passes the baby to the man sitting next to him, rearranges the angle of his jumper so it drapes over his shoulders in just the way he wants it to, and carries on flirting with the woman sitting opposite him.

I love Italians. I think I might want to be reincarnated as an Italian; never mind a butterfly or a higher being or whatever it is Buddhists believe you can aspire to if you spend years in an orange dress being careful not to tread on anything. Just coming back Italian would do me. And the food's great too.

Alfie's usually pretty firm about not eating anything he doesn't instantly recognise, but he loves being made a fuss of by Luca's mum, who spends most of the meal putting things on his plate and cutting them up, and then nodding encouragingly and clapping her hands with delight when he eats them. He even snuggles up to her for a quick cuddle at one point, which goes down very well.

We don't get back to the hotel until nearly one in the morning, but at least Alfie doesn't wake up and kick anybody when Luca carries him into our room. In fact he sleeps right through until nearly half-past nine, which is a record for him and something I hope he's really going to get the hang of while we're here.

We spend the morning racing round with Em, getting things ready for the wedding. Em meets a friend in town who's so pregnant I'm amazed she's still able to stand up, let alone go shopping, until Em explains she's having twins, which apparently are common on the island, and sure enough during the morning we see three more sets of twins, including the two men who run the butcher's, who are identical, and both stand behind the counter like extras in a Fellini film.

Apparently one of Luca's brothers has twin girls, and Em is pretty nervous about her chances.

'But in a way it would be lovely, wouldn't it? Having two at once.'

'Oh yes, lovely.'

I'm not going to tell her what I really think, just in case. I remember thinking that twins might be nice when I was pregnant with Alfie. For about five minutes. My god, I must have been mad.

We go back to the hotel for lunch and Marco offers to take us out for a boat trip round the island later on.

'We can take bread to feed to the little fish, and it will be perfect, yes?'

Well, no, actually. I'm not that keen on the idea of Alfie in boats, mainly because I just know he'd fall out before we even got out of the harbour. But of course he thinks it's a brilliant idea, and is already halfway out of the door, and Em whispers that Marco is very reliable and we can all go, and it really is the best way to see the island. So in the end we all go down to the harbour and the boat turns out to be an uncle's fishing boat, which Marco seems very at home in.

We stop at a small fishing village, where Marco says we can swim. There's a low wall surrounding a pool of sea water, which Alfie loves, and Marco spends ages showing him how to snorkel with the mask we bought in town this morning. Alfie gets so excited every time he sees a fish he nearly swallows the tube and has to be hoicked up by Marco by his shorts until he gets his breath back.

It's a perfect way to spend the afternoon and Em gradually relaxes and says that she supposes it won't be a complete disaster if the extra lilies don't arrive in time. Whereas this morning she got completely hysterical about it and I had to practically force feed her ice cream in a café before she'd calm down.

When we get back the dressmaker's arrived and we try Alfie in his suit, which is in pale-blue linen. He looks so sweet in it I wish Mum was here to see him. He's never had a proper suit before, and looks very grown-up but also somehow smaller. It fits him perfectly: Em bought it in Milan along with her dress and mine, and god knows what it cost because she won't tell me. The deal was I paid for our tickets out here and for Em's tiara thing, which we brought over with us. It's silver with little glass beads. She's been wearing it round the hotel ever since we arrived. To practise, she says, but I think she just likes wearing it.

Her dress is beautiful. It's a proper bride's dress but not too fussy, in creamy white silk with tiny glass beads and a little bit of embroidery in white and cream on the hem. It fits perfectly, but the woman wants to adjust the hem a little, and is obviously a professional because she doesn't make Em stand on a table like I had to when Mum was doing my summer dresses for school.

Em's still talking about aubergine for my dress, and I'm getting seriously worried when a lovely pale-yellow dress emerges from the bag in a mixture of linen and something else so it doesn't crease before you even get it on. It's very elegant and has a little jacket to go with it, and the same embroidery round the hem that Em has on her dress. The dressmaker fixes the hem, which looks fine to me but she insists a little shorter would be better, and when she's pinned it you can see she was right, and then she packs everything away on hangers and says she will be back tomorrow morning.

We try to explain to Alfie again about how he has to walk down the aisle dropping flower petals. He says he thinks it's silly but he'll give it a go, and Em tells him she's got a special present for him, which he can have tomorrow if he manages not to stand on her dress. And I tell him I'll get him a present too, if he remembers to drop his petals a few at a time and not all in one big heap by the door.

The next morning is chaos. After so many mini-dramas that I'm getting close to hysterics everything suddenly goes all peaceful and quiet, and we have a blissful half-hour sipping champagne and putting the finishing touches to Em's nails, because she can't decide between Nude Blush and Sugar Frost, which look identical to me, but at least she has to sit still while I paint them.

Alfie's watching the video of *Mary Poppins*, which Em got for him, and we all end up singing 'Feed the Birds' and getting a little bit tearful. Well, not Alfie, obviously, who thinks we're both being very stupid.

The wedding makes me cry too, and we're not talking elegant sniffing and dabbing either. Em looks beautiful, and

Alfie does his bit really well. She does the whole thing in Italian too, which I somehow hadn't expected, and I'm so proud of her, and then I notice Luca wiping his eyes when he thinks nobody's looking, and that makes me even worse.

The service takes hours. Alfie falls asleep, and I notice quite a few other people seem to be having a little doze, but eventually we get to the bit where they actually get married, and Luca's voice goes all wobbly and they put their rings on and turn round, and the smile on Em's face is just perfect. And then she looks at me and winks. Which just about finishes me off completely.

We go back to the hotel and everyone's waiting and there are cheers and lots of hugging, and we drink champagne on the terrace, and even Em's mother looks pleased. Luca's mum spent most of yesterday in the kitchen, and now she and practically every other female relation of Luca's are taking over the kitchen again to make all sorts of traditional wedding delicacies for tonight's big meal. They've deferred to Em's mum on the cake, which is a traditional English wedding cake that they all seem rather in awe of. God knows how she managed to get it out here, but there was a huge fuss yesterday about the icing, which had cracked slightly, but she managed to fix it, and it does look beautiful.

Luca makes a speech and everyone laughs, and then he very sweetly does the whole thing again in English, 'for my new English family', and says when he first met Em he thought she was a terrible stubborn Englishwoman, and now he knows her really well he realises he was right, and she's a terrible poker player, but she is also the woman who he knows he will love until he is dead. I think it probably sounded slightly more romantic in Italian, but he looks so happy you can tell he really means it.

There's a buffet lunch with bowls of salads and cold meats for anyone who's hungry, and then the plan is that we all lounge about a bit and have a sleep and then there's the big wedding meal this evening.

Alfie's outraged when I suggest we go and have a sleep and

I only manage to persuade him by telling him there'll be fireworks tonight, and he can stay up to watch them but only if he has a sleep now.

'Yes, but I'm not tired. I am not.'

He falls asleep within minutes. And so do I.

I'm desperate for a cup of tea when I wake up, which is a bit pathetic really, but Alfie's thirsty too so we head off to the kitchens, with his hair sticking up in little tufts from where he's been asleep. Luca's mum is still beavering away but she stops to make Alfie a little snack, and pats down his hair while he's eating it, which he doesn't even notice because she does it so casually. And what's really clever is that she doesn't make me feel it's my fault it was all sticking up in the first place.

Em comes in, also in search of tea.

'Oh good, I've been looking for you. I've got presents.'

Alfie starts squeaking with excitement as we follow Em to her room. Luca is fast asleep in the middle of the enormous bed, looking very pleased with himself.

'Oh ignore him – he'll wake up in a minute. Actually, Alfie, do you think you could wake him up?'

'Em, are you sure that's a good idea?'

But Alfie's already leapt on the bed and is jumping about yelling 'Uncle Luca', 'Uncle Luca', and to his credit Luca doesn't wake up screaming, but simply wraps himself in the sheet a bit tighter and says hello.

Em gets a huge box from her wardrobe and gives it to Alfie, and Luca obviously knows what's in it because he sits up and watches him expectantly. Alfie rips it open to reveal an enormous toy St Bernard dog, which is almost as big as him, and he shouts 'Nana', and throws his arms around its neck and rolls around on the bed.

'Oh Em, you shouldn't have. It must have cost a fortune.'

'It did. But he's worth it, my special page boy. When I saw it I couldn't believe it, it was just so perfect. And who knows, this way you might not have to get the real thing. Oh, and this is for you.'

She hands me a posh-looking box, and inside it there's a silver locket, with a tiny picture of Alfie inside and an engraving: 'To Alice. Love Em and Luca.' God, I think I'm going to cry again. I give them both a hug and then manage to get Alfie and Nana out of the door so the poor man can get up and get dressed without an audience.

Alfie's in bliss playing with Nana in our room, while I have a shower. I've completely fallen in love with the shape of the houses here and I love the domed ceiling in the bathroom: it's like being in a medieval chapel. Luca's explained to me that they just fit the stones together, with no cement, and they make the domed roofs by putting lots of thick wooden props into the room once the walls have been built, and then they fit the stones together into the shape they want, again with no cement. And then they take the props out, and if they've got it right the whole thing stays up. Whoever gets to remove the last prop must have to be very nifty on their feet, or a very confident builder.

Alfie's busy making Nana a dog basket in the middle of my bed with all the pillows and blankets while I get ready, and we even have to leave her a glass of water in case she gets thirsty.

The restaurant's been transformed and there are flowers and candles everywhere. Marco comes over and says we're sitting with him at dinner, he has arranged it.

'I hope this is OK, but I need your help. My cousin's friend, this Mariella, she is very determined.'

'No problem, as long as you don't mind Alfie helping himself to anything he fancies on your plate.'

'Ah.'

The dinner is amazing, and so many different dishes are brought out from the kitchen that I lose count. Alfie's on red alert for squid, which he ate inadvertently the other night and pronounced delicious but has now decided is the most disgusting thing in the whole world, and Marco keeps himself busy flirting like mad with everyone under seventy because he's still trying to shake off Mariella, who's giving me pointed looks from across the room, and then some of the tables are moved back and people start dancing.

Luca's given Alfie a glass of water with a tiny bit of wine in it, and after a bit of dancing he gradually slows down and then falls asleep at our table. I must remember to try this at home.

Em's mum has drunk far too much and keeps gripping hold of my arm and telling me that she still doesn't know why we couldn't have had the whole thing in England. But apart from that everyone seems to be enjoying themselves.

At some point after midnight the fireworks start, but Alfie's still fast asleep. I'm standing out on the terrace, watching the fireworks and Em and Luca, who seem completely blissed out, when Marco comes over.

'I think there is still one tradition left we must do.'

'Oh, what's that?'

'At a proper English wedding I think there is a tradition?'

'What, like it pours with rain and then there's a fight?'

'No. The bridesmaid. She has to kiss the best man. I think?'

'Well. Actually.'

'Oh yes. I have read about it. And it is very bad luck if there is not enough kissing.'

'Not at English weddings. Possibly at Italian ones.'

'Oh yes. At Italian weddings everybody must kiss.'

He is rather gorgeous. Oh, what the hell. I kiss him. And he kisses me back. And then I kiss him again. Blimey.

'I'd better go and see if Alfie's woken up.'

'I think we hear him if he is woken up.'

'Probably.'

'I think we should stay here. I think this is much better.'

I think he's right.

We're still locked mid-clinch when Em comes round the corner.

'Oh sorry.'

'No, it's fine. Really. I was just going to check on Alfie.'

Crikey. My legs have gone all wobbly.

'No, I shall go. You stay here and I shall tell you.'

'God, I'm sorry, Alice, I didn't mean to interrupt anything.'

'You didn't. I mean it just sort of happened. There's nothing to interrupt. Really. I just kissed him, that's all. He asked me to. So I did.'

'I bet that surprised him.'

'Not half as much as it surprised me.'

'He's lovely, you know.'

'I know.'

'And just think, if it worked out we'd be related, and you could come and live out here and we'd be sisters-in-law, and you could design new *dammusi* and we could meet in town every morning, and –'

'Em. You don't think you might be reading a tiny bit too much into one little kiss, do you?'

'Possibly. But he's been giving you longing looks ever since you arrived.'

'He has not.'

'Oh yes he has. It's just like buses, isn't it? Just when you give up hope two come along at once. First Harry and now Marco.'

'Yes, and that's another thing. I mean I'm sort of with Harry, aren't I? Not that we've had any big talks or anything, but it still feels like cheating. And I really hate that. I don't know what came over me really. Maybe I'm drunker than I thought. I don't normally come over all brazen, and I really don't want to make things complicated.'

'Complicated's good, you know, sometimes. Sometimes it's how it is.'

'I know. But it was only a kiss. He was probably just being friendly.'

'Alice. He wasn't just being friendly. Trust me.'

'Well, whatever he was being I should go and get Alfie. And say goodnight to everyone, and you should get back to your husband.'

'My husband. I still haven't really got used to saying it. Are you sure, about Marco, I mean?'

'Yes. Really.'

'All right. I think you're mad, but all right. And thank you, for making everything so perfect. Today, I mean. I had the best day.'

'Oh sweetheart, I'm so glad.'

Marco's very nice about my deciding to call it a night, and says he'll see me tomorrow. Em and Luca walk us back to our room, and Luca says he hopes his brother has not been annoying me, and I say no, almost the exact opposite really, which makes him laugh.

I can't quite work out how I feel about the unexpected kissing thing, but I also can't work out where I've put my toothbrush, so I'm definitely more drunk than I realised.

Alfie wakes up for a brief chat with Nana but soon settles again, and after a few moments of realising that the room is actually whirling around quite a bit when I lie down I fall asleep pretty much instantly too.

The next morning we see Marco on our way to find some breakfast. Alfie's insisted on bringing Nana, and I'm too hungover to do much about it. Marco's very charming and says he has to go back to Milan today for business, but maybe we'll come back for another holiday and he'll take us out on the little boat again, and I say maybe, and he smiles, and then Alfie starts barking and says Nana is Very Hungry.

Later we see Marco driving off in his car and I feel quite a pang. Part of me would really have loved to have stayed on that terrace. And he was a really great kisser, but that might have been the champagne. Maybe I'll see him again. Em's invited us over for Christmas, and you never know.

But then there's Harry, and I'm feeling a bit guilty about that, because I'd be pretty bloody livid if he announced he'd been kissing some total stranger on a terrace while we've been away. Not that we've sworn undying devotion or anything, but still.

It's all a bit confusing, especially with a hangover. And anyway there are more important things to worry about right now. Like how I'm going to get Alfie to stop barking. And how we're going to fit a massive toy dog on to the plane on the way home.

We spend our last day lazing in the sun and having little swims in the pool until Nana falls in and has to be rinsed out in the shower and then dried in the sun.

Em takes us to the lake in the middle of the island in the afternoon, which is called the Mirror of Venus, and is such a brilliant blue it's almost unbelievable. It's like swimming in a warm bath. The sulphurous mud that surrounds it is supposed to be terribly good for you and all round the lake there are little groups of people smothering themselves in it and then lying in the sun to bake. It does make your skin feel wonderful, even if I just know Alfie's going to try the same thing with the mud in our back garden when we get home.

He's had such a lovely time here, and even though I've been smothering him in Factor 200 he's starting to go a lovely golden colour already. Maybe we should come back at Christmas, or maybe next Easter when Em says the island is covered in flowers and the weather is starting to warm up. Or maybe we should just stop here and Alfie can learn Italian and I can buy our sausages from the twin butchers, and learn how to build domed houses.

The journey home is really exhausting, partly because the flight from Sicily is delayed so we have to spend four hours trying to amuse ourselves in Palermo airport, which isn't easy, but mainly because I don't really want to go home. It's been so lovely spending time with Em, and the island's so beautiful.

But Alfie's glad to be back, and watches his video of *Peter Pan* surrounded by all his toys, in celebration.

The garden has gone completely rampant while we've been away, and Charles and Lola are away at a villa in France, so Molly and I try to do our bit in the new garden too so Mr Channing and Frank don't end up doing it all.

We spend nearly a whole morning weeding, and I tell Molly all about Italy, and she says it sounds fantastic and she wishes she had a friend who lived somewhere lovely like that.

She thinks that Marco sounds lovely too and says that although kissing total strangers on holiday is not technically perfect behaviour, it's not like Harry ever needs to know, and anyway it was only a kiss.

And then we talk about taking Alfie and Lily into school, for their visit to the reception class to prepare them for starting school in September: Alfie's determined to take Nana with him, and Lily says she might go, but only to have a look because she hasn't made her mind up yet.

'I can't really believe they're starting school, you know. They seem too little.'

'I know. I've been trying to teach Lily to put her shoes on herself, but she just won't do it. Although she sometimes does it for Dan.'

'I've got Velcro ones for Alfie – he'd never manage with laces. What time are we supposed to take them in?'

'Half-past one, and then there's a meeting in the hall at two-thirty when they'll be selling the school sweatshirts and stuff.'

'I hope they like it. God, wouldn't it be awful if they come and say they hate it and they're not going back.'

'Yes, but we've got the whole summer to work on them. Janice is already knitting Lily a school jumper, by the way, and she says she'll do one for Alfie too, if you like.'

'Oh dear.'

'I know. I've told her they wear sweatshirts, but she's got the wool and everything. At least she can't do it in pink. She says she's going to make it a bit big, so it'll last.'

'Oh great. Nice long arms she can roll up.'

'Oh stop it – I don't want to think about it. Tell me more about Italy.'

'Well, there's not much more to tell.'

'Have you seen Harry since you've been back?'

'Not yet. He's coming round later, actually.'

'Did you miss him?'

'Not really. I can't work out if I'm just a bit more relaxed than I used to be, or if it means I don't really care about him.'

'I think it all changes when you have kids, you know. I was thinking about it the other day. You sort of get to a point where you're pretty settled and not much is going to shake you to the core. Well, not a man anyway. I mean obviously I'd be devastated if something happened to Dan, but if we're bickering, or he's a bit off for a while, it doesn't seem like the most important thing in the world any more. It just feels like it's part of the deal, and there's no point getting too wound up by it.'

'Yes, I think you might be right. Maybe we've grown up. God, that's a bit scary, isn't it? We're the big girls now.'

'Yes. And some of us are bigger than others at the moment.'

Lola rings in the afternoon and says she hates France.

'It's full of bloody British people traipsing round in their sandals whining about how all the prices have gone up. Jesus. There's nobody interesting, and the kids are driving me mad. France is definitely off the list now – everyone's going somewhere else. Ezra keeps falling in the bloody swimming pool, and the au pair we've hired has taken a fancy to a waiter in the local pizza place and keeps disappearing. And Mabel's got some hideous heat rash so she looks appalling. We've bought her some stuff from the local pharmacy and it smells disgusting. She looks like she's got the plague. Honestly, I've got a good mind to leave them all to it and check into a hotel somewhere. Charles seems perfectly happy to spend hours with the children, doing absolutely nothing. It's so boring.'

'Is the weather nice?'

'No. It's fucking boiling. The locals keep saying it's the worst summer they can remember.'

'What a shame. Still, at least you've got away – change of scenery and all that.'

'Oh yes, it's a change all right. I'm going to need another holiday to get over it when I get back. Actually, that's why I'm ringing. Do you fancy coming to a health farm with me or something? There's a new one that's getting great reviews.'

'I'd love to, Lola, but money's a bit tight at the moment, what with going to Italy and everything, and I'm a bit pushed at work.'

'Oh. Well, think about it, and let me know, I'm on the mobile.'

Bloody hell. I'm very glad I'm not in France at the moment.

Harry arrives early on Friday night, and wants to hear all about Italy. I give him the edited highlights, and then I try to tell him about Alfie's first afternoon at school and how I'm feeling nervous about it, but he doesn't seem that interested.

'I can't remember much about mine. We were packed off pretty early, and it's all a bit of a blur. I hated the first few days every time. I used to be sick, every morning. I can remember the feeling, waiting for the train. It was awful. I'm sure he'll be fine.'

'I suppose so.'

'I mean you'll be there, won't you, to collect him every afternoon?'

'Oh yes, or Mum, but it'll still be a long day for him. I mean the afternoon is only a trial, to get them used to the idea, but I really hope he doesn't hate it.'

'Yes, but at least he gets to come home.'

I can't help feeling slightly narked that he seems to think that because Alfie's not being sent off to boarding school he'll be fine. I suppose if I'd been sent off when I was tiny I'd probably think the first day at a local village primary wasn't much of a challenge, but it still feels like a fairly big deal to me. I try to explain this but it all ends up getting rather tense.

'What's the matter? You're building up to something, I can feel it. You've been funny ever since I arrived. Are we going to have A Talk? The one where you say you want a commitment and I say I like things the way they are?'

192

Bloody cheek.

'Not necessarily. I might say I want to slow things down a bit.'

'Oh. Right. And do you?'

'No, but now you mention it, it might be nice if we talked about things more.'

'Like what?'

'Oh I don't know, anything.'

'Look, can't we just leave it? I mean we have fun, don't we?'

'Yes. But what if I want more than fun? I mean, I don't know, say I wanted another baby or something.'

I don't really know why I've said this. I don't want another baby. Well, definitely not at the moment and definitely not with Harry. But for some reason I want to see his reaction. He looks pretty horrified.

'Hang on a minute. We didn't say anything about babies.'

'I know we didn't, of course, but shouldn't we be able to talk about things like that?'

'I suppose so. I mean I don't mind Alfie, of course, but I really don't want one of my own. I'm not ready for anything that serious, not yet. I don't know if I ever will be, to be honest.'

'Oh.'

'Is that a problem then?'

'It's just I think maybe being away has made me realise I want a bit more than that. Not just a sort of regular fling, no strings attached.'

'Damn.'

'I know.'

'I'm not sure I'm up for that.'

'I know that, Harry, and I'm sorry, I really am.'

'Oh well. Maybe we've just run our course, or whatever it is they say.'

'Yes.'

'Should I go now then?'

'I suppose so.'

I really don't want him to go. But somehow I don't really want him to stay either.

He gets up and walks towards the door.

'I'm sorry, Harry.'

'Me, too.'

Damn. I really didn't mean that to happen. Not that it's not true, but I just hadn't realised I'd made up my mind until we started talking about it. Bugger. I'm really going to miss him. Double bugger.

I ring Molly who comes round with emergency chocolate.

'I bet he'll call you.'

'Maybe, but we didn't have a fight or anything. We sort of agreed, so I don't think he will. Being in Italy and seeing Em and Luca made me think, and I really don't want to settle for a Mr In Between any more, someone with potential, who with lots of work might turn into something wonderful. I get enough bloody conversions at work. It's got to be a brief bit of passion that doesn't pretend to be anything else, or it's got to be the real thing. Someone who'll love Alfie almost as much as I do, not just put up with him as part of the package. Mr In the Middle just doesn't do it for me any more.'

'Well, good for you. I think you're absolutely right. Do you want a Flake, or a Crunchie?'

8

AUGUST

Mad Dogs and Englishmen

Garden Diary

Pick herbs to dry and store in airtight containers. Order bulbs for spring. Fertilise roses before autumn. Water lawns and flowerbeds in hot weather, making sure to water thoroughly and deeply. Maintain weeding regime.

The weather turns boiling hot so I buy a plastic sandpit for Alfie and a few bags of play sand. He plays in it quite happily for about five minutes while I'm trying to pick herbs, and then spreads the sand all over the lawn. I try to stop him but end up tripping over a bag of sand and falling flat on my face into the herb bed. The smell is wonderful and I lie there for a bit slightly stunned, hoping that nothing is going to be hanging off at a funny angle when I get up. Alfie thinks I'm playing, and leaps on top of me. The fennel gets bent and the mint's rather flattened but once I've trimmed off the worst bits it all looks OK, and I end up with a huge pile of herbs to hang up to dry in bundles round the kitchen. Feel very virtuous, like a good countrywoman laying down stores for the winter. Even if I can't actually remember what they're called, I bet they'll add interesting flavours to soups. Although technically Alfie won't eat soup, but maybe I could pretend it's some sort of sauce.

MOLLY AND I ARE planning a day out at London Zoo with the kids, even though Molly's definitely at the heavily pregnant waddling stage now.

'I can't even fit in the bath any more. I can get in, but it's pretty tricky getting out, and I can't sleep in this heat.'

'Neither can I. Have you had any more arguments about cereal?'

Molly and Dan had a rather ferocious argument yesterday about the right way to open a packet of Shreddies.

'No, but we've made up, sort of. I apologised last night and he watched a Bruce Willis film, to make sure I understood I was still on probation, and I didn't say anything. I just tried to do my knitting for the baby, but that's driving me round the bend too – it's gone all circular. Maybe I could make a cape?'

'That's a good idea. I bet all the really trendy babies are wearing capes. Look, are you sure you fancy this zoo thing?'

'I've got six weeks to go yet. What could happen?'

'You could go into labour while we're on the train or something. That's what could bloody happen. I'm not terribly good at being calm in a crisis. You might as well know that right now.'

'Oh don't worry. I've got a feeling it's going to be late, just like Lily.'

'Well, I hope you're right. Because I don't fancy appearing on the six o'clock news, helping you give birth surrounded by lions and penguins.'

The zoo's full of shrieking kids and animals, and Alfie's wearing his new safari hat and baggy shorts, which make him look like he's about to appear in a Morecambe and Wise sketch.

Within twenty minutes of our arriving I suddenly realise we've lost him: one minute he was there, and the next minute there's this Alfie-shaped hole where I think he should be standing, and the air's sort of shimmering. I want to start looking under seats and behind bushes as if he might have mysteriously shrunk or something: if I pretend that I can still see him then maybe he can't really *be* lost. He's only been gone for a minute and I'm already cracking up.

Just as I'm about to get completely hysterical I catch a glimpse of him, standing down the side of one of the cages talking to a malevolent-looking eagle through the bars. I can't decide whether to cuddle him or go berserk so I do a bit of both, and Molly has to sit down because she's pretty close to tears too. He promises never ever to wander off again, and I hold his hand, much to his annoyance, and try to calm down, which isn't easy; but short of tying them on a long bit of rope I can't see what else you're supposed to do, except blame yourself for eternity if they do manage to give you the slip.

We have lunch in the café, which costs a fortune, and the weather has gone all stormy and humid so everyone's grumpy. Lily drops her sandwich on the floor and shrieks until Molly gives her most of hers, and then Alfie decides he needs another bag of crisps and will whine until he gets one. I tell him he won't ever have crisps again, ever, if he doesn't stop it, and he starts to cry, and a woman at the next table, who has two perfectly behaved children with her, gives me a horrible superior look.

I distract Alfie with the promise of ice cream if he packs it in, and then one of her kids squirts juice in the other one's face and they both start kicking, and I try to give her exactly the kind of look she gave me.

We do the penguins and seals after lunch, and the children's zoo, which isn't nearly so much fun now you're not allowed to molest the animals, but Alfie still manages to get chased by a goat, and nearly loses his new hat, and then we have a drama in the gift shop and practically have to call for armed assistance to get them both out without giant pandas. Whichever bright spark decided to stock the gift shop with giant stuffed animals deserves a really big slap.

The train home is late and filthy and Alfie invents a new song which consists of singing a selection of his favourite rude words quite loudly. We try ignoring him, but there's only so long you can ignore someone repeatedly singing 'Bum willy Bum' on a rush-hour train. I try a bit of threatening, but he's beyond caring, and then Molly summons up the energy from somewhere to tell them a story, and they turn into little angels who take it in turns to add unusual twists like great white sharks suddenly appearing in people's baths. It constantly amazes me how quickly children can change. One minute you want to throttle them and then suddenly they go all sweet.

I've left my car at the station and while I'm driving us home I offer to make supper, to give Molly a rest.

'Oh yes please. I'm so tired, that would be great.'

'I've got salad, and some ham, and a few strawberries. Not many though, but enough for the kids.'

Molly says there are stacks in the new garden and Frank says we should pick as many as we fancy, so after a cup of tea and a rest we walk up with a bowl to pick strawberries, and then take some over to the house because it feels a bit cheeky to just wander up and nick them all. There's no sign of anyone but the back door's open so Lola's probably in her office upstairs.

'Actually, come to think of it, Charles said something about taking them over to his mother's for the day. Let's just leave some strawberries and not bother her – she's probably working.'

'OK. No, Lily, stay in the kitchen.'

Lily's already run off, heading for the playroom, and Alfie's about to follow her.

'I'll go, you watch Alfie.'

It feels rather weird being in someone else's house without them knowing. I don't want Lola to think she's got burglars, and I'm just about to shout hello as I reach the bottom of the stairs when I hear Lily yelling 'Daddy'. And then I hear someone say 'Christ', and everything sort of goes into slow motion.

Lola appears at the top of the stairs clutching a sheet, and Dan bounds down wearing only his jeans, which he's still doing up. He looks really pale, as if he's just been told some really bad news. Which I suppose in a way he has.

'Moll, it's not what you think. I'm sorry, wait, let me explain.'

Molly has come into the hall. She stands very still for a moment, and Dan falters slightly, and then she makes a weird noise, a mixture between a cry and the kind of noise you make just before you're sick, and runs out of the house. I follow her, with the kids, who seem rather quiet as if they know something's up but can't quite work out what. We walk back down the lane in silence.

I feel pretty shaken by the time we get indoors, so god knows how Molly's feeling. I open a big bag of crisps and my emergency bag of Smarties, and stick *Peter Pan* on. Molly's sitting at the kitchen table, staring at the fridge.

'I can't even have a fucking drink.'

'I'll make tea.'

'I don't want tea. I feel sick. Tell me what we just saw. I want to hear you say it out loud.'

'I don't know, Molly, I think, Christ, I just don't know.'

'Fucking bastard. How could he? I wonder how long that's been going on. He's been weird for ages. I thought he was just working hard, but he was probably out seeing her. God.'

I think she really is going to be sick. She gets up and goes over to the sink.

'Did you see his car? I didn't see his car. She must have picked him up somewhere. Maybe it's back at our house.'

Saying the words 'our house' seems to upset her all over again and she starts crying.

'Do you want a glass of water or something? Oh god, there's someone at the door. Molly, it might be Dan. What do you want me to do?'

'Tell him to fuck off. I can't see him now, I can't.'

She looks really panicked.

It's Charles.

'I thought you might like one of these. We've been over at my mother's at one of her village things and I thought they were – Sorry, is this is a bad time?'

'No, it's – they're lovely.'

He's clutching a sunflower in a little pot.

'I got some for the garden too, for the children. I've always loved sunflowers – they're so cheerful, aren't they? Oh hello, Molly.'

Oh god. She looks furious.

'Molly, calm down.'

'I'm perfectly calm. I've just found out Dan's a complete bastard, but I'm quite calm about it really. I am. It's funny, in a way. I was feeling guilty about not paying him enough attention. But it looks like someone else has been taking care of that one for me, doesn't it?'

'What? I don't understand. What do you mean?'

'I mean your bitch of a wife and fucking Dan, that's what's I mean. We just walked in on them, up at the house. We'd been picking strawberries for tea, and –'

She starts to cry, and he goes bright red for a moment and then he starts to walk back to his car.

'Molly, go back in and sit down, and Charles, don't go. Come in and have a drink or something – you can't go home like this. I'll get the kids in – just go into the kitchen and talk to Molly.'

Charles has sort of frozen by the gate, looking helpless, but he turns round and they both go into the kitchen, and then Lily comes outside and dances about getting increasingly agitated, and Alfie starts joining in, and I say something really stupid about how it's all right, it's just that Mummy doesn't like sunflowers, which strikes me as especially ridiculous the moment I've said it, but I can't really think of anything else to say. We get Mabel out of her car seat and then Ezra and Alfie start bickering about whether to watch *Peter Pan* or cartoons.

Molly and Charles are both sitting in the kitchen looking shell-shocked, but when the kids barge in they manage to rally slightly, and we end up having a surreal conversation about the zoo and all the animals we saw, while I make some tea. I dole out more crisps and gradually the kids settle down with the telly, although Ezra and Lily keep wandering back into the kitchen, and have obviously picked up on the underlying tension.

Molly's gone weirdly quiet, which is almost more scary than when she was sobbing. Charles keeps shaking his head, and staring into space, and in the end they go out into the garden and pretend to be looking at plants, and Charles puts his arm round her and I can tell she's crying again.

He says he thinks he'd better go home, but he'll ring us later, and Molly says if Dan's still around could he please tell him not to bother coming home because she doesn't want to see him.

She looks really pale and I can't help thinking maybe I ought to call a doctor. I mean it can't be good for pregnant people to have big shocks like this. I do what I always do in a crisis and call Mum, and she says she'll come right round, and I'm to keep a close eye on Molly and if she starts going faint or anything we're to go straight to the hospital. Which really worries me, so I ask Molly if she's sure she's feeling all right, and she says no, she feels like she's been run over by a truck but she promises she'll tell me if she starts to feel weird in a need-to-go-to-hospital kind of way.

I end up taking Molly and Lily home, and Mum takes Alfie to stay at her house. The phone's ringing when we get to

Molly's but she won't answer it, and in the end she unplugs it.

I've got my mobile with me, and Charles rings and says that Lola was out when he got home, and he'll ring us later if she turns up. He sounds really distant and exhausted.

Lily falls asleep quite quickly after I've given her a bath and Molly's read to her for a bit, and we have supper sitting out in the garden watching the chickens. It's quite calming watching them pecking about and fluffing up their feathers, but Molly still looks very pale.

'I don't know what to do. I keep thinking, but I can't work it out. All I know is I can't cope with seeing him. Not just yet. I feel really strange, but it's like I just want to put everything on hold.'

'I know, sweetheart, but there's no rush. You can talk to him tomorrow.'

'Or maybe not. Maybe I'll just never speak to him again.'

My mobile rings and it's Dan.

'Look, Alice, is Molly there? She won't answer the phone and I've got to talk to her.'

'Hang on a minute.'

Molly shakes her head.

'I can't.'

'Did you hear that?'

'Yes. Just tell her I'm sorry, will you? I can explain. Is she OK?'

'Not really.'

'Alice, I just, oh god, it's just complicated.'

'Tell it to Molly, Dan, not me. Ring her tomorrow.'

God, I'm so furious with him, I'm shaking as I put my phone back in my bag. At least I didn't have to find Patric and Cindy together. At least he had the decency to sit me down and tell me. And at least I wasn't pregnant. Poor Molly, it's so unfair. I can still feel the shock and humiliation of it all, that sense of complete betrayal. It's like an old bruise that still hurts when you press it. And she's only just at the start of it all. Christ.

*　　*　　*

202

Charles rings around eleven and says Lola came home and they had a blazing row and now she's gone to stay in London for a few days.

'She said it's all my fault. Apparently I'm really boring.'

'Oh Charles.'

'Is Molly all right?'

'Sort of. And what about you?'

'Same really.'

'Look, call me, any time – really. I'm at work in the morning but I'm around in the afternoon. If you want someone to talk to.'

We get to bed late, and I fall asleep almost immediately, and have all sorts of complicated nightmares about losing Alfie at the zoo mixed in with Patric moving out and then coming back with Lola and Dan, which makes me feel rather guilty in the morning because I only meant to doze so I was ready to spring into action if Molly needed me.

I'd planned on getting up early to make her breakfast too, but she wakes me up with coffee, and says she's been up for ages, but didn't want to wake me. She seems calmer, and says she'll call me later and come round this afternoon. She just wants to spend some time with Lily and try not to think about anything.

I go home and get changed and get into work late, but Janet and Malcolm are away in Spain so there's nobody looking at their watch and being sarcastic.

Mum calls and says she'll bring Alfie home this afternoon, and he's been lovely although he nearly gave Dad a heart attack leaping into their bed at dawn for a cuddle.

'He slept in your old bed, he looked really tiny, and I've been thinking, you know, and I never liked that Lola. I always thought she was a nasty, selfish piece of work, but I'm surprised at Dan. He always seemed such a nice boy. I bet his mother's mortified.'

I hadn't thought about how Doreen's going to take the news of the chosen one's fall from grace. Every cloud has a silver lining, even if it's only a really tiny one, although I'm not actually going to say this to Molly. But I'd quite like to see Doreen's face when she finds out.

I collect up some papers at lunchtime and take them home. I haven't got anything urgent on, and Brenda says she'll cover for me. There's a note from Mum – she must have popped in on her way to playgroup. She says there were three messages on the answerphone, all from Dan last night trying to track Molly down, and Charles has called and she's told him I'll call him back, and she'll bring Alfie home later.

She loves answering my phone in case she picks up any interesting bits of news that I'm trying to keep from her. She likes knowing even trivial stuff, like what I had for lunch or where I've been shopping. She's the same with Jim: she once spent nearly half an hour talking to the receptionist in his office before he realised who she was talking to, but it was too late by then and she'd already told her the winkle story. He had to buy the woman coffees from Starbuck's on the way into work for months to get her to keep quiet.

I hear a car arrive, and then I see Lola walking up the path. Fucking hell.

'Hello, am I *persona non grata*?'

'If you mean am I furious with you, then yes. I am.'

'It was only meant to be a fling, you know. It wasn't serious or anything.'

'Well, it bloody was for Molly.'

'I know. But honestly, she was never meant to know. It was pretty much over really.'

'I don't want to know the details, Lola.'

Actually, I do, but I'm rather ashamed of this.

'We just sort of got together vaguely for a while, that's all. I wasn't going to try to take him off her or anything. God forbid.'

'I think that almost makes it worse. At least if you'd fallen madly in love with him I could understand it.'

'Don't be ridiculous. With Dan? Please. If you hadn't been creeping round my house nobody would ever have known.'

'Lola, we weren't creeping anywhere, we were bringing you some strawberries.'

'Charles is furious.'

'I don't blame him.'

'I don't really care. It hasn't been working for ages.'

'Well, get a divorce then. Find a way to make it all right for the kids, and get on with it. But leave other people out of it.'

'It's been really hard for me too, you know.'

'I'm sorry, Lola, but my sympathy's all used up, I've been with Molly all night. Heavily pregnant Molly.'

'I know. I do feel a bit bad about that.'

'A bit bad. Jesus, Lola, you're unbelievable.'

'But you don't understand. It was just a fling, just something to keep me sane while I made my mind up. It's all right for you – I'm under real pressure. They don't give you the kind of money I earn if you're not totally committed, and it doesn't matter if I'm in the office or at home, they still call me. I'm surrounded by bastards who want my job.'

'Well, maybe you should let them have it. It can't just be about you, Lola, I mean surely it's about the kids too. You need to sort things out for them. They need to come first, don't they?'

'I never did, not with my parents. My mother made that perfectly clear.'

'Oh for god's sake, Lola, get over it. Just because you had a crap mother doesn't mean it's all right for you to be the same. Look, I don't know what you came round for but I don't think I'm up for it, whatever it is.'

'I've got to decide what to do, and it's really difficult. You know what it's like, coping on your own, and I'm just not sure if I'm cut out for that kind of thing. I could move back to London, and be like a divorced father. See the kids at weekends, shower them with presents and then fuck off before bedtime. But maybe I should take them with me – we could get a house in London. I don't see why Charles should keep them – they're my children too. He seems to think I'll just move out and leave him with everything.'

I think she'd be quite happy to leave the children if only it didn't mean Charles having them.

'Are you serious then, about splitting up?'

'Oh yes. This was just the final straw. It's been building for ages. But I just don't know what I really want yet. I mean I haven't even got a decent nanny sorted out, and if they stay with Charles he'll probably demand maintenance or something. Christ, wouldn't that be ironic, me having to pay him to look after the children?'

'Lola, it can't just be about money.'

She gives me a very supercilious look.

'Oh Alice. You really don't get it, do you? He's very rich, his family's absolutely loaded.'

'Well, that's OK then, isn't it?'

'No, it bloody isn't. If we're getting a divorce I should get half of everything. I'll have to get a good lawyer, make sure his bastard family don't cheat me. We're talking about a great deal of money here, but most of it's in family trusts, and they're bound to try to keep it. His mother's always hated me.'

I can't really believe she's only talking about the money. Suddenly I feel very angry.

'Oh well, if it's only the money you're worried about then I'm sure you'll be fine.'

'If you're just going to be sarcastic I might as well go. Jesus, you're so fucking superior. I didn't think you'd be so suburban.'

She's got a horrible sneering look on her face and somehow this just finishes me off.

'I'll tell you what's suburban, Lola. What's really fucking suburban is being obsessed with money, and having the right car and the right house, and giving endless rounds of dinner parties, when it's all completely fake. It's all about who you know, and what your friends will think. It's like the worst kind of cliché: nobody understands me, I'm so bloody special the normal rules don't apply to me. You live in some sort of parallel universe – do

206

you know that? You're like a black hole, it's all about you and what you want.'

Blimey. I'm so angry I've actually gone a bit shaky. Lola storms off, banging the front door nearly off its hinges as she goes.

I call Em to try and calm myself down.

'What, Dan? Lola's having it off with Molly's Dan? God. What a cow.'

'I know.'

'Poor Molly. What's she going to do?'

'I don't know. I don't think she knows yet.'

'What a bastard.'

'I know. I can't believe it really either.'

'Well, tell her she can come out here, after the baby, if she wants to. For a nice long rest. Luca's mum will whip the baby out of her hands as soon as she lands.'

'Thanks, Em. I'll tell her.'

'And you too. It'll help cheer you up after binning Harry. I'll ask Marco down, if you like.'

'I didn't bin him, Em, we both agreed. It just wasn't going anywhere.'

'Yes, but he'd have carried on popping round for a bit of action, wouldn't he?'

'Probably. Actually, I wouldn't mind a bit of action now – take my mind off all this business with Molly and Dan. It's so depressing, and I hate seeing her so upset. It's so unfair.'

'Well, come over here any time, sweetheart, and I'm sure that can be arranged.'

Molly rings as soon as I've finished talking to Em and says she's going to meet Dan later, at the house, and we arrange for her to drop Lily off with me for a bit so they can talk. She seems fairly calm when she arrives, and looks very determined, but I can't really talk to her because the kids are both being quite clingy. She looks exhausted when she gets back, but she's brought sweets and lemonade with her, so the kids soon perk up and run round the garden trailing sand everywhere.

'So how did it go?'

'Fine. I've told him I can't make any big decisions until after the baby. I really can't. He kept trying to tell me it didn't mean anything, and it was only a few times, like that makes any bloody difference. But I've told him I want him to move out for a few weeks. We can tell Lily he's off on some big job – he's done that before. He can come back on Sundays and see her and everything. And then after the baby's born I'll be able to think properly.'

'Are you sure?'

'Yes. Absolutely. I know I didn't want this baby at first, but I really do now, and I know I just won't be able to cope if I try to sort it out now. It can't be good for the baby, can it? The tension of just seeing him today made me realise. I know it sounds loopy, but I know I can't do it – I'm too tired. So I'm going to try to pretend nothing's happened. Just for a few weeks. Does that sound mad?'

'No, not really.'

'And I think it will do us both good. Give us a bit of distance. I'm so angry now, if I started I don't think I'd ever stop. Not just about Dan, it's everything really. Trying to keep everybody happy, do the right thing by Lily, and him, and work. I'm just so tired and I haven't got the energy. It's not that I don't care or anything, but I just can't face it. You know what I mean, don't you?'

'Yes, of course I do.'

'And I'm so fucking disappointed in him. I thought he was better than that. I mean I know things have been tough lately, but I never thought he'd do something like this. And it's no good blaming it all on Lola.'

'No, I suppose not.'

God, that's so typical of Molly, always trying to be fair. And I know she's right, but somehow I'm more angry with Lola than Dan, which doesn't really make sense. It's just that I know it wouldn't have been Dan's idea. I mean he might have gone along with it, got caught up in all the attention and excitement, but Lola would have been in charge. It would have been her idea. Because everything always is.

'There is one thing, though.'

'What?'

'Will you come with me to the hospital? I mean I'm sure I'll be all right with the midwives, they all seem really great, but it'd be nice to have a friendly face.'

'Of course I will. But I'll be crap, I'm warning you.'

'You won't. But it's OK. I mean if it gets too much you can go out for a walk – I won't mind. But I don't think I want Dan there. I mean I might change my mind at the last minute, but I don't think I will. You don't think I'm mad, do you? You would tell me, wouldn't you?'

'Of course. And I'd love to be there. Only I'm not sure I'd choose me to rely on when push comes to shove. Oh sorry.'

'Very funny.'

'Do you want a drink, or anything to eat?'

'No, but I'd love a little sleep. Is that awful? It's just that I'm so tired. Would you mind, only for half an hour? And then I'll take Alfie home with us or something, so you can get a bit of peace.'

'Don't be daft, sleep as long you like. I'm not doing anything. I've got to go to the supermarket later, but that's all.'

'OK, how about I have a sleep and then I'll stay here with the kids while you go shopping. How's that? Save you taking Alfie round?'

'Now you're talking. And I can get some stuff for you too if you want.'

'I really fancy spaghetti. I've been craving pasta all day. I'll make supper, if you like. Does Alfie like mushrooms?'

'Yes.'

'OK. I'll do my special spaghetti. And we can have ice cream for pudding. Dark chocolate for us, vanilla for the kids. Actually, I'm not sure I'm supposed to have dark chocolate – I think it's full of caffeine. Well, bugger it. Oh this is great. All I have to do is sleep, and then make a list. Lovely, just like being a princess.'

I can't really think of anyone less like a princess, bless her. She waddles off upstairs, and I sit with the kids and try to avoid getting covered in wet sand.

Christ. This just gets worse. Molly's back at home and has just rung to say Doreen's turned up on her doorstep in a terrible state, saying that Dan's staying with her and he's told her all about it, and she just wanted a word.

'And then she told me that these things happen, and apparently Dan's dad did something similar, with a woman who worked at the local pub. Dan was three and his brother had just been born, and his dad went off for a fortnight and then came home and pretended nothing had happened. And she says she just got on with it, and in the end it was fine and she got over it. But I don't think she ever really got over it, not really.'

'Well, that explains a lot of things.'

'I know. I felt almost sorry for her, all that anger bottled up. No wonder she's such a nightmare. I really don't want to end up like that. And then she said didn't I think it would be best if Dan came home.'

'She didn't? God, what a cheek.'

'She said she knew it wouldn't be easy, but really what choice did I have, with the new baby and everything. And then I lost my temper and said I had lots of choices and that it wasn't the dark ages any more, and women didn't have to just put up with crap if they didn't want to. I told her we might split up, and I'll go it alone and be much happier, or we might work things out. But I'd decide when I was good and ready.'

'Oh good for you, and what did she say?'

'Well, she took it rather well, to be honest. She said she admired me – it was funny, it was like she really meant it. And she squeezed my hand. It was odd. It was like she was almost proud of me. It was a bit annoying really. I thought she'd storm off and I could feel victorious. And then she said she wanted to help, and if I needed any cleaning done she'd be more than happy to come over. Any time. I won't ask her, of course, but can you believe it?'

'Not really. But my bathroom's filthy if you think she'd be interested.'

Charles has been trying to avoid telling anyone where Lola is, but it's getting quite tricky. Mrs Bishop has been asking questions, and so far he's just said she's busy at work and is staying in town for a few days. But she's not convinced and the Garden Society have been busy going into overdrive: it's only a couple of weeks until the judges come round for the competition, so they're all spending hours weeding and generally making everything as pristine as possible.

'I just don't want anyone knowing until we've sorted things out.'

'Of course not.'

'Her latest plan is that we all move back to London and we give it another go.'

'Oh.'

God, I really hope he doesn't fall for it.

'But I don't think there's any point. I mean she's done it before – that's why we moved down here really – and she's bound to do it again. But I don't know. What do you think? Should I give it another go?'

I really want to say no, she's a complete bitch and you're better off without her but I don't think I should. I mean apart from anything else he might still love her or something.

'I don't know, Charles. Do you want to give it another try?'

'I don't, if I'm honest, but I want to do the right thing for the children. Actually, I think the only reason she doesn't want a divorce is money.'

I think he's absolutely right, but I don't want to make things worse.

'Why do you say that?'

'She's always been obsessed with it, and she keeps going on

about wanting half of my family money – it's all in trusts – but we own the house jointly, so I should be able to give her half the value of the house, and a bit more, but that's not enough. She always wants more. Anyway, I don't want to move back to London. I hated it there, I always felt slightly useless, but down here I don't. And I love the garden. I know it's daft, but I do. And she'd only do it again, I know she would. Things haven't been right for ages. It's my fault. I should have sorted something out ages ago but I just couldn't face it. I thought it would be better for the children, you know, that sort of thing. Stupid of me really.'

He's gone bright red and looks very upset.

'No it wasn't. You were trying to do the right thing. That's never stupid. Where's she staying at the moment?'

'With a friend in town, but she'll be home at the weekend, she says, and she wants to take the children – I mean if we don't all move back to London. She says when she gets settled she'll have them live with her, but I already know she won't. She just needs to find a way to explain it to her friends and she'll be quite happy leaving them down here with me, seeing them for the occasional weekend. I just need to give her enough money so she can get the right kind of house. It all comes back down to money. I know that sounds dreadful, but it's true. Sometimes I think it's the only reason she married me.'

'Oh Charles, that can't be true.'

'Maybe. In the beginning we were pretty happy, but she was different then. She's got worse over the years, which is probably my fault. Anyway, I think I'm going to say no. To the new start, I mean. I don't think it'll do the children any good. They pick up on all the tension.

'She was talking about sending Ezra off to boarding school – did you know? Over my dead body. I might be hopeless but at least I can spare him that. I hated mine. Really hated it. And she knows that. I think that's when I knew really, that there was no point. I won't have him packed off. He can stay with me. That's got to be better, hasn't it?'

'Yes. I'm sure it is.'

'Anyway, sorry for going on like this. I'm sure it will all sort itself out eventually. How's Molly?'

'Fine. I mean she's still a bit shell-shocked, but she's hanging on for the baby before she decides anything.'

'I must say I do feel dreadful about that – about Molly, I mean.'

'Well, it's hardly your fault.'

'Oh it is, in a way. It always takes two people to screw up a marriage, you know, Alice.'

'I suppose so.'

God, he's such a grown-up. But I know he's right really.

'Anyway, I meant to say, about the garden, Frank was saying he thinks we stand a chance, you know, he thinks they'll like it. I really hope so – we could all do with some good news for a change, and they've all worked so hard on it.'

'You've worked hard too, Charles. And for what it's worth I think you're probably right about Lola, and the children are bound to be better off if you're both happier, when things are sorted out.'

'Do you think so?'

'Yes. And I hope we win something for the garden, because it'll drive Lola crazy, missing out on all the glory.'

'Knowing her, she'll find a way to take all the credit.'

'Oh I think she'll have a hard job. Not if Mrs Pomeroy's got anything to do with it.'

The weather's gone all hot and stormy again, and we're all completely fed up with it. Cindy's managed to drag Patric off to Majorca to some posh hotel that must be costing a fortune. I hope his heat rash isn't playing him up too much.

Molly and I decide to take the kids to the beach for the afternoon, because they're driving us crazy being stuck at home. They run in and out of the sea up to their knees giggling until Alfie falls over and gets soaked, but at least we're all slightly cooler. Then they move on to building sandcastles and collecting buckets of water for their moat, while we sit on the sand on a blanket supervising, drinking tea from the thermos, sneaking the occasional biscuit when they're not looking.

'Are you sleeping any better?'

'Not really. I feel like I'm in a permanent fog. It's quite nice actually, as long as I don't try to do anything.'

'How was Dan on Sunday?'

'Oh fine. I mean he arrived, and he stuck to the deal, and didn't say anything. He just played with Lily and then I made lunch and she seemed all right, like everything was normal. And then he said he had to go off to work and she didn't seem that bothered, to be honest.'

'And how did you feel seeing him again?'

'Oh, still pretty furious, but somehow this deal about not doing anything until after this one's born really helps. You do think I'm right, don't you?'

'Yes, I've told you. I mean how can you possibly know now how you're going to feel? God, by the last few weeks with Alfie I was so overwhelmed by it all I really wouldn't have noticed if the entire world had collapsed as long as the maternity ward was still open.'

'Good. Because sometimes I think it means I don't love him, and there's no point. I mean if I really loved him I'd want to kill him, wouldn't I? Actually, I do want to kill him, but I just can't summon up the energy at the moment.'

'There you are then. I think the only thing it means is that you're pregnant.'

'True.'

'God, look at him.'

A rather gorgeous man is walking down the beach, with a little girl balanced on his shoulders. She's wearing a sunhat that is about three sizes too big, and a pink sundress.

'Oh sweet. Lily had a dress a bit like that.'

'He's gorgeous.'

'Yes. But he knows it. And just watch, some poor woman

will stagger along behind him in a minute, carrying all the bags. Just you wait.'

Sure enough a young woman appears, quite a way behind him, and she's got one of those trendy three-wheel buggies, which looks like hard work on the sand. And she's draped with all sorts of bags, and an umbrella, and a blanket.

'Typical.'

We do a quick survey of the beach to reassure ourselves that behind the façade of happy families there's actually quite a lot of seething tension. There seem to be lots of men sauntering along with the car keys and a small bucket, while the women trot along behind them, loaded down like donkeys. We do spot one man who's carrying all the kit, while his wife, who's wearing a sarong, carries a magazine and her mobile phone. She's obviously furious, probably at finding herself on a British beach instead of St Tropez.

Then a young couple arrive who are sharing their bags pretty equally. They've got a small baby who must be having his first trip to the seaside. They've brought every bit of kit going: one of those special tents that blocks UV rays, with mosquito netting, an umbrella, a playmat, a huge bag of toys, just in case he gets bored, and a video camera so they can capture the moment when he first claps eyes on the sea.

They both look knackered, and handle the baby like he's an unexploded bomb, constantly changing the position of his tent, or his hat. But they look so proud of him, and Molly says, 'Dan and I used to be like that once,' and goes all quiet.

But just when I think she might get upset a really horrible red-faced man arrives and starts yelling at his wife and kids. He's practically marched them on to the beach in formation, and a pale, tired-looking woman is carrying an enormous cool bag, and the minute she puts it down on the sand he yells, 'Not there, Maureen,' and she has to move it.

Then he gets out his rubber mallet and puts up windbreaks in a huge square with a tiny gap as the entrance to his camp. He'll probably be posting sentries later. He shouts at the two boys to take up their positions for a game of Frisbee, but the smaller one is useless at catching things, and gets yelled at repeatedly, and told he's an idiot.

'I can't stand it. I'm going to have to go over and say something. I hate bullies like him.'

'Oh Molly, don't. He'll probably shout at you too.'

'I hope he does – I could do with a good shout. He might get more than he bargained for.'

But before we have time to get Molly up and on her feet something completely marvellous happens. The little boy who's been told he's an idiot throws the Frisbee back to his father and it whizzes past his head, missing him by inches. As he leaps up to catch it he loses his balance and falls flat on his face, into the wet sand at the edge of sea. It makes a really satisfying squelching noise, and almost the entire beach has seen it, you can just tell. Everyone smiles, and someone even claps. Actually, I think that might have been Molly.

'Thank God for that.'

He gets up and walks rather stiffly back to his camp. And just when we're all having visions of terrible retribution inside the windbreaks the wife comes out, and cuddles the little boy. And gives him what looks like a KitKat, only we can't quite see. If I'd known it was going to be this fascinating I'd have brought binoculars. Mum's got some, Jim got them for her for Christmas, and she loves them. She says she uses them for watching the birds but actually she spends ages watching the neighbours.

'This is better than *EastEnders*. Look, that snooty woman in the sarong's going into the sea. She's going to get a terrible shock – I bet she doesn't realise how cold it is.'

She seems to hesitate, as if she can't quite believe how cold the water is, and wants to make a formal complaint to the management, but she's very determined and ploughs on. Maybe she's trying to get to France.

We eat our picnic, with sand, and then we have a paddle.

'The baby's at the seaside too, isn't it, Mummy?'

'Yes, Lily.'

'Does it want to come out and have a swim? It can borrow my armbands.'

'Not yet, poppet, but thank you for saying you'll share your armbands. That was very nice.'

Alfie looks at Molly's tummy, and then moves a bit closer and shouts very loudly, 'Come out, come out. We're at the seaside, and we've got armbands,' and then he knocks, as if he were knocking on a door. Luckily Molly doesn't seem to mind.

'He must be asleep. I bet he'll be cross when he's waked up and knows he missed the seaside.'

Not nearly as cross as Molly's going to be if she ends up giving birth on the beach.

'Actually, Alfie, I think you're right, the baby's having a sleep at the moment. Shall we have another paddle?'

Alfie and Lily start trying to jump over the waves just before they break on the shore.

'Actually, I've been meaning to ask you about that, Moll. Is there some book I should be reading, or a pamphlet or something, from the hospital?'

'What, like how to be a good birthing partner?'

'Yes.'

'No.'

'Great. Well, have you got a birth plan or anything?'

'No, but I'll tell you what I want, if you like.'

'OK.'

God, I hope it's not a water birth. I don't really fancy having to plodge around for hours in a lukewarm paddling pool.

'I want to start off naturally, with no drips or monitors or bright lights. And no popping.'

'What?'

'I hate it when they say just pop yourself over there, pop up on to the bed, that sort of thing. I hate it. It makes me want to scream.'

'Right.'

'I mean if anyone is less likely to be popping herself

anywhere it's got to be a woman who's nine months pregnant. Stagger would be better, or heave. The Consultant says it all the time. I've only seen him once but he didn't actually make direct eye contact once, and he's really pompous. Mr Hamilton-Parr. It might be good if you could give him a quick slap if he turns up.'

Actually, I'm not really sure I'm up for this after all, but it's a bit late to say so now.

'OK. Well, that sounds good to me. Slapping, and no popping. I can do that. No problem.'

9

SEPTEMBER

If You're Happy and You Know It Clap Your Hands

Garden Diary

Plant winter cabbages and spinach, clean borders and take cuttings. Plant bulbs by throwing them in handfuls and then plant them where they fall to give a natural effect, avoiding clumps or dark shade. Put netting over ponds to keep out leaves.

Plant bulbs in a tub by the back door: I tried the throwing-them-in-handfuls thing but half of them disappeared under the hedge. I also rake up some leaves and add them to the bonfire pile. At the weekend I try to light it, after spending ages poking through with a rake trying to make sure we're not about to cremate any hedgehogs. Actually getting the bloody thing to light isn't as easy as I'd thought and I end up using all the Sunday newspapers and three long-burning fire lighters before it finally catches, and then flames shoot into the air and look like they'll burn down the fence, and possibly the house. Alfie goes into pyromaniac mode, and leaps about being a Red Indian. I stand by with a

219

bucket of water to throw on him if he doesn't calm down. He's desperate to throw things into the fire, and just when I've finished explaining that this is in fact very dangerous and completely forbidden by Boy Scouts etc he throws one of his slippers into the flames, and cackles in a Lord of the Flies-*type way. Jesus. Who knew bonfires could be so stressful.*

A LFIE'S FIRST DAY AT school turns out to be less traumatic than I feared, and he looks really sweet in his school sweatshirt: I don't understand why some primary schools insist on jamming four-year-olds into stiff shirts and ties. It looks vaguely fetishistic to me.

Both Alfie and Lily go in perfectly happily, Alfie swinging his new Batman lunchbox and Lily chatting to the teacher, who seems very jolly. It's slightly disconcerting when she walks up to us and says hello, mummies, are we excited about our first day? but Alfie and Lily seem to like it. I've had nightmares about Alfie clinging on the gate and refusing to go in, but in fact the only one near to tears is me. I'm sure he'll be fine. He liked the practice afternoon, and he knows loads of the other kids. But still.

When I get into work Mum is on the phone straightaway, wanting a full account. She says she's been sitting on the edge of her seat since dawn, but didn't want to ring in case it made us more nervous.

'Oh well, thank heavens he went in happy.'

'Yes, and he knows lots of children already, from playgroup.'

'He'll be fine.'

'Yes.'

'Ring me the minute you get in – promise?'

'Yes, Mum, I promise.'

'Or you could call me on your mobile in the car, when you're driving home. As long as you pull over and stop. I'm not having you driving along talking into that headset thingy. I saw a man doing it the other day, and he was swerving all over the place. I wrote down his number plate, just in case, and I've got a good mind to ring up the police, so they can keep it on file, in case he does it again.'

'All right, Mum, I promise.'

Home time turns out to be a bit of an anticlimax too, thank god, and Alfie doesn't announce that he's never going again or has already been bullied by a horrible big boy at playtime, which were my top two worries. Instead he comes out, looking shattered, with only one sock on, for some reason, and no lunchbox, and says it was quite nice, and he did drawing, and Mrs Trent said he was a very good boy, and then he wants to know what's for tea, and says he hates pasta, in fact he has always hated pasta and will not be eating it under any circumstances.

I offer baked potato and tuna, which apparently would be even worse and would make him actually have to be sick, and we end up compromising on sausages and peas with mashed potato, but only if I make sure it isn't lumpy, and doesn't have those black bits in. I only put pepper in once, but he's never really got over it.

Molly says Lily seems fine too, although she says her lunch was horrible and other girls had juice, not bottles of water, and she wants Sunny Delight like Natasha.

'It's started already. Now we're at the mercy of what the other kids have.'

'I know. And Sunny Delight's full of rubbish. Do you think if I bought a bottle I could fill it up with something less disgusting?'

'Yes, but I don't think it's a very good idea.'

'I know, but in her first few weeks I just want her to be happy.'

'Well, maybe you could do it for a bit. Oh, and buy a few bottles.'

'Why?'

'Because once Alfie works out she's got it, he'll want it too.'

* * *

221

Patric calls just after tea to talk to Alfie about his first day at school, which is quite sweet of him. Actually, I've noticed he doesn't seem to be annoying me so much lately, and at least he turns up to see Alfie fairly regularly, and that's what counts. He made a big fuss of his new school sweatshirt at the weekend, and took photographs and everything.

Even though he usually finds something to be irritating about, I just don't feel so angry with him any more. I think it's finally starting to fade. I can't see that he'll ever be top of my list of people I'd want to be stuck on a desert island with, because apart from anything else he'd be moaning so much I'd probably have to drown him, but as long as he carries on being around for Alfie then I think we'll be fine.

I'm even starting to feel slightly sorry for Cindy. She told me at the weekend that the holiday was a bit of a disaster. Apparently he insisted on working for most of the first week, and was either on his laptop or the mobile, and then the heat-rash situation went to code red and she had to call a doctor who turned up and gave him an enormous injection, for some reason, probably just for a laugh because he was making such a fuss. And then he slept for nearly forty-eight hours and she was worried he'd gone into a coma.

I've just finished making Alfie's packed lunch ready for the morning when Jim phones, to see how his first day was, and then he asks me how Molly's doing, and ends up confessing that he thought something might happen, because when he went to the pub with Dan he sort of hinted that something was going on with Lola.

'And you didn't think to tell me? You total pillock.'

'Oh well, Scouts' honour and all that, and anyway he didn't actually say anything. It was more vague than that, and I did tell him to steer well clear.'

'Well, he obviously took that to heart then, didn't he? What exactly did he say?'

'Not much, just that she was always flirting with him, when he was round doing the garden and stuff, nothing

222

definite, and how he was finding it pretty hard-going with Molly.'

'Well, I still think you might have told me. I could have kept an eye out, and warned Molly or something.'

'You couldn't have, you know. You can't go around accusing people of having affairs until you know they are. And by then it's too late.'

'I suppose so.'

'Anyway he's a silly sod – she's lovely, Molly, and that Lola's a nightmare, if you ask me. Anyone could see that. What a prick.'

'Well, if he rings you I'd avoid that line, if I were you. Try to talk to him.'

'Oh I'd never have thought of that. Thanks so much. Anyway I don't think he'll call me – he knows I'll be on the girls' side on this one. I was telling him about some bloke in the office who left his wife when she was pregnant, and we agreed that it was real pond-life behaviour.'

'He hasn't left her, you know – he's just staying with his mum while they sort things out. Molly can't handle any more drama until after the baby's born, but they haven't decided anything.'

'Back at his mum's. Poor sod. I bet she's giving him a right bollocking.'

One of Molly's chickens has run away from home. Actually, it's probably been eaten by a fox, but Molly's convinced it ran away and is getting really obsessed with it. I think it's some weird version of the nesting phase you're supposed to go into just before you give birth.

'It must be so horrible living with me – even the chickens are running away.'

'Molly, Frank said it was bound to be a fox, didn't he?'

'Yes.'

'Well, then. Stop it. How was the doctor's?'

'Oh my blood pressure's still up a bit, but nothing serious.'

'Pop up on the couch?'

'Yes. That's probably why my blood pressure was up. And all this lounging about is driving me mad, and I really am worried about the chickens, you know. I thought maybe I could get another two. That would take it up to six, and that's a good number, apparently. I've been reading up on it, and you have to be really careful introducing new ones or they get henpecked.'

'So what do you have to do then? Get them all counselling or something?'

'No. But you have to make sure the new hens are old enough, at least twenty weeks, and you have to let them get used to each other. You can buy special rubber things called bumper bits, to put on the beaks of the bullies to stop them pecking the new girls. I wish we had them at school.'

'Blimey. It's not very *Little House on the Prairie*, is it? Rubber devices for chickens.'

'I know, but will you come with me? I want to get them tomorrow, and start getting them settled.'

'Oh all right.'

Great. I've got loads of work to do, and now I have to go out and help Molly choose chickens.

We go to some batty birdwoman Elsie recommends, who breeds chickens and ducks, and end up with two hens who take ages to catch. We put them in the run when we get them home, while the others are roaming round the garden, and they all eye each other up a bit. God, even I feel a bit tense, and we haven't actually got the rubber things, and Christ knows how we'd get them on even if we did. Molly thinks Poppy in particular would very much mind having a rubber device stuck on her beak. But they all seem fairly friendly, thank god, so we let the new girls out for a trial run and there's a bit of barging and shoving, but no seriously threatening behaviour.

'What a relief. But I think I'll still keep them separate at night, though. They can sleep in the run when the others are in the henhouse, and I'll introduce them gradually.'

'OK.'

'You think I'm losing it, don't you?'

'No. Well, maybe slightly. But I can see it would be pretty tragic to end up with a bullied chicken on your hands on top of everything else. I'm just glad you didn't decide to go in for sheep. God knows what they get up to.'

'Did you know chickens can only count up to two, so if they're really broody you only have to leave them two eggs and they're fine. I think I might let Poppy have some chicks. She keeps hiding her eggs in the hedge and she seems very keen. And she really pecks at you when you try to collect them.'

'Right.'

'Don't look at me like that. I do realise I sound like a total nutter, you know.'

'Good. You had me worried there for a minute.'

'Coffee? It'll have to be decaff, I'm afraid – it's all I've got.'

'Fine.'

We sit in the kitchen watching the chickens bonding and Molly says Dan came round last night with a cardigan from Doreen for the baby.

'But I think he was just hoping for a chat.'

'And how did that go?'

'I went and had a bath – I couldn't face it. I just don't want to see him at the moment, I really don't. It's like I can almost pretend he's off on some job if I don't actually see him. Lily showed him her new reading book, though, and it was nice for her, I think, him coming round. But I just can't cope with it, not when I'm feeling like this. It's just too much. Actually getting myself out of bed's a bit of a challenge at the moment. Do you think that's just the baby and everything, me zoning out ready for the birth?'

'I'm sure it is.'

'Good, because I can't seem to get the energy up to do anything much. I was going to go up and see the garden today, but I was just too tired. And I really want to see it, before tomorrow. Did Charles say what time the judges are due?'

'Any time after ten, I think.'

Charles rang up in a state of high excitement yesterday. The judges came down last week and they'd just called to say we'd made it through to the final round of the competition. Apparently Mrs Pomeroy got so excited she actually kissed Mr Channing, so now they're both in shock.

'I've taken the morning off work, but I should go in for the afternoon. I hope they don't hang about.'

'I'll come to you after the school run and we can walk up the lane, if you like. If you promise to go slowly.'

'OK. I can't work out what to wear, though. I mean I know we're supposed to be amateurs but I want to make the right impression.'

'You look lovely in your new skirt. That velvet one. And that's not too businessy.'

'OK, I'll wear that. God, I hope they don't ask me any tricky gardening questions. I don't want to let the side down.'

'You'll be fine.'

I'm really nervous about the judges. I so want them to like the garden, and I'm terrified they're going to ask me something and I'll get it wrong. Name this plant, that kind of thing, or a trick question about the best way to pollinate fruit trees.

Molly and I are sitting in the summerhouse waiting for them to arrive, and I'm trying to take deep breaths in the hope that I'll stop feeling quite so sick.

'They're here, don't panic, they've just arrived.'

Mrs Pomeroy looks very close to panic to me.

'You stay here, and we'll introduce you on our way round.'

We catch glimpses of Charles and a huddle of judges, being tailed by Frank and Bill and Mrs Pomeroy and Graham Poltney. They spend ages looking at plants and we can hear them talking. It all sounds pretty technical to me, and lots of Latin plant names are being bandied about, although occasionally you hear something familiar like carrots or lavender from Charles.

'And this is Alice, and Molly. They both helped us get the project started. Alice is our designer and this is her first garden, but I'm sure it's just the first of many. She's obviously got a talent for it, don't you think?'

Blimey, Mrs Pomeroy's laying it on a bit thick. But the judges nod and start asking me about the ideas behind the design, and why I went for such a linear water feature, so I blather on about wanting moving water, both for the noise and the light reflected on to the plants and the bricks, but nothing too deep since the children use the garden quite a lot, and they all nod and say very sensible, terribly dangerous some of these deep ponds.

The two older judges are very friendly, especially the woman, who's got a lovely smile and very nice earrings that look like silver daisies, but the younger man is more tricky and says I seem to have drawn on lots of influences in my design and did I have one overall concept, or what? Oh dear. I'm assuming it won't go down very well if I say I just looked through stacks of books and nicked anything I liked the look of and then tried to put it all together.

'Well, I wanted to suggest a secret garden, but one with a structural sense to it. And I wanted it to feel like you're going on a journey as you walk round the different pathways. I knew the Garden Society would come up with wonderful planting ideas, but I wanted to give them a definite framework. And I didn't want it to feel totally traditional so I tried to make it a space that could be used differently by different people, especially the children.'

Everyone seems rather impressed by this. In fact I'm pretty impressed with it myself. I knew reading all those gardening books would come in handy one day.

'If you follow me, I'll show you the children's play house, and their vegetables. They're particularly proud of their tomatoes.'

Right on cue Mrs Bishop arrives with Mabel, in her party

dress, and she leads the way, taking the hand of the younger judge and telling him all about growing beans, and how Jack climbed up his beanstalk but we don't do that because it might break. God knows how Charles arranged it. He must have had Mrs Bishop on standby hovering just outside the doorway, but the judges are enchanted.

They make another circuit of the garden, and ask a few more technical questions, and there's a slightly tricky moment when Mr Poltney and the woman judge end up bickering about the best type of apple for a really reliable crop, but then we all move into the house where Mrs Bishop's made lunch.

The judges say there's really no need to feed them, and coffee would have been fine, but Mrs Bishop says oh no, you can't come all this way and only have a cup of coffee, and anyway it was no trouble, the ladies from the WI did it, and they love any excuse to put on a spread.

Elsie introduces herself and says they're a terribly nosy lot and didn't want to get left out, more like, while Mrs Pomeroy glares at her. The judges all smile.

'I can see this is a really village project.'

'Oh yes. They're all taking it really serious, and you'd better give them the top prize – they've worked really hard, you know, the lot of them. The whole village, practically. If they haven't given plants they've given barrowloads of compost. Me and Frank drove up and down in that car collecting it all, and it took us hours, I can tell you. But as my old dad used to say, spend a penny on the plants and a shilling on the hole, and it's certainly paid off, hasn't it? I've never seen such healthy veg. Even my Ted, god rest him, he would have been hard put to match it, and he was a champion, you know. Won the gold medal for his cauliflowers, three years in a row. And caulis can be tricky, as you know. Well, you probably do know, being judges.'

'Oh yes, quite.'

'Do come and meet some more of the team.'

Mrs Pomeroy firmly steers the judges away from Elsie,

who doesn't seem at all bothered and concentrates on getting her wine glass refilled.

Molly says she's feeling a bit hot, so we go back outside into the garden with Charles.

'Well, I think that went all right.'

'Yes. And it was a brilliant idea to have Mabel show them the play house.'

'Oh that was Mrs Bishop's idea. Do you want some coffee, by the way? I got some decaff specially for you, Molly.'

'Lovely.'

'I won't be a minute then.'

He goes off back to the house, and I notice Molly's gone a bit pale.

'Are you all right, Moll? You seem a bit quiet.'

'Yes. I'm fine. But promise you won't panic.'

'What do you mean? No, I won't bloody promise. What?'

'Well, I think my waters just broke. Either that or this seat's suddenly got wet.'

'Oh my god.'

I leap up, and sure enough she looks like she's sitting in a small puddle.

'Jesus Christ. All right, don't panic.'

'I'm not panicking, I'm fine. It's you that's panicking. Just calm down and take deep breaths.'

I don't believe this. She's the one about to give birth, and she's telling me to take deep breaths.

'Oh god, all right, just hang on, and I'll go and get the car.'

'You might have trouble fitting it through the garden gate, don't you think?'

'Oh right. Yes. OK, well, can you walk? We can take it slowly, and get you to my car. Oh bugger, we walked up. My car's back down the lane.'

Molly smiles and says she'll be fine walking, and then Charles comes back.

'I'm afraid I can't find the decaff – Mrs Bishop must

have put it somewhere, but I can make tea. What's the matter?'

'Molly's gone into labour and my car's down the lane and I don't think she should walk, do you? I think it's too far.'

'I'm fine, really.'

'What? Oh. You mean? Oh. Right. Well, use my car, yes, take mine. I'll go and get the keys. And he rushes off to the house.

He says he'll pick up Alfie and Lily from school later, in my car, and I give him my car keys, which I finally find in the bottom of my handbag after another mini panic. Jesus, I'm going to be a complete wreck before we even get to the hospital.

By the time we drive off everyone seems to know that Molly has gone into labour, and they all wave us off, and Elsie heartily recommends that Molly has an epidemic like her June, who apparently said they could have cut her legs off and she wouldn't have known a thing about it. So that's encouraging. Actually, I think I might need one if I don't calm down soon.

The judges seem very impressed that Molly has put in an appearance even though she's in the middle of giving birth, and I hear one of them saying they're obviously all terribly dedicated while I'm getting Molly into the car.

I make her get in the back, just in case she needs to lie down or anything.

'Are you all right?'

'Yes.'

She's puffing quite a lot.

'You can stop that puffing right now. You're not at the puffing stage, are you? Jesus Christ, tell me you're not at the puffing bit yet.'

'No. I'm just practising.'

'Well, bloody stop it. Just breathe. Are you getting proper contractions?'

'Oh yes. I have been for quite a while.'

'How many minutes apart?'

'I haven't really timed them – I've lost my watch.'

'What? Well, why on earth didn't you say?'

'Oh, it's bound to take hours – stop fussing.'

'Molly. If you're getting one-minute contractions and start pushing in the back of this car, I will never forgive you. Is that clear? Oh I know, I've just had a really good idea. I'll call an ambulance on my mobile and get them to meet us, some-where along the way. Shall I do that?'

'No, really, it's not anywhere near every minute yet. I'm sure it'll be hours.'

It's really weird driving through town with Molly in the back panting and puffing. People are going to the supermarket, and generally dithering about, and I want to wind down the window and yell at them to get out of the way.

Actually, the car is so flash it has electric windows and all sorts of buttons, which I don't really understand and don't dare push, and we have to listen to 'Here We Go Round the Mulberry Bush' quite a few times because I can't work out how to turn off the CD player. I daren't fiddle about with it in case I find the emergency airbag-testing button or something interesting like that.

I've got a funny feeling I may have pressed the button that warms up my seat, because it feels really hot, but that might just be residual panic warming up the leather. But at least it's automatic, and Charles said you really can't go wrong unless you put it into four-wheel drive, and then it might make a funny noise. It feels very high up, and I can almost under-stand why Range Rover drivers are always such pricks. It makes you feel so superior. Well, if you haven't got a woman in labour on the back seat it probably does.

I'm driving quite fast, and I'm sort of hoping a police car will pull us over and then escort us to the hospital with flashing lights. But naturally when you really need a police-man to tell you off for speeding they're all back at the police station polishing their helmets.

*　　*　　*

231

When we arrive at the hospital I want to drive right up to the front door, but Molly insists we park properly or Charles will get his car clamped. It takes me ages to find a space, and then I can't get the bloody thing parked because it's so enormous. I finally manage but then I can only open the door about three inches, and realise I'll have to limbo out. Which won't really work with Molly, so I have to reverse back out, help her out and then drive back in. At this rate the baby will be born in the bloody car park.

'Come on, let's go. Are you all right?'

'I think so.'

'You're doing brilliantly. Just take your time. Shall I go and find a wheelchair?'

'Don't you bloody dare. Ooh, here comes another one.'

We stand in the middle of the car park, and she turns to face me and puts her arms on my shoulders. And then she presses down, really hard, and I almost fall over.

'Oh that was great, that really helped.'

'Good.'

Bloody hell. If she's going to do that all afternoon I'm going to end up about three foot six.

The labour ward seems fairly efficient, apart from the retarded receptionist who takes ten minutes to type Molly's surname into her computer before pressing the wrong button so she has to start all over again. But they soon have us in a room, with Molly hooked up to a monitor. She's at four centimetres, apparently, which could mean she's got ages to go yet, or it could mean all hell will be let loose in the next hour and a half.

She's being very calm, and talking about having a go with the gas and air, but so far she's managing with deep breathing and the odd bit of squeezing my hand. I'm trying really hard to avoid too much of that pressing-down-on-my-shoulders thing.

'I haven't got my bag. I've got things for the baby, but it's all in my bag at home. I've got my tapes in there as well – I wanted to have music.'

'I can ring Janice, or Mum, and get them to bring it in, if you like.'

'Yes, that's a good idea. Go and call Janice, she's got keys, and could you ring Doreen, actually maybe Janice could pick Lily up from Charles's, and then she can stay with her until my mum gets here. I called her this morning, because I had a feeling this might happen, so she's already on her way. And while you're at it get yourself a coffee or something. You look like you need one.'

'All right, if you're sure you'll be OK on your own for a bit. Do you want anything?'

'Opal Fruits.'

'What?'

'Opal Fruits. I had them last time, and I really want some now. Except I think they've got a stupid new name now.'

'Like Snickers.'

'Yes. Whoever thought that one up must be a total moron.'

'Anything else?'

'Yes, chocolate. Mars Bar or a Topic. And maybe some juice?'

I ring Mum, who gets very excited and says she'll ring Janice and one of them will bring Molly's bag over. I find the hospital shop and stock up on chocolate bars and juice, and Opal Fruits/Starbursts, and then have a quick look round to see if they've got anything else Molly might fancy.

They've got the most tragic collection of baby clothes you've ever seen, all in horrible pastel colours with teddy bears in white satin on the front. Why can't they just have plain stretchy towelling ones? I mean who really wants a peach Babygro with a satin lamb on the front?

But lurking at the back is a plain white cotton sleepsuit, which is a newborn size and looks so tiny it makes you want to burst into tears just looking at it. I buy it in case Molly's bag doesn't arrive in time. And then I see some face wipes and some lip balm, which I remember wanting when I had Alfie, so I buy them as well, along with a couple of bottles of mineral water. The cafeteria is right next door so I have a quick cup of possibly the nastiest coffee I've ever tasted and then go back to Molly.

She loves the sleepsuit, and drinks the juice. Various doctors and midwives troop in and out and all say something slightly different, but basically she's doing really well and the baby's heartbeat is fine, and we walk about a bit, and then I rub her back, and she does a bit of rather tight hand-holding and shoulder-pressing and I lose all the feeling in my fingers, and then she really starts to find it a bit tough, and she says it's much worse than it was with Lily and she wants an epidural. And she wants it Now.

I go out and find the midwife. She's sitting having a cup of coffee and I don't really like to interrupt her. But on the other hand I don't want Molly in pain while she sits here having a coffee break. She gives me a filthy look.

'Yes.'

'Um, she's finding it a bit hard now. She'd like an epidural.'

'Right. Well, I'll be along in a minute.'

'I'll just wait here for you, shall I? While you call the anaesthetist? Only I think someone told us that only an anaesthetist can do it, and they sometimes take a while. So if you don't mind I think I'd rather you phoned now, and then finished your coffee. I mean there's no reason why she should wait any longer than she needs to, when she's in pain. Is there?'

I give her what I hope is a rather determined look, but I think it might have gone a bit threatening. She reaches for the phone.

They rig up a mobile epidural so Molly can still move about but she can't really feel anything, and she gets a lot more chirpy and eats her Mars Bar while nobody's looking.

The nurses are changing shifts and a new midwife comes on, called Billy, who is very obviously gay, and reminds me of

Graham Norton, although without the shiny suit, obviously, or the celebrity guests.

'Hello, my darlings, and how are we today?'

I like him already.

'Fine now the epidural's kicked in. What on earth is that?'

He's brought in a giant pink rubber ball with him, like a space hopper only with no ears to hold on to.

'It's a birthing ball. You sit on it and bounce around and it opens up your pelvis.'

'I'm not sure I really fancy bouncing just at the moment.'

'Oh no, it's not for you, not with your epidural. It might get a bit tricky, you might get all tangled up with your line or something. No, I thought I might have a go, to cheer you up. I think you need a laugh when you get to this stage, don't you? And some women like to give it a good kick. Actually, one of my patients threw one at her husband last week. Nearly knocked him over, although I wouldn't recommend that. But he was a right prat, so I didn't blame her. Now, would you mind if I had a quick look, sweetheart, just to see how you're doing? If that's OK with you?'

No popping. Excellent.

'Fine.'

'Ooh six centimetres. Well done. Well, this baby's not hanging about. IVF, was it?'

'What?'

'IVF. My friends Amy and Donna, they went IVF. Did you two have to wait long? Only it took ages for them to get on a list.'

It takes a minute for this to sink in, and then Molly laughs and says, 'Um, we're not actually a couple. This is my best friend, Alice. My partner's away at the moment, working.'

'Oh. Well, I've just made a right tit of myself then, haven't I? Oh please don't tell anyone – they're in a terrible flap out there trying to be all PC. We don't get a lot of lesbian couples in here, and Sister's trying so hard not to be shocked. Bless.'

'Oh. Right. Well, I won't say anything.'

'I can just tell we're going to get on – you're going to be one of the ones I really like. I'll be back in a minute – is there anything you want? Water, or ice or anything? We've got ice chips now, like on the telly.'

'Oh, well, yes, ice chips would be great.'

'Okeydokey. Back in a jiff.'

'Bloody hell. Shouldn't one of us have shorter hair or something? I mean if we were lesbians wouldn't one of us have short hair?'

'Alice. Don't be a twit.'

'Sorry. It's rather flattering really, but I hope they don't say anything to Mum when she brings your bag in. She'll have a complete fit.'

Billy, who says all his friends call him Silly Billy and we can as well, only not in front of the doctors, says that Molly is doing brilliantly. But gradually over the next hour he stops cracking jokes and starts watching Molly quite closely, and she goes very quiet and says she feels sick, and Billy says that's normal and she says she knows it is, but couldn't she just have a little sleep?

She's lying down now, and Billy's put her back on the monitor, which suddenly starts bleeping. He fiddles with the switches and says everything looks fine but I think he's getting worried, and so am I.

Then in the space of about ten minutes everything gets really scary. Billy is doing her blood pressure, which he says has gone up. A lot. She looks really pale now, and then she starts to ramble a bit, and mutters something about the chickens and how tired she is, and then she says she's got a terrible headache and she starts to cry.

I stroke her back, and Billy goes off and comes back with a doctor, and the next thing I know she seems to be almost asleep and they're rushing her bed along the corridor to a theatre for an emergency Caesarean. It's all really frightening, and I've got a horrible feeling I might be sick.

A nurse takes me into a cubicle outside the theatre and tells me to put on a gown and mask, and a hat, and hurry up because they're not going to hang about. They're green elastic J-cloth things, and I spend quite a long time trying to put the hat on before a nurse tells me that that bit is actually meant to go over your shoes, and the hats are on the shelf over there.

By the time she leads me into the operating theatre Molly is already on the operating table. They've put a green cloth screen up over her chest so she can't see what they're doing, and she still looks really pale, but now she looks frightened as well. I hold her hand and she starts saying something about how if anything goes wrong I'll look after the baby, won't I, but I pretend not to hear.

'You will, won't you? Promise me, Alice.'

'Yes, I promise, but it's going to be fine.'

'And Lily too?'

'Yes. Now stop it.'

If she carries on like this I'm going to end up in hysterics, and I bet they throw you out of theatre if you start sobbing.

There are two doctors and an anaesthetist who's fiddling around with all sorts of wires, which he's attaching to Molly by a clip that goes on one of her fingers, and she's got another drip in her hand now. There are three nurses as well as Billy, and one of them is wheeling over a trolley full of instruments, all of which look pretty terrifying, and then another doctor comes in and says she's a paediatrician, and she'll be checking the baby over as soon as it's delivered, so we're not to worry if they don't pass it straight over. Billy says this is just a precaution and they always get the paediatrician in for C-sections. Jesus Christ. I was bloody worried enough before the paediatrician turned up.

Molly's crying again, but silently. Tears are sliding down her cheeks and on to the green sheet she's lying on, making a dark circle which starts to spread outwards, and I watch it getting bigger and keep stroking her hand, and then she starts to shiver, which Billy says is quite normal, and often happens when they top up an epidural ready for a Caesarean.

God, I hope it's nothing to do with her having eaten that

Mars Bar. I briefly wonder if I should tell them, because I'm sure you're not supposed to eat things in case you're sick when you're unconscious. But if she's not unconscious it must be all right. Although when she closes her eyes she looks pretty close.

I try not to look over the screen, and keep stroking her hand, but somehow I can't help it, and then without any warning at all, which frankly I could have done with, the young woman doctor picks up a scalpel and cuts a line across Molly's tummy and I come so close to fainting it's a miracle that I actually remain upright. I can't believe Molly hasn't leapt off the table in agony, but she looks like she hasn't felt a thing. God, this is amazing. It's so shocking that you want to scream at them to stop, but at the same time it's completely fascinating.

One of the doctors asks Molly if she's chosen any names yet.

'Jack if it's a boy, I think, and Alice, if it's a girl.'

Oh god, I really am going to cry now. I feel a tear rolling down my cheek into my mask. I wonder how many other people have stood here, crying into their masks. I keep thinking, Please let it be all right, let them both be all right, while I squeeze her hand and she smiles, very faintly.

The nurses have been chatting and checking the instruments, and the doctor's describing what she's doing using all sorts of medical terminology, so I think the other doctor must be some kind of junior and she's training him, when suddenly they all go quiet.

The doctor seems to be rummaging about and everyone is looking at Molly's tummy. The room is totally silent except for the beeping of machines. I hold my breath. And then suddenly a tiny foot appears and a second later a baby is lifted into the air and the doctor says, 'Well, here's Jack.'

He's sort of waxy and purple, and then suddenly he starts to go pink, and he spreads his arms out like he's trying to catch hold of something, and his hands are like tiny starfish. And then he gives a little cry like he's been startled out of a long sleep and the doctor hands him to the paediatrician. She takes a quick look and carries him round to Molly, all wrapped up tight in a little green sheet.

And when she sees him. The look on her face. It's just magic. She smiles and her eyes fill with tears and she says hello, and then she breathes out. A really long deep breath, like she's been waiting all these months and now she can finally relax.

And he's got those dark navy-blue eyes newborns have and thick waxy black hair and he's looking at Molly and he's perfect. I can see Alfie when I look at him and for a moment I don't think I'm going to be able to stop myself from running out and going home to find him.

But then Billy hands the baby to me and tells Molly that we're going to take him upstairs to the ward to get him washed and dressed.

'So he'll be ready for you when you come up.'

'Yes, but let me have a few more minutes with him first.'

So we stand there while she looks at him. And he looks at her. And she puts her hand up to his face, the hand with the needles in for the drip, all covered up in white surgical tape. And she strokes his hair, with one finger, and smiles.

Billy pats her shoulder.

'He's lovely. Well done.'

'Thank you.'

'We'll get him upstairs now.'

'Alice.'

'Yes.'

'You'll stay with him, won't you, until they bring me up?'

'Of course I will, sweetheart.'

Wearing a mask means I can't give her a kiss, so I put my hand on her cheek and say I'm so proud of her and he's perfect and I notice one of the nurses stiffens slightly. Blimey, word must have got round.

'I'll watch him for you, and I won't let him out of my sight, I promise.'

*   *   *

239

We put him in his little plastic tank when we get out of the theatre, and wheel him through the corridors and up in the lift and everyone who sees him smiles. Billy washes him very gently with cotton wool, and he just blinks and stretches and doesn't make any kind of fuss, and at one point he locks his gaze on to mine and I just stand there, staring into his eyes, and I can't believe he's only just been born.

'This is the best job in the world, at moments like this.'

'Oh yes, I can see that.'

'It still gets me. Every time. Look at him, little poppet. And he's big too – just over nine pounds.'

I put him in the sleepsuit, which is only just big enough, and I'd forgotten how tiny newborns are, and about the cord and everything, and I feel very clumsy.

Billy wheels the cot round to a bed on a side-ward, and says he'll leave us here for a minute while he goes to get Molly's notes. And then one of the nurses brings Mum in. She says they've kept her waiting downstairs for ages, with Molly's bag.

'Mum, this is Jack.'

'Oh bless him, isn't he lovely? Where's Molly?'

'Still downstairs. She had a Caesarean but she's fine.'

'And what about you?'

'What? Oh fine. Oh Mum, it was so amazing.'

And to my horror I find myself clinging on to her and sobbing. Which is pathetic really, because everything's lovely, and he's perfect and Molly's fine. So god knows what I'm crying about. Mum pats my back like she used to do when I was little.

'He's lovely. I'm so proud of you.'

'Oh Mum, it's nothing to do with me. It's all down to Molly – she was just brilliant.'

'Yes. But I'm still very proud of you.'

No wonder Patric said that being there when Alfie was born was the most terrifying thing he's ever done. I mean when you're the one on the trolley it's bad enough, but somehow standing there all helpless and trying to be strong and encouraging when you're actually frightened out of your wits is almost worse. And Molly made much less fuss than I did – she was so amazing. I almost feel tempted to ring him, just to say I understand a bit more now. But he'd probably think I was trying to make some point and end up getting all defensive.

I sit holding on to the crib while Mum goes off to find some tea, and then a nurse and a porter arrive with Molly and lift her on to the bed, and get her settled. She looks tired, but very happy.

'Let me hold him.'

I pick him up and put him into her arms and she cradles him and strokes his hair.

'Do you want a pillow under your arm?'

'Please.'

I prop two pillows from the next bed under her arm.

'Thanks, Alice. Thanks. You were great.'

'So were you.'

'He's pretty fantastic, isn't he?'

'Amazing.'

'He looks quite like Lily when she was born.'

'Does he?'

'Yes. Only he's got more hair.'

'Well, he's perfect.'

'Mum's brought your bag in. Do you want me to unpack it for you?'

'Oh yes please.'

'She's just gone for some tea. Do you want some? Or a drink? Can you have anything yet?'

'I don't know. They said I'll have to have this catheter in until morning, and this drip too, probably. But they didn't say anything about drinking.'

'I'll go and find out, shall I?'

'Yes. In a minute. Just stay here with me for a while. I still feel a bit weird.'

We sit and she asks me to hold him, but so she can still see him, and then a nurse arrives and says they've got the blood results back and Molly needs a blood transfusion, and she puts another drip stand by the bed and hangs a big bag of blood from it. It looks almost black, and slightly menacing, but within a few minutes the drip's doing its thing and Molly starts to go a bit pinker.

The nurse hovers and keeps checking her blood pressure, and then Mum comes back with the tea and says congratulations, and he's the most beautiful baby she's ever seen.

And then she says she'd better go and get Alfie, and I walk her to the lift and she says she hoped I didn't mind about her saying Jack was beautiful, because of course Alfie was much more beautiful, which is so sweet it makes me tearful all over again.

I creep back into the ward and we sit and whisper about how lucky she is to have such a perfect son, until they both start to fall asleep. A new nurse comes in and smiles at me and hands me the baby while she very gently checks Molly's blood pressure without actually waking her up. So I sit there giving him a cuddle, and then I put him into his crib on his back, and roll up a blanket and tuck it down one side like I used to with Alfie so he felt all snuggled up.

'I'll come back tomorrow, first thing. Tell her, when she wakes up. I'll be back in the morning.'

'OK. And congratulations. He's lovely.'

When I get out into the car park I can't find the car. After about ten minutes I remember we came in the Range Rover and I'm just about to get in when Dan walks over and says hello, rather tentatively.

'Is she all right?'

'Yes, she's fine. She had to have a Caesarean because her blood pressure went a bit weird but she was wonderful.'

He makes a coughing noise like he's being strangled and then the tears start, but without any noise, like he's not even aware that he's crying.

'I'm sorry, just ignore me, I'm so sorry. I've fucked everything up, haven't I? And Mum rang and told me and I didn't know what to do. I've been so worried.'

'Of course you have. Oh Dan, I'm sorry, but she's fine. And the baby's lovely.'

Somehow it just doesn't seem right to tell him that he's got a son while we're standing in a car park, like he's just some interested passer-by, so I put my arms round him and give him a hug, and whisper into his ear, 'He's lovely. A lovely big beautiful boy, and Molly says he looks like Lily did when she was born. And she made me get her Opal Fruits, just like you did last time.'

And then he breaks down and sobs. Really sobs. We stand there for ages, and he says he doesn't want to go in, in case she's asleep or it upsets her, but he'll call later and come back tomorrow. And then he asks me about the baby again, and what colour hair he's got, and am I sure Molly's all right.

He looks so lost when he walks back to his car I have to sit and pull myself together a bit before I drive home.

When I get back there are no lights on at home so Mum and Alfie must still be up the lane with Charles. I drive up and park the car, and find Charles sitting in the kitchen surrounded by teapots.

'I made tea, but then it got cold, so I made some more.'

'Right. Lovely.'

'The children are fine. Molly's mum collected Lily, and Alfie's upstairs watching a film with your mum. She's terrific, isn't she? She was so excited when she got back from the hospital, and so full of how great you'd been.'

'Oh well, I don't know about that. I nearly fainted and I've been crying half the afternoon. Not exactly a rock.'

'And Molly's all right?'

'I think so. They've given her a transfusion and she seemed much better when I left. I mean tired, obviously, but a much more normal colour and everything.'

'Oh I'm so glad. Here, I've made you some sandwiches – I thought you might be hungry. Actually, Mrs Bishop made some much nicer ones, but the children ate them. So I've made some more. They're not very delicate.'

He passes me a plate of very thickly cut cheese sandwiches.

'Great. I'm starving. But I want to see Alfie first.'

I go upstairs for a quick cuddle, but he's not really that keen because he's deeply involved in his film. Mum tells me to go back down and get something to eat because I can't have had a thing for hours, and then we'll go home when the film finishes.

The sandwiches are great, and we talk about babies and birth and Charles says the first time he saw Ezra he remembers thinking he was going to try to do everything he could to make sure he was always happy and felt safe.

'But it hasn't really turned out like that. I mean at least my father managed to hang on to my mother. We probably shouldn't have had children, you know. I don't know why we did really. Lola just decided and that was it. It was as if we'd got the house and the car so we'd better have the children, like they were some sort of – what's that phrase Lola's always using – consumer something, consumer durable, that's it, like children were some sort of consumer durable.'

'Well, they certainly consume a great deal.'

'I was reading something in the paper the other day, about Alpha women, and you know, I think the trouble is that Lola's an Alpha woman, definitely, whereas I'm a Delta. Or an Effer, if they have Fs, I can't remember. Anyway, what she needs is an Alpha male.'

'Well, whatever an Alpha male is, he'd have his work cut out for him.'

'True. But I do feel guilty. About the children, I mean. Did I tell you Ezra's started wetting the bed again?'

'Charles. You've got to stop it, you know. You can't go on like this, blaming yourself for everything. Lola may well be an Alpha woman, but she's also an Alpha bitch, and you're better off without her. You've just got to start being happy and upbeat for the kids. Sorry, I'm really tired – I didn't mean to be rude.'

'No, it's all right. I think you're probably right.'

'I think you're a great dad, I really do. You try your best, and that's what really counts, in the end, whatever letter of the alphabet you are. Everybody knows that, and I'm sure Ezra does too.'

'I hope so. Sometimes he looks at me as if I'm such an idiot, it's almost frightening.'

'Oh they all do that. Alfie does it all the time. It's just part of growing up, I think, looking at your parents like they're morons.'

'Oh. Right. Well, that's a relief.'

Mum comes home with us and then says she'd better be off to sort out something to eat for Dad, who sends his love and says he's glad that the baby arrived safely.

Alfie is very excited about the new baby being a boy, and has already chosen a sword to lend him when he comes round to play. It takes me ages to get him settled, and then Molly rings and says she's got the nurse to wheel a phone to her bed.

'Mum's bringing Lily in tomorrow morning, but will you come in first? I want to look nice for Lily, and I'll need to put a clean nightie on, and could you bring a bit of make-up or something, so I don't look too washed out? I haven't got any, and I must look dreadful, and I don't want her to get worried.'

'You look fine, but of course I'll come.'

'Do you think she'll like him?'

'Oh sweetheart, do you want me to come back? You sound a bit wobbly.'

'No, I'm fine. It's just the hormones, I think, or this morphine stuff they're giving me.'

'Is there anything else you need?'

'No, I don't think so. He's asleep and I think I'll sleep too, in a bit. I just keep looking at him. He's so lovely.'

'He's perfect. Get some sleep, and I'll see you in the morning.'

*   *   *

Mum says she'll take Alfie to school, so I go into the hospital early and they've both slept a bit, and Molly looks much better. She gets really nervous before Lily arrives, but she's so happy to see Molly it's fine, although she's still slightly annoyed that the baby's a boy. But at least he's got her a present, a Barbie, with a car, so she's pretty impressed. Molly must have had it all ready in her bag.

And then Dan arrives, and stands at the end of the bed looking slightly awkward.

'You can hold him, if you like.'

Molly smiles. He walks towards her and picks up the baby from his crib, and looks close to tears before walking very fast straight out into the corridor.

'Where's Daddy going?'

'Oh I think he's just having a little walk. He'll be back in a minute.'

And sure enough he comes straight back, and has obviously pulled himself together.

'He's pretty special, isn't he?'

'Yes.'

'But not as special as Lily, of course.'

'Oh no, nobody could be as nice as our Lily.'

And Lily nods and I suddenly feel I'm intruding, so I say I'm going off in search of tea and will be back in a bit. When I get back Dan and Lily have gone.

'He seemed pretty knocked out with him, didn't he?'

'Yes. But then we all are. He's a very special baby.'

'They're all special, Alice.'

'I know. But he's extra special.'

'Yes. He is. He slept nearly all night, you know.'

'Blimey. Well, don't count your chickens.'

'Talking of which –'

'Yes. I know. I will feed them, I promise. I forgot last night but I'll go round later.'

'I'll get Mum to do it. I forgot to tell her, but I'll call her later.'

'It's all right.'

'No, you've done more than enough. I can't ever really tell you what it meant to me, you know, having you there. You were great.'

'Well, I wouldn't have missed it for the world. I really wouldn't. It was wonderful.'

'Not even my death-grip shoulder press?'

'Well, maybe not that. You could have warned me, you know. I think one of my shoulders is lower than the other one now. Maybe I should get a parrot.'

'Dan had backache for weeks after Lily.'

'Now you tell me.'

'What am I going to do, Alice?'

'I don't know, sweetheart. There's no rush. Wait until you get home and see how you feel.'

'Yes, but what if I don't know how I feel? Half of me just wanted him to stay today, and for us to pretend that nothing happened, but the other half just can't get over it.'

She starts to cry. Oh god.

'I know. It'll take time, Moll. Just give it time.'

'Do you want a cuddle?'

'What, and freak out the nurses, you mean?'

'No, the baby, you fool.'

'Oh yes please. I thought you'd never ask.'

10

OCTOBER

Hickory Dickory Dock

Garden Diary

Collect fallen leaves. Harvest spinach and greens before frost. Move tender plants into pots and place in sheltered areas. Plant out winter tubs and baskets.

The gutters are filling up with leaves and overflowing every time it rains, so I find the step-ladder and poke about with a stick. Thankfully Alfie's at school, or he'd definitely be standing at the bottom of the ladder shaking it. I end up with a bucketful of horrible leaf sludge, which is rather satisfying in a weird way, and I decide to start a compost heap. I pile it up in a corner behind the garage along with the leaves I've raked up from the lawn, but then I'm not really sure what you're supposed to do next. Before I get a chance to read up on it when I get him home from school, Alfie decides that leaf sludge is the perfect thing for SAS-type camouflage manoeuvres, and spreads it all over his face and hands, and comes into the kitchen crawling on all fours and threatening to blow the house up if I don't give him some biscuits. Great.

MOLLY AND JACK ARE coming home from hospital today, and half the village is on standby to welcome them back. I've been given so many tiny blue cardigans I've lost count. Practically every single woman in this village must be a champion knitter, and even Elsie has done him a hat, which is very sweet of her, and at least it's not pale-blue; although I'm not completely sure lime-green is going to be his favourite colour either.

Molly's all ready to go when I arrive to collect them, and is desperate to get home. Jack sleeps all the way in his car seat, which is probably a good thing because I'm driving very slowly so Molly doesn't get too jiggled about. In fact I'm driving so slowly other cars start flashing at me, and I have to do that daft waving-your-hand-out-of-the-window-in-a-sort-of-circle thing to tell other cars to pass us, and a man in a Jag gets a slightly different sort of hand signal, that only requires the use of one finger, when he pulls alongside us and toots and tries to look threatening. Creep. If he'd woken Jack up I would have taken his number for Mum to include him on her 'Dangerous Drivers I've Spotted Recently' report for her Neighbourhood Watch Group. Apparently some poor police liaison officer has drawn the short straw and now he has to visit her group, and Mum's determined he'll get plenty of good information to take back to the station.

Molly's mum Mary is waiting for us when we get in, and the entire house is sparkling. She's probably even washed the chickens. Mum's been round to help, and so has Doreen, and it turns out they all share the same views on the right way to clean a kitchen: in other words properly, on your hands and knees, not just squirting a bit of Dettox and wafting a J-cloth about. Mary's even made shepherd's pie for lunch, which was Molly's favourite apparently when she was little.

'I've used that vegetarian meat stuff, Quark or whatever it's called. I don't know what it'll taste like, mind, but it looks all right. So whenever you're hungry just you let me know, pet. It won't take ten minutes to heat up.'

There's a pile of presents on the chair in the living room.

'Thanks, Mum. Who are all these from?'

'Oh well, things from your Aunty Pam, and me and your dad – just a few little bits to start him off properly. Alice, you will stay for lunch, won't you? There's plenty.'

'I really should be off. I've got work I should be getting on with.'

'Well, what about a cup of tea then, before you go?'

'Oh yes please. And Molly, I meant to say, I've got loads more presents at my house. I'll bring them round later. Your boy is not going to be short of a cardigan, put it that way.'

'It's so lovely to be home, it really is.'

She's started opening some of the presents, and seems to be having a little cry. But it's one of those hormonal everything's-perfect-so-why-do-I-keep-crying moments, rather than anything serious, so I decide to pretend I haven't noticed while Mary makes the tea.

Jack wakes up and we all fuss over him, which he seems to like, and then I leave them to have lunch and say I'll see them tomorrow. Mary's taken over feeding the chickens so I'm looking forward to a quiet evening.

I'm just finishing the washing up after tea when a mouse runs out from under the fridge and disappears under the cooker. Alfie's absolutely thrilled, but I think I'm going to be sick. I can hear it scratching at something; at least I think I can. It's probably three fields away by now. But it might not be. It might be watching me from under the fridge. Oh god, I think I really am going to be sick.

I briefly wonder about dialling 999, but I'm fairly sure the police would take a pretty dim view of being called out to deal with a mouse. Maybe Mum's neighbourhood watch one might come round, though. I wonder if she's got a hotline number or something. Bugger, bugger.

Alfie's lying on the floor shouting under the cooker, 'Come out mousey, come out.'

It better not bloody come out.

'It's lovely, isn't it, Mummy? It can be my pet. I can call him Eddie, like my chicken.'

Christ. If this latest episode in my perfect bloody life is going to involve using poison or traps or anything I'll have to keep it secret from Alfie or he'll be picketing the front door. I can just see him marching round the front garden with a placard, chanting 'Save Our Mousey'.

In the end I decide to call Charles, and he tells me about special mousetraps, where the mouse walks in and a little plastic door shuts behind it.

'Oh great. And then what do you do?'

'Take it out into the fields and let it go.'

'Oh, all right. That sounds OK. You don't have to actually touch it, do you? Only I couldn't cope with that.'

'No. You just hold the box. I've got one if you want to borrow it – we had mice when we first moved in. Well, one, at least. I didn't tell Lola – I knew she'd insist on having the whole house fumigated. It's probably just a field mouse.'

'Well, it should be in a bloody field then, not under my fridge.'

'Go and buy some chocolate mousse and I'll bring the box down.'

'What?'

'Chocolate mousse. They love it. Gets them every time.'

Bloody hell. We go to the village shop and buy chocolate trifle, which is the closest they've got, and Alfie tells the lady behind the till it's for our mousey, but luckily she just smiles at him and obviously thinks he's talking rubbish.

Charles arrives with Ezra and Mabel, who are mad keen to see the mouse, and we fill the plastic box with trifle, which the children think is a shocking waste of good pudding, and then we sit in the living room and have a drink and a biscuit and try to take their minds off anything to do with rodents. But when Charles goes back into the kitchen to make some more tea the bloody thing's already gone into the box, and is now scratching about, covered in chocolate.

Alfie lies down next to the box and has a little chat.

'Please can we keep him?'

Luckily Charles is ready with all the answers.

'He's a field mouse, Alfie. He needs to be free. Keeping him indoors would be very cruel.'

And more importantly it would completely freak me out.

'He needs to be out playing with his friends.'

Oh great. They have friends. I'll end up like the Pied Piper, and I'll have to bulk-buy chocolate trifles.

'What if it's a norphan?'

'A what?'

'A norphan, with no mummy and no friends.'

'It won't be. I promise.'

We eventually convince them all that we should take it out into the fields and release it. I'd quite like to drive it somewhere a few miles away, but I don't want to risk it escaping in the car, so we walk down the lane, looking like nutters, with the children singing 'Hickory Dickory Dock' and 'Three Blind Mice' at the top of their voices. It's almost dark as we climb over the gate and crouch down at the edge of the field.

'OK, mousey, off you go.'

We lift the door up, but the bloody thing won't move, and only peeps nervously out of the box. It looks rather sticky, and a bit pissed off, to be honest. It's tiny, and a very dark brown colour – but that might be the trifle – with a rather sweet little tail, not one of those horrible sick-making long things. Maybe it's a vole.

'Charles, do you think it might be a vole?'

'I think voles are bigger. Why?'

'Well, if I tell Mum we had a vole under the fridge she might not freak out so much.'

'Fair enough. A vole it is then. A chocoholic vole.'

It finally plucks up courage and darts off, straight across the field towards the woods. But as we walk towards the house I'm sure I can see it running along the edge of the field. The bastard thing's probably racing us back home to see if there's any trifle left.

As we get in Charles says he'd better get the children home. Ezra's still sulking because he wanted to keep the mouse in his bedroom.

'Thanks, Charles, really. For lending us the box and everything.'

'My pleasure. Just don't call me if it's spiders. I hate spiders.'

'Oh I don't mind them. At least you don't have to buy them trifle.'

There are no more scratching noises, but as I'm getting into bed I'm sure I can hear something. The flaming thing's probably come back. After totally freaking myself out for about ten minutes I put the duvet over my head so I can't hear the noise, and decide that it's time to get serious. No more trifle. I'll call the council tomorrow and get the poison man round. I know it's cruel. But I don't care. Even if they are voles, they're bloody noisy ones. And they're not living in my ceiling. Or under my fridge.

Molly's finding it rather hard-going with her mum and Doreen. They've developed a sort of dual fussing routine, involving lots of cups of tea and suggestions that Molly might like a nice little nap.

Her mum's just dropped her off with Jack while she goes to the supermarket.

'They're both being so sweet, and I'm really grateful, honestly, but they keep washing everything, and every ten minutes there's another bloody snack.'

'Tell me about it. Mum's gone into a complete frenzy since I told her about the mouse. She's been on a bleach fest ever since.'

'Did the council turn up?'

'Yup. He's put loads of trays up in the attic, and he's

coming back next week. Your mum will be going home soon, though, won't she?'

'Next week, after I've been to the hospital. As long as they say I'm fine. Dad's coming down at the weekend to collect her. She must be really tired, you know. She gets up every time he cries, even in the middle of the night. Actually, I'm really going to miss that.'

'I bet you will. And how's Dan?'

Dan's taken to calling in at teatime, and he picked Lily up from school yesterday.

'He seems fine, but Lily got stroppy when he left last night. He said he had to go to work, but she didn't like it. That's the first time she's really minded. He was quite upset. But we had a long talk yesterday, and he finally said how unhappy he was. He's never admitted that before.'

'Well, that's a good sign. I mean if you're really talking about things now.'

'I know, but it's bloody hard. It'd be much easier just to blame it all on him, but that's not completely fair. I've been shutting him out, for quite a while in a way, sort of taking him for granted. I was so busy with everything else, I just never noticed how unhappy he was.'

She looks close to tears.

'Don't get me wrong. I don't want to turn into one of those women who say it was their fault when some bastard hits them. No, he made a mistake. A big mistake. And it's going to take us a long time to get over it. I hate the idea of him with her, I really do. But in a way that sort of helps. It's made me realise how much I love him. Otherwise I don't think I'd care, would I?'

'No, I suppose you wouldn't.'

'And I don't want us to split up, not really. If I could rewind and wipe out all that stuff I would. But I can't.'

I don't think she can quite bear to say Lola's name.

'And then there's Lily, and Jack, and I want to do the right thing by them. But if it's not right then I think we're all better off out of it. I mean I think staying together for the sake of the children is just bollocks – it doesn't help anybody. I mean poor old Doreen tried that, and look how happy she is. But he is a really great dad. And that counts for something, doesn't it?'

'Oh yes. It counts for an awful lot.'

'So I was thinking maybe the grown-up thing to do is to forgive and forget.'

'Maybe.'

'But I don't feel very grown-up.'

She says this in a very small voice.

'I know, sweetheart, but maybe you could have a trial few days or something?'

'No, I've thought about that, but we'd both be watching all the time for the slightest thing. It would make us too nervous. I think we need to have a fresh start, and really give it a go, for a month or two, not keep picking away at it. I think I'm going to ask him to move back in for a few months, and see if we can get past it. And if we can't, then at least I'll know.'

'You're an amazing woman, you know that, Molly.'

She smiles.

'So should I tell him then?'

'Yes. Ring him up. Ring him now, if you like.'

And she does, while I go and rake up leaves.

She comes out into the garden and says he sounded very relieved.

'And then he went all quiet.'

She looks close to tears again.

'You really love him, Moll, don't you?'

'Yes. I think I've finally realised that I do. Despite everything. I do.'

Molly's mum's finally gone home, and Dan's moved back, and even though it's all very fragile they seem to be coping. Molly says it's a bit like walking on eggshells, but Lily's much more settled. I don't envy her – it must be hard work having to tiptoe round things all the time.

I'm still on my nightly mouse alert, but at least Alfie's

decided that mice are boring, and he's back to wanting a pet rabbit. Some helpful person from the RSPCA brought one into school last week, so he thinks he's an expert now. I might get him one for Christmas, as long as I can get him to promise not to dig rabbit holes all over the lawn again.

I can't really believe I'm thinking about Christmas already, but Mum keeps going on about making lists, which is starting to make me panic. She rang up yesterday morning at half-past seven to ask me if I thought she should get a present for Stella this year, and if so what did I think about a travel iron, because she'd seen a nice one in Debenhams. Sometimes I just don't know how Dad copes.

I'm round at Molly's for my daily cuddle with Jack when Charles arrives, looking all pink and flustered.

'Oh good, you're both here. I called at your house, Alice, but you weren't there. It's fantastic news. We won a silver medal, in the competition. A silver medal. Isn't that great?'

Apparently Mrs Pomeroy is euphoric, and says the competition people want to come down and take pictures for a magazine article, and she thinks we might even get on the telly. It's really exciting, and even though I know it's all down to the plants, and the fact that Molly went into labour in the middle of the judges' visit, I can't help feeling a tiny bit pleased that my design didn't actually make any of them laugh out loud.

'I must go, I want to make sure someone's told Elsie. But it's fantastic, isn't it? I'm so proud of everybody. Especially you, Alice. Well done.'

And he gives both me and Molly a kiss, and goes even more pink, and then rushes off to tell Elsie.

'God, isn't he nice, going round to tell Elsie. I've been thinking about having a tea party or something, to say thank you to everyone for all the things they made for Jack, and show him off. But now it can be a double celebration. What do you think?'

'Great, if you're sure it won't be too much work.'

'Well, I've got an ulterior motive, to be honest. I want everyone to know Dan and I are back together. I mean nobody's said anything, but they all know he wasn't around, and they must have put two and two together.'

'And made six probably.'

'Yes, so I thought if they see us together it would kind of clear the air. The only problem is Charles.'

'What do you mean?'

'Well, I want to ask him, of course, but I don't want him to feel uncomfortable. You know how he is, he won't want to say no, but I think he might want to avoid being in the same room as Dan. What do you think? I thought I might ring up and ask him how he'd feel about it, but then I realised that might not be very tactful.'

'So you'd like me to have a go?'

'Well, yes, but only if you don't mind. I really want him to come, but I don't want him to feel he has to.'

'All right. I'll try to sound him out next time I talk to him.'

I decide to go up to the garden just before lunch, in the hope that he'll be there. It's still looking lovely. Mr Channing has planted new things in the beds where the strawberries and tomatoes were, including some purple cabbage that looks great. The bay tree in the middle of one of the herb beds looks much bigger now, and all sorts of new shapes are emerging now the autumn has arrived.

Charles is tidying up the paths, and I clear the rills of leaves and then we stop for a coffee.

'How's Molly doing? She looked much better this morning.'

'Yes, she is. And Dan's moved back – did you know?'

'Has he? Oh good, I'm so glad.'

'Are you?'

'Oh yes. I don't really blame him, you know. Lola can be pretty determined. I mean I don't think I'll ever count him as a close friend, but I'm pleased for Molly, I really am.'

'Well, that's very grown-up of you.'

'Oh I don't know. I mean it would be different if we were the perfect couple before it happened. If I'd been madly in love I'd have wanted to kill him.'

'Well, if you're really sure. She's having a little tea party, to sort of show the baby off, and say thank you to everyone, and she wants you to come. But only if you won't mind, with Dan and everything.'

He smiles.

'Oh. No, I think I could cope with that, and it would stop people gossiping. Mrs Bishop keeps asking me about Lola.'

'I bet she does. She'll be on a mission to find out.'

'I just say it had been coming for a while, and it was a mutual decision and all that. I mean I don't want people feeling sorry for me.'

'Of course not.'

'Actually, coming to tea at Molly's might be quite handy. Put pay to any rumours.'

'Good. Well, it's next week, but I'll get her to call you.'

'Fine. I spoke to her earlier, Lola I mean. She rang, mainly to let me know she's seeing someone else, someone from work, and she's rented a flat. She's coming down this weekend to see the children. She had to cancel last weekend at the last minute – too much work or something.'

'God, I don't believe her sometimes.'

'And she definitely wants a divorce now – she's hired a lawyer. Some really expensive one. I'm sure I've seen his name in the papers.'

'Do you mind?'

'No. I thought I might but I really don't. It's a bit of a relief, actually. I suppose I'll have to sort out someone to act for me, maybe someone local.'

'Oh that's a good idea. And then Lola's flash London lawyer can completely screw you. Honestly, Charles, don't you dare. Get someone really expensive, who can give as good as they get.'

'You're probably right.'

'Sorry. I didn't mean to be bossy, but just don't let her walk all over you, all right?'

He gives me a funny little smile.

'I promise.'

There's a slightly awkward silence.

'I've been meaning to ask you about the village school, actually. What do you think of it? Only I thought I might move Ezra.'

'I think that's a great idea. It's nice and friendly, and the teachers are really kind. I'm sure they'd keep an eye on him.'

They'll have to, because he's been worse than usual lately, which isn't surprising, I suppose. But even so I'm glad he won't be in Alfie's class.

'He can be so sweet sometimes, you know. I mean admittedly he's being pretty revolting at the moment. But really he's quite shy and he desperately wants people to like him.'

I feel rather mean now.

'They're all revolting sometimes.'

'Yes, but the trouble is he's so jealous of Mabel. I don't think I've handled that very well. I mean we got all the books and we talked about it but somehow we never really followed anything through.'

'Why don't you make a time, once a week or something, when just the two of you go out, just you and him. Drop Mabel off with me, if you like. And you can tell him how proud you are of him.'

Bloody hell. He's gone quite red. I hope I haven't said the wrong thing.

'Oh Alice, that's such a great idea. I think he'd really like that. Especially if Mabel was banned. Are you sure you wouldn't mind? I could ask Mrs Bishop. Actually, my mother's been offering to help. Maybe she could have Mabel once a week or something. She finds Ezra rather hard-going. I'll call her tonight.'

'Good. Well, let me know if she's busy.'

I hope she can do it, because I'm really frantic with work at the moment, and Alfie's going through a phase of not sleeping too well, so I'm extra knackered. I think it's something to do with starting school – Mum says we were both the same when we started school, and he'll soon settle down. I bloody hope so, because it's very annoying being calm and reassuring at three in the morning.

And I hope Charles gets something sorted out with Ezra. It's really sweet how hard he's trying. I don't suppose being packed off to boarding school is exactly the ideal preparation for parenthood, but at least he's giving it his best shot. And I know it shouldn't be more impressive when a man worries about his kids, Molly's right, it really shouldn't be, it's absolute bollocks. But somehow it just sort of is, although I wouldn't actually admit this out loud to anybody.

Molly's tea party is a big success. Mrs Pomeroy's in her element, and spends most of the afternoon showing people all her photographs. Everyone seems to have decided not to mention Lola. Apart from Elsie, of course.

'So where's your Lola got to then?'

'Elsie, really.'

But you can tell Mrs Pomeroy's agog for the answer too.

'Well, nobody's seen her for weeks. Gone off to London, has she? Well, good riddance, I say. Always seemed a bit too fond of the sound of her own voice, that one. She wasn't good enough for you, if you ask me.'

Charles laughs.

'Oh, that's very nice of you, Elsie, but I'm sure she wouldn't agree.'

'I bet she'll turn up when the magazine people are here.'

'I don't think so. She's rather busy at the moment.'

'Oh she'll find time, if it involves a bit of glory. Like some other people I could mention. We didn't see a lot of them when it came down to digging in the pouring rain, did we? But now we've won a prize they're all here.'

Mrs Pomeroy leads Elsie away, and makes a face at us behind her back, and Charles laughs.

'I don't know why you're laughing – she's right, you know. I bet she'll turn up and try to take over.'

'Oh no she won't. We've already talked about it, and she told me to make sure she got proper credit, since it was all her idea. I told her to get stuffed.'

'You didn't.'

'I did. It was marvellous. I said the Garden Society would keep any prizes, because they did most of the work, and the credit was all yours, for the design. She wasn't very pleased, I can tell you.'

'Oh good for you.'

I wish I could have seen her face.

Mr Channing comes over and starts to talk to Charles about winter-planting ideas, and Molly passes Jack to me.

'He'll scream if I put him down, but I need to collect up some cups.'

'No problem. Is Alfie still in the garden with Dan?'

'Yes, they're looking at the new chicks.'

'Jack's really getting bigger now, isn't he? He feels a lot heavier.'

'That's probably down to the fact that he never stops feeding. The only thing he's not terribly keen on is sleeping at the moment.'

'Alfie got a bit better when he started having baby rice and stuff. I think that helps.'

'I've got a funny feeling it's going to take more than baby rice to shut this one up.'

We walk into the kitchen and I sit down, but Jack starts to cry so I have to stand up and jiggle him a bit. I'd forgotten about the jiggling thing.

'Doreen says Dan was a terrible sleeper too.'

'How is she?'

'Fine. Sort of. She still comes round and takes him out for walks, which is great. And she's still being really bossy, but she's saving most of it for Dan now.'

'Oh dear.'

'And I keep finding myself getting really angry with him for no reason, and then I see him sort of shut down and I hate it. But I can't see any way out of it – I think we've just got to get through it. There are good bits too, when we're all together and he's playing with Lily or Jack, and he smiles at me. Things like that. But it's a lot harder than I thought it was going to be.'

'It's bound to take time, Moll.'

'I know. It just feels like it might be quite a long time.'

'Well, at least you won't have to worry about the gossip now. Everyone seems to have accepted you're back together.'

'Yes. Oh but I didn't tell you, it was really sweet. Frank had a little word with Dan the other day, when he brought some onions round. Dan was mortified. He told him he hoped he realised what a bloody fool he'd been, and how he was glad he'd come to his senses, and did he realise how lucky he was that I'd let him come back.'

'Oh bless him.'

'Yes. And Bill's still not speaking to him, not really. I mean he's polite and everything, but he avoids him.'

'He'll get over it.'

'I know. I'm rather touched really. Dan is too in a funny sort of way.'

I take Jack out into the garden to see if a change of scenery will settle him down, and find Mr Channing and Frank hiding from Mrs Pomeroy.

'She'll find you in a minute.'

'Yes, but at least we'll have had a breather. She's writing an article for the local paper now, you know. There's no stopping her.'

'Well, that's quite a good idea, isn't it?'

'Yes. But she just takes over. I mean we might have a few ideas. Bill's on the committee too, you know. But she just goes off without asking and does what she thinks best.'

'Have you got any ideas then?'

'Well, no, not as such, but we might. Give us time. We need to raise money to sort the roof out, that's for definite. Or we might as well have our meetings outside. The rain was pouring in the other day.'

We talk about jumble sales and raffles and then Frank says we could do a calendar.

'Like that WI one. They made a fortune.'

He's very proud of himself for coming up with such a brilliant idea. But I don't think Bill's so sure.

'What, with us all starkers, you mean? Oh she wouldn't like that.'

Frank looks even more keen now.

'Well, so what? Elsie would be game, and we could stick Mrs P behind a wheelbarrow. If we could find one big enough.'

Actually, I'm not really sure I want to see Frank and Bill with just their hats on, but they're getting really enthusiastic about the idea.

'What are you three laughing at? It must be good, I could hear you in the house.'

'Charles, Frank's had a brilliant idea. We're going to do a gardening calendar, to raise money for the new roof. Naked Gardeners. What do you think?'

'Christ, you're not serious, are you?'

'Yes, we are. And we've elected you to be the person who explains it to Mrs Pomeroy.'

'Good God.'

Alfie tells me on the way home that he thinks babies are really boring.

'Lily says Jack just sleeps and cries all the time. That's not very nice, is it Mummy?'

'Well, all babies cry sometimes.'

'Yes. But chickens don't. And dogs don't. I think we should get a puppy, you know. It would be lovely. Much better than a silly baby.'

'You were a silly baby once, you know, Alfie.'

'Yes, but now I've growed up. And I want a dog. Everybody at my school has got a dog except me. It's awful.'

'Alfie, that's not true. Lily hasn't got a dog, for a start.'

'No, but she's got chickens. And anyway she's a girl. Girls don't have dogs, they have rabbits.'

'So you don't want a rabbit any more then?'

'No. They're stupid. I want a dog.'

'Alfie, I've told you, when you're bigger, maybe.'

'I can't wait that long. I can't. I hate you, Mummy. I double hate you.'

I'm at home trying to work on plans for another barn conversion which Malcolm has just dumped on me, but I keep getting interrupted. It's all very well being part of village life, and doing the garden has definitely meant I feel much more part of things now, but it does all tend to mean people keep ringing up or dropping in.

So far this morning Mrs Pomeroy's rung to say that the magazine people are coming down next week, and do I think we should let Elsie come, only you know what she's like. And then Charles calls to say we must make sure Elsie's not pushed out, and Frank drops in to say he's not sure he wants to be in a magazine, and do I think he has to wear a suit, only Mrs Pomeroy says he does, but we're meant to be gardeners and nobody wears a suit to do the garden except for poor Mr Pomeroy.

I suggest he checks with Mr Channing on the dress code, and then on his way out he tells me the roses need pruning and he'll do it for me if I like, and by the time he's left he's spotted loads of other important jobs that need doing in the garden, and says he'll bring Mr Channing round to help. So that will mean I'll have both of them twittering on for hours, which is very kind of them, obviously, but god knows how I'm supposed to get any work done.

I've just sat down after getting rid of Frank when there's another knock on the door. This is getting ridiculous. I open the door, ready to tell whoever it is to sod off and let me get on with some work.

It's Harry.

'Oh. Hello.'

'I was just passing, so I thought I'd call in. Is that OK?'

'Of course. Come in.'

Bugger. I'm wearing a tragic old jumper and jeans and I haven't even brushed my hair this morning. Not that it matters, of course. But still.

'Are you sure you're not busy?'

'No, not all. I was just going to make some coffee – do you want some?'

'Please. The front garden's looking pretty good. How's the back doing?'

'Go and have a look. I'll bring the coffee out, if you like. It's not too cold out there, is it?'

'Not in the sun, no, it's quite warm.'

'We won, by the way, a silver medal, for the new garden.'

'That's great, congratulations.'

'I'm sure your herbs helped.'

'Good.'

Naturally I've run out of fresh coffee, so I make do with instant and take the mugs out into the garden.

'So how are you then?'

'Fine. But it's all been a bit frantic. Lola and Charles have split up, and Molly and Dan nearly did too. Actually, they still might, I suppose.'

'Bloody hell, what brought all that on?'

'Lola and Dan were having an affair.'

'Crikey, he must be a total idiot. Why on earth would you want to go off with someone like Lola if you've got a woman like Molly at home?'

I've remembered why I liked him so much. Damn.

'Well, it's all right now. I mean Molly and Dan are back together, and they're trying to make it work. And the baby's really lovely.'

'Good, and how's Alfie?'

'Fine. He's started school.'

'Oh, of course. Does he like it?'

'Yes, so far. Although he's not too keen on dance. He tends to gallop about instead of being a tree.'

'I hated dance. We had to learn how to waltz with other boys. It was dreadful. And then they brought the girls in at the end of term, and that was even worse.'

'Alfie's not too keen on girls at the moment either. They're going through a rather macho phase in reception.'

'Oh I'm sure he'll come round eventually. Most of us do.'

Oh god, I think he's going to Say Something.

'I was wondering, actually, if you might fancy a drink or something one night. Maybe?'

'Oh Harry. I don't know. The past few weeks have only made things more complicated really. It's so hard just to avoid damaging each other, let alone getting it right. It's sort of made me even more determined not to screw everything up, for Alfie mainly, but me too, I suppose. I think it has to feel overwhelming if it's going to work. Like you just don't have a choice.'

'Oh. Right. Bugger. Well, I'm sure you're probably right. Just thought I'd mention it. You do know you're supposed to cut that parsley back, don't you? It'll go all leggy if you leave it like that. And that lavender needs cutting too.'

We talk about the garden for a bit, and I end up with another long list of vital jobs.

'Well I'd better be off, but thanks for the coffee. And maybe I'll see you, after a decent interval and all that, for me to get over my heartbreak.'

'I'd like that. And you're not really heartbroken, are you, Harry?'

'No. Disappointed, but not heartbroken. I'm not really the heartbroken type.'

Thank god for that. I really don't know what I would have done if he'd said yes, he was completely devastated. Seeing him again has reminded me just how much I like him, but I'm sure now that I've done the right thing. I just wish you could sleep with someone sort of off the record; although everyone knows that off the record has a horrible habit of becoming right back on the record just when you least expect it.

As he walks down the path to his car I'm very tempted to say I've changed my mind, because I've always really liked the way he walks, and he's got such great shoulders. But I manage to resist. Which is a good job too because apart from anything else I've still got the bloody plans to finish, and it's nearly time to pick Alfie up.

Alfie's learning the recorder, which is bad enough, but the really bad news is that he has to bring the flaming thing home to practise. Every night. Lily's learning too. They're both standing tooting away in the playground when we arrive to collect them. Molly's walked up, and Jack is fast asleep in his pram. Not for long, I bet.

'Lily, that's lovely, but put it in the pram now, and we can walk home.'

They both run around tooting.

I ask Molly if she thinks I can throw Alfie's recorder out of the car window on the way home, and blame it on a freak gust of wind.

'Good plan. Let me know if it works, and I'll try it tomorrow. I don't remember signing any forms for this. In fact I'm sure I didn't.'

'Yes we did, at the start of term – don't you remember? I thought they'd just do it in school time. Honestly. They might have said. If I'd known the idea was they brought them home I'd have said no.'

Alfie has found a new use for his recorder now, and is batting a small boy on the head with it.

'Alfie, stop that.'

'He started it.'

'Well, you stop it, right now. Come on, get in the car.'

'No. I want to walk home with Lily and Baby Jack. We're going to play our corders all the way home.'

'He can if he wants, I don't mind, and you know we should be looking on the bright side really.'

'How do you make that one out, Pollyanna?'

'Well, they do the trumpet at my school. Just think. They could both have trumpets.'

'Christ. Really?'

'Oh yes. And drums. Or violins. They're the worst, I think – it goes right through you. We have to have a rota for our music assemblies at school, otherwise everyone just hides in the staff-room.'

'I wish I could just hide somewhere – look at him. He's using it as a sword now. Alfie, stop that. You can't have a recorder if you're going to be silly with it.'

'Oh yes I can. Mrs Trent said I can have one, and she's in charge.'

'Get in the car. Now. Or there'll be no cartoons.'

'Yes, come on, Lily. Let's go. Don't do that, darling, you'll frighten Jack.'

'Alfie. I mean it.'

I've just had a really good idea.

'I know. Let's go home and ring up Daddy, Alfie, and you can play him a lovely tune down the phone.'

A trouble shared is a trouble halved. And anyway he was only telling me last weekend that I should be doing more to encourage Alfie's creativity.

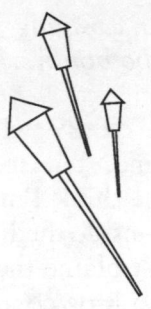

11

NOVEMBER

Rocket Man

Garden Diary

Sow over-wintering varieties of vegetables. Prune shrubs. Protect any late vegetables with fleece in frosty weather.

I go into a pruning frenzy with Frank and Mr Channing, who cut back all the bushes to small stumps. I can't believe they'll ever grow to full size again but they promise they will. We cut down the last of the herbs, and the smell is wonderful, and then we have another bonfire to get rid of all the pruned bits of bush, and I take the precaution of putting Alfie in his wellies, which he can't actually get off without help, so that we don't lose any more slippers. He wants to pretend we're camping, and cook sausages by poking them into the fire on sticks, but since I know this will end in tears or food poisoning, and most likely both, I persuade him that frying the sausages indoors and then eating them outside will be just as good. It's all going rather well until it starts to pour with rain, and Alfie drops his sausage in the mud. I try telling him that this makes it even more like proper camping but he's furious and throws his fork into the bonfire.

A LFIE'S DRIVING ME CRAZY with his recorder. Mum doesn't seem to mind, but if I have to hear 'Little Donkey' one more time I think I'm going to crack. Molly says the chickens all run inside the hen house whenever Lily starts to play, and I don't blame them.

The school's planning a little concert for the end of term, which should be a laugh. They're going for a modern theme and are putting on a musical extravaganza called *Music From Around the World. Music to Drive You Round the Bend*, more like it. Apparently the top class have got bongos, and Alfie's very jealous. So that's something to look forward to: bongos from year six, and 'Little Sodding Donkey' from reception.

I'm on the parent-helper rota for Alfie's class this afternoon, and I'm down to help with arts and crafts. I'm not really looking forward to it, to be honest, and Molly's been giving me her top tips.

'Wear clothing you can burn afterwards, and try to spot the trouble-maker as soon as you arrive.'

'How am I supposed to do that then?'

'Oh it won't be hard – believe me. It'll probably be a boy, although girls can be lethal too. And he'll be wandering about while everyone else is sitting down, and he won't make direct eye-contact, or if he does he'll just stare at you.'

'Jesus.'

'Just take him to one side and offer him a fiver if he cuts you some slack and behaves. That usually works.'

'Thanks so much. That's very encouraging.'

'And if anyone sees you just tell them it's positive-behaviour modification. That'll shut them up.'

Alfie's nowhere to be seen when I arrive, and Mrs Trent says he's making models with Miss Pilchester in the hall.

'Do go and have a look, if you'd like to, before you start with your group. I thought papier mâché, they all enjoy it so much, and we're making masks for our concert.'

Oh how fabulous, papier mâché. My favourite. I wander along to the hall and only just manage to see Alfie, since he's hidden behind the enormous box that he's painting red. At least he's got his painting pinny on, although he's still got quite a lot of red paint on his trousers and shoes.

'Hello, Mummy, look at my rocket.'

'It's lovely.'

Miss Pilchester, who must be at least eighty and has been a general helper at the school for decades, seems to be having a lovely time. She's sitting surrounded by pots of glue and lots of cardboard tubes and bits of shiny paper, cutting up a large sheet of black card.

'I'm helping Emily make booster rockets.'

'That's very nice.'

Christ. I don't think I can do this.

My group are all sitting waiting expectantly in their aprons when I get back to the classroom, and Mrs Trent's already briefed them, and they're raring to go.

'Now, Beaver Group, say hello to Alfie's mummy. She's going to help you make your masks.'

Bloody hell. Within five minutes there's glue everywhere. I think one small boy's actually stuck to his seat. We're tearing up newspaper like our lives depend on it, and our balloons are deflating rapidly. They're quite hard to keep hold of and keep shooting out of our hands and sticking to the floor, which requires lots of getting up and running round squealing. Mrs Trent's already had to come over twice, to restore order, and Andrew's already popped his balloon and had to start all over again.

'When can we paint them?'

'I think they have to dry first. Probably in a day or two.'

'I'm going to do a tiger.'

'That'll be nice. What about you, Andrew?'

'A larn.'

'Lovely.'

'Yes. A big larn to eat people right up.'

A couple of the girls look rather worried.

'It could be a nice lion, couldn't it? Like Elsa in *Born Free*. Have you seen that film?'

'Yes. But my dad says it's crap.'

'Oh, I quite liked it.'

He gives me a pitying look.

'My best film is Hannibal. He eats people, you know.'

He treats us all to quite a good impression of Hannibal Lecter, and the girls look even more worried. Actually, I'm feeling slightly nervous myself. I wonder if I should offer to slip him the fiver now, or wait until later.

'I think that's just made up, to make the film more exciting. It isn't real, you know.'

'Yes it is. My dad says. He says they ought to bring back hanging. That's when they kill you, on a bit of rope.'

We've finally covered our balloons, clothing, chairs and most of the table with small pieces of newspaper soaked in glue, so I think we're about done, when Mrs Trent claps her hands and says 'Fingers On Lips, Everybody. Now.' Some of my lot will probably get their fingers stuck to their mouths permanently.

Everybody who's finished tidying up has to sit on the mat and choose a book to read, quietly, and we have to be quiet little mice, and must tiptoe and make very tiny noises. So we all tiptoe about, until people start squeaking a bit too much, and Andrew says he's going to be a rat and bite Louis, and then Mrs Trent finds a special job for him, helping her with the paint pots.

Alfie comes back in with the rest of his group, and Miss Pilchester seems to have managed to get them all cleaned up and out of their aprons without any fuss at all, which is more than I can say for most of my group who are still trailing about with bits of newspaper. She helps me finish tidying while Mrs Trent sits down and starts reading them all a story.

Just before home time she gives them all a leaflet from the Fire Brigade.

'Now, everybody – Andrew, stop that, dear, that's not very nice, is it – do you remember the lovely fireman who came to see us in assembly?'

Yes, they do.

'Well, he's given us these leaflets to take home, to remind us. Sydney, if you keep doing that you'll have to go and sit in the home corner. To remind us all about how to be safe with fireworks. Can anybody remember some of the things he told us? Some of the things we have to remember not to do on Bonfire Night? Andrew, I hope you're not being silly again.'

Lots of little hands go up in the air.

'George?'

'Not to stick sparklers in your eye.'

'Well, yes, but I think he said not to wave them about too much, didn't he? Especially not near your face, or anybody else's.'

'Yes, and you've got to wear your gloves.'

'Well done, George, that's very good remembering. We must all wear our gloves, to keep our fingers safe. Anything else? Louis?'

'You're supposed to keep your fireworks with your biscuits?'

'Very good. We have to keep our fireworks in a biscuit tin, not a cardboard box. Does anybody know why? Sydney, please stop wriggling and sit up properly. Tommy?'

'What?'

'Do you know why we're supposed to keep our fireworks in a biscuit tin?'

'In case you want a biscuit?'

One or two of the girls snigger, but Tommy doesn't seem to care.

'I like biscuits.'

'That's very nice, Tommy, but I think there's another reason we're supposed to keep our fireworks in a tin. Alfie, do you know why?'

Oh dear.

'Yes, so the box doesn't catch on fire and blow you up, because it's very hard to set fire to biscuit tins, unless you've got a bomb. If you've got a bomb you could blow it right up.'

'Thank you, Alfie. Well done.'

I feel quite proud of him – he must have been really listening to Fireman Sam in assembly. What a rotten job that must be, touring round schools talking to mixed infants and trying not to give them all nightmares. Unless you get to bring your fire engine, of course. I bet that goes down extremely well.

'Let's all line up nicely with our coats on now. Natasha, I don't think you were first, were you? Go and sit back down on the mat. I think I'm going to choose people who are sitting nicely today, and the first person to go and get her coat and line up by the door can be Hannah.'

Alfie and I talk about the firework leaflet on the way home, and I congratulate him on remembering about biscuit tins.

'We can use our biscuit tin, can't we, Mummy? And I can eat all the biscuits.'

'We're not having the fireworks at our house, remember? Mabel's having a firework party for her birthday, isn't she? And Charles is doing the fireworks.'

'Has he got a biscuit tin?'

'I'm sure he has.'

'And gloves?'

'Yes.'

'Good.'

Charles calls to ask me if I think Mabel would prefer a Barbie cake for her birthday, or one of Mrs Bishop's special creations.

'Barbie, of course.'

'Oh. Right. Only Mrs Bishop's already started on hers, I think.'

'Well, that's all right – let her make one too. They're fabulous, her cakes, and there'll be loads of people round. Tell her you don't want to waste one of her special cakes on the kids, but if she could make one for the adults you'd be really grateful.'

'That's a good idea. She'll like that.'

'Has Lola decided if she's coming yet?'

'No, she's not, thank god. She's got some party at work, and anyway she's furious with me again.'

'Why?'

'Mainly because the article about the garden was so nice, I think, and nobody rang up to ask her for her comments on gardening.'

'Good job they didn't really. Bully someone else into doing it, and then try to take all the credit. Not very Vita Sackville-West, is it?'

'That's never stopped her before. She loves giving her opinions on stuff – she thinks it makes her look important. Every time I talk to her now I realise how much happier I am. I really think you've got it right, you know.'

'Got what right?'

'Being a single parent. It's so much simpler.'

'It's not always simple, you know. I mean for a start most of us don't have a big house in the country. Are you still getting deluged with food parcels, by any chance?'

'Yes. Fishcakes yesterday, from Mrs Norris, and some lovely vegetable soup from Elsie. And Mrs Bishop, of course, casseroles ahoy.'

'Well then. Nobody's even made me a sandwich, let alone a casserole. Well, apart from Mum, obviously, but you know what I mean. People don't usually rally round for single mothers – you're either a brazen hussy or an idiot.'

'Oh. So are you a brazen hussy then? How lovely. Do you have a special outfit? Because you don't usually look very brazen.'

God, how annoying. He's making fun of me now.

'It's not funny, Charles. A man only has to walk down the street pushing a bloody buggy and everyone thinks he's a hero.'

'Sorry. Well, you can have some of my soup, if you like. It's rather good, actually.'

'Alfie hates soup, but thanks. And I'm glad it's all working out, I really am.'

'Well, the children are definitely much happier, and that's the main thing, isn't it? I was thinking about it the other day, actually, and I don't think I was a very good father to them when Lola and I were together, you know. Somehow they seemed to get lost in the middle.'

He goes silent. I think he's remembering just how unhappy they all were.

'And I really enjoy looking after them now. Well, apart from the squabbling and the endless bloody searching for things. They seem to lose things the whole time – I think we've got some sort of black hole in our house, a sort of anti-matter chamber that absorbs socks and PE kit. But I'm enjoying it.'

'I always knew you were a good dad.'

'Oh Alice, what a lovely thing to say.'

'Well, it's true.'

Actually, I really love vegetable soup. I wonder if there's any way I can try to backtrack slightly on the soup thing.

Janet's still sulking about our winning the silver medal and my not having insisted on a mention for the firm in the magazine article. She's whining on at me about the state of my desk, and I'm just about to tell her to get stuffed when Brenda comes in and says there's a call for me, from a new client who'd seen the job I did for the Franklins. When she puts the call through it's actually her, back on reception, saying Janet's an old bag and I should just ignore her.

And then Mum rings to say Alfie's brought his spaceship home, because Mrs Trent says they haven't got room for it in the classroom.

'I had to get your father to put the roof rack on, and then I kept worrying that it would rain and the car would get covered in red paint. Have you seen the size of it?'

'Well, yes, I saw him painting it. It's just a big box, isn't it?'

'No, it's three big boxes, glued together. It's huge. It must have taken him hours.'

'Oh. Well, I can't wait to see it.'

'You won't be able to miss it – it's too big to get up the stairs. I've put it in the middle of the living room and it'll have to stay there until you can persuade him to take it apart and get it up to his bedroom. I've tried telling him but he won't have it. I hope you're not planning on having any visitors round.'

I'm sure she's exaggerating, but when I get home I realise she's not. Houston, we have a problem. It's absolutely enormous.

'Alfie, it's lovely. But I can't get into the kitchen very easily. Do you think we can move it a bit?'

'All right. But we're not going to unstick it. Nana says we can, but she's just being stupid.'

'Alfie. Don't be rude. Say sorry.'

'Sorry, Nana. Look, Mummy, it's got writing on.'

'For The Queen of the Galaxies' is written on the side, in glittery paint. I'm assuming he means the star systems, and not chocolate bars.

'Mrs Trent helped me, doing the writing. It's for you. It's a present. You can take it to your work, if you like. Or you can sit in it, or anything. It's your very own starship. Look, I've drawed on the handles and the buttons and everything. And it's got missiles.'

We sit in it and have a quick tour of the planets while Mum lays the table for tea. I never actually knew I wanted a starship before, but now I realise what I've been missing, and at least if I do take it into work Janet will be pleased. She's been trying to get me back in my box for ages.

'It's lovely, darling. Thank you so much.'

I'm going to have to build up really slowly to getting it upstairs. Maybe I can do it while he's asleep.

I'm on my way back home after dropping Alfie at school the next morning when I notice a large 'For Sale' sign has appeared by the turning into our lane. Christ. There aren't any other houses round here. Charles must have put the house up for sale. Bloody hell. He might have said. I drive up to the house and find him in the garden, digging over a flowerbed.

'I saw the "For Sale" sign.'

'Oh. Sorry about that. I meant to say.'

'You meant to say? Well, thanks a lot. Honestly, I thought we were friends, Charles. When were you going to mention it – when the removal van arrived?'

'No, but–'

'Well, I think you're mad. I mean why on earth sell now? It's ridiculous. The children are only just starting to settle. And what about the garden? What are the Garden Society supposed to do? Hope the new owners will let them in occasionally?'

'Look, it's sweet of you to be worried but –'

'I'm not being sweet. Don't be so patronising. And I'm not worried. Jesus. I just thought we were friends, that's all.'

'Alice. If you'd just shut up for a minute, I'll explain.'

Oh. Bugger. He's smiling.

'I'm not selling. I only asked them to value it, but you know what they're like, estate agents, always pushing their luck. I've just been talking to them, actually, and it'll be gone by this afternoon. The sign, I mean. So there's no need for the lecture. And we are friends. I hope.'

'Oh.'

'Quite.'

He's actually laughing now.

'Sorry. It's just –'

'Blast – what's he doing here?'

'Who?'

'My father, heading this way. Damn. My mother must have sent him round on a mission to lecture me about something. I wonder what I've done wrong now.'

'Well, I'll be off then, and sorry, about the sign thing, I just thought –'

'Oh no you don't. You can jolly well stay and give me some moral support – make up for your appalling hectoring. Hello, Dad, what are you doing here? We were just going to make some coffee. Alice, I think you met my father at Ezra's birthday party, didn't you?'

'Yes. Hello, Gerald. Lovely to see you again.'

'Hello, my dear.'

Charles smirks at me and walks back towards the house. Damn. Gerald seems quite agitated.

'I've given your mother the slip. Thought I'd pop over for a quick chat. No names, no pack drill, that sort of thing. So I'd appreciate it if you didn't mention it. You know how she gets.'

'Yes, you can't get a word in edgeways sometimes, can you?'

Charles gives me a very pointed look.

'Yes, well, I wanted a word, about your getting shot of that frightful woman, and not a moment too soon, by the look of things. What on earth is that sign for, by the gates? You're not selling up, are you? Bloody stupid time to sell. You're not falling at the first hurdle, are you? You need to stand up for yourself, you know.'

'Dad.'

'I thought you told me you liked it here, or your mother did. Have you called that chap I told you about? He's the bee's knees, you know, top barrister and all that. Of course he won't be cheap, charge you hundreds just for writing a letter. Bastards. But that's what you want, because you take my word for it, she'll be getting one. Anyway, that's why I wanted to talk to you – I've got a couple of little funds that your mother doesn't know about. And I want to keep it that way. Do you understand?'

'Yes, Dad, but –'

'So I don't want you doing anything stupid, letting her walk all over you. There'll be more than enough to see her off, and some left over, I shouldn't wonder. And you seem so happy here, and this gardening thingy, well, it's marvellous, winning medals and all that. Your mother's very proud of you, you know, and I am too. I mean a chap has to have a hobby. And well, that's it really. It's there if you need it. I just wanted you to know. And as for selling up you can just forget about that right now. I've never heard anything so bloody stupid.'

He's gone quite red, and Charles looks very touched.

'I've just been explaining to Alice, Dad. The house isn't on the market. I'm just getting a valuation, so I've got some figures together.'

'Right. Well, that's what I said. Good. Well, that's sorted then. And the money's yours, if you need it. No point keeping it until I'm gone. You might as well have it now. Only don't tell your mother, for god's sake. Now, what does a chap have to do to get a drink round here?'

As I'm leaving Charles is showing his dad some paintings he's just bought, and the old man seems very impressed.

'Well, lovely to have met you again, my dear.'

'Yes. Thanks for popping round, Alice. It's always nice to see you.'

Bugger. He's back to doing the smirking thing again.

Jim and Stella are having supper with us, on their way down to Brighton for the weekend. I've hidden Alfie's recorder because we've had 'Little Donkey' three times already, and Jim says he's gone deaf in one ear. Stella's upstairs reading to Alfie while we do the washing up.

'So how are Molly and Dan doing?'

'Fine. I think it's all still a bit fragile, but they seem to be all right.'

'Good. And what about you? No more visits from Harry? Still sure you did the right thing?'

'Yes.'

'Good, because I don't think we need any more nutters in this family.'

'He wasn't a nutter.'

'Oh yes he was. Growing herbs. Honestly. Waste of time, if you ask me. Bit of lawn and a flowerbed. What's wrong with that?'

'I'd never have thought of that. God, that would probably have won us a gold medal at Chelsea.'

'Oh, and I meant to tell you, I saw that Lola woman the other day, in a flash restaurant. She was throwing a fit about something. She didn't see me, though, thank god. So how's old Charlie boy coping then, without her? Bloody relieved, I should imagine.'

'Yes.'

'You've gone all red.'

'I have not.'

'Yes you have.'

'Well, it's just I made a bit of a fool of myself the other day. I thought he was selling the house and I went storming up there and told him off and it turned out he was only getting it valued.'

'Would that be a problem then, him selling? Oh, I see, you're getting keen on him. Is that it?'

'No, I just know he doesn't want to move, that's all.'

'Right. So you wouldn't mind at all then?'

'No. And anyway that's not the point.'

'Oh yes it is. Look, if you fancy him, what's your problem?'

'I didn't say that. I've never thought of him like that, and anyway he's still getting over Lola.'

'Yes. I can imagine she'd take a bit of getting over.'

'Exactly. And then there's the children. And I don't want Lola thinking I was after him, because I wasn't. I mean, I'm not. I didn't even really like him when they were together.'

'Fuck what she thinks. What do you care?'

'Well, I don't, not really. But I don't want people thinking I

281

had anything to do with them splitting up, and I don't want it to get tricky.'

'Tricky can be nice, you know. I mean by all means be a bit discreet, if you like, take it slowly. Pick a time when the kids aren't around, and go for it.'

'They're always around.'

'Well, ask him out for a drink.'

'Oh that's a great idea. And then Mrs Bishop can tell the whole village, and Mum can quiz me when I get back. That'll be very low-profile then.'

'Stop making excuses. Go for it, and may the force be with you.'

'Look, I've told you, there's nothing to go for.'

'You're a great one for putting things off.'

'Yes. And so are you. When exactly are you planning on telling Mum about you and Stella moving in together?'

'How did you know about that?'

'Stella told me.'

'God, she'd be a crap secret agent.'

'She's really happy.'

'So am I, and I was going to say, but I don't want Mum knowing just yet, or she'll start going on about us getting married. You know she will. She's pinning all her hopes on us now, for the full monty white wedding. It's all your fault.'

'Oh well, that makes a change.'

Charles has had to cancel his firework party, twice, because of torrential rain. It was so stormy last week you could barely stand upright, let alone light a sparkler. But the weather's finally cleared and the party's back on for tonight. Mabel's had her birthday tea party earlier with her friends from playgroup, with Mrs Bishop and Molly helping out, and apparently it was bedlam, but they all enjoyed themselves, and Jack loved watching the children running around.

The firework party has turned into quite a gathering and Charles has ended up inviting nearly the whole village. Frank's doing the bonfire, and he's been collecting wood and bits of old furniture for days now, and covering it all up with plastic and tarpaulin in a big heap in the middle of the lawn, where Charles is planning a new flowerbed. He's putting the finishing touches to it, and telling me that a good fire really helps a garden.

'Purifies the earth, fire does. And wood ash is a great fertiliser. It'll give everything a head start.'

'I didn't know that. Should I be putting the ashes from my fire round the flowerbeds then?'

'Yes, but dig it in well. This reminds me of when we used to have a big bonfire on the village green, you know, when I was a boy. We used to gather up the wood for weeks, and go round the other villages on our bikes and nick bits of their wood too. It took a bit of skill, I can tell you, cycling home with big planks of wood balanced on your handlebars. Not like nowadays, everyone having bonfires in their back gardens. It's not the same.'

'I'm not sure I'd be too keen on Alfie cycling round with planks.'

We all stand in the back garden, drinking mulled wine, which Mrs Bishop has made using her special secret recipe. I've got no idea what's in it, but even though it's freezing out here, nobody's feeling the cold. The children have all got sparklers, and Charles has taken the firework code very seriously and put buckets of sand all over the place. In fact I've just nearly tripped over one, but that might be because I'm on my second glass of mulled wine. Mr Pomeroy and Bill are doing the barbecue, and the smell of charcoaled sausages is making me really hungry.

Molly's just been over to check on their progress.

'I think they're nearly ready.'

'Thank god for that. Where's Lily gone?'

'Off with Dan for a little walk, and a chat about not poking her brother with her sparkler.'

'Oh dear. She was doing so well when he first came home.'

'I know. It comes and goes. I think she quite likes him

really, but not all of the time, and especially not if anybody's making a fuss of him.'

Frank and Bill are trying to light the bonfire, but it must have got wet despite the plastic sheeting because nothing much is happening, until they pour some petrol on. Then it lights with a huge whooming noise and the guy shoots about fifty feet into the air and lands on a small bush and sets fire to it, and the children all clap. Frank looks rather dazed for a minute, and Mr Channing gets a bucket of water and puts the bush out, and they stamp on a small bit that's fallen off and is still burning. I hope neither of them are doing the fireworks or we're going to have to lie face down on the grass for the entire evening.

The bonfire's really burning now, and the heat's amazing. The children are fascinated, and keep edging closer, but Frank and Bill are keeping an eye on them and anyway you can't really get too close before you feel your cheeks start to crinkle up.

We all stand expectantly, looking up into the sky, and then suddenly the first rocket shoots up in the air with a really loud bang, and sends out a shower of pink stars. Charles must have spent a fortune on all the fireworks. One of the rockets goes sideways instead of up, and gives Mrs Pomeroy a bit of a nasty moment. But apart from that they're all lovely.

The grand finale is one of those things that produce a torrent of small silver stars that explode into lots of different colours. Everyone claps and then we light more sparklers and try to stop the children from shoving each other, or their hats, into the fire. Alfie's got one of his gloves off, so I make him put it back on and say if he takes it off again we'll have to go home, and then Dan gets each of them a sausage in a bun.

Molly's trying to jiggle Jack about for a bit longer and con him into thinking he's not hungry. Alfie wants a drink, and Lily does too, so I go into the kitchen in search of juice.

'Were they all right, the fireworks? It's a bit hard to tell when you're lighting them.'

Charles looks like he's been out on a covert mission with the SAS in their black balaclavas. He's got sooty marks all over his face, and a really mortifying old woolly hat on.

'I didn't realise there'd be quite so much smoke. The bonfire was blowing in my direction most of the time. Actually, I thought I was going to choke at one point.'

I can't help laughing. He looks so funny.

'I know, it's not very *Mission Impossible*, is it? Passing out lighting a few fireworks. God knows how they manage when they throw smoke bombs into rooms to rescue people.'

'I think they wear masks.'

He smiles.

'Oh. Right. Well, that makes sense. I must remember that.'

'What, for the next time you're out with Special Forces liberating an embassy or something?'

'Yes. But I'm not supposed to talk about it. I could get into terrible trouble.'

'Well, the fireworks were great, and the kids loved them.'

'Good. Do you want a glass of wine, by the way? There's some decent stuff in that bottle over there. I've been hiding it from Mrs Bishop, or she'd have put it in her mulled wine. She's chucked in all sorts, you know.'

'I know. I've been drinking it for the past hour, and it's all right, actually.'

'Well, I might try some then, if you think it's drinkable. I didn't want to risk it before I did the fireworks.'

'Very wise. Have a sip of mine, if you like.'

I pass him my glass and he takes a fairly hefty swig.

'Good god. That's lethal. I think my feet are melting.'

'I know. It's good, isn't it?'

He takes another swig.

'Yes, once you get used to it, it is rather.'

'Well, get your own glassful then.'

'Alice. I've been meaning to say, and I hope you don't take this the wrong way, but I saw Harry's jeep outside your house, you know, a few weeks ago, and I just hope, well, the thing is, I just wanted to say that, if you were thinking of seeing him again, or something, I think you can do better.'

He's gone very bright red under his black smudges now. But that could be the mulled wine. He looks a bit like an embarrassed chimney sweep.

'I'm not.'

'I mean I know he's a decent bloke and all that, and he knows all about herbs, and that's very interesting, of course, fascinating, but I just don't think he really appreciates you. Not properly.'

'Charles, I'm not. It's over. Definitely.'

'Oh thank god. Oh sorry, I didn't mean to say that. Oh fuck it.'

And then completely out of the blue, with no warning at all, he kisses me. And before I know it I'm kissing him right back.

'Crikey. I didn't really mean to do that.'

'No, neither did I.'

'You've got black marks on your face now. Sorry.'

'That's all right.'

'Shall we do it again?'

'Yes.'

And just as we're really getting the hang of it Mrs Bishop walks in.

'Oh thank the lord, and about time too. Me and Elsie were just saying we hope you two get a move on. Honestly, you should see the way he looks at you sometimes, and you're no better. Right under your noses, both of you. I don't know what's took you so long, I really don't. And he's a lovely man, you know, Alice, you could do a lot worse. Although he does make a terrible mess leaving his papers all over the place. You'll have to train him up. And she's a lovely girl too, Mr B, much nicer than you-know-who. Sorry if I'm speaking out of turn, but I'm just so pleased.'

'Oh. Well, that's good.'

Charles looks even more embarrassed now.

'Anyway, you two, don't you mind me. I'll just take out this juice for the children, and I'll keep them out of your way for a bit.'

And before we can stop her she's shot back out into the garden clutching a carton of juice, with a big smile on her face.

'Bugger. Well, that'll be halfway round the village in the next five minutes.'

Charles looks very serious all of a sudden.

'Yes. So we might as well give them something to talk about then, don't you think? See if I can't get any more black marks on your face.'

And he puts his arms around me, and even though this might all get terribly complicated, and his face is really filthy, and that hat really does make him look slightly mad, it feels great. It feels like coming home.

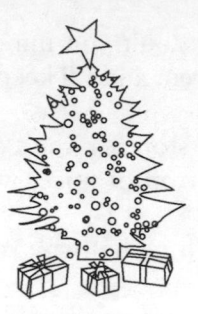

12

ONE YEAR LATER
Jingle Bells

CHRISTMAS WEDDINGS ALWAYS SOUND so romantic, and I still can't believe that we've managed to persuade Alfie to wear a kilt. I really didn't think we stood much chance until Molly came up with the brilliant idea of renting *Braveheart* on video. I had to keep diverting his attention by tickling him during the most gory bits, but the kilt was no problem after that, although persuading him that he couldn't paint his face blue was a bit tricky. Mum's been in a frenzy for weeks. She spent so long choosing her wedding outfit that I really thought I was going to have to sedate her: we visited practically every shop in Western Europe, and even then she couldn't find a hat.

The church is freezing, but smells wonderful and the flowers are fabulous. Stella's arranged hundreds of little scented candles that are flickering all over the place. The ceremony's been a bit of a blur so far because I've been trying to keep an eye on Alfie: he's been perfect up till now but you never know when he might decide to launch into a bit of 'Scotland the Brave'.

'Do you take this woman to be your lawful wedded wife?'

Oh god. I didn't think I was going to cry. But I am. He looks so happy, and sort of nervous too, like it's all just a tiny bit too much for him and he might lose it at any moment.

'Yes. I do.'

Yup. Crying now.

God, I'm a complete sucker for all this weddings-in-churches business. I wonder if I can fish a tissue out of the tiny little pocket in my skirt without anyone noticing.

The Vicar goes on about let no man put asunder and everything, and then we walk back up the aisle. Everyone is looking and smiling. Mum's dabbing away with her hankie, and Dad's blowing his nose, and I'm concentrating on not dropping my flowers, because they're tied up with velvet ribbon and it's quite hard to get a grip without squashing them.

My shoes are killing me, but I'm trying to walk elegantly rather than doing anything reminiscent of hobbling. Alfie's starting to speed up a bit and looks quite eager to get outside, so if I don't manage to slow him down in the next twenty seconds he'll be overtaking everybody.

We've got to do the signing-the-register thing now, and the photographer's lurking. Charles is carrying Mabel, who's almost asleep.

'You look lovely, and you were right about those shoes. The other ones were nice, but those are better.'

'Actually, they're killing me at the moment, so I might have to get the other ones from the car. Where's Ezra?'

'Outside, waiting for Alfie.'

'Great. Well, we've just got to do photographs and then we can all go and get something to eat. I'm starving – I was too nervous to eat much earlier.'

The reception and the food are lovely. Wedding food can be so boring, but the hotel has come up with a huge buffet breakfast, in a trendy brunch rather than a Little Chef kind of a way: bacon, sausages, kedgeree, even porridge. Actually,

Alfie and Ezra have had a competition to see who could eat the most porridge, which I'm not really sure was the best idea in the world, and I've eaten so much I've had to undo one of the buttons on my skirt.

'You look great in that outfit. It really suits you.'

'Oh thanks, Moll.'

'It was a lovely service, I thought, and Alfie did really well.'

'All thanks to you and Mel Gibson.'

'Happy to help. Oh god, Jack's off again. He just wants to walk all the time now. You can't get him to sit still for more than five minutes, and Lily keeps teaching him new words. She was trying to get him to say bugger the other day.'

'Doreen will love that. Has he stopped saying puke yet?'

'No, but only me and Dan notice it really, and Janice. It's so annoying at mealtimes – he says it all the time.'

'Well, give him to me then – it might come in handy in a minute. I think I might have eaten a bit too much.'

Jim and Stella come over, looking very pleased with themselves.

'So you did it then?'

'Yup. Looks like it.'

'Happy?'

'Blissed out, to be honest. And thanks.'

'What for?'

'Oh for being my clever little sister and stopping Mum from driving us completely round the bend. And for getting Alfie to wear his kilt. You win the best bridesmaid award, definitely, doesn't she, Stella?'

'Yes. Really. Thank you, it was all just perfect. Just how we wanted it.'

'My pleasure. God, I'm going to miss you both.'

'Oh don't you start, you'll set Mum off again.'

Telling Mum about Jim's big new job in Boston was a total nightmare. His company are paying for him to move out there to run their American office, and they're getting him a house and everything, but they'd only pay for Stella if they were married. We told Mum about the wedding first to distract her, but it didn't help much and it still took us nearly an hour to calm her down.

'It's not that far, you know. You can come over, and we'll come back, and I'll have meetings in London all the time.'

'I know, but it still feels like a big deal.'

'Stop it right now.'

'I'm coming to the airport, you know. I don't care what you say. I'm coming.'

Jim gives me a really sweet look.

'Just promise you won't bring Mum.'

'Do I look that daft? Why on earth would I bring Mum and have the whole place in an uproar when she goes into hysterics? Charles will keep Alfie and I'll come by myself. Just me, and a wet hanky.'

'Alice.'

'Yes.'

'If you don't stop it right now I'm going to have to give you a Chinese burn, and don't think I won't, just because I'm in this get-up. I know what you're up to, you know. You're just trying to divert attention away from the fact that you're still refusing to do the decent thing and give Mum the wedding she's really been waiting for. You'll be next. Once you and old Charlie boy stop playing squires and peasants, you'll be the next one up the aisle.'

'Oh no I won't. Mum's had her family wedding now, and that'll have to do.'

'Still my naughty little sister then?'

'Definitely. And we're not playing squires and peasants.'

'He lives in the big house, you live down the lane in the little one. Squires and peasants. It's obvious. What do you call it then?'

'I call it a semi-detached relationship. Just how we like it.'

'Semi-detached? Sounds more like a bungalow than a relationship.'

'Well, it works for us.'

Charles comes over.

'Hello, squire. How's it going?'

Stella and I start to laugh.

'What?'

'He thinks he's being funny. He thinks you're being a snooty squire living in the big house, and I'm being the poor peasant stopping in mine. Just ignore him.'

'I have asked her, you know. I want to make that perfectly clear. But she won't have it. People in the village must think I'm a terrible bounder. I might put a notice in the parish newsletter: "To whom it may concern, I have asked her, but she keeps saying she likes things the way they are."'

'But I do.'

'I know. So do I.'

'She's always been stubborn, you know. It's not like the good old days, is it? When women knew their place.'

'Jim, do shut up. Please ignore my husband. Oh, I quite like saying that.'

'Oh I see. Starting already, is it? Telling me to shut up in public.'

'Yes. And I've been learning how to do Chinese burns. So watch it.'

We gather on the steps of the hotel to wave them off on their honeymoon, and Stella tries very hard to throw her bouquet at me, and I have to hide behind a pillar. I can tell Mum's watching me and shaking her head. Stella's friend Gemma catches it in the end, which is good because she's very keen on getting married, apparently, although her boyfriend gets a rather hunted look on his face when she walks towards him proudly clutching the flowers.

We have another quick drink, and Mum says how well Alfie did, and wasn't it all perfect, although she thinks Stella's mum might have made a mistake going for fuchsia-pink, and then we round up the kids and drive home. Mabel falls asleep fairly quickly, while Alfie and Ezra sit listening to tapes on their Walkmans.

'You don't really mind, do you?'

'What?'

'About us not living together. I mean I know we've talked about it, but I'd hate it if you secretly minded.'

'No, I think you're right.'

Charles has a habit of not talking about things that really bother him. It's like getting a limpet off a rock trying to get him to talk about his feelings. He tends to say he's fine, even when it's obvious that he's not. And even when it comes to small things like the way he likes his coffee he doesn't make a fuss. It took me nearly three months to work out he prefers it black. He just never said. It's one of the things I really love about him. That he's so relaxed. But it also drives me round the bend.

'Are you sure?'

'Yes. And anyway the children have had enough to cope with. I mean obviously at some point I'd like us all to be living in the same house, but for now I think it's fine.'

'Fine?'

'Sorry. I forgot you were allergic to fine. Fantastic. Brilliant.'

'Good. Well, at least now we've got the wedding over with we can start panicking properly about Christmas.'

'Just run it by me one more time, how we ended up with everyone coming to us.'

'Look. I've said I'm sorry. Only we usually go to Mum, and with Jim away it's even more important she sees us, but then your mum was so keen too and I didn't have the heart not to ask her as well. I really didn't mean to ask them both on the same day, honestly. But Lola's not due until teatime, and your mother will have gone by then, so there shouldn't be any awkward scenes or anything. And Mum and Dad have promised they'll just ignore her, whatever she says.'

'Famous last words.'

'I know.'

'What if she starts ranting on again, like last time, about how badly behaved the children are or something?'

'How nobody was fussing enough around her, more like.'

'I know. But that's what I mean. What if she starts? If she has a go at Alfie your mum will kill her. Actually, that might be rather good.'

'Yes. But I don't care. It's Christmas, and the children will love it and I don't care about anything else. And I'm going to get some spare presents for anyone she's horrible to.'

'You'd better get a lot of extra presents then.'

'I know. What do you think we should get for her?'

'Swastika armbands might be good. She could wear them to boss people about. I saw some in that catalogue you were showing me, with the dressing-up outfits. They had all sorts, nurses, policemen, everything.'

'Yes, but not Nazis, Charles. Nobody buys their children Nazi dressing-up kits.'

'Well, it's my best idea so far, but I also thought of one of those giant slipper things that you put both feet in. I saw them in one of the catalogues, in all sorts of colours. I thought bright-yellow might be nice. It would look like a giant banana.'

'You're brilliant, do you know that? A giant yellow slipper. Perfect. And my dad gave my mum oven gloves once. She was quite pleased, but I always thought that was a particularly manky present, so maybe the children could get her some oven gloves. Actually, you know, I've been think-ing, if you told me what your surprise present's going to be that would be a big help. I could factor it in, sort of thing.'

'You don't think I'm going to fall for that, do you?'

'You might.'

'I'm not telling you. It's a surprise.'

Bugger. I really want to know.

'You've got to tell me at some point.'

'I do not.'

'Yes you do. Because it might be another of your really bad ideas, like your brilliant plan to take us all fishing.'

'Look, I thought you agreed you wouldn't keep mention-ing that. It was perfectly calm when we set off. You said so yourself.'

'I never knew children actually contained that much sick.'

'They would have loved it if it had stayed calm. You know they would.'

'Well, at least none of them will ever be tempted to run away to sea.'

Charles laughs.

'Are you coming back with us tonight?'

'No, I thought a quiet night in with Alfie, if you don't mind. Talk him out of his kilt and have an early night. I'm knackered.'

'All right, but come up for breakfast tomorrow morning?'

'Sure.'

Molly rings when I've just settled down with a cup of tea and a nice little pile of digestives.

'I thought the wedding was lovely.'

'Yes, it was, wasn't it? Did you get home all right?'

'Fine. They both fell asleep in the back of the car. And then Dan and I had another fight about what to do for Christmas. Doreen's still on at us to go to her, but then we'd have to go to Mum's for New Year, and Dan really wants to be at home, with just us. I can't make my mind up. Families are so complicated, aren't they?'

'Well, come to us for New Year, and bring your mum. We were talking about it the other day – we thought we'd have a sort of gathering on New Year's Eve, just low-key, with everyone from the Garden Society. Mrs Bishop can make her famous mulled wine. What do you think?'

'Sounds great to me. Oh well, that's decided then, we'll stay here. Your mum was on at me about telling you to get married again today. Did I say?'

'Oh god, was she? Sorry.'

'I told her I thought you'd got it pretty well worked out, actually. Never mind a room of your own, I want a house of my own too.'

'I know, it's the best of both worlds really.'

'I'm not sure people should live together, you know. Not all the time.'

'But you and Dan are still all right, aren't you?'

'Oh yes, we're definitely back on track and everything. I don't think about it much now, you know, all that stuff before Jack was born. It seems like years ago. But that doesn't stop it feeling like bloody hard work sometimes. I think it was much easier when we all lived in caves and gathered berries. The women looked after the kids together, and when the men came home they all had a feast, and if they'd got eaten by a buffalo that was fine too. The problem is our hunters come home every night.'

'I don't think buffalo actually eat you, do they? They probably just squash you about a bit; that must be why buffalo mozzarella's so bloody expensive. Milking a buffalo must be a bit dodgy. Actually, I'm not sure Charles would be very good at the hunter thing, to be honest – he's a bit too squeamish. He tried to make steak-and-kidney pie last week but it ended up just steak because he said the kidneys were so revolting he couldn't touch them.'

'I don't blame him. Dan wouldn't be much cop either, come to think of it.'

We arrange to meet up for coffee tomorrow, and I get back to my biscuits. Molly's definitely much happier now, but I know she still finds it hard sometimes. I mentioned something the other day about when she was pregnant with Jack, and she said she couldn't really remember much about it – she just remembers crying in the bath for hours.

And if I ever mention Lola's name, if I'm saying something about the children, or Lola's latest visit or anything, she sort of flinches. Actually, I usually try to avoid mentioning Lola's name, not that Molly's said anything, but I can tell it still hurts. The echoes just go on and on. But they're getting there, and that's the main thing.

Patric wasn't too pleased when he found out about Charles, and we had a weird conversation where he said maybe we ought to consider giving it another go, for Alfie's sake, and I said that for Alfie's sake we probably shouldn't. I think it was just sour grapes really.

He still comes down every fortnight or so, and he's almost civil to Charles. Although I'm a bit worried about Cindy, who seems to be getting more and more obsessed. It's as if she thinks if she can just make everything perfect for him he'll be happy. And the harder she tries the more he treats her like a doormat. If she doesn't snap out of it soon Molly and I are going to send her on some sort of emergency assertiveness course.

Charles has been a complete revelation, and it just keeps getting better. Sometimes I can't believe how lucky I am. He's calm and patient, and great with Alfie, but he's also really passionate, and he makes me laugh. A lot. Although sometimes not on purpose, like when he tries to be masterful and macho and it all goes wrong. He tried to cut down one of the old trees behind the garden wall in the summer and nearly knocked himself out when a branch fell on him. He just isn't that practical really. But he doesn't sulk about it for weeks if it turns out you're better at something than he is.

And even though it's complicated trying to work out my role with Ezra and Mabel, and how to handle Lola, who was furious when she found out and is still being pretty nightmarish, it's definitely worth it. Definitely. Ezra seems happier, and much calmer, and Mabel's a sweetheart most of the time, although she's inherited her mother's stubbornness, which can be a bit scary sometimes.

But there's no rush, and we can take our time working out what we're going to do next. I love spending time back at our house, just me and Alfie, and I don't think I ever want to give that up completely and get locked into coupledom for every minute of the day, every day of the week. But not because I'm not happy with Charles or trying to keep my options open or anything. I'm not looking for anyone else and I can't see that changing. But there is room for me, and I like that. And me and Alfie. And Charles gets to spend time on his own with

Ezra and Mabel, which they need, I think. Space. The final frontier, well, in relationships it is anyway. And I think we've almost cracked it, I really do.

Christmas lunch is a triumph. It ends up being a bit of a team effort with Charles and Dad doing the vegetables, and Mum doing the gravy. And the turkey takes care of itself, once it's in the oven, so all I have to do is set the table. The children have made all the decorations – with lots of paper chains and tinsel – which aren't very elegant but we're very proud of them. Ezra's made a robin on a log, which he's covered in glitter, even though it looks more like a dodgy vulture, and Alfie and Mabel have made angels out of pipe cleaners and white crêpe paper, which are dangling all over the place.

It's a bit more *Blue Peter* than Martha Stewart, but with the Christmas tree and the fairy lights it all looks very festive. Actually, I think I might have gone slightly overboard with the fairy lights. I even got some of the disco flashing ones that have different settings, at least two of which make you feel slightly sick if you watch them for too long.

Em calls to say Happy Christmas, and says she really wishes she could come over to see us all. She's eight months pregnant now, and getting slightly nervous. But at least it's not twins. Luca is being great and his mum's thrilled, and I'm going to go over when the baby's born. I've arranged it with Luca, as a surprise, and Charles is going to come too. Mum says she'll stay with the children so we can have a nice little break. I'm really looking forward to it, and I can't wait to see the baby.

The really major success of the day is Charles's surprise present, which arrives in a large wicker basket, which his father carries in from the car. The children guess what it is before he's even got it in the house. It's a small but very noisy Labrador puppy, a distant relation of a dog Charles had when he was little. The children are ecstatic.

'I know, but before you say anything it can stay here with

us, and I'll do all the cleaning up and everything. And we've had him checked out by the vet, and he's already had all his injections, and he'll be good-natured and easy to train.'

'Right.'

Alfie's delirious.

'Oh thank you. Thank you for ever.'

They all crowd round the puppy and stroke him. He's wagging his tail so hard he's almost falling over, and he keeps making little excited yelping noises.

Bugger. He's very sweet.

'Don't you think we might have enough to cope with, without a puppy as well?'

'I know. But Ezra and Alfie both wanted one so much. It seemed so mean not to let them. And I really will do all the work – you won't even know it's here.'

'I'll be holding you to that.'

'It is rather sweet, isn't it?'

'Yes.'

'And look at Alfie's face.'

'I know. Charles, you know that thing they put on those car stickers: "A dog is for life not just for Christmas?"'

'Yes.'

'I rest my case.'

'Right.'

'And you'll be the one out with a shovel clearing up the lawn, right?'

'Yes. I've already got one, actually, and a proper bucket thing. You bury it in the ground and put chemicals in and the whole thing biodegrades.'

'Oh how lovely. Well, that'll be a nice feature for the new garden, won't it? We can include that in our plans for the new lawn. And then we can leave the lid off and one of the children can fall in.'

'It's only a small bucket. Nobody could actually fall into it.'

'Want to bet?'

'Yes. Well, I'll make sure the lid is on at all times. I promise.'

'Charles.'

'Yes.'

'You're a twit, you know that, don't you? A nice twit. But a twit nonetheless.'

'There is one other thing I should mention.'

'What?'

'Lola hates dogs. They make her nervous. She's not that keen on puppies either.'

'Right. Well, yes, that does help, slightly.'

Lola arrives rather late for tea, with Julian, who does something that earns him amazing amounts of money in the City, and who wears impeccable suits, even at weekends. I can't imagine him ever being crumpled, or slightly grubbed up after a session in the garden. He probably has absolutely spotless wellies, if he's got wellies at all.

Lola's got so many presents for Mabel and Ezra that they have to make four trips to the car. She's also brought Alfie a jigsaw and a book, and she's got me one of those expensive-looking books that are full of beautiful pictures, on how to arrange flowers properly. I don't know why this is so annoying, but it is.

I'm in the kitchen making another pot of tea with Charles, who's still trying to recover from opening his present and being confronted with a pair of enormous white fleece pyjamas with sheep all over them. Mabel thinks they're lovely. But then she also likes Lola's new giant slipper. We couldn't get yellow so we went for shocking-pink.

'Oh good, I wanted to get you both on your own for a bit. Marvellous decorations, by the way, very home-made-looking, although I think you might have got the lights slightly wrong. And I'm not sure about all that tinsel.'

Does she imagine we're entering some sort of Christmas-decoration competition or something? How can you not be sure about tinsel? I wish I could think of something annoying to say back. Good. I've just thought of something.

'Oh the children love all the tinsel. But not as much as they love the new puppy, of course. He's so sweet, isn't he?'

'I just hope they realise they can't bring it with them when they come to us for the weekend. We've just bought some very expensive Persian carpets. And I hate dogs, you know that.'

Charles smiles. I think he's quite enjoying himself now.

'That's why I didn't buy a puppy for you, Lola. He'll stay here with us, and Alfie. After all, he's Alfie's dog too.'

'Yes, I know that, Charles, thank you. I just thought I ought to make it clear, that's all. Anyway, I've got some good news, well, wonderful news really. I've just been offered a fabulous new job, CEO and President of the London office. It'll be a huge challenge but it's going to be brilliant. And also – and Julian and I are really thrilled about this so I hope you will be too – we're going to get married, in June probably, or possibly July. I haven't decided yet.'

She pauses with a rather nasty look on her face, for the full shock-value of her announcement to sink in.

'Marvellous, isn't it? We'll be buying a bigger house, of course. We thought possibly Islington, or maybe somewhere more central – we'll have to see. And we'll need to talk about how to tell the children, because I'll want them to play a big part in the wedding. I thought Mabel would make a lovely flower girl, although I'm not too sure about Ezra. Maybe he can be an usher or something. And then I'm thinking about another baby – I thought next spring might be nice. Julian adores children.'

You could have fooled me.

'Though obviously I won't say anything to the children about that just yet. I mean a new brother or sister might make them feel terribly jealous at first, but I'm sure they'll be thrilled once they get used to the idea.'

Charles smiles at me. And I know just what he's going to say.

'It will be a new half-brother or -sister, actually, not a new brother or sister. We've been talking about it quite a lot

301

recently. Because you see we've got some good news too. Well, more than good really. Fantastic.'

'What? Honestly, Charles, I wish you'd try to make a bit more sense sometimes.'

'Our baby, Alice's and mine. Due in early June, actually, isn't it, darling?'

'Yes.'

Lola looks absolutely furious.

'But where will you live? I thought Alice was still in her cottage.'

'Oh she is, in her cottage, I mean. We think we'll keep both places, for the moment anyway. We think it's probably better for the children, and we both like our independence. But at some point I'm sure she'll move up here, and we can use the cottage for guests, or rent it or something. And Alice has some wonderful ideas about work she wants to do to the house, changing the bedrooms round, and moving the play-room downstairs, that kind of thing. We thought we might extend the kitchen too. I mean we've thought about moving and buying somewhere bigger, but the children love this house and anyway there's the garden. It means too much to both of us to move. And we were thinking, we might even go in for a swimming pool – it would be so lovely in the summer.'

I think he might have overdone it a bit with the swimming pool. Lola looks like she might be about to explode.

'Have you told the children yet?'

'About the baby, yes, a few days ago, but we're keeping it fairly low-key. They seemed quite pleased though.'

'I do think you might have consulted me, Charles.'

'Yes, perhaps I should have. I didn't think you'd be that interested, to be honest.'

She glares at him.

'Well, I've been thinking, and I'll want to see the children more, for proper weekends, that sort of thing, when I get the new house ready. I know I've had to cancel a few times lately, but I'd like to get into more of a routine in the new year.'

'Fine.'

'So we won't be able to carry on like things are, with me coming down here to see them, you know. It's madly inconvenient.'

'I'm sure they'd love that. And you can always drive down here and collect them, for the whole weekend, any time. Because we won't be able to drive them to you, because we'll be busy with the new baby, so it would be madly inconvenient for us too.'

I think she might be going to hit him in a minute. But he has got a point, because over the past few months she hasn't spent more than a couple of hours with them.

'I thought you were looking a bit fat, Alice, but I didn't like to say anything. I thought it might be that jumper.'

'No. It's all me. I'm really looking forward to that bit.'

Actually, I'm not, but I'm not telling her that. I didn't mind the getting fat bit, although I don't remember being quite this big so early on last time, which is a bit worrying. But I did get fed up with not being able to bend down or get out of the car, or sleep properly. Still, it's all part of the deal, I suppose, and I'm so pleased, so deep down seriously delighted, that I don't really care. My only worry was Alfie, but he seems quite pleased. I'm sure he won't always be, but I think he's big enough now to be able to cope with it, and I'm going to try really hard to make sure he never feels left out.

So far the only person who's had a major problem with it is Patric. He started saying something about how he supposed I'd be moving into the big house now, and he had no intention of paying me maintenance if I was living with someone else, but then he remembered he doesn't actually pay any maintenance, so he just sulked.

But I think he was really narked because Cindy's getting keen on having a baby, and has been talking about it a lot recently. She even asked me for advice last time they were down, which is a bit ironic if you think about it. I said I thought she should go for it, as long as she was ready to go solo if Patric bolted like last time. And I said that being Alfie's mum is definitely the best thing I've ever done, and I thought she'd make a lovely mum. She seemed quite cheerful when they left.

Lola leaves straight after tea and says she's off to Barbados for a week with Julian, because they're both exhausted and need a break, and then she'll call us when she gets back. Nice work if you can get it. Mum and Dad are dozing on the sofa, with Mum cuddling Mabel, who's now fast asleep. She got a bit upset when Lola left, but soon cheered up when Mum offered to read her a story.

Charles and I take the boys and the puppy out for a quick walk down the lane before supper.

'Mummy, when the new baby does come will you do swearing?'

'What?'

'Ezra says when the baby's born the mummies do lots of swearing, and they say the F word and everything. He seed it in a film.'

'Oh I don't think so, Alfie. I think I'll just be happy. What about you, Ezra? Do you think you might be a bit happy?'

'I might. If it's not a girl. I hate girls.'

'You do not. You love Mabel, you know you do.'

'Sometimes. I suppose.'

'And I'll still be your best boy, won't I, Mummy?'

'Yes, Alfie, you'll always be my best boy.'

Ezra suddenly looks quite nervous. He's such a sweetheart under all that bluster.

'And what will I be?'

'You'll be my special big boy, Ezra, and the baby's biggest brother.'

He smiles and looks at Charles for a bit of extra reassurance.

'And you'll be my best boy Ez. You know that, don't you? You'll always be my best boy.'

'Yes, Dad, I know that. I was asking Alice, actually.'

'I'll be counting on you quite a lot, Ezra, to be honest,

because babies can be pretty boring, you know. I'll want to be playing with you and Alfie all the time but I'll have to take it for walks in the pram instead. Do you think you might be able to help me out with that?'

'I might.'

'That would be great.'

Ezra puts his hand in mine. God, this is complicated. Alfie doesn't seem that bothered, but you never know.

'Alfie was a lovely baby. I hope the new baby is half as nice as he was.'

'I spect it won't be. Nana says I was a delight.'

Good old Mum. He wasn't such a delight in the middle of the night, that's for sure, although I've been trying not to think about that.

'Have you two decided on the puppy's name yet, by the way? Only I'm not sure about Merlin – I think it's quite a grown-up name for such a little puppy.'

Merlin's their favourite so far, but there are lots of other contenders, including Bilbo, because Ezra's been getting heavily into *Lord of the Rings*. I'm secretly lobbying for this because I think it will serve Charles right having to march round in public yelling Bilbo.

'Race you to the gate and back?'

'Here, Dad, hold the lead for a minute. All right. Ready. Steady. Go.'

And they race off down the lane.

'God, I'm knackered.'

'Me too.'

'And I'm hungry.'

'Again?'

'Yes.'

'All right. Let's get them home and I'll make you some supper. You don't think there's any chance it might be twins, do you? Only my mother reminded me this afternoon that twins run in our family.'

'That's not very funny, Charles.'

'I'm not joking. They really do. I'd sort of forgotten.'

'Sort of forgotten?'

'Sorry. I suppose we'll know soon enough, though, won't we? When's the scan again – next week?'

'The week after next.'

'Well. They'd show up on that, wouldn't they?'

'They? Less of the they, if you don't mind. Jesus Christ, you certainly know how to put a girl off her food. I don't feel quite so hungry now, for some reason.'

'Not even for toasted cheese?'

'Oh well, maybe toasted cheese. With lots of ketchup. That might be quite nice.'

We walk back to the house. The boys have run ahead, carrying the puppy because he got fed up with walking. I'm definitely going to call him Bilbo and see if they get used to it. Charles is walking along whistling. I really do fancy some toasted cheese now. I wonder if I can get him to speed up a bit. The fairy lights are twinkling through the hall windows. It's really cold, and slightly foggy, and the light is fading quickly now.

I'm trying not to panic, but it's no use. Christ. Twins. Oh. My. God.

A NOTE ON THE AUTHOR

Gil McNeil is the author of the bestselling *The Only Boy for Me*, and has edited two collections of stories, *Magic* and *Summer Magic*, with Sarah Brown. Gil is currently working on a new novel, *In the Wee Small Hours*, and is also a consultant at Brunswick Arts, and helps run a new charity, PiggyBankKids, which supports projects that create opportunities for children and young people. She lives in Kent with her son.

The Only Boy for Me Gil McNeil
£6.99 0 7475 5776 4

Soon to be a major TV series

'A portrait of childhood to rival Roddy Doyle's and an angst-ridden love life to match Helen Fielding's' *Glamour*

Most people would think Annie Baker had it all: an idyllic life in the country and a fabulous job as a film producer. And so would she, if it weren't for the men in her life. Her six-year-old son Charlie gets traumatised if she buys the wrong kind of sausages. Her tempestuous boss Barney is a Great Director, but keeps getting stuck with dog-food commercials, and as for Lawrence, well, he just wants to get her fired. And then she meets Mack ... Funny, heartbreaking, truthful and uplifting, Gil McNeil's brilliant first novel will make you laugh and cry.

'Funny and sparkling ... a profoundly moving study of motherhood and true love. Charlie is its hero, more lovable than any fictional lover, worth any sacrifice, absolutely the only boy for me. Breathless for more, you have to read it at one sitting' Ruth Rendell

'A joy: a laugh-out-loud account of Annie Baker's life and loves ... a heartbreaking, funny look at parenting and passion' *Elle*

'Imagine what might happen to Bridget Jones if she'd grown up a bit, got married, had a kid and still wasn't quite ready to give up her boozy nights out with the girls ... Anyone who thought Paddy Clarke and Nick Hornby had cornered the market in cute kids should think again' *Hello!*

To order from Bookpost PO Box 29 Douglas Isle of Man IM99 1BQ www.bookpost.co.uk
email: bookshop@enterprise.net fax: 01624 837033 tel: 01624 836000

bloomsburypbks

www.bloomsbury.com/gilmcneil